THE
PERFECT
WIFE

Also by JP Delaney

The Girl Before
Believe Me

THE
PERFECT
WIFE

JP DELANEY

Quercus

First published in the USA in 2019 by
Ballantine Books
Penguin Random House
New York, United States

This edition first published in Great Britain in 2019 by

Quercus Editions Ltd
Carmelite House
50 Victoria Embankment
London EC4Y 0DZ

An Hachette UK company

A CIP catalogue record for this book is available
from the British Library

HB ISBN 978 1 78648 852 7
TPB ISBN 978 1 78648 853 4
EB ISBN 978 1 78648 854 1

This book is a work of fiction. Names, characters,
businesses, organizations, places and events are
either the product of the author's imagination
or used fictitiously. Any resemblance to
actual persons, living or dead, events or
locales is entirely coincidental.

Extract from *Four Quartets* by T.S. Eliot by permission of the publishers,
Faber and Faber Ltd.
Extract from *Is There a Nutmeg in the House?* by Elizabeth David
by permission of the Estate of Elizabeth David.

Every effort has been made to contact copyright holders.
However, the publishers will be glad to rectify in future editions
any inadvertent omissions brought to their attention.

10 9 8 7 6 5 4 3 2 1

Typeset by CC Book Production
Printed and bound in Great Britain by Clays Ltd, Elcograf S.p.A.

MIX
Paper from
responsible sources
FSC www.fsc.org **FSC® C104740**

Papers used by Quercus are from well-managed forests and other responsible sources.

When Pygmalion saw the way these women behaved, he was disgusted by the many faults nature has instilled in the female sex, and for a long time lived as a bachelor, without a wife to share his bed.

Ovid, *Metamorphoses*

What is love but another name for positive reinforcement?

B. F. Skinner, *Walden Two*

1

You're having that dream again, the one where you and Tim are in Jaipur for Diwali. Everywhere you look, every doorway and window, there are lanterns and candles, firecrackers and fairy lights. Courtyards have become flickering pools of flame, their entrances surrounded by intricate designs of coloured rice paste. Drums and cymbals throb and sizzle. Surrendering to the din and confusion, you surge with the crowd through a market, the stallholders urging platters of sweets on you from every side. On an impulse you stop at a stall where a woman decorates skin with beautiful Hindi patterns, the smell of sandalwood from her brushes mingling with the acrid, savoury cordite from the firecrackers and the aroma of *kaaju*, roasting cashew nuts. As she paints you, deft and quick, a cluster of young men dance past, their faces painted blue, their muscular torsos bare, then they come back, dancing just for you, their expressions deadly serious. And then, the final touch, she paints a bindi on your forehead, right between your eyes, telling you how the scarlet dot marks you out as married, a woman with all the knowledge of the world. 'But I'm not,' you protest, almost pulling away, fearful you're going to offend some local sensibility, and then you hear Tim's laugh and see the box he produces from his pocket and, even before he goes down on one knee, right here in the midst of all this noise and mayhem, you know this is it, he's really going to do it, and your heart overflows.

'Abbie Cullen,' he begins, 'ever since you erupted into my life, I've known we have to be together.'

And then you're waking up.

Every part of you hurts. Your eyes are the worst, the bright lights searing into your skull, the ache in your brain connecting with the stiffness in your neck, soreness all the way down your spine.

Machines beep and whirr. A hospital? Were you in an accident? You try to move your arms. They're stiff – you can barely bend your elbows. Painfully, you reach up and touch your face.

Bandages encase your neck. You must have been in an accident of some kind, but you can't remember it. That happens, you tell yourself groggily. People come round from crashes not remembering the impact, or even having been in a car. The important thing is, you're alive.

Was Tim in the car as well? Was he driving? What about Danny?

At the thought that Danny or Tim might have been killed, you almost gasp, but you can't. Some change in the beeping machine, though, has alerted a nurse. A blue hospital uniform, a woman's waist, passes at eye level; she's adjusting something, but it hurts too much to look up at her.

'She's up and running,' she murmurs.

'Thank God,' Tim's voice says. So he's alive, after all. And right here, by your bedside. Relief floods through you.

Then his face appears, looking down at you. He's wearing what he always wears: black jeans, a plain grey T-shirt and a white baseball cap. But his face is gaunt, the lines deeper than you've ever seen them before.

'Abbie,' he says. *'Abbie.'* His eyes glisten with tears, which fills you with alarm. Tim never cries.

'Where am I?' Your voice is hoarse.

'You're safe.'

'Was there an accident? Is Danny OK?'

'Danny's fine. Rest now. I'll explain later.'

'Have I had surgery?'

'Later. I promise. When you're stronger.'

'I'm stronger now.' It's true: already the pain is receding, the fog and grogginess clearing from your head.

'It's incredible,' he says, not to you but the nurse. 'Amazing. It's *her.*'

'I was dreaming,' you say. 'About when you proposed. It was so vivid.' That'll be the anaesthetic, you realise. It makes things richer. Like that line from that play. What was it? For a moment the words elude you, but then, with an almost painful effort, a *clunk*, you remember.

I cried to dream again.

Again Tim's eyes fill with tears.

'Don't be sad,' you tell him. 'I'm alive. That's all that matters, isn't it? We're all three of us alive.'

'I'm not sad,' he says, smiling through his tears. 'I'm happy. People cry when they're happy, too.'

You knew that, of course. But even through the pain and the drugs, you can tell those aren't everything's-going-to-be-all-right-now tears. Have you lost your legs? You try to move your feet and feel them – slowly, stiffly – responding under the blanket. Thank God.

Tim seems to come to a decision.

'There's something I have to explain, my love,' he says, taking your hand in his. 'Something very difficult, but you need to know right away. That wasn't a dream. It was an upload.'

2

Your first thought is that you're hallucinating – that this, not the dream about him proposing, is the bit that isn't real. How can it be? What he's saying to you now – a stream of technical stuff about mind files and neural nets – simply makes no sense.

'I don't understand. Are you saying something happened to my brain?'

Tim shakes his head. 'I'm saying you're *artificial*. Intelligent, conscious . . . but man-made.'

'But I'm fine,' you insist, baffled. 'Look, I'll tell you three random things about myself. My favourite meal is salade niçoise. I was angry for weeks last year because my favourite cashmere jacket got eaten by moths. I go swimming almost every day—' You stop. Your voice, instead of reflecting your rising panic, is coming out in a dull, croaky monotone. A Stephen Hawking voice.

'The damage to that jacket was six years ago,' Tim says. 'I kept it, though. I've kept all your things.'

You stare at him, trying to get your head around this.

'I guess I'm not doing this very well.' He pulls a piece of paper from his pocket. 'Here – I wrote this for our investors. Maybe it'll help.'

FAQ

Q: What is a cobot?

A: 'Cobot' is short for 'companion robot'. Studies with prototypes suggest the presence of a cobot may alleviate the
loss of a loved one, providing solace, company and emotional support in the aftermath of bereavement.

Q: How will cobots differ from other forms of artificial
intelligence?

A: Cobots have been specifically designed to be empathetic.

Q: Will each cobot be unique?

A: Each cobot will be customised to closely replicate the
physical appearance of the loved one. Social-media
records, texts and other documents will be aggregated
to create a 'neural file' reflecting their unique traits and
personality.

There's more, much more, but you can't focus. You let the sheet
fall from your hand. Only Tim could imagine that a list of factual
questions and answers could help at a time like this.

'This is what you do,' you say, remembering. 'You design artificial
intelligence. But that's something to do with customer service –
chatbots—'

'That's right,' he interrupts. 'I *was* working on that side of it.
But that was five years ago – your memories are all five years out
of date. After I lost *you*, I realised bereavement was the bigger
need. It's taken all this time to get you to this stage.'

His words take a moment to sink in. *Bereavement.* You've just
realised what he's trying to tell you.

6

'You're saying I died.' You stare up at him. 'You're saying the real me died – what? Five years ago. And you've somehow brought me back like this.'

He doesn't reply.

You feel a mixture of emotions. Disbelief, obviously. But also horror at the thought of his grief, at what he must have been through. At least you were spared that.

Cobots have been specifically designed to be empathetic . . .

And Danny. You've missed five whole years of his life.

At the thought of Danny, a familiar sadness washes over you. A sadness you firmly put to one side. And that, too – both the sadness, and the putting aside – feels so normal, so *ordinary*, that it can't be anything except your own individual emotion.

Can it?

'Can I move?' you say, trying to sit up.

'Yes. It'll feel stiff at first. Careful—'

You've just attempted to swing your legs onto the floor. They go in different directions, weak as a baby's. He's caught you just in time.

'One foot, then the other,' he adds. 'Shift your weight to each in turn. That's better.' He holds your elbow to steady you as you head for the mirror.

Each cobot will be customised to closely replicate the physical appearance of the loved one . . .

The face that stares back at you above the collar of a blue hospital gown is *your* face. It's puffy and bruised-looking, and there's a faint line under your chin, like the strap of those hats soldiers wear on ceremonial parades. But it's still unarguably *you*. Not something artificial.

'I don't believe you,' you say. You feel weirdly calm, but the conviction sweeps over you that nothing he's saying can possibly be true, that your husband – your brilliant, adoring, but undeniably obsessive husband – has gone stark raving mad. He's always worked too hard, driven himself right to the edge. Now, finally, he's flipped.

'I know it's a lot to take in,' he says gently. 'But I'm going to prove it to you. Look.'

He reaches behind your head and fiddles with your hair. There's a sucking sound, a strange, cold sensation, and then your skin, your face – your *face* – is peeling away like a wetsuit, revealing the hard, white, plastic skull underneath.

3

You can't cry, you discover. However great your horror, you can't shed actual tears. It's something they're still working on, Tim says.

Instead you stare at yourself, speechless, at the hideous thing you've become. You're a crash-test dummy, a shop-window mannequin. A bundle of cables dangles behind your head like some grotesque ponytail.

He stretches the rubber back over your face, and you're you again. But the memory of that horrible blank plastic is seared into your mind.

If you even *have* a mind. As opposed to a neural net, or whatever he called it.

In the mirror, your mouth gapes silently. You can feel tiny motors under your skin whirring and stretching, pulling your expression into a rictus of dismay. And, now you look more closely, you realise this face is only an approximation of yours, slightly out of focus, as if a photograph of you has been printed onto the exact shape of your head.

'Let's go home,' Tim says. 'You'll feel better there.'

Home. Where's home? You can't remember. Then – *clunk* – a memory drops into place. Dolores Street, in central San Francisco.

'I never moved,' he adds. 'I wanted to stay where you'd been. Where we'd been so happy.'

You nod numbly. You feel as if you ought to thank him. But you can't. You're trapped in a nightmare, immobile with shock.

He takes your arm and guides you from the room. The nurse – if she *was* a nurse – is nowhere to be seen. As you walk with painful slowness down the corridor, you glimpse other rooms, other patients in blue hospital gowns like yours. An old lady gazes at you with milky eyes. A child, a little girl with long brown ringlets, turns her head to watch you pass. Something about the movement – just a little further than it ought to go, like an owl – makes you wonder. And then the next room contains not a person but a dog, a boxer, watching you exactly the same way –

'They're all like me,' you realise. 'All . . .' What was his word? 'All *cobots*.'

'They're cobots, yes. But not like you. You're unique, even here.' He glances around a little furtively, his hand increasing its pressure on your elbow, urging you to go faster. You sense there's something he's still not telling you, that he isn't supposed to be whisking you away like this.

'Is this a hospital?'

'No. It's where I work. My company.' His other hand pushes insistently in the small of your back. 'Come on. I've got a car waiting outside.'

You can't walk any faster – it's as if you're on stilts, your knees refusing to bend. But even as you think that – *your knees* – it gets a little easier.

'Tim!' a voice behind you calls urgently. 'Tim, wait up.'

Relieved at the chance to pause, you stop to look. A man about

Tim's age, but more thickset, with long, straggly hair, is hurrying after you.

'Not now, Mike,' Tim says warningly.

The man stops. 'You're taking her away? Already? Is that a good idea?'

'She'll be happier at home.'

The man's eyes travel over you anxiously. His security pass, dangling round his neck, says *Dr Mike Austin*. 'She should be checked out by my psych team, at least.'

'She's fine,' Tim says firmly. He opens a door into a large open-plan office area. About forty people are sitting at long, communal desks. No one is pretending to work. They're all staring at you. One, a young Asian-looking woman, raises her hands and, tentatively, applauds. Tim glares at her and she quickly looks down at her screen.

He guides you straight through the office towards a small reception lobby. On the wall behind the front desk is a colourful street-art mural framing the words *IDEALISM IS SIMPLY LONG-RANGE REALISM!* Something about it seems familiar. You want to stop, to look more closely, but Tim is urging you on.

Outside, it's even brighter. You gasp and shield your eyes as he steers you past a polished steel sign saying *SCOTT ROBOTICS*, the initials *S* and *R* like two upended infinity symbols, towards a waiting Prius. 'The city,' he tells the driver, while you struggle to fold your unresponsive limbs into the back. 'Dolores Street.'

Once you're both in and the Prius is moving off, his hand reaches for yours. 'I've waited so long for this day, Abbie. I'm so happy you're finally here. That we're together again, at last.'

You catch the driver looking curiously at you in his rear-view mirror. As you leave the parking lot he glances up at the sign, then back at you again, and something dawns in his expression. Understanding. And something else as well. Disgust.

ONE

The very first we knew of Tim's plan to hire an artist-in-residence was when we heard him talking to Mike about it. That was typical of Tim. He might exhort all of *us* to work more collaboratively and openly, but the same directive blatantly didn't apply to *him*. Mike was one of the few people he would sometimes actually listen to, on account of them starting Scott Robotics together in Mike's garage, almost a decade ago. Even so: it might have been Mike's garage, but it was Tim's name on the company. That told you pretty much all you needed to know about their relationship.

So, regarding the artist-in-residence proposal, it wasn't as if Tim was discussing it with Mike so much as telling him. But it was also typical of Tim that his announcement had to be prefaced by a loud, passionate tirade about what was so stupid and wrong and screwed up about the way we currently did things, even though we were only doing them the way he'd argued equally passionately for the last time he made us change everything.

'We need to wake the fuck up, Mike,' he was saying in his rasping British accent. 'We need to get more *creative*. Look at these people –' and here his gesture took in all of us, working away in Scott Robotics' open-plan HQ – 'and tell me they're thinking outside the paradigm. They need to be *stimulated*. They need to be *excited*. And we're not going to do that with free bagels and Pilates.'

Tim once told a reporter that having an idea about what the future would look like and then waiting for it to happen was like being permanently stuck in traffic. He's not a patient man. But he is the closest thing to a genius most of us have ever worked with.

'Which is why we're hiring an artist,' he added. 'Her name's Abbie Cullen. She's smart – she works with tech. She *excites* me. We're giving her six months.'

'To do what?' Mike asked.

'Whatever the hell she likes. That's the whole *point*. She's an artist. Not yet another time-serving worker-drone.'

If any of us were offended by that description – among our number we counted quite a few millionaires, veterans of Silicon Valley's most notable start-ups – none of us showed it, although we were already wondering how long the free bagels would now continue.

Mike nodded. 'Great. Let's get her in.'

We waited for the cry of 'Listen up, people!' that usually prefaced Tim's announcements. But none came. He'd already gone back into his glass-walled cubicle.

Many of us, of course, were already typing *Abbie Cullen artist* into our search engine of choice. (When you actually work in tech, using Google or Bing is a bit like a craft brewer drinking Budweiser.) So, pretty much instantly, we knew the bare facts about her: that she had recently exhibited at SXSW and Burning Man; that she was originally from the South; that she was twenty-four years old, a redhead, tall and striking and a surfer; and that her website said, simply, *I build artifacts from the future.* We had also found, and circulated, some video clips of her work. *Seven Veils* was a circle of electric fans, pointing inwards at one another to create a vortex in which thin strips of coloured silk tumbled and twirled perpetually. *Earth, Wind, Fire* was a cyclone of flame, bouncing like a roly-poly toy atop a gas burner as it battled competing blasts of air. Most spectacular of all was *Pixels*, a grid of dozens of what looked like table tennis balls that floated as if on a cushion of air, but also interacted with the gallery visitor. Sometimes the balls seemed to flicker, like a shoal of fish; sometimes they pulsed lazily, like water streaming behind a boat, or formed almost-recognisable shapes: a head, a hand, a heart. In one clip, a child visiting the exhibit clapped her hands, causing the globes to drop abruptly to the floor before warily creeping back up, the way a herd of heifers noses up to a hiker. They were beautiful and strange and playful, and although they had no meaning or message you could easily take away, they also had a kind of purpose; they expressed something, even if what that something was couldn't be put into words.

What had they to do with us? We were engineers, mathematicians, coders, developing intelligent mannequins for high-end fashion stores – *shopbots*, Tim's big idea, the idea that had pulled in nearly eighty million dollars in start-up funding over the last three years. What did we need with an artist? We didn't know. But we had long ago learnt not to question Tim's decisions.

He was a visionary, a wunderkind, the whole reason each one of us was at that company in the first place. What Gates was to personal computers, Jobs was to smartphones or Musk was to electric cars, Tim Scott was to AI – or would be, very soon. We idolised him, we feared him, but even those who could not keep up and had to be let go respected him. And there were many of the latter. Scott Robotics was not just a business. It was a mission, a first-to-market blitzkrieg in a war to mould the future of humanity, and Tim was not so much a CEO as a battlefield commander, charging from the front, our very own Alexander the Great. His gangling physique, rock-star cheek-bones and goofy giggle failed to mask his iron determination, a determination he demanded from each of us in turn. Twenty-hour days were so common they were barely worth remarking on. The postdocs fresh out of Stanford who were his usual hires felt empowered, rather than exploited, by the insane work ethic. (On which subject, his interview technique was legendary. You were ushered into his cubicle, where he would be working on emails, and waited patiently for him to say – without looking up – 'Go.' That was your cue to pitch why you wanted to work at his company. Assuming you passed, next came what was known as 'The Timbreaker'. Sometimes it was a computational question: 'How many square feet of pizza are eaten in the US each year?' More often, it was philosophical: 'What's the worst thing about humanity?' Or practical: 'Why are manhole covers round?' But mostly it was to do with code. Such as: 'How would you program an artificial politician?' And the answer you were required to give was not just theoretical: Tim expected you to come up with actual lines of working code, one after another, without the use of pen and paper, let alone a computer. If you did well, it was signalled by a single word, delivered in the direction of the emails he was still working on: 'Cool.' If he said quietly, 'That's pretty lame,' you were out.)

His impatience – which was also legendary – was somehow

another aspect of his charisma: proof that the mission was time critical, that every second was precious. He even peed quickly, one employee reported after standing next to him at the urinals. (The employee, meanwhile, was afflicted with pee-shyness.) His speech was even faster – curt, precise, bombarding you with instructions or, occasionally, invective. Senior managers, or those who very badly wanted to be senior managers, were often noted to have picked up a trace of the same clipped London accent, so different from the languid, questioning inflections of Northern California. It was as if he were a force field that buckled those around him. If Tim looked you in the eye and said, 'I need you to go to Mumbai tonight,' you felt exhilarated, because you alone had been given a chance to prove yourself. If Tim said, 'I'm taking over your assignment,' you were crushed.

It was sometimes cultish. Not for nothing were we known in Silicon Valley as 'the Scottbots'. The mission could be refined, but it could not be challenged. The leader might have his foibles, but he could not be wrong. At costume parties – paradoxically, Tim *loved* costume parties – where most people went as characters from *Star Wars* or *The Matrix*, he went as the Sun King, complete with buckled shoes, frock coat, outsized wig and crown.

His background was another part of the legend. The impoverished childhood; the bullying that made him leave school at eleven to self-educate. The growing interest in chatbots, just at the time when people were starting to interact with e-commerce sites on their smartphones. The creation of Otto, a customer-service bot that, instead of being robotically polite and frustratingly obtuse, was efficient, smart, geeky and cool – not unlike Tim himself, as many commentators remarked. Otto didn't always spell correctly or use capital letters. He peppered his responses with emojis and witty allusions to nerd culture – quotes from *South Park*, catchphrases from sci-fi films. When you encountered Otto, you were convinced you'd just been put through to some wizard-level teen genius who would fix your problem for the sheer thrill of it. No one was surprised when Google bought Otto for sixty million dollars.

Then, at the age of twenty-three, Tim walked out of Google to found Scott Robotics, taking Mike with him. Their first success – put together in the aforementioned garage – was Voyce, a telephone-helpline bot that was consistently ranked higher than human operators. More successes followed. Tim was obsessed by the idea that AI interactions should be lifelike. 'One day the keyboard and mouse will seem as outdated as punch cards and floppy disks do now' was his mantra, along with, 'You don't change the future without changing the rules.' The shopbots were a daring progression. Nothing like this had been attempted before – an AI that interacted with people physically, in person, without the medium of a screen or phone. But it made good, even brilliant, business sense. High-end retail mannequins already cost tens of thousands of dollars; sales assistants, too, were expensive, given that they often stood around doing nothing, and personal shoppers with a good eye and an exhaustive knowledge of a store's inventory were time-consuming to train. Combining the three was a no-brainer. It was a sector ripe for disruption, and Scott Robotics – our tiny band – was going to be the first to disrupt it.

And now we were to have an artist to help us. Had we known, of course, where it would lead – had one of our expert futurologists been able to predict how things would turn out – we might not have been so sanguine about that. But even if we had known, would we have said anything? Frankly, it was unlikely. It was not the kind of company where you debated the direction of travel.

4

Tim's silent on the way home. He was never one for small talk, but this is different. He seems almost exhausted.

This is what he was like after a big presentation to the investors, you remember: after weeks of living in the office, sweating every detail, he'd simply collapse, so drained of energy he could barely speak.

For your part, the sense of shock returns. The driver's disgust is nothing to your revulsion and self-loathing.

'It was what you'd have wanted,' Tim says at last. 'Please believe that, Abs. I know it must feel strange right now, but you'll get used to it. You were always the bravest person I knew.'

Were you brave? Memories flicker around the edges of your brain. Surfing a big wave at Linda Mar. Welding an artwork, the fiery sparks spitting into the blue lenses of your goggles. But then there's nothing. Just fog.

You turn and look out of the window, avoiding with a shudder the faint glimmer of your own reflection. San Francisco looks both familiar and new, like a foreign country you're returning to after many years. An exile you don't even remember. The buildings are mostly the same. It's the details that have changed: the smartphones in people's hands that have become larger instead of smaller; the electric bicycles everywhere; the white Priuses that have all but replaced yellow cabs. And the Mission has become even more gentrified, artisanal coffee shops on every block.

Then the driver makes a turn, and suddenly you don't recognise anything. One moment, everything is familiar. The next, fog has taken it away.

'Why don't I remember this?' you say, panicked.

'Creating memories takes a lot of processing power. I had to be selective. The gaps will fill themselves, eventually.'

A garbage truck passes in the opposite direction, noisily crunching a plastic bottle under its tyre. That's what you'll do, you decide. You'll wait a few days, then throw yourself under a truck. Death would surely be preferable to this repulsive travesty of existence.

But even as you think it, you wonder if you're really brave enough to do that. And if you were, would Tim's technicians simply gather you up and put you back together again, like Humpty Dumpty?

Again . . . You realise you still have no idea what happened to you.

'How did I die?' you hear yourself ask.

He looks across at you, his face tense. 'We'll talk about that. I promise. But not yet. It might be too much, right now.'

The Prius pulls up at some electric gates. Behind them you recognise your house, a handsome white clapboard mansion. Despite the astronomical prices in central San Francisco, you could have lived somewhere even grander if you'd wanted to. Tim's wealth was huge, even by tech standards. But ostentation was never his

style. You wonder if the garage still contains the same beaten-up Volkswagen.

'Welcome home,' he says softly.

The front-door lock sticks, and it takes him a few moments to get it open. For some reason that, too – the way he's hunched, patiently working the key – is familiar. You look around and see a small security camera over the door. Another upload.

Inside, everything is dimly recognisable, like visiting a house you lived in as a child.

'I'll show you around,' he says reassuringly. 'Fill in any gaps.'

The kitchen first. Flooded with sunlight, comfortable, but with a professional gas range. Mauviel pans jangle gently overhead like some massive copper wind chime. You open a cupboard at random. Inside are spices – not ready-ground, but whole, in precise rows of glass jars, each neatly labelled in your own handwriting.

'You love to cook,' Tim explains.

Do you? You try to think of anything you've ever cooked, and fail. But then – *clunk* – it comes to you. All those Instagram pictures, hundreds upon hundreds of them. You even had followers, eagerly copying whatever you made.

You point at a bowl of almost-spherical objects on the counter, so vibrant they hurt your eyes. 'What are *those*?'

'These?' He picks one up and hands it to you. 'These are oranges.'

The word makes no sense. 'Orange is a colour.'

'Yes. A colour named after a fruit.' He's watching you carefully. 'Like lime. And peach.'

'But they *aren't* orange, are they?' You examine the one you're holding, turning it over curiously in your hands. 'At least, not as orange as a carrot. And in hot countries, oranges are green.' Something else strikes you. 'My hair is this colour, too. But people call it red. Or ginger. Not orange.'

'That's right. But ginger isn't a colour. Or a fruit.'

'No – it's a root. Once associated with a fiery temperament.' *Clunk.* You stop, confused. 'Did I remember all that, or just guess it?'

'Neither.' A smile pushes the exhaustion from Tim's eyes. 'It's called Deep Machine Learning. Without you even being aware of it, your brain just compared millions of examples in the cloud and came up with a rule for colours and fruits. And the insane thing is, even *I* couldn't tell you how you did it. That is, I could plug in a screen and see the maths happening, but I couldn't necessarily follow it. I tell my employees: the *A* in *AI* doesn't stand for "artificial" anymore. It stands for "autonomous".'

You can tell from the way he says all this how incredibly proud he is. *You breakthrough, you.* A part of you wants to bask in his approval. But you can't. All you hear is, *You freak.*

'How can you possibly love me like this?' you say desperately.

For a moment there's a flash of something fierce, almost angry, in his expression. Then it softens. *'Love is not love which alters when it alteration finds,'* he quotes. 'Sonnet 116, remember? We read it at our wedding. Four lines each, in turn. Then the final couplet together.'

You shake your head. You don't remember that, no.

'It'll come back to you.' You wonder if he means the memory, or the sentiment. 'My point is, those weren't just empty words to us. You were always unique, Abbie. *Irreplaceable.* A perfect wife.

A perfect mother. The love of my life. Everyone says that, don't they? But I really meant it. After I lost you, plenty of people told me I should move on, find someone else to spend my life with. But I knew that was never going to happen. So I did this instead. Was I right to? I don't know. But I had to try. And even just talking to you now, for these few minutes – seeing you *here*, in our house, hearing you speak – makes all the years I put into this worthwhile. I love you, Abs. I will always love you. Forever, just like we promised each other on our wedding day.'

He stops, waiting.

You know you should say *I love you* back. Because you do love him, of course you do. But it's still too raw, too shocking. And right in this moment, telling Tim you love him would feel tantamount to saying, *Yes, this is fine. You did the right thing, my husband. I'm glad you turned me into this freakish, disgusting lump of plastic. It's worth it, to be here with you.*

I, too, love and worship thee more than life itself . . .

'Shall we continue?' he says after a moment, when you don't say anything.

5

He leads the way upstairs. You have to hold on to the banister, your legs stamping cautiously on each step.

'Those were all yours,' he says as you pass a huge floor-to-ceiling bookcase. 'You loved books, remember? And that's Danny's room.'

The bedroom he indicates, the first one off the landing, doesn't look much like a child's room. There are no curtains, no carpet, no pictures or toys of any kind. Apart from the bed, the only furniture is a small TV and a shelf of DVDs. To anyone else it might seem spartan, but to a child like Danny, you know, it's relaxing. Or at least, less stressful.

'How's he doing?' you ask.

'Making progress. It's slow, of course, but . . .' Tim leaves the sentence unfinished.

'Will he recognise me?'

Tim shakes his head. 'I doubt it. I'm sorry.'

You feel a stab of sadness. But then, even a normal child might forget their mother after five years. Let alone a child like Danny.

Danny has childhood disintegrative disorder, also known as Heller's syndrome. It's so rare, most paediatricians have never seen a case. Instead, they'd tell you patronisingly that children simply don't reach the age of four and then get struck down by profound autism over the course of a few terrifying weeks. That they don't suddenly regress from whole sentences to talking in squeaks and groans and little snippets of dialogue from children's TV shows. That they don't start urinating on carpets and drinking from toilet bowls. That they don't pull out their own hair for no reason, or bite their arms until they bleed.

When a child dies, the world recognises it as a tragedy. The parents grieve, but there's also the possibility of grief lessening, one day. But CDD takes your child away and swaps him for a stranger – a drooling, broken zombie who inhabits your child's body. In some ways it's worse than a death. Because you go on loving this beautiful stranger even while you're grieving the sweet little person you lost.

A strange reverse psychology takes place: when someone finally tells you what your child has, you don't want to believe it, because there's no treatment. Instead, you cling to the hope it might be a brain tumour, or epilepsy, or something you read about on the internet. Anything that offers a tiny glimmer of hope.

'Where is he now?' you ask.

'He goes to a great special-ed school across town. Sian – she was one of the teaching assistants there, until I hired her as a live-in nanny – takes him every morning, then comes back to work with him on his therapy programme afterwards. It's not close, but it's the best place for kids like him in the whole state.'

You've missed so much, you think. Danny's at *school*. A school you didn't even know existed.

Tim opens another door. 'And this is the master bedroom.'

You step inside. It's a large room, dominated by the self-portrait, almost life-size, on one wall. The woman in the painting is red haired, her mid-length braids – dreadlocks, almost – casually piled on top of her head. Her left ear, the one turned to the viewer, has three large studs in it. She's wearing a striped shirt, the lower part of which is covered in coloured smears, as if she simply wipes her paintbrush on it as she works. She looks cheerful: an optimistic, sunny-natured person. On her neck a tattoo, an elaborate Celtic pattern, disappears under the shirt collar and emerges from one sleeve.

You look down at the flesh-toned rubber of your own arm.

'We can't do tattoos,' Tim explains. 'It would compromise the skin material.' He gestures at the picture. 'Other than that, it's pretty accurate, wouldn't you say?'

He means you're an accurate copy of the painting, you realise, not the other way round. They must have used a scan of it to construct you.

Is the woman in the painting really you? She seems too self-possessed, somehow, too *cool*. And too confident. You look at the signature, a dramatic squiggle in the lower left corner: *Abbie Cullen*.

'You didn't usually work in oils,' he adds. 'It was your wedding gift to me. It took you months.'

'Wow . . . What did you give *me*?'

'The beach house,' he says matter-of-factly. 'I had it built for you as a surprise. There's a big garage there you used as your main studio – you needed space for your projects.' As he speaks, he's opening another door, directly opposite the master bedroom. 'But you worked in here when we were in the city. This is where you painted that self-portrait.'

The floorboards in this little room are flecked with paint. On a trestle are jars of dried-out paintbrushes and tubes of solidified acrylics. And a silver pen in a stand. You go and pick it up. The barrel is inscribed *Abbie. Always and always. Tim.*

'The ink will have dried by now, I expect,' he says. 'I'll get some more. I'd better start a list.'

Numbly, you pull at the hospital gown you're still wearing. 'I'd like to get dressed.'

'Of course. Your clothes are in the closet.'

He shows you the walk-in closet off the main bedroom. The dresses hanging there are lovely – boho-chic, casual, but made from beautiful materials in bold, bright colours. You glance at the labels. Stella McCartney, Marc Jacobs, Céline. You had good taste, you think. And a good budget, thanks to Tim.

You pick out a loose Indian-styled dress, something easy to wear. 'I'll leave you to it,' he says tactfully, stepping out.

Remembering that hideous plastic skull, you avert your eyes from the mirror as you pull the gown off, but then you can't help looking. Your body hasn't been this toned for years, you catch yourself thinking: not since you gave birth to Danny . . .

But this isn't a body. Those limbs were put together in an engineering bay, your skin colour sprayed on in a paint booth. And below the waist you simply fade into smoothness, as blank and sexless as a doll. With a shudder, you pull the dress over your head.

There's a sudden crash from downstairs, the front door slamming open. Feet pound the stairs.

'Danny, don't run,' a female voice says.

'Don't wrun!' a small voice mumbles. 'Wrunning!' The running feet don't slow down.

Danny. Spinning around, you catch a glimpse of dark hair, deep-set eyes, a taut elfin face, as he hurtles down the landing. Maternal love sluices through you. You can't believe how big he is! But of course, he must be almost ten. You've missed half his life.

You follow him to his room. He's already pulled an armful of toy trains from under his bed. 'Line them up. Line them uuuuup,' he mutters feverishly as he sorts them, biggest to smallest, placing them precisely against the skirting board.

'Danny?' you say. He doesn't respond.

'Danny, *looking*,' the woman's voice prompts firmly behind you. Danny does look up then, his gaze passing blankly over yours. There's nothing in it, no hint of recognition that you're even a person, let alone his mother.

'Great looking. Good *job*.' The woman steps past you and crouches next to Danny. She's in her twenties, blonde and cheerful, her hair tied back in a ponytail. 'High five, Danny!'

'Sian, this is—' Tim begins.

'I know what it is,' Sian interrupts, giving you a look even blanker than the one Danny just did. 'High five, Danny!' she repeats.

Without lifting his eyes from his trains, Danny flaps his hand in her direction. She moves her own hand so he makes contact with it. 'Good looking, good high fiving,' she says encouragingly, 'but now we're going to go back and walk upstairs properly. Then you'll get extra time with Thomas.' She holds out her hand. When he doesn't respond, she says clearly, 'Stand up and hold my hand, Danny.'

Reluctantly, he gets up and takes it. 'Well done! Good standing,' she says as she leads him away.

'She's a very good therapist,' Tim says when they're out of earshot. 'When she joined us, Danny wasn't engaging with anything except food and his trains. Now we're getting about a dozen exchanges a day.'

'That's great,' you say, although that *it* still stings. 'I'm so proud of you both.'

You say it, but you remember your excitement when the two of you first discovered applied behaviour analysis, this way of teaching children with autism that, according to some studies, was even capable of curing them, or at least making them indistinguishable from other kids. If you'd known then that, five years later, Danny would still be working on eye contact, would you have had the energy to keep going?

You push the thought aside. Of course you would. Any gains, however hard won, are better than none.

Danny stamps up the stairs again, more slowly this time, with Sian at his heels. When he reaches his bedroom, she produces a blue train. 'Good walking, Danny. Here's Thomas.'

'Here's Thomas,' Danny echoes as he flops down and aligns the train with the others.

Then, without warning, his troubled eyes flick up to yours.

'Muh,' he says. 'Muh-muh.' Then he laughs.

'Did he just call me *Mummy*?' you say, amazed.

Tim's already weeping with joy. You would be too, if you could cry.

TWO

It was a couple of weeks after Tim's announcement before Abbie Cullen actually showed up. Finishing a commission, we speculated, or maybe having second thoughts about working with us at all. We didn't get many visitors – our backers were paranoid about security, and our location had been chosen for its low cost per foot rather than its potential for social activities. So to say that Abbie made quite an entrance probably says less about her than it does about the smallness and focus of our lives.

Even before Tim's cry of 'Listen up, people!' most of us had spotted her in reception – and, if we hadn't, we'd certainly seen the way Tim himself hurried over to greet her. She was tall, for one thing, almost six feet, with ripped skinny jeans and knee-high Cuban-heel boots that, along with the coil of reddish-brown braids piled atop her head, made her seem even taller. A black, inky tattoo – a Hawaiian design, someone said later, or maybe Maori or Celtic – sprawled from her neck all the way down her left arm. But the thing that struck us most was how young she seemed. In an industry like ours, where you could be a veteran in your twenties, she had a freshness about her, an innocence, that marked her out as not one of us.

'Abbie Cullen, everyone. Our first artist-in-residence,' Tim said, escorting her into the open-plan area. 'Her work's amazing, so look it up online. She'll be here for six months, working on some projects.'

'What kind of projects?' someone asked.

It was Abbie who answered. 'I haven't decided yet. I hope it'll be informed by what you guys are doing.' Her voice had a twang of the South in it, and her smile lit up the room.

Whether someone deliberately activated it we couldn't say, but one of the shopbots chose that moment to approach her. 'Hi, how're you doing today?' it said brightly. 'This jacket I'm modelling would look really great on you.' Needless to say, it wasn't actually wearing a jacket – that was just a sample pitch we'd coded into the prototype. 'Shall we go around the store together, and I'll pick out some things for you to try? You're about a size eight, right?'

'You got me,' Abbie said, laughing, and for some reason, even though it wasn't particularly funny, we all laughed along with her. It was like our child had said something inappropriate but cute to a visiting VIP.

Tim laughed too, the high-pitched boyish giggle that was one of the few geeky things about him.

'Abbie will be based in K-three,' he said, naming one of our meeting rooms, but she stopped him.

'I'd rather have a desk out here, where I can get a feel for what's going on. If that's OK by you.'

'Whatever you like,' he said, shrugging. 'People, give her every cooperation. And learn from her. Asset-strip her brain.

Reverse-engineer her creativity. Remember, she's here for your benefit, not hers.'

Which, when we thought about it later, was not the friendliest way he could have welcomed her. But that was Tim for you.

6

It'll take three weeks, he predicts. Three weeks for you to adjust to this new reality.

Like most things Tim says, this isn't plucked out of the air but based on hard data. In the 1950s, a plastic surgeon called Maxwell Maltz recorded how long it took facial reconstruction patients to get used to the results of their surgery. He published his findings in a book called *Psycho-Cybernetics*, which became one of the bibles of Tim's industry.

For three weeks, therefore, Tim plans to stay home, helping you adjust. He starts with the simplest things, bringing you objects from the garden – a curiously shaped stone, a leaf, a bird's wing – or reading you articles from newspapers. His pleasure when he finds something your brain has missed, like the oranges – something he can teach you – is infectious.

As if you're a child, he limits your time online, and vets the sites you visit. Too much information at once, he believes, may be more than your new brain can handle. *Go, go, go, said the bird: human kind cannot bear very much reality.* You know you once knew who wrote that, but it's gone. Your memories are piecemeal, dependent on what happens to have been included in the uploads

Tim made before you woke up. Or booted up, as he sometimes refers to it.

Then – *clunk* – it comes to you, plucked from the cloud. *T. S. Eliot.*

For the same reason, he still won't talk about the circumstances of your death. The closest he comes is a brief reference to *the accident* before clamming up. No one has ever been in a position to recall their own annihilation before, he explains. It might be unbearably painful. Mind-blowing, even.

But you suspect it's not only for your benefit that he avoids the subject. Revisiting that period would clearly be painful for him as well. And Tim was never one to dwell on past defeats. Now he's got you back, he'd rather behave as if the intervening years never happened.

You try to imagine what he's been through, what those last five years must have been like. In some ways, you realise, you had it easy. You simply died. He's the one who suffered. You see it in the deep lines on his face, the thinning hair, the small junk-food belly that juts from his once marathon-running frame: remnants of the terrible grief and loneliness that drove him on, night after night, in the obsessive quest to create you. Already he's hinted at near-breakdowns brought on by overwork, arguments with his investors, employees walking out. The first cobots were abject failures, he tells you, million-dollar experiments that went nowhere. But he refused to give up, and around about the fifth or sixth attempt it started to come together. 'But I didn't want to make *you* until I'd got the technology right. I couldn't bear to have you come back as some half-arsed beta.'

'So what am I? A prototype?'

He shakes his head. 'Much more than that. A quantum leap. A paradigm shift. And, most importantly, my wife.'

Sometimes he just sits and stares at you, drinking you in. As if he can't quite believe he's actually done it. As if he's succeeded more than he ever thought possible. Then you smile at him, and he seems to come out of a trance. 'Hey. Sorry, babe. It's just so good to have you back.'

'It's good to *be* back,' you tell him.

And gradually, slowly, you almost come to believe it.

7

He's tried to minimise the differences between this body and your old one, you discover. Your chest rises and falls, just as if you breathe. You shiver when it's cold, and if it's warm have to take off a layer of clothing. You blink, sigh and frown in ways you can't always control. And at night you go to a guest bedroom, so as not to disturb him, and sleep; or rather, enter a low-power mode, during which you recharge your batteries and upload more memories. Those are the best times. Somehow your dreams seem infinitely richer than the waking world.

During one of those sessions, you find yourself remembering the day after he proposed to you. You'd travelled east to the Taj Mahal, where he'd paid a fortune for a private tour without the crowds. You were in a daze of fuzzy euphoria the whole way, leaning against him in the back of the air-conditioned Mercedes, occasionally stealing glances at the enormous red diamond on your finger.

Later, the guide explained how the palace was built as a funeral monument for the shah's favourite wife, Mumtaz Mahal.

'If I die before you, I'll expect at least a palace,' you informed Tim mock-seriously.

'I won't let you die before me.' And even in the upload, you can hear the absolute conviction in his voice.

On the fourth day, some paints arrive.

'I hope these are all right,' he says as he unpacks them. 'You were very particular about which brands you used.'

Were you? You don't remember that, either. 'I'm sure they'll be fine.'

But what to paint? You feel no desire to create anything. It so clearly matters to Tim, though, that you force yourself to try.

The oranges, you decide eventually. A still life. You take the bowl upstairs and set it in your art room.

Four hours later, you're almost done. You go to show Tim.

'That's incredible,' he says encouragingly. 'See? You've kept all your talent.'

You look at the canvas doubtfully. It seems to you that what you've retained is technique, not talent. Your painting is as accurate, and as devoid of personality, as a photograph.

But Tim is delighted. He gets you to sign it: *Abbie Cullen-Scott*. The swooping, confident signature looks like yours. But it's a forgery, whatever anyone says. A digitally generated facsimile. Just like the rest of you.

Next he orders a selection of gym equipment. Not to burn calories – your weight will be forever fixed at 160 pounds – but to make your movements more natural. There's even a Wii. It's difficult at first, and more than once you crash to the floor playing *Dance Party* on the lowest setting. But with every session you become a little less awkward.

You braid your hair the way it is in the self-portrait upstairs. You even experiment with make-up. You barely used it before, but this new face requires a more hands-on approach. It's a good thing you're an artist, you think. Gradually you work out how to soften your blank, rubbery features with highlights and shadows, until they could almost pass for the real thing.

At Tim's suggestion, you try yoga. You're surprised to find you can do all the poses, even the most advanced – the King Pigeon, the Peacock, the Tittibhasana. He watches with quiet pride. Your body is as perfectly engineered as a racing car, you realise. You just have to learn how to drive it.

His third gift is an Olympic-sized trampoline. Watching the delivery men assemble it on the lawn, you have a sudden memory of one of the first dates he ever took you on, to House of Air, the indoor trampoline park near Golden Gate Bridge. That was when you'd realised that, as well as being ferociously driven, Tim could also be fun.

Afterwards, you'd walked the Bay Trail together to Fort Point, where you sat looking out over the ocean, holding hands.

'We should go to Fort Point again,' you say now, suddenly nostalgic for that time. 'I loved that date.'

Tim hesitates. 'That's a good idea. But not just yet.'

'Why not?'

'Going outside might be tricky right now.'

You look at him, puzzled. 'You mean I can't leave the house?'

'Soon, yes,' he says quickly. 'We just need to . . . prepare you, that's all.'

When the delivery men are done, he kicks off his shoes and

climbs aboard the trampoline. 'Ready?' he says, holding out his hands.

Gingerly, you get on. It's hard to balance at first, and he keeps tight hold of you, bouncing you gently to build up momentum.

'That's it,' he says encouragingly. 'You're getting it.' He does an impression of a NASA countdown, timing it to his bounces. 'T minus *twelve* and *counting . . . eight, seven, six, five . . . Main* engine start. *Lift-off!*'

As he says *Lift-off*, he gives one last, harder push. You feel your knees bend, one-two-three, and then suddenly everything falls into place and you're airborne. He lets go of your hands and you're soaring, higher and higher with every bounce, your braids flying, legs scissoring, the two of you laughing and shouting as you leap together, pulling absurd shapes in the air.

And for the first time since he brought you home, you feel it: the joy that's indistinguishable from love; the happiness that only comes from being happy with one particular person, the person you trust to protect your happiness with his life. *I love you*, you think ecstatically. *Tim, I love you.* And though what comes from your mouth as you tumble through the air is just a wild shriek of exultation and delight, you can tell from his huge grin he understands.

8

On Saturday, Danny has time off from his therapy. You find him sitting on the side of his bed, aimlessly bouncing himself up and down. It gives you an idea.

'Shall we play on the trampoline, Danny?'

He groans. It's often hard to interpret Danny's noises. Tim says most are probably just vocal 'stims', self-stimulations. No one knows why people with autism do this, he says, but there's a theory it gives them a sense of control in an overwhelming world. The bed-bouncing, which Danny can do for hours, is another example. When he gets stressed he creates bigger sensory inputs, for example by biting the backs of his hands.

'Danny?' you repeat. 'Would you like to come outside and play?'

After a moment he shakes his head. 'Nuh!'

Encouraged by the fact he answered at all, you hold out your hand. 'Come on, Danny! It'll be fun!'

'Whoa!' Sian's voice says behind you. 'What are you doing?'

You turn around. The therapist is standing there, watching disapprovingly.

'I'm trying to get Danny on the trampoline,' you explain, although surely it was perfectly obvious what you were doing.

'Well, you're doing it wrong. You need to break it down into a series of clear instructions. Say, "Danny, stand up." Then, "Danny, hold my hand." Then, "Danny, walk downstairs with me," and so on. Each time he complies, you say, "Good job," and give the next instruction.'

'I'm his mother. I was trying to sound friendly.'

Sian gives you a strange look, and for a moment you think she's going to call you on that word *mother*. But all she says is, 'Maybe, but what you did was confusing to him. You asked if he wanted to go outside, and he answered accurately by telling you that no, he didn't. You should have praised him for identifying his response and then articulating it. Instead, the consequence of him answering correctly was that he got asked the same question all over again.' She shrugs. 'When you said, "Would you like to . . . ?" what you actually meant was, "*I* would like you to." Sure, it sounded nice, and most kids soon pick up on what we really mean, but it's unfair on those like Danny who find language difficult.'

You feel criticised, but it also strikes you that in some ways Danny and you are in the same boat, both struggling to make sense of a world you don't really fit into.

'Could you teach me? The way you work with him, I mean? I want to learn to do it properly.'

For a moment she hesitates. Then she says, 'Sure, why not?' in a less-than-enthusiastic tone.

'Danny, touch your nose.'

You count to three, then prompt him, taking his hand and guiding it so he touches his own nose. 'Good touching!' you say, as if he'd done it all by himself. 'Here's Thomas!'

You hand him the train and make an entry on the data sheet. He gets thirty seconds with Thomas as a reward, then you take the train away and do it all again. He needs a fraction less prompting this time. That, too, is recorded.

'Danny, look at me.'

He swings his eyes in your direction. They don't lock on to yours – there isn't that spark you normally get when two people make eye contact. But it's an attempt, and that's what matters. 'Good looking!' you say encouragingly. 'Here's Thomas!'

'Not bad,' Sian says reluctantly. 'You're getting the hang of it.'

Danny's programme consists of hundreds of these exercises – 'trials' or 'drills' in the therapists' jargon. Each is one tiny step along a giant path, with raisins or a short burst of playing with his trains as a reward. Once he's discovered he'll get a treat for doing something, he'll need less prompting next time.

That's the theory, anyway. The data sheets show he's done some of these drills over a thousand times. But Sian stays relentlessly positive.

'Good trying, Danny! Good job!'

You have a sudden memory of Danny before his regression, playing hide and seek. How he used to hide himself and then, unable to contain his excitement, shout out, 'Where could he be? Is he under the table? NOOOO! Is he under the bed? NOOOO! Is he in the shower? NOOOO!' It was so sweet, you always went along with it, looking in all the places he named. Later, a psychiatrist speculated that maybe, even then, Danny didn't have something called theory of mind, the ability to put himself in another person's shoes.

'Did I do the ABA programme with Danny before?' you ask Sian.

'You did, yes.'

'Was I good at it?'

She pauses before replying. 'When you wanted to be.'

'What does that mean?'

'ABA can be hard for parents. Sometimes they're too emotion-ally involved. Sometimes Abbie would say, "Why can't we just let him be himself?" But these procedures are evidence based. And it's unfair to kids like Danny not to help them reach their full potential.'

You notice she tends to say *Abbie*, not *you*. But at least she's moved on from *it*.

Every day you fall in love, and every day your heart is broken.

The mother of a child with autism knows her feelings for him will never be reciprocated. Her child will never say *I love you*, never draw a Mother's Day card, never proudly bring home a school project or a girlfriend or a fiancée or a grandchild. He will never tell you about his day, or confide his deepest fears.

Yet he will always need you, more than any other child could need you, precisely because he can't fight his battles on his own. He needs you to stop the world from crushing him. He needs you to be his translator, protector, bodyguard, advocate. He needs you to think twice before turning on the vacuum cleaner or the microwave or the hair dryer or whatever else might cause him agony. To do battle with doctors, waiters, teachers, fire alarms, the marketing idiots who changed the colour of a Cheerios packet on a whim without realising it would make him inconsolable for days.

He may never be able to accept a hug from you, let alone to hug you back. But instead you can stand before the world with your body braced and your arms outstretched, deflecting the blows that would otherwise rain down on him.

He will need you to teach him, slowly and painfully, the basics of everyday life: how to imitate, how to ask for food, how to choose clothes. How to recognise the difference between a smile and a frown, and what those strange contortions of a human face might actually mean.

And because of that, your love for him has a quality no other love can have. It burns with a fierce, undimmable energy. It's the love of a warrior who would die defending her position, sooner than step aside.

One evening, you're getting Danny ready for bed when you remember you left a saucepan boiling downstairs. When you get back, you discover he's taken his toothbrush and, very carefully, squeezed a tube of your new acrylic paint over it. And not just over the bristles: he closed his little fist tightly around the tube as he walked around. A long sine wave of Indian Red now adorns the white carpet on the landing.

He looks at you and smiles. That's when you discover he also cleaned his teeth with it. He looks like a cheerful little vampire.

'Well done, Danny,' you say, amazed. 'Good copying.' Because, while there's no point in telling him off for something he didn't know was wrong, the fact that he tried to imitate something he'd seen you doing is a breakthrough.

'Well, fizzle my fenders,' Danny mumbles dreamily, parroting one of his favourite expressions from *Thomas the Tank Engine*.

9

The three weeks are nowhere near up when Tim gets a call.

'He's done *what*?' he says incredulously. Then, 'No, I'll do it. I don't trust that idiot to fix this.'

He puts his phone down. 'That was Mike. Some stupid screw-up at the office. I'm going to have to go in.' He grimaces. 'If that's all right. I don't like leaving you.'

In truth, you'd known three whole weeks was going to be a stretch. Your honeymoon was only ten days, and even then Tim sneaked into the bathroom every morning to answer emails.

'I'll be fine. Besides, I want to finish going through my books.' You've devoured everything in the bookcases downstairs, but the big double-height bookshelves on the landing remain untouched.

'Well, if you need anything, just call me.' He takes something from his pocket. 'Here. It's time you had this again.'

'This' is a beaten-up old smartphone, scratched and battered, the screen a little chipped at the corners. It's encased in a papier-mâché shell made from layers of vintage wallpaper.

'You made that case yourself,' he adds. 'You were so good at things like that.'

Before he leaves, he kisses you on the forehead. 'Love you, Abs. See you later.'

'Love you too,' you echo.

As soon as he's gone, you turn on the phone. Tim still won't talk about what happened to you, but perhaps there's something here that will satisfy your curiosity.

You go into the texts. The most recent one was five years ago, sent to someone called Jacinta G.

Sure! Count me in for Pinot and character assassination! Abs xx

You've no idea who Jacinta is. But here you were, planning a girls' night. And then you died. Out of the blue, never expecting that text to be your last.

You keep scrolling. Most of the names mean nothing, lost in the fog. Then, suddenly, one pops out.

Lisa.

Your sister. Your finger hovers over the call button. But then you wonder how much Tim has told her. She may know nothing about this. About *you*. You can't just phone her out of the blue without some sort of warning. Reluctantly, you move on.

You see Tim's name. Your last text to him simply read:

Things going well here. OK if I stay another day? Xx

His reply came just a few minutes later:

Of course. As long as you like. x

You scroll up further, stopping at random.

Still up for date night? Reservation's @7 Axx

Tim's answer was badly typed – under the table of a meeting, perhaps:

Sadly mty date toniht will b w Ted's bozo coders. Going tp pull a late one.

No worries. Takeout? Xx

I'll piuck up grocries. Steak? candles? wine? choc dess?

You had me at choc dess. Xx

It was a happy marriage, you think. Despite Danny, despite Tim's Type-A personality, the two of you made it work.

You scroll on, stopping occasionally, until you reach a whole decade ago.

Thank you for a beautiful evening. And an even more beautiful night. Tim x

The pleasure was all mine, believe me! Axx

You feel a sudden pang of emotion. Eventually you and Tim may be able to go on date nights together. You can dance, hold hands, even kiss. But the special physical connection of love-making is another matter.

Unbidden, the exact word for what you feel about that lands in your thoughts, ready-made.

Your emotion about those texts is *envy*.

You're about to put the phone down when you spot the Safari icon on the menu bar. You tap it and a search engine appears, the box blank and inviting.

At last. Quickly you type in *Abbie Cullen-Scott San Francisco death accident? How?*

An agonising moment while it searches. And then –

Page Blocked.

You look at it, wondering. Blocked how?

Then you realise. Tim must have set up some kind of filter. Like one of those parental-control apps, with the details of your own death as the blacklisted content.

It's because he loves you, you tell yourself. He guessed the temptation would be too great. It's a sign of how well he knows you. How much he cares about protecting you from pain.

You wonder if he'll be sent some kind of alert now. You hope not. It would be nice to keep your weakness to yourself.

And nicer still if your husband had trusted you in the first place, you can't help thinking. Even as you ruefully acknowledge that he was right not to.

You wonder what else he's screened from you. Picking up the phone again, you try Facebook, then Twitter, then Instagram. Only Instagram loads, and even then, links to certain accounts seem to be blocked.

Are there horrors here he has chosen to shield you from? What insinuations does he not want the roiling, restless multitudes of the web to whisper in your ears?

Then you remember the disgust in the eyes of the Prius driver who brought you home. Imagine that, being flung at you online!

Tim's right, you decide. Too much reality right now would not be a good thing.

THREE

Abbie Cullen didn't do very much, to begin with. She sat at a spare desk. We pointed out to her the break room, the free bagels and tubs of cream cheese, the restrooms, and where to put the recycling. Jenny Austin – Mike's wife – brought over a spare laptop, and there was a rush to be the one to help Abbie connect it to our network. (Tim refused on principle to have an IT administrator, on the basis that if you weren't smart enough to do that kind of stuff yourself, you shouldn't be working for him.) And then she just kind of sat around, chatting.

There was a pool table in the office, but it almost never got used. Nobody wanted to be the person who was shooting pool when Tim Scott walked by. It was generally just a convenient place to stack late-night pizza deliveries, and its soft blue baize was stained like an old mattress with their leakings. But when Abbie Cullen picked up a cue, turned to the nearest person – who happened to be Rajesh – and said, 'Wanna play?' we not only tolerated it, we went to watch.

She was not even quiet. When she won a shot, she whooped.

Pretty soon she developed a programme of going around and asking people to explain to her what they did. She would squat down next to our chairs, so she didn't tower over us, or sit on our desks, swinging her long legs, asking us questions. And she seemed genuinely interested, even amazed, by what to us was now fairly everyday and mundane. She was *sweet*. She had a way of reaching out and resting her hand on our arms to make a point, which was – well, *flirtatious* would be the wrong word. It was more like she saw no reason not to be tactile, and no one in her life had ever seen any reason to make her feel self-conscious about it.

We didn't either, of course. We were charmed.

The second day, she wore a Debbie Harry T-shirt under an old leather jacket, and ripped jeans. Some of us did wonder if that was a bit too casual, for the office. But then she was an artist, not a regular employee.

Someone asked her if she knew what her first project would be, and she shook her head. 'I'm still waiting for an idea.' Not, *I'm working on it*, or even, *It'll come*; she was just waiting for something to show up and announce itself. We admired her confidence, but we also worried for her. What if no idea ever came? At what point would she give up? And if she gave up, would she leave us?

So we waited along with her, and gradually What Abbie Might Do became a topic – perhaps even *the* topic – of conversation in the break room.

'She's talking to the form-cutters this morning. I expect she'll want to use the 3-D printer.'

'I heard she's thinking of doing some portraits of us.'

'She's interested in how the bots are coded. I bet she'll incorporate that into her project.'

It was when she started talking back to Tim, though, that she reached another level in our affections.

It was quite a small thing, the first time. Tim was tearing a strip off one of the new developers. We felt for the guy; we had all been in his position, though we also experienced a secret thrill that it was now someone else's turn. We called these bawling-outs 'Tim-lashings' or 'getting Timmed', just as we called all-nighters 'Tim time' and pre-dawn was 'Tim o'clock'. And, to be fair, his outbursts were rarely unwarranted, merely excruciating. With Tim, the particular failings of the task you had messed up on were never merely errors. They were much worse than that: an indication that you didn't subscribe to the same perfectionist worldview as him, that your standards or your commitment were somehow eternally compromised. He could move from the particular to the philosophical in a nanosecond.

'We don't do *workarounds*,' he was snapping at the hapless developer. 'We don't do *betas*. And we particularly don't do *failure*. If something's not good enough, don't fix it – *reinvent* it. You think Elon Musk set out to build a better car? *Wrong*. He set out to build the thing that would *replace* the car. While you, my friend, are still polishing *fenders*.'

To which Abbie said, 'What's wrong with a bike?'

It was not a particularly smart or witty remark. But the fact she said it at all – that she acknowledged the way Tim was yelling at the poor guy within earshot of everyone – broke the unwritten rule, the fourth wall that separated us from him. And silently, inwardly, we applauded her for it.

He gave her a blank look. 'Nothing's wrong with bikes. Any time you want to invent a self-driving bike, feel free.'

And so it began.

10

Upstairs, you spread out some old sheets and get to work on the bookcase, methodically removing a shelf's worth of books at a time. The tops are grimy – clearly, no one else has touched them in years. You wipe each one with a cloth before separating out those you intend to read. With the more interesting ones, you flick through in search of notes or annotations too. For a moment, you can't recall the right word for that kind of thing. Then it comes to you. *Marginalia*. Of course. You are a person who enjoys such words, you are discovering.

You wonder if you always did, or whether it's something to do with your new, deep-learning brain.

The big shelves at the bottom mostly contain cookbooks. *Happy Abbie-versary*, Tim's written inside a book of Venetian recipes, *Best trip ever!* Inside *The Unofficial Harry Potter Cookbook* you find the cryptic inscription, *Present number thirty-seven!!* A copy of *Dishes from India* is inscribed, *To Ms Abigail Cullen, soon to be Mrs Cullen-Scott. From the happiest engineer in the world.*

Tucked into the flap is a theatre programme, something experimental at the Cutting Ball. Scribbled on the back, in your handwriting and Tim's, is an exchange:

Asleep??

Not quite.

I'm thinking about FOOD.

Mmmm . . .

Italian?

Oysters!

Bail?

I'm right behind you.

And a hand-painted Valentine in the shape of a heart. *Dearest Tim, I give you my heart.*

Another word comes to you, equally satisfying. *Ephemera.*

As you pull out Elizabeth David's *French Provincial Cooking*, it falls open at a page crusted with pink cooking stains. A sentence has been underlined: *It is useless attempting to make a bouillabaisse away from the shores of the Mediterranean.* In the margin, your earlier self has written, *YOU'RE ON!!!!* Below is what looks like a shopping list:

> *Rascasse*
> *John Dory*
> *Galinette (substitute Gurnard?)*
> *Saffron*

And, in a different pen:

> *N.B. Next time, simmer the tomatoes TWICE as long as*
> *this tyrant says.*

Smiling, you put the book to one side. You can't eat anything yourself, but you like the thought of cooking something nice for Tim that you cooked before.

You're halfway through the bookcase when your phone pings. For a moment you wonder who it could be. But then you remember: Tim's the only person who knows your phone's in use again.

U OK? Hate that I'm not there with you. X

Affectionately, you text back:

Your job needs you! I'm fine. Love U. Xx

You wait, but he doesn't reply.

Reaching up, you pull another book from one of the upper shelves, almost falling backwards as the cover comes away from the pages. A broken binding. It must have been a favourite, you think, for you to have kept it even in this poor condition. Perhaps it can be rebound.

Carefully, you open it. Then you realise something. The book inside is smaller than the cover. In fact, you now see, it's a different book altogether, a paperback that's had its own front and back covers ripped off. But you can still read the title, printed at the top of every page.

Overcoming Infatuation. Some kind of self-help book.

Flicking through, you see that some passages have squiggles next to them. And at the end of one chapter, a paragraph has been underlined:

> Limerence, or infatuated love, is outwardly almost identical to the real thing. But just as a little salt seasons meat while too much poisons it, so love and limerence are actually two sides of a coin.

You put it aside to show Tim. Perhaps he can explain it.

As you turn back to the shelves, your phone pings again. You pick it up eagerly, thinking it's Tim's reply. But the sender's name simply says *FRIEND*.

Puzzled, you open it. On the screen are just four words:

This phone isn't safe.

You stare at it. There are no earlier texts above it, nothing to indicate who 'Friend' might be.

As you watch, the message slowly fades from the screen. Some kind of Snapchat-type spam, you decide.

Putting the phone down, you continue with the books. You're almost at the end of the row when you notice a volume of poetry, *Ariel,* by Sylvia Plath. A memory leaps in your mind. You read those poems as a teenager and fell in love with them, the way only a teenager can.

You pull the volume out. But this cover, too, simply slides away from what's inside. Intrigued, you prise the contents from the shelf. This time, though, it isn't a book that the cover's concealing.

It's a small electronic tablet. An iPad Mini, hidden away here, where no one would ever think to look for it.

Unlike your phone, there's no arty personalised case, nothing to indicate whose it is. But it must be yours. No one else, surely, would hide something among *your* books like this.

Who's it hidden from? Danny?

No. Back then, if you'd wanted to keep it away from Danny, you'd simply have placed it somewhere his five-year-old hands couldn't reach.

From Tim, you realise. It can only be hidden from Tim.

Are you the kind of woman who keeps things from her husband? The thought is disturbing, almost shocking. But, at the same time, not entirely surprising. It feels . . . It feels *right*, the way a word or a fact sometimes does.

After all, Tim is the very opposite of laid-back. Perhaps you'd wanted to avoid a lengthy debate about something. A woman has a right to privacy, even within a marriage.

But a whole hidden iPad? an inner voice objects. *That feels like more than just privacy.*

That feels like secrecy.

And then there's Friend. How strange is it that you get a message saying your phone isn't safe at the exact moment another device turns up?

You hold down the iPad's power button. Nothing happens – the battery's long since depleted. You take it down to the kitchen and plug it into the charger. As you turn back upstairs, the intercom buzzes, startling you. Behind the coloured glass of the front door, a face fragments into orange and red. The straggly hair looks familiar.

You go and open it. On the doorstep is Tim's colleague, the one who tried to stop you from leaving the office. A black laptop case hangs from his shoulder. You search for his name. *Mike Austin*, that's it.

'Abbie,' he says. 'Hey.'

'Tim's not here. He's gone to the office.'

He nods. 'I know. I just came from there.'

'Then why—'

'It's you I've come to see,' he interrupts. 'I wanted to talk to you alone.'

11

You make him coffee.

'Is it strange,' he says carefully as you put the cup down in front of him, 'not being able to drink that yourself?'

'Believe me, that's the least of what seems strange about all this.'

'I guess so.' There's a short silence while he blows on his coffee, watching you over the rim of the cup. 'What do you remember about *me*, Abbie?'

'I saw you at the office. You work with Tim.'

'That's true. But I'm much more than a colleague. I'm Tim's oldest friend. The co-founder of Scott Robotics. I was best man at your wedding . . . You don't remember that?'

You don't, no. 'Tim said something about having to be selective. Not giving me too many memories all at once.' You pause. 'He won't even tell me how I died.'

'Did he explain why not?'

'He said it might be too much to handle.'

Mike takes a mouthful of coffee before replying. 'Well, he's correct about that. Creating a sentient AI from scratch in less than five years – it's an extraordinary achievement. But Tim's been . . . Tim's been pretty driven about it. The only thing that mattered was speed. Getting it done as fast as possible. Getting to *you*.'

You don't understand the point he's making. 'And he did it. Against all the odds, here I am.'

'Yes – here you are. But as for *how* you are . . . Have you heard of an AI called Tay?'

You shake your head.

'Tay was an adaptive-learning chatbot that Microsoft's research division put out on Twitter a couple of years back. Its first tweets were charming – telling everyone how cool humanity was, how happy it was to be here, that kind of thing. Within twenty-four hours it was tweeting that feminists should burn in hell and Hitler was right about the Jews. The adaptive learning had worked *too* well.'

'Well, I'll try not to go crazy. Or go on Twitter.'

You meant it as a joke, but Mike nods seriously.

'Look, I probably understand the way your brain works better than anyone. But even I couldn't swear we got everything right. We didn't always have time to check our steps.' He swings his laptop case up onto the table. 'Really, it was pretty irresponsible of Tim to take you away before we'd run some tests. But I can check you out right here.'

'This is what you do, isn't it?' you remember. 'That's what your job really is – to go around after him, sorting out whatever he's been too impatient to deal with first time around. When he cuts a corner, you go back and check it. When he's overhasty, you take care of the detail.'

Mike gives a thin smile. 'I prefer to think of it as complementary skills. Tim's like an architect – he sees the big picture. But an architect is only ever as good as his builder. Stand up, would you?' He pulls a cable from his bag.

You get to your feet. 'And you're sure Tim won't mind?'

'Actually, I wouldn't mention this to Tim if I were you. You'd probably just set him off unnecessarily.' Mike bends down. You hear the click as his cable slots into your hip.

You're uneasy. Doing something like this behind Tim's back feels wrong.

But then, you think, you don't intend to say anything about that iPad, either. At least, not until you know what's on it.

A series of beeps issue from Mike's computer. 'What are you testing for?' you ask.

Intent now on his screen, he doesn't look up. 'Like I said, Tim was in something of a rush. So, rather than design an artificial mind from scratch, it seemed easier just to construct a digital replica of the human brain. Or rather, the human *brains*, plural. Most people don't realise, but the main part of our brain, the bit that looks like a big walnut, is a relatively recent addition – it evolved after we learnt to use language. Beneath it, there's an older, smaller organ called the limbic brain, which dates back to the first mammals. That's where the emotions are generated – friendship, love, all the things that make us sociable.'

'And that's where my empathy comes from?'

'We believe so,' he says cautiously. 'And then, underneath *that*, there's an older brain still, the reptilian brain. That's what controls our unconscious compulsions – breathing, balance, the survival instinct. How the three structures interact is still something of a mystery. And, of course, sometimes the balance gets out of whack. It's not a great design by any means, at least not on paper – it's like a house that's been extended multiple times over the centuries, instead of being conceived from the ground up. Mostly it works fine, but when it goes wrong, it's a bitch to fix. In theory, you could be susceptible to all the same problems humans can have – personality disorders, psychosis, confabulation . . .'

'Confabulation?'

'Self-deception. Making things up without realising it.'

You stare at him. 'Are you saying I can't trust my memories?'

'No one should ever entirely trust their memories. I take it you haven't noticed any problems?'

'No,' you say curtly.

'Good.' Mike's hands scuttle across his keyboard. The clicking sets your teeth on edge.

Something else occurs to you. 'If you're his best friend, why hasn't Tim uploaded any memories with you in them? Why can't I remember you at all?'

Mike looks up from his laptop. 'Probably because he knows I don't like you very much,' he says calmly. 'That I loathe you, in fact.'

12

'Me then? Or me now?' you say, taken aback.

'Both,' Mike says. 'Although "loathed" might be too strong a word to use about the original Abbie. I mean, it was pretty hard to dislike you all that much. You were this idealistic, fresh-faced twenty-something, without a cynical bone in your body. You were even into tech, for Christ's sake. It was hardly a surprise Tim fell for you. It wasn't you who was the problem. It was *him*.'

It was a whirlwind courtship, Mike explains. Tim was completely head-over-heels in love.

'It's an issue in our industry. In school, the geeks aren't cool enough to get the girls. Even the good-looking ones find themselves in all-male study groups. Then, after college, they're trying to get a start-up off the ground and there's no time for a social life. Until they raise some serious funding, and then – *wham*. Suddenly they're rich, they're flying around the world giving speeches, they're offered the best tables in nightclubs and they're being interviewed by *Vanity Fair* and *Time* magazine. Half of them are still virgins at that point. It's no wonder they lose their heads to the first beautiful woman who comes along and tells them how fascinating they are.'

You frown. 'Tim didn't lose his head. He lost his *heart*. It's not the same.'

'Maybe,' Mike says, shrugging. 'But you didn't exactly fight it. You only had to mention some designer's name and Tim was beating on their door, buying you the latest dress or bag. Which, as often as not, you'd take back and swap for something you liked better. He had terrible taste, as you often liked to remind him.'

The clothes in the walk-in closet, you think. Those expensive boho-chic labels. 'Are you saying I was some kind of gold-digger?'

Mike shakes his head. 'Tim was well aware some women only wanted him for his money – founder-hounders, they're called around here. He was pretty good at spotting those. And, to be fair, you weren't materialistic. But you did lap up his attention. You were on the rebound from some toxic relationship or other, and I guess it felt good to be adored.'

His coffee cup is almost empty now. Absent-mindedly, he turns it round by the top with his fingertips as he speaks, as if it's a dial he's slowly cranking up to maximum.

'Tim couldn't see the problems. To me, they were clear as day. People say opposites attract, but study after study shows it's actually similarities that make for solid long-term relationships. Similarities – and pragmatism.

'When Tim gives you his full attention, it can make you feel like the most important person in the world. Add to that the whole jet-setting lifestyle – the houses, the cars, the red carpets, the fund-raisers – and it's a bit like you've bought into a fairy tale. But that's just on the surface. Really, his life is about the all-nighters, the funding deadlines, the endless emails, the coding crises. That's what motivates him and consumes a hundred per

cent of his energy. People like Tim need quiet, supportive partners who are happy to stay in the background. Not grand passions
that only serve to distract them.'

Mike sounds almost sad, you think. And with a flash of insight
you realise what really happened back then.

Mike was *jealous*. Back in the garage, he'd had Tim all to himself. Little by little, as the company grew, that relationship had
been diluted. But at least it was still all about their baby, this
enterprise they'd created together.

The last thing Mike would have wanted was for Tim to fall in
love with someone outside the company's magic circle. To be
diverted from the mission.

You don't say any of that, though. Instead, you say mildly, 'And
now? What's your problem with who I am now?'

'Where do I start?' he says with a rueful smile. 'Don't get me
wrong – it's nothing personal. And losing your wife is a tragedy
I wouldn't wish on anyone, let alone my best friend. After you
died, Tim pretty much fell apart. And the company almost fell
apart with him – after all, he *is* the company, as far as our backers
are concerned. When, about a year later, he suddenly announced
he wanted us to start working on an AI with emotional intelligence, I thought it was a sign he was finally getting over you,
thinking about the business again. So I said, "Sure, let's go
for it."'

You doubt Tim had been asking for Mike's permission, but
again you keep the thought to yourself. 'And?'

'Oh, he threw himself into it. His determination was extraordinary, even for him. He drove our employees like a bastard –
some couldn't take it, but Tim just went out and hired more,

irrespective of cost. It was eighteen months before he told me what his plans really were. I couldn't believe it. Everything we'd done – every cent we'd borrowed, every mortgage we'd signed, every all-nighter we'd pulled – it had all been about *you*. And now he's got you . . .'

'Yes?'

'For all the millions we've spent, what have we actually proved?' Mike asks quietly. 'That we have the technology to build a very approximate replica of a dead human being. Yes, it's a breakthrough, but – so what? Only a man deranged by his own grief could think that's a direction society should be travelling in. How does it make the world more productive? What does it *change*? Nothing – it simply fossilises the past. People die – it's a tragedy, sure, but there are other people to fall in love with, and so life goes on. Compared with driverless cars, or nanosurgery, or even a drone delivery for your groceries, you're a cul-de-sac. Extraordinary technology, yes. But yoked to a pointless application.' He stops. 'At least, I'm pretty sure that's what Tim would have said about it, if it had been anyone else but him and you.'

'He loves me,' you say defensively. 'Some men build a memorial. He built an AI.'

'Memorials bring closure. You're the exact opposite. Think about it – for as long as you exist, he'll never get over the death of the real Abbie, or know what it is to have the love of a new woman in his life. At best, you'll only ever be a pale shadow of the person he once loved. How is that a meaningful relationship? Another woman, someone who isn't Abbie Cullen and isn't even trying to be – *that* woman might have had a chance of healing him, of helping him move on. And now she'll be denied that

67

chance. Your existence deprives Tim of the very thing he was trying to achieve.'

You feel a flash of anger, not least because you can see Mike's point. 'And if he *had* moved on and met someone else, you'd be jealous of her, too. You'd resent *her* for being the focus of his attention, instead of you and your precious company.'

Mike smiles thinly. 'You think you're the first to say something like that to me? I know my place in Tim's life. I made my peace with it long ago. Sure, I stand in his shadow. But that's a pretty big place. And *I'm* lucky enough to have a rock-solid marriage of my own.'

'To Jenny. One of your own employees.'

'To Jenny,' he agrees. 'The most brilliant programmer I've ever worked with. Who understands that a long-term relationship is about kindness and compromise and, yes, hard work sometimes.' He closes his laptop. 'The good news is, you're working fine. But that may be down to good luck rather than good coding.'

There's a ping from across the room. Guiltily, you turn towards it, thinking it might be the iPad, but then you realise it's just your phone. You go and pick it up. Another text.

Love u too. How u doing? Not bored? x

'Tim?' Mike asks.

'Yes.' Quickly, you text back.

All good! X

'Did you tell him I'm here?'

You shake your head.

'I think that's the right decision. We'll keep this between ourselves.' Mike starts winding up his computer cable. 'This is something you'll soon learn, Abbie. With Tim, honesty is not always the best policy. The secret to managing him successfully is to be selective.'

'I'm not trying to *manage* him at all. He's my husband.'

Mike doesn't reply for a moment. Then he says, 'You know, we have something in common, you and I. We both want what's best for Tim. Just remember how fragile he still is, would you? The very last thing he needs is any more emotional upheaval. Any more *hurt*. Right now, that could destroy him.'

His eyes hold yours. This has nothing to do with the tests he just carried out, you realise: in fact, you're pretty sure now those were simply a pretext, an excuse to come here and have this conversation.

Mike's warning you about something. Something you don't even know yourself yet. But whatever it is, he wants you to keep it a secret.

13

When Mike's gone, you go and look at the iPad. Thirteen per cent charged now. You thumb the switch. The Apple logo appears, followed by a message saying the operating system needs to check for updates.

Finally, a keypad appears. *iPad requires passcode after restart.*

You search your memory for numbers that might have some significance for you. You try your birthday, then your year of birth. Each time, the iPad shakes the screen. *Wrong.*

You grimace, frustrated.

The simplest thing, of course, would be to tell Tim. He could give the iPad to his tech people to unlock. You start to put it somewhere he'll see it when he returns. But then you stop.

If there *are* secrets on that iPad, they're *your* secrets. You didn't want Tim to know about them back then. Until you know what they are, isn't it best to play it safe and say nothing, at least for now?

And then there's Mike's warning. If whatever's on the iPad will cause Tim grief, it might be better for him not to know about it.

You try not to listen to the small voice inside you that's saying, *You're worried it's something that'll make him think less of you.*

Because the thought has crossed your mind: what if, before

you died, you were having an affair? You have no memory of that, obviously. But from what you've understood of Tim's explanations, your memories were constructed from your digital footprint – social media, texts, emails, videos and so on. By definition, anything you kept hidden from the world would be a blank.

You don't think you're the sort of woman who would ever be unfaithful to her husband. You love him. But if you can't remember, how can you rule it out?

And then there's that book. Who was it you were infatuated with, exactly? Tim? It seems unlikely, after so many years of marriage. And if it *was* him, why hide the book away?

How horribly ironic it would be if, after he'd spent five years obsessively recreating his perfect wife, Tim discovered within a few weeks that she wasn't so perfect after all.

You stare at the front door, thinking.

There's a tiny phone shop near the corner of Mission and Cesar Chavez that does iPad repairs – or used to, five years ago. You remember there was a handwritten sign in the window: *Smartphones/tablets unlocked.*

It's time to leave the house.

FOUR

Who was the first to add her on Facebook? It was probably Bethany or Cath; it would have looked creepy if it had been one of the guys. But, because we had pretty much all friended each other anyway, one day there she was, showing up in our 'People You May Know' feeds, initially with one friend in common, then two, then twenty. Abbie Cullen was accepting us!

So now we knew not only what she was like in the office, but also what she did with her weekends, what her family looked like at their last Thanksgiving, and what her political opinions were. (Not that they had been hard to guess.) She 'liked' other artists, mostly, supporting their shows and openings, but there was enough detail on her timeline to satisfy our curiosity in other areas too.

We learnt that she had started off as part of an all-female collective that built surreal metal sculptures at rock festivals. We learnt that her parents were divorced, and that her father was a minor celebrity, an East Coast academic who had fronted several thoughtful TV documentaries. We learnt what she looked like on a surfboard (impressive), on vacation in a swimsuit (stunning), and which college she had attended. (That she'd gone to Stanford was both a surprise and a cause for delight; many of us were graduates of that institution, although we had majored in subjects like mathematics and symbolic systems rather than art.) We learnt – and this caused a minor flurry of excitement, or would have done if we had not been carrying out these researches privately, covertly, each on his or her own initiative – that, according to Google's image-recognition app, the heavily tattooed young man in many of her timeline photographs was Rick Powell, frontman of The Purple Fireflies, who – again according to Google – was now in a relationship with Heidi Joekker, the Victoria's Secret model.

Was Abbie newly single? We wondered, but Facebook wasn't saying. One of us would ask her eventually, though. We were sure of that.

We didn't expect it to be Megan Meyer. Megan was not one of us. She was a Silicon Valley dating coach whose company, Meyer Matching, specialised in pairing high-net-worth executives. Her website made no secret of her fees, which were – frankly – astronomical: $1,500 for the initial interview, $25,000 for entry-level membership, which guaranteed at least one date a month, and $5,000 for a one-to-one coaching session, which might encompass anything from a fashion consultation to practice dates. Oh, and if you settled into an exclusive relationship with one of your Meyer Matches – each of whom was personally vetted by Megan herself – you coughed up a bonus of $50,000. For the big triple M – a Meyer Match Marriage – you were talking $250K, payable every five years, for as long as the marriage continued. Given those kind of charges, it was no surprise that her clientele came almost exclusively from the C class – CEOs, CFOs, CTOs.

The first time we spotted Megan in Tim's office, a few years back, it caused a ripple of interest. But on reflection, we felt almost sorry for her. The very fact that Tim had summoned her to his workplace for the initial interview suggested she'd bitten off more than any matchmaker could reasonably be expected to chew.

Shortly after, a profile appeared on her website, under the heading *Bachelor #4*:

ARE YOU A MATCH FOR BACHELOR #4?

Our bachelor is an extremely successful entrepreneur: passionate, dynamic and motivated.

As CEO of his own highly successful start-up, he has many demands on his time. But he is also someone who thinks deeply about the future, and is now fully committed to finding the right person to share his own future with.

A man of extremely high standards, used to making far-reaching decisions on a daily basis, he believes he would know within minutes whether he had met his lifelong partner.

His perfect match is 22–25 years old, petite, brilliant and ambitious. She has feminine curves, unfussy hair, and a natural, healthy appearance without heavy make-up, tattoos or coloured nail polish. She will likely have a background in molecular biology or calculus. She is smart, poised, loving, family orientated, nurturing, altruistic, and a non-smoker. She is excited to forge a remarkable future with a world-class partner.

Candidates should apply, in writing, here, with a CV and six recent photographs.

That had been a while ago now, and if Tim had been dating since, we certainly weren't aware of it. (There was that thing with

Drunk Karen at the summer party; no one was surprised when, a few weeks later, now-sober Karen quietly moved on.) Megan strode into the office from time to time on her three-inch Manolo Blahniks, showed Tim some headshots on her iPad, then went away again, shaking her head. One time she was heard to sigh loudly as she climbed into her top-of-the-line convertible Jaguar.

About three weeks after Abbie started her residency, Megan came in for one of her usual sessions with Tim. But afterwards, instead of leaving, she followed Abbie into the break room. Sol Ayode was in there, assembling a bagel, so he heard it all.

'Megan goes up to Abbie, all bright-eyed and smiley,' he reported. 'And Megan's like, "Hi!" and Abbie goes, "Hi!" right back. Then Megan introduces herself and gives Abbie her card, and Abbie says sorry, she doesn't have a card to give in return, because she's an artist. So then there's a bit of discussion about Abbie's art. Then Megan asks her straight out if she's ever considered signing up with an executive dating agency, because she – Megan – happens to have some really good clients she thinks Abbie would be perfect for.

'To which Abbie says –' at this point, Sol paused for dramatic effect – '*Abbie* says, "I don't think a dating agency's my kind of thing. Whatever happens, happens, right?" To which *Megan* says, "No, really, we vet all our clients personally; you couldn't hope for a better introduction to some of the most fascinating and successful men in the Valley." To which *Abbie* says –' another pause – '"That's really not what I'm looking for."

'"Oh?" says Megan. "So what *are* you looking for?" And Abbie goes . . .' Here, Sol was clearly torn between his desire to insert yet another dramatic pause and his eagerness to deliver the next line just as quickly as he possibly could. 'Abbie goes, "Well, my last relationship was polyamorous."'

Her last relationship was polyamorous. Of course it was. What did we expect? She was an artist. She was so much cooler than us.

It was Ryan – workshop Ryan, not developer Ryan – who was the first to speculate, after hearing this story, that Megan Meyer might not have struck up a conversation with Abbie on her own initiative, but had actually been acting on Tim's instructions. Had he expressed an interest in Abbie, even then? Or – we soon built on Ryan's suggestion – had Megan picked up on Tim's interest somehow and decided that, if a relationship was on the cards, better that it happen with her own involvement, and therefore commission, than not?

And, if so, had she pointed out to her client that Abbie barely met a single one of his stated criteria, from her height right through to the hand-rolled cigarettes she occasionally smoked by the fire escape?

The fact is, we didn't know if this was what had happened or not. But it fed into the obsessive mythology we had already created around Tim Scott. So that was what we chose to believe.

14

You find a coat, then – remembering the disgust in the eyes of the Prius driver who brought you home – add a hat, scarf and dark glasses.

At the front door, you hesitate. Tim didn't actually forbid you from going out, but he certainly warned you against doing it too soon.

Screw it, you think. You can't hide away at home forever.

As you reach for the door handle, you catch sight of yourself in the mirror. You look ridiculous. You take off the scarf.

Once through the gates, you turn right, heading south. When the sky doesn't fall in, you start to feel less tense. A jogger runs past with a dog on a leash. Both ignore you. A young Latino gives you a brief glance, but it's one of appreciation, nothing more. A child in a stroller smiles at you tentatively. His mother, chatting on her phone, doesn't even look in your direction.

Mission Street seems different – cleaner, smarter than it used to be; there's no sign of the guy, brain fried on crack, who used to drag an electric toaster around by its cord and talk to it as if it were a pet. But the phone shop's still there, next to the Korean restaurant, its tiny window piled high with phones and SIM packs. The handwritten sign is still there too, almost crowded out by

IPHONES JAILBROKEN and an illuminated dot-matrix sign flashing *LAPTOP REPAIRS*.

Inside the shop, a nerdy hipster with an elaborate beard leans over the counter, carefully picking a broken screen out of a phone with tweezers.

'Hi,' you say, a little nervously.

'With you in a sec,' he says without looking up.

You wait for him to finish. He has a mass of very curly black hair. You find yourself gazing at it, fascinated by the way it moves.

'How can I help?' he says at last, pushing the phone to one side.

'It's this.' You produce the iPad. 'I've forgotten the passcode.'

'Sure you didn't steal it?' he asks as he takes it.

'Of course not. It's mine.' You don't seem to be able to blush, which is good.

'Just kidding.' He presses the power button and looks at the screen. 'Why don't you restore it from the backup?'

'I forgot to set a backup,' you say lamely.

'Hmm.' You can tell he doesn't believe you. 'Well, if it *is* yours, there's a way of getting access to some of the apps.'

He presses the home button. For a moment, nothing happens. Then an electronic voice says, 'What can I help you with?'

'Siri, open the dangle-dally app,' the young man says.

'You don't seem to have an app named dangle-dally. We could see if the App Store has it,' Siri says helpfully.

'Sure, let's do that.'

As if by magic, the App Store screen appears. The young man taps the button again, and there's the home page.

'That's amazing . . . What was that you just downloaded?'

'Nothing. Just a non-existent application to fool Siri.' He looks at the screen again and frowns. 'Which is not to say your problems are over. This iPad's been wiped. Those are just the default apps you're seeing there.'

'Oh,' you say, disappointed. 'Isn't there anything else we can try?'

'I could run a recovery program. It'll take at least twenty-four hours, though. Come back in a couple of days and we'll see what we've got.' He reaches for a receipt pad. 'Name?'

You don't like leaving the iPad, but you don't really have a choice. 'I'm Abbie.'

While you've been talking, a middle-aged couple have come into the shop. You've been vaguely aware of them behind you, whispering, the woman's voice occasionally rising in urgency. Now she says suddenly, 'It *is* her. I'm going to ask.' Putting her hand on your arm, she says, 'Excuse me, are you Abbie Cullen-Scott?'

'Yes . . . Why?' you say, surprised.

'Oh my God! And you're all right?'

'I'm fine. Thank you for asking.'

'My goodness! And do you mind . . . I mean, it's none of my business, but – what happened?'

'What do you mean?' Then you realise. They think you're the old Abbie, somehow come back from the dead.

'I . . . Well, I don't actually remember . . .' you begin.

'You lost your memory!' She turns to her husband triumphantly. 'You see? I told you. I always said it wasn't him.'

'I thought you said it was.' Her husband barely sounds interested. He looks at the man behind the counter. 'We've come for the Galaxy that got dropped in the bath.'

'No, I didn't,' the woman insists. She turns back to you. 'What caused it, if you don't mind my asking?'

'Perhaps she doesn't remember that, either,' her husband suggests.

'Let her answer, Steve,' the woman says sharply.

'Actually, your husband's right,' you say. 'I don't remember anything about it—'

'But you're here now!' the woman announces, as though it's somehow her doing. 'You're back! And with your husband?'

'Honey . . .' her husband remonstrates, but the woman presses on.

'We signed the petition. Just so you know. He had so much support around here.'

You're barely listening. It's just occurred to you that public news of your so-called miraculous return might not fit in with Tim's plans at all.

'There's been a mistake. I'm not . . .' Suddenly the little shop seems terrifyingly claustrophobic. 'Excuse me,' you say desperately, trying to push past them to the door.

'She isn't well!' the woman exclaims. 'Steve, call the police.'

'What with?' he says lugubriously. 'You dropped my phone in the bath while you were playing *Candy Crush*.'

'We're in a phone store!' the woman snaps. 'Oh, *I'll* do it.' She pulls a mobile phone out of her pocket.

'Please, stay here,' she says to you as she dials. 'Everything's going to be all right.'

'Are you calling the *police*?' the young man behind the counter says incredulously. He starts taking phones from the shelves and dropping them into a box.

'You've got this all wrong,' you insist. 'There's really no need—'
But the woman's already talking to an operator, giving the address,
saying they need to send a police car and isn't it amazing, she's
found her, she's found Abbie Cullen-Scott.

15

You're standing there, wondering what to do, when your own phone rings. The caller ID says *Tim*.

'Where are you?' He sounds worried.

'At a phone repair shop.'

'Why? Is something wrong with your phone?'

Now's hardly the moment to tell him about the iPad. 'It was nothing – it's sorted now. But some people saw me and they've called the police—'

'Don't talk to the police,' he interrupts. 'Do you hear me, Abbie? Get out of there. Go west one block, then take a right on Bartlett—'

'How do you know which street I'm on?' you say as you start walking.

'I can see you on Find My Phone. I got worried when you didn't answer the house phone just now. Go quickly, will you?'

'Tim, I'm so sorry,' you say miserably. 'You said not to go out.'

'Don't worry about that now. Are you moving?'

'Yes. As fast as I can.' You look over your shoulder. The couple are following you, the woman still on her phone, the man lagging behind, embarrassed. In the distance, you hear a siren.

'I think the police are coming,' you add. 'What do I tell them?'

Tim sighs. 'Tell them the truth. But Abbie – don't believe everything they tell *you*, OK? I'll come and get you.'

'Why? What might they tell me? Tim, what do you mean?'

'It's complicated—'

'Abbie? Abbie Cullen-Scott?' A uniformed policewoman, short and stocky, absurdly overdressed, with as many bits of equipment hanging off her as a mountaineer, is touching your arm. 'Mrs Cullen-Scott, you need to come with us. We'll get you looked after.'

FIVE

It was Darren's turn to get Tim-lashed, and he was getting the whole nine yards.

'I wanted it *seamless*,' Tim yelled at him. 'I wanted it *immersive*. And instead, you've brought me this *garbage*.'

'It *will* be seamless,' Darren said nervously. 'It's still under development.'

There was a pause, but only because Tim had taken a breath, as if he was genuinely *startled*, shocked even, by the idiocy of Darren's response.

'I *know* it's under development. That's why I hired a *developer*. Except I didn't, did I? I hired a third-rate *bozo* who doesn't know development from *diarrhoea*.'

'I just don't think what you're asking for is possible—' Darren began.

And now it was our turn to draw in our collective breath, because we all saw that Darren had committed a terrible error. The statement he had just made – that he was being asked to do the impossible – never went down well with Tim in any case. Not for nothing did he have a framed quotation by Muhammad Ali on his wall, something to do with the word *impossible* not being a fact, just someone's opinion. But more importantly, what Darren had just said was inconsistent with his own previous statement, that he would fix it in due course. He wasn't the first to lose his nerve under a Tim-lashing, but we all knew he was about to get ripped apart for it.

Except Abbie didn't know that. Abbie looked across at Tim and said, in a tone of genuine curiosity, 'Why do you have to be so *aggressive*?'

Tim stared at her.

'Why don't you try being *nice* for a change?' she went on. 'It's not as if it's going to make the poor guy any more productive.'

We braced for the explosion. But it never came. Instead, in a voice so calm it was almost eerie, Tim said, 'Actually, you're wrong about that.'

'*How* am I wrong?'

'Take a look at the *Journal of Experimental Psychology*, volume forty-seven, issue six. The authors designed a study to look at the effects of different moods on creativity. People who are angry not only have more ideas more quickly, they also tend to have ideas that are judged more original by their peers.'

'That's bullshit,' Abbie said disbelievingly.

Tim shook his head. 'The results have been replicated several times. There's a good one in the *Personality and Social Psychology Bulletin*, volume thirty-four, number twelve. Subjects gave a short presentation that received either negative or positive feedback on a randomised basis. They were then asked to complete a creative task, which was evaluated by a group of experienced artists. Those who had been given harsh feedback significantly outperformed the other group. The higher and more unreasonable a leader's standards are, the better people will perform.'

Abbie stared at him. To be honest, we all did.

'And *that* is why you shout at people?' she asked incredulously. 'Because you think it makes them better workers?'

'No,' Tim replied. 'I shout at them because I get frustrated. But I was curious to know *why*. So I did some research on it.' He pointed at her. 'You're angry now. That's good. Maybe you'll come up with a half-decent idea, instead of playing pool and distracting my employees.'

'*You* were the one who told me—' Abbie began furiously, but it was too late. Tim had already gone back into his office.

16

The cop's male colleague drives, while she sits with you in the back. Neither says much, for which you're grateful. Tim's words are churning around in your head. What did he mean by *Don't believe everything they tell you*?

You're met at the station by a grey-haired man in plain clothes. He looks questioningly at the female cop, who shakes her head. 'We haven't discussed anything.'

'Good. Abbie, come with me.'

'I'm not . . .' You stop, still unsure how to put this.

'You're not sure that's who you are?' he says, guiding you towards an interview room. Over his shoulder, to the policewoman, he says, 'FMO, please, Sandy. Full exam.'

'No, it's . . .' *Tell them the truth*, Tim said. You take a deep breath. 'It's more complicated than that. I'm a robot.'

'You think you're a robot,' he repeats. 'OK. In a short while a medical officer will be along to take a look at you. In the meantime, is there anything you need?'

He thinks you're insane, you realise. He thinks you're Abbie-who's-had-some-kind-of-breakdown.

'My husband works in robotics,' you try to explain. 'He built me.'

'That's right,' the policeman says, nodding. 'I know Tim. I'm Detective Ray Tanner. We've been looking for you for a long time, Abbie. But you're here now, that's the main thing.'

Despite the gentleness he's trying to put into his voice, he sounds peeved. Almost as if you turning up has proved him wrong about something. Something important.

'No,' you say miserably. 'You don't understand. I don't *believe* I'm a robot. I *am* a robot.'

Looking at his kindly, concerned face, you realise there's only one way to convince him. You reach up behind your neck. You've touched the seam there many times, but you've never been brave enough to pull it all the way open, the way Tim did. Even the thought makes you feel sick.

'What are you doing?' Tanner says uneasily. 'Abbie? Jesus Christ!'

You feel the same sucking sensation, the same coldness as before, and then Detective Tanner has recoiled away from you, knocking over a chair in his astonishment.

17

Twenty minutes later, the atmosphere is very different. The medical officer has given you a brief inspection and announced that you are far beyond her area of expertise. The IT officer, ditto. And now there are three people sitting across a table from you. Detective Tanner, a man in a grey suit who introduced himself as the deputy chief of investigations, and a female detective sergeant.

'But why?' the deputy chief wants to know. 'What was the purpose of building you?'

You shrug. 'Emotional support.'

'Or to fool people into thinking that the real Abbie had returned alive and well?' Tanner suggests.

His comment is directed to the deputy chief, not you, but you shake your head firmly. 'Of course not.'

'If the people who found her had put it on Twitter instead of calling us, who knows what story might have gone around,' Tanner says, still to the deputy chief. 'He's toying with us. Trying to make it look like we got it all wrong.'

'What do you mean, "wrong"?' you say, puzzled. 'Wrong about what?'

The deputy chief looks at you. 'You have no knowledge of that?'

'Knowledge of what?'

'That, four years ago, Tim Scott was put on trial for the murder of his wife, Abigail.'

You stare at him, stunned. A long moment passes. You can't believe it – surely Tim would never have kept something as important as this from you. But then – *clunk!* – you feel it, a cascade of images tumbling into your mind. Newspaper reports, video feeds, tweets and blogs and snatched paparazzi images. Tim, gaunt and unshaven, being led towards some courtroom doors –

'Should I have a lawyer?' you say faintly.

The deputy chief looks at Tanner, who shrugs. 'Legally speaking, we believe she's computer equipment. She certainly has no rights.'

'Well, I'm not saying anything else,' you tell them defiantly. 'Not until my husband gets here.'

Tanner leans forward. 'You call him your husband. But he isn't, is he? You're not married to him. You can't be – you're a *machine*. Before you feel sorry for him, feel sorry for *her*. For Abbie. And if you know anything that can help us solve her disappearance, even at this late stage, tell us. For her sake.'

Disappearance. The word, with all its ramifications, echoes around your head.

The silence is broken by a knock on the interview-room door. Tanner sighs in frustration. 'Enter.'

A policewoman comes in and whispers something in his ear. 'Tim Scott's here,' he says reluctantly. 'With a lawyer. We're going to have to let her go.'

Relieved, you get to your feet. 'I'll walk you out,' he adds.

At the door he stands back to let you go before him. As you

pass, he suddenly leans forward, blocking your way with his arm, forcing you to stop. Speaking in a low voice, so only you can hear, he says, 'I spent twelve months building a case against Tim Scott. You tell him from me, I'm not going to give up just because he's made himself a Barbie doll.'

18

'I see now why you didn't want me going out. But you might have told me the reason.'

Finally, you're back at Dolores Street together. Tim grimaces. 'I know. I'm sorry, Abbie. It wasn't that I expected you to stay cooped up here forever. I just didn't know how to tell you. These past two weeks have been such a special time for me. A second honeymoon, almost. And I suppose I was worried you might react the way everyone else did, back then. I thought if I could just re-establish the connection between us first . . . and then somehow it was easier to keep putting it off.'

'I understand,' you say, although understanding isn't the same as forgiving him, not quite. 'But, Tim, what happened? You have to tell me now. The police used the word *murder*, but they also talked about my *disappearance*.' You hesitate. 'And what made them think *you* could have had something to do with it?'

He nods decisively. 'You're right. Let's talk.'

It was a surfing accident, he says. He stresses the word *accident*.

'There'd been a storm – high winds and rain. You were at the beach house on your own, working on a new project. I stayed here in the city, with Danny. The whole point was to give you some time alone, to let you rediscover your spark.'

Even now, five years later, you can tell how difficult this is for him. He stares into space, his eyes unseeing. Fixed on memories that are still almost too much to bear.

'You often went night-surfing, even in poor conditions – you found high waves exhilarating, and you were easily skilled enough to cope with them. You said it cleared your head when you'd been working. There were plenty of people who could confirm that. It was only later the coverage got so . . . I kept some, actually.'

He gets up and comes back with a USB stick that he plugs into his laptop. When he turns the screen towards you, you see he's put together a kind of digital scrapbook, a slideshow of screen grabs from newsfeeds and social media. He sits back and watches intently as you click through them, scouring your face for signs of your response.

The first articles just tell the bare facts of your disappearance:

Air Search Fails to Find Storm Victim

The search continues today for Bay Area artist Abbie Cullen-Scott, whose vehicle was found parked overnight near San Gregorio State Beach in strong winds. The mother of one, who with tech-entrepreneur husband Tim Scott owns a $10M beach house nearby, is known to be a passionate surfer.

Residents expressed surprise anyone would risk going out in the heavy breaks seen Friday. The area is known for unusual offshore rock formations that, under certain conditions, funnel freak waves as high as fifty feet.

You reach back into the past, searching for memories that would confirm any of this, but nothing comes. You have no recollection of that time at all. And that, somehow, insulates you from the horror of it. It's as if you're reading about someone else. Not your own final moments.

You continue clicking through. It was the *Chronicle* that first made the connection with Danny, and by implication raised a different possibility:

Search Halted for Tragic Abbie

The search was called off today for missing artist Abbie Cullen-Scott. The 30-year-old mother was 'struggling' with her autistic son, Danny, according to friends. Danny is currently being cared for at the couple's home in the Mission by tech founder Tim Scott, 40, who has requested privacy through his legal representative.

The next day, Tim issued a statement. Clearly, at least part of his reason was to combat the *Chronicle*'s insinuations.

Abbie is a wonderful person, a beautiful wife and exemplary mother, an incredibly optimistic, forward-looking individual who cares deeply about art and the positive effect it can have on people's lives. Now that the search for her has been scaled down, I have to confront the devastating possibility I will never see her again. If so, I have lost not only my wife, but my soulmate. I ask that the media respect my privacy, and that of our son, at this difficult time.

The statement caused a ripple of interest on Circle of Moms and other parenting sites.

- A woman in Australia drowned herself and her daughter. There's a ton of stuff about it online if you do a search.
- There's no support. My cousin and her husband have a child with autism and they can't even go out.
- My friend's boy screams if they make a left in the car.
- Not so tough if you're a millionaire tho IMHO!!
- I'm sorry but there's no excuse for depriving a child of his mom, however bad your life is.

Ten days later, however, the *Chronicle* reported that detectives were *now investigating the possibility that Abbie may have been the victim of a criminal act.*

The next slide shows a police search team coming out of the house, carrying plastic crates. The caption reads: *Detectives take away computers and other equipment belonging to tech founder Tim Scott. Investigators have brought in cadaver dogs trained to sniff for human remains.*

You look over at Tim. His face is still impassive, but you can only imagine what being the object of those suspicions must have been like for someone as private as him.

And still the insinuations kept coming. The next article highlighted the similarities between your own disappearance and another death, four years earlier:

Police Probe Abbie 'Copycat' Indications

Detectives are looking into 'striking similarities' between the disappearance of missing artist Abigail Cullen-Scott from San Gregorio Beach last month and another case four years ago.

Twenty-seven-year-old Kerry-Ann Brookheimer's vehicle was also found abandoned near the beach after a storm, prompting a major search by air, land and sea. Ms Brookheimer's body was never found, something a spokesman from the county sheriff's office attributed at the time to the area's unusual rip currents.

'Police are investigating whether Abbie, or anyone close to her, were aware of the circumstances of Kerry-Ann's disappearance,' said Detective Ray Tanner, the officer leading the hunt for Ms Cullen-Scott, yesterday.

The hint was clear – someone might have tried to make the more recent death look like an accident, knowing that a body washed into the sea in that area might never reappear.

In the absence of any facts, the mood on social media turned against Tim.

- I'm not saying he killed her. But maybe he drove her to it. You can't ever tell what goes on behind closed doors.

- You only have to look at him to see what kind of man he is.

- I knew someone who worked for him once. People think he's some kind of guru but she said he was the most arrogant jerk she'd ever come across.

- That coast is so quiet at night, it would be easy to drive a body down to the water.

And then, out of the blue, the *Chronicle* came up with a different angle.

'I Met Missing Abbie on Cheating Site,' Claims Company Director

A married man claims to have responded to a profile created by the missing mother on Discreet Liaisons, an online forum for married people seeking affairs. 'She was using a different name, but I'm a hundred per cent certain it was her. We chatted on several occasions, and she initially seemed keen. But when I pressed for an actual hook-up, she said she'd chosen someone else.'

The article purported to be a serious investigation into the popularity of such websites, but it kept coming back to salacious speculation.

Women who sign up for these sites may be taking risks with their personal safety, as sites rarely vet clients or run identity checks. Did Abbie meet someone online who was involved in her disappearance? And did her husband know about, or become aware of, her activities?

The site, which is based in Romania, failed to respond to requests for a comment yesterday.

You glance at Tim, but his expression is still unreadable. A little uncomfortable – you still haven't told him about the hidden iPad – you turn back to the screen and click on to the next item. More social-media posts.

- Why haven't they charged him? CLEARLY he killed her when he found out what she was doing.

- Surely any jury would convict on the balance of probabilities.

- I disagree. A jury would likely give credit to a husband whose wife drove him to it with her infidelities.

- The police have made so many errors, they're probably scared of being shown up in court.

As if in response, the headlines then broke a new development:

TIM SCOTT ACCUSED OF MURDER
Tech Titan Charged Despite Absence of Wife's Body

19

You click again, but that's the end of the document.

'The police thought they'd found a motive,' you say, understanding now. 'They thought, if I'd had an affair, that could be your reason for killing me.'

Tim's eyes hold yours, very still. 'That seemed to be their thinking, yes.'

'Tim—' you begin, just as he continues, 'It was crazy, of course. You would never do something like that, never. Integrity is very important to you.'

He sounds utterly certain. But then, Tim is confident in all his opinions.

Once again, you find yourself wondering what could be on that iPad.

'It's clear to me what must have happened,' he adds. 'You were – are – an exceptionally beautiful woman. Someone stole a picture of you for their online profile, that's all.'

'But I'm also quite distinctive,' you object. 'Isn't the whole point of catfishing – that's the word, isn't it? – that the person doing it finds someone who looks a bit like them? Otherwise, when they turn up in person, it's obvious they've been lying.'

He shrugs. 'They could say they'd changed their hairstyle. Or used an old photo. Women do that all the time, don't they?'

'I guess,' you say doubtfully.

'I ran image-recognition software,' he adds. 'The police said they would, but I had no faith in them by then. So I hired server space from Google and did it myself. There were thousands of pictures of you online – mostly on news sites, of course, because of your disappearance. But not a single photo on any dating site. There was so much media interest by then, though, that the authorities were under pressure to justify all the money they'd wasted on the investigation. So, rather than admit they'd been incompetent, they decided to charge me. After that, of course, they were even less interested in looking at alternative explanations.'

'Could I . . . ' You hesitate. 'One of those articles suggested I might have killed myself.'

'Again, I just don't believe it – even if you could have done that to *me*, you would never have abandoned Danny.'

You feel the same. From what you recall, while mothers of autistic children did take their own lives sometimes, they almost always killed their disabled child too, rather than abandon them to an uncertain world. You remember one heartbreaking story about a mother who jumped off a bridge along with her six-year-old son. When they were found, she still had her arms wrapped tightly around him, the maternal urge to protect him unshakable even as she took them both to their deaths.

Though Mike would probably say it was just her emotional brain and her reptilian brain wanting two different things, you reflect.

'It's true you'd been a little depressed,' Tim adds. 'But things were getting better – we'd finally decided on the right treatment for Danny, got him into that school . . . You were feeling more optimistic about the future. We both were. You went surfing, that's all. You even took your board with you. Why would you have done that, if you were intending to kill yourself?'

'I took antidepressants,' you say as another memory returns to you. 'Citalopram and lurasidone. Dr Fenwick prescribed them after Danny's diagnosis.'

'That's right.' Tim hesitates. 'Though you didn't always take them. Not regularly. They kept you on an even keel, but they also muffled any positive feelings you had – made it almost impossible for you to work creatively. After your disappearance, the police found a stash of loose pills in the bathroom. You'd been removing the right number from the bottle each day, so I'd think you were still taking them, then hiding them.'

You stare at him. 'So I *was* clinically depressed? If I had meds I wasn't actually taking—'

He shakes his head. 'If anything, you were excited – you'd had an idea for a new project. I think that must have been why you stopped taking them – you really wanted to give it your best shot.'

That makes sense, you think. But then a fact slots neatly into your brain. *Side effects of citalopram in women include low libido and loss of sexual function.*

If you *were* having an affair, might that, rather than a new project, explain your excitement? And also explain why you didn't take those particular meds?

'What was the project?' you ask.

Tim shrugs. 'I don't know. You never talked about ideas until they were finished. And it hardly seemed the most important thing, afterwards. Whatever it was, it's still in your studio, I guess. At the beach house.'

You understand those last texts between the two of you now.

Things still going well here. OK if I stay another day?

And his reply:

Sure. As long as you like.

Even so, the picture you're getting of your marriage is a mixed one. A woman who pretended to her husband she was taking antidepressants when she wasn't. A husband who counted the pills in the bottle. Periods apart, focusing on work. Were these the ordinary, healthy accommodations of marriage, the give and take of a relationship that had settled down for the long term? Or the tiny cracks that signalled the beginnings of a broken partnership?

Tim says softly, 'We were happy, Abs. So happy. Perhaps our marriage wasn't entirely conventional, but what marriage is, when you look under the hood? I'm not always an easy man to live with – I know that. But I never wanted some colourless Silicon Valley wife who spent her days having hair treatments and planning fund-raisers. I met that kind of woman all the time, and they bored me stiff. You, on the other hand . . . Right from the start, you captivated me. Sure, we didn't always agree on everything, but that was part of the fun. Whenever you were around, there were sparks. You were – you were *alive*.'

An unfortunate choice of word, you think ruefully. Because isn't *alive* the one thing you can never truly be, now?

Outside, you hear sounds coming from the street – shouts, some kind of commotion. The entry phone starts buzzing – not regularly, but in short sharp bursts.

Tim goes to the window. 'I wondered how long it would take the vultures to get here,' he mutters.

Two big, sleek vans – one from KGO-TV and one from KPIX – have pulled up outside the gates. From their roofs, satellite dishes rise up smoothly on hydraulic runners, pointing skywards like the weapons of some strange armoured vehicle: the shock troops of a new kind of warfare. Men and women with video cameras on their shoulders swarm out, surrounding the gates.

'They'll all be here soon,' he adds. 'All the news stations. Then the photographers, the radio journalists . . . The whole fricking circus. Just like before.'

You go and put a hand on his shoulder. 'At least this time you've got me.'

'At least I've got you,' he agrees. 'That makes it bearable.' He puts his hand over yours.

You stay like that for several moments. Then you reach for the blinds, meaning to close them, but he stops you. 'I'll do it. It's not me they want this time.'

He's right. Already, seeing you at the window, lenses are swinging in your direction. Beyond the gate, a reporter with her back to you, doing a piece to camera, is pushed out of the way by her own cameraman in his eagerness to get the shot. He goes down on one knee to film you, the heavy camera balanced on his shoulder, eyes intent on his viewfinder, and again you're reminded of heavy weaponry: a fighter with a rocket launcher, crouching down to take aim.

Tim's phone rings. He checks the caller's name on the screen before answering. 'What?' he says curtly, then, 'No. Tell them nothing.'

The person at the other end talks for a long time. You can tell from Tim's expression that he's getting angry. But his tone, when he eventually responds, is polite.

'Thank you, Katrina. It certainly *is* what I pay you for. But the answer's still no.'

'Who was that?' you ask when he rings off.

'The woman who heads our PR agency.'

'What did she want?'

'To give me the benefit of her advice.' Tim grimaces. 'She said if she picks a network and sets up an exclusive interview with you, the others will stop hounding us. Once they know they haven't got the scoop, they move on to their next victim, apparently.'

'I'm not sure I could do an interview,' you say nervously.

'You won't have to.' Tim reaches for his car keys. 'There's another exit at the back. We can get out that way.'

'Where will we go?'

'To the beach house. It's a gated community – they won't be able to get at us there.'

'What about Danny?'

'Sian can bring him after school. I'll pack him some things.' He turns towards the staircase, then stops. 'I'm glad we're going to the beach house, actually, although obviously I wish the circumstances were different. You always loved that place.'

'Yes,' you say. 'It'll be good to see it again.'

Despite everything, you feel a little frisson of anticipation. Because, however frustrating it is to be driven from your home like this, you're going *there*. To the place where it all began, or ended, or both. The place where you died.

SIX

After her spat with Tim, Abbie sat at her borrowed desk, staring into space and frowning. Occasionally her lips twitched, like someone talking in their sleep. We knew what was happening – it happened to us all after a Tim-lashing: she was rerunning the conversation in her head, saying all the things she wished she'd come up with first time around.

Suddenly she sat up and typed something into a web browser. Again, we knew why: she was checking out the studies on anger Tim had referenced, in the hope he'd got them wrong – how satisfying would that be! And again, we could have told her she was wasting her time; not just because Tim was almost never wrong, but because we'd already looked up the studies ourselves, as soon as he'd mentioned them. If anything, he'd understated the results.

After that, she folded her arms across her chest and looked mutinous. And finally, with a sigh so loud you could hear it right across the office, she got up and strode outside to have a cigarette.

When she came back, she was looking thoughtful. She went over to the printer and took some loose paper from the tray. Sitting down again, she sketched something on the topmost page.

Someone asked her if she wanted a macchiato – they were

about to do a Starbucks run. Abbie silently shook her head, then went back to her scribbling.

After a while, she sat back and looked at what she'd done.

'Well, son of a gun,' she said out loud.

Getting up, she cracked her knuckles and stretched. (How we loved it when she stretched! There was something wholesome about it, something *healthy*: we liked the way she never tried to make herself insignificant or fade into the background.) Then she went over to Jenny.

'How would I set about getting hold of some discarded robot parts?' she asked cheerfully.

20

Tim takes the 280 along the valley, past San Andreas Lake, before crossing over the reservoir and turning up into the hills. Within minutes you've left the congestion of San Mateo behind. Forests of oak and evergreen enclose you on every side, dark and silent, the road an endless switchback, winding through the woods, always pointing upwards.

'We used to say, when driverless cars make this commute easier, we'd move out of the city for good,' he comments. He drives well, all his attention on the road, keeping his speed down between bends.

As you traverse the long, winding ridge towards the Pacific, you find yourself thinking about the day's events. There's something about the account of your disappearance in Tim's slideshow that's nagging at you, something you can't quite put your finger on. Once again, you find yourself curious about what's on that iPad. *Come back in a couple of days*, the guy in the phone shop had said. That might be tricky now you're leaving the city.

And then, like a fanfare, you've crossed the far side of the ridge and the view opens up. Below you, in the distance, the setting sun glints orange off the ocean, dazzling you.

'Not too long now,' Tim says, pulling down the visor.

You pass pumpkin farms and hiking trails on the winding road down, but mostly you just drive through empty coyote bush and eucalyptus. It seems incredible that, less than forty minutes away, the world's most connected companies – Google, Apple and the rest – are huddled together in one tiny, polluted patch of urban sprawl.

It's getting dark by the time you reach Half Moon Bay. Even though it's not that late, the shops are mostly closed, and the bars and restaurants have a forlorn, just-about-hanging-on air. Tim doesn't stop, heading south down the coastal highway. A few miles further on, he pulls off at an unmarked metal gate. Reaching for his phone, he taps in a code and it swings open. Inside, the road forks. One branch leads down to what looks like a small cluster of houses. The other – newer and better maintained – goes left, along the cliff. A discreet sign says *Cullen-Scott Residence*. An automatic barrier – thick pillars that look as if they could flip a vehicle over if they came up under it – sinks silently into the asphalt.

A minute later, Tim pulls up by a long, low building. As he kills the engine and the headlights fade, the lights inside the house come up, as if in response. It's mostly built of glass, with a few walls of brushed concrete and red cedar panelling, its lines layered and angular. There's no garden, just some walkways and steps enclosing patches of the same scrubby wild grass that stretches away as far as your eyes can see in the light now spilling from the massive windows.

Below you, beyond the house and the cliff edge, the ocean is an endless, restless presence, silvery-black as a piece of split coal.

'Wow,' you say, amazed. 'It's beautiful.'

He nods. 'When I found this place, there was a decrepit old ranch house here. The architects knocked it down and constructed this in record time. I waited until they were three months from completion before I proposed to you.' He gestures towards the cliff. 'And that was where we got married. Right there, with the ocean behind us and the house in front. That day was the first time you'd seen it . . . You should have seen the look on your face.'

Just for an instant, you can picture it – you, in your wedding dress, staring open-mouthed at what he'd done for you.

'I'd like to remember that,' you say wistfully. 'Our wedding, I mean.'

'Of course. We can upload the footage tonight.'

Inside, the house is just as beautiful as it is outside. There's even more art here than in the city house – street art, vibrant and cartoonlike. It gives the interior, which might so easily have seemed soulless and grand, a youthful, art-student feel.

'What an incredible life we had,' you say, marvelling. 'Everything was so perfect for us, wasn't it?'

Tim picks up a small sculpture – a child's doll, cast in glass, with a lightbulb for a head – and gives it a half turn before replacing it on its plinth. 'Perfect,' he repeats. 'Because you made it that way. Which is another reason I had to bring you back. And don't think, by the way, that just because we had a good life we didn't engage with the world. You always used our wealth to try to make a difference. You never stopped caring about gender politics, the arts, the homeless . . . And special education for children like Danny.'

'Yes,' you say, nodding. 'That was the one part of our life that wasn't perfect, was it? Danny.'

'It was a shock, of course. And yes, it meant we had to reassess a few things. But you took it in your stride. Things happened for a reason, you said. If we'd been given Danny, it was because we were the best people to take care of him. Which we did.' He hesitates. '*You* did. We were lucky – we could afford help – but it was *you* who talked to every doctor on the West Coast, *you* who researched all the different therapies. You were amazing. Not that I was surprised. But what happened, and how you responded to it, just made me love you even more.'

'Thank you … But don't underestimate what *you've* done, either. All those years bringing him up alone.'

'I love him,' Tim says simply. 'Just as I love you. His problems will never change that.'

'I love you too.' It's the first time you've said those words to him properly since all this began, you realise. 'Tim, I love you too.'

You look around at this place where you got married, and imagine what you felt then – the optimism of two young people stepping out together on a journey, an adventure. You can almost remember it – how excited you were, how certain that, whatever problems you faced in life, you would overcome them together.

And you feel it now, too: a sense of possibility, an eagerness for the future. The journalists, the lingering self-disgust, the physical limitations – none of those really matter, not if you've got each other.

I can do this, you think. *I can live this life. So long as I've got Tim, we can make this work.*

SEVEN

Abbie begged and borrowed from all of us. From Hamilton she got the frame of an old shopbot, the Mk II. From Rajesh she got a couple of Mk III arms. Kathryn gave her some wiring, and Darren – developer Darren, who worshipped her rather too obviously since she'd put herself between him and Tim's tongue-lashing – wrote some code. We all wanted to know what it was for, of course, but Darren wasn't telling.

'I promised her I'd keep it a secret,' he kept saying. 'You have to wait and see.'

The gas burners, pneumatic tubing and welding tools were Abbie's own, lugged from the back of her beat-up old Volvo.

This was another Abbie entirely, this slim, lanky figure in dark-blue overalls and even darker welding goggles who knelt in a corner of the parking lot, day after day, spraying sparks. And when she was finally done, it was to the parking lot she summoned us. Of course, we all went – even Tim and Mike. Nobody would have missed this.

'I made something for you all,' she announced. It came out as *y'all*, the trace of the South in her voice showing us how excited she was. 'I call it *Electra Dancing*.'

We noticed she had a fire extinguisher standing by. 'You should probably give her some room,' she added.

She pulled a sheet off the thing that stood next to her. It was a kind of sculpture, we saw straight away, not dissimilar to the shopbots we were all familiar with. Some of the shopbot parts, though, had been replaced with junk – the head was an old motorcycle headlight, the fingers were bicycle chains, and there were bits of old telephones and typewriters incorporated into the design. It was wearing a pretty vintage dress in bright yellow cotton.

As we watched, the bot abruptly raised both arms. Flames shot from its wrists – one forward, one back, like a Catherine wheel. It started to spin, or at least its body did. The head remained motionless. And suddenly flames started shooting from its head and that started spinning too, the opposite way to the rest of it. It was a dancing dervish, a pirouetting top, a whirligig of flame.

'I'm pretty!' the robot announced in a mechanical recorded voice, like a truck reversing, even as it was consumed by fire. 'I'm pretty!' Its torso erupted in flames, the yellow dress turning to lace and dropping to the ground. We thought – or said later we'd thought – of witch burnings, autos-da-fé. But mostly we just stood and gaped. 'I'm pretty!'

It was all over in less than a minute. First the bot fell silent, then it stopped spinning, its smoking carcass completely incinerated. An acrid, cordite stench wafted over the parking lot.

'What went wrong?' someone asked – some *idiot*: most of us decided later it was Kenneth. But Abbie didn't seem to mind.

'Oh, it was supposed to do that,' she said cheerfully, surveying the charred wreckage. And, turning towards us, she added, 'I like to play with fire.'

She did indeed, as some wit pointed out later. Because, although we were not very good at art or its interpretation – felt rather uniquely unqualified to judge it, in the normal way of things – it was absolutely clear to us that *Electra Dancing*, or 'the firebot', as we christened it, was Abbie's way of telling us that she thought the shopbots sucked.

21

While you wait for Danny and Sian to get to the beach house, you plug Tim's USB stick into a computer and look through the next document. It's another slideshow – of articles about the trial, this time.

Once again, he watches intently as you read.

The first cuttings relate how Detective Tanner listed to the court the steps taken to find you, the subsequent widening of the search to include the possibility you'd been harmed, and the switch of focus from accident to murder. The jury was told that police cadaver dogs had found two 'areas of interest': one in your car, and one in the kitchen at Dolores Street.

Under cross-examination, Detective Tanner admitted the sniffer dogs might have been reacting to the smell of raw meat previously stored in your kitchen. You'd been given some venison by a friend not long before your disappearance, which you transported in the car and subsequently hung in your larder.

He also admitted that the switch to a possible murder investigation came after air and sea searches around San Gregorio had drawn a blank.

'In other words, you were keen for it to look as if you'd finally made some headway?' Tim's defence lawyer, Jane Yau, suggested.

Not surprisingly, Detective Tanner rejected this, maintaining that it was reasonable, when no evidence emerged to support the most likely explanation, to switch his team's attention to the next most likely.

'So you *can* confirm that the transition to a homicide investigation – a widespread, costly, well-publicised homicide investigation – was prompted, not by any actual evidence that a murder had taken place, but by the *absence* of evidence of accident or suicide?' Jane Yau pressed.

Reluctantly, Detective Tanner conceded that this was indeed the case.

The jury then heard from an old college friend of yours, Sukie Marenga, also an artist, who said you'd told her you were having problems in your marriage. You'd also complained that Tim was reading your emails. Sukie told the court that, around that time, Tim and you wrote down your feelings about each other on two pieces of paper, which you burned together in a Buddhist-style ceremony.

'They were trying to parcel up their bad energies and release them to the universe,' she explained. 'It's a reiki ritual to cleanse yourself of negativity.'

'Do you happen to know whether the ceremony was effective on this occasion, or whether some of those negative energies in fact persisted?' Mark Rausbaum, the prosecuting attorney, asked – a question which was immediately challenged by the defence, but which no doubt planted a suspicion in the jurors' minds that the ritual had not been one hundred per cent effective, after all.

Rausbaum then introduced phone records showing you'd used your phone far less frequently in the weeks preceding your disappearance than you usually did. The state's contention, he explained, was that you had become aware your husband was spying on you, and this had brought the existing problems in the relationship to a head. Tim subsequently killed you, drove you to the beach in your own car, and disposed of your body in the ocean.

Supporting this theory was the fact that your wetsuit was still hanging in the wet room at the beach house. The prosecution suggested this meant you couldn't have been surfing that night.

Tim's lawyer highlighted a number of weaknesses in this scenario. Not only was there no body, there was no evidence that the problems in your relationship were anything other than the usual ups and downs of a high-pressure marriage. Tim had explained to the police that, a month before your disappearance, you'd left your phone on a bus, and it was a while before it was found by the transit authority – something the transit authority confirmed. In the meantime you'd been using a temporary phone, which had vanished with you. There were no signs of violence in either of your houses, or in the car, or at the beach.

Jane Yau also pointed out that San Gregorio was a well-known clothing-optional bathing area and that you'd been known to surf there naked on more than one occasion. Perhaps you'd simply forgotten your wetsuit that night? What was more, data from the GPS locator in Tim's phone showed no evidence he'd been anywhere near the beach house on the night in question. Admittedly, the phone had been powered off at the time – but that was simply due to a flat battery, Tim had explained. The defence requested that the case be dismissed.

And, perhaps remarkably, given the intense level of media

interest, the judge agreed. Quoting the ancient principle of corpus delicti, he said in a written statement that, while it wasn't absolutely necessary for the prosecution to produce a body in order to prove a murder had taken place, it was certainly necessary to prove that a murder had taken place before somebody could be accused of it. The standard of proof in corpora delicti cases must therefore be higher than a mere 'balance of probabilities'. He was dismissing the charges with immediate effect.

In the period following the trial's collapse, a twenty-six-year-old woman from San Jose was charged with posting an offensive message about Tim on Twitter. In a separate case, a thirty-one-year-old woman from Los Angeles who posted something on Facebook was given a six-week suspended prison sentence. A petition to the government to change the law so that corpora delicti cases required a lower standard of proof in future received over twenty-five thousand signatures, and was then quietly ignored.

Detective Tanner gave a TV interview on the courtroom steps, in which he said the police would not be looking for anyone else in connection with Abbie's disappearance.

After some of the judge's comments in previous trials were publicised on social media, a separate campaign to force judges to retire at sixty-five received over fifty thousand signatures.

The police subsequently clarified that, while there were no outstanding lines of enquiry, 'a team of officers is available to respond at any time to any new information that is received regarding Abigail Cullen-Scott.'

Tim Scott declined to give any interviews whatsoever.

22

You sit back, relieved. Of course, you're biased, but the case against Tim was clearly paper-thin. The prosecution had no body, no CCTV and no forensic evidence. An attractive, high-profile young mother had vanished, and, in the subsequent media frenzy, someone had to be found to blame for it, that's all.

You'd known all along there was no way Tim could have been involved, but you'd been half-dreading that the trial might have turned something else up, that your husband – never the humblest or most patient of men – could have been goaded by some wily prosecutor into saying something that showed him in a bad light. But, as it turned out, he'd never even had to take the stand. He'd been completely exonerated. And if a few crazies on social media had a hard time accepting that – well, that was their problem, not his.

All the same, it strikes you that you, Abbie, were a strangely absent figure from the proceedings. The allegations of affairs weren't even touched on, nor the evidence of your depression. You'd hoped reading about the trial might give you an insight into what was really going through your mind in those last few weeks, but – just as with the contents of your phone – there's nothing.

'Do you believe me?'

Startled, you look up. Tim's eyes are boring into yours.

'Do you believe I had nothing to do with what happened to you?' he repeats.

The question must be burning him up for him to even ask. His certainty is usually as fixed a part of his personality as his grey T-shirts.

'Of course.'

He grimaces. 'Don't say, "Of course." "Of course" means "I have no choice but to believe my husband." Your mind's better than that, Abbie.'

Is this why he built you? you wonder. So you could pronounce him innocent from beyond the grave? To hear you say out loud the words the jury foreman never got to say?

'But it *is* "Of course." And I didn't need to read those articles to think that, either. I *know* you, Tim. I know you'd never deliberately harm anyone. But especially not me.'

Tension leaves his shoulders. 'Of course I wouldn't.' You both smile at his choice of words.

You hear the sound of a car pulling up. It's Sian, arriving with Danny. 'Hi, Danny,' you say eagerly as he runs into the house. He ignores you, instead making a beeline for the long wall of windows overlooking the ocean, which he greets by rubbing his face happily over the glass. You know you should really follow through, make him go back and say hi in response, but he looks so delighted to be here that you don't have the heart.

'He loves this place,' Tim says, watching. 'He used to spend hours down on the beach, jumping in the waves with you.'

'Maybe that's something I can do with him tomorrow, then. I'd like that.'

Tim hesitates. 'I'm afraid not. You going in the ocean would be like me taking my smartphone into the pool. Water – particularly salt water – would wreck you in a second.'

'Oh.' You think of your earlier self, the thousands of hours you spent on a board. That was why Tim built this house, after all – so you could be near your beloved ocean. And now even that's off-limits.

'We might be able to address that, though, in time,' he adds. 'And the hiking here is terrific. We should think about getting a dog—'

You shake your head. You don't want a dog.

You make pasta. The four of you sit around the massive party-sized table on the sun deck to eat it, but conversation is fitful. You try to draw Sian out, but she seems to regard your questions as just some random computer-generated chit-chat. Sometimes she ignores you altogether. Only when you ask her about Danny's school does she become more animated. Meadowbank is, she says, exceptional, the only place in the whole state where kids like Danny get the consistency and intensity of support they need. The results there have been incredible.

You can't help looking at Danny, who's taking no part in the conversation, dreamily twirling a forkful of pasta tubes in front of his eyes before finally putting it in his mouth. Automatically, you smile at him – his fine, ethereal face is beautiful, whatever his condition – but 'incredible' isn't the word you'd have used.

'You should have seen him a few years ago,' Sian says defensively. 'He was self-harming – headbanging, biting the back of his hands, pulling out his hair . . . He's made giant strides.'

'Of course,' you say quickly. 'You've done a great job.'

Later, Tim and Sian clear the dishes while you stay with Danny. You've devised a simple game: you read one of his Thomas books out loud, but every now and then substitute a silly word for one of the originals – 'gorilla' for 'train', say – or deliberately get 'Toby' and 'Terence' mixed up. Since Danny knows the text backwards, this is indescribably amusing to him. Sometimes he laughs so hard he can hardly make the thumbs-down sign, his way of saying, 'Wrong.'

'Thomas, you are a really useful *elephant* . . .'

You pause for effect. From the kitchen, you hear Sian say conversationally, 'It's incredible how quickly you forget she isn't real. For a while, back there, it was just like talking with a person.'

Outraged, you wait for Tim to slap her down. But his reply is brief and noncommittal, a low rumble you can't quite catch.

'Well, maybe you could train her to add a bit less salt to the pasta,' Sian adds primly. 'Still a couple of things a robot can't do as well as a human, I guess.'

Danny taps your arm insistently to make you go on mangling the story, and you don't hear the rest.

After dinner, thankfully, Sian retires to her room with her laptop. You watch TV with Tim while Danny plays with his trains, lining them up against the skirting board in endless, exact permutations.

'I'm sorry about the salt,' you say eventually.

'What? Oh, that. Don't worry about it.'

'Sian doesn't seem too keen on me.'

Tim shrugs. 'She's worried you'll replace her, that's all. She'll come around.'

You hadn't thought of it like that. 'Replace her? Why?'

'If you think about it, therapy work's another sector that's ripe for automation. The whole point is to be consistent and repetitive. There's plenty of evidence a bot could do that side of it far more effectively than a human.'

'Well, of course I'm not going to replace her. She's good for Danny. And he likes her.' Even so, you feel better.

The news comes on. You're the second item. *'Tech titan Tim Scott, who four years ago was controversially cleared of murdering his wife Abigail, has created an eerie robotic replica of the missing woman.'* It's illustrated with a long-lens shot of you closing the blinds.

Abruptly, Tim raises the remote and the picture dies. 'I'm going to bed,' he says with a sigh.

'We talked about uploading some wedding footage,' you remind him.

'Oh – so we did. We can set that up now.'

As you follow him upstairs, you pass a painting on the landing. You stop to look at it more closely. It's a portrait of Danny at a few months old, half asleep, one eye squinting lazily up at the viewer. It's smaller than the other paintings around it, barely larger than a paperback. Even the brushstrokes are finer and more detailed, as if the painter's whole world has shrunk to this tiny face, those dark eyes, the crinkle of pouchy skin beneath each eyelid.

There is no way, you think, no way on God's earth, that the woman who painted that portrait could have abandoned her son. No matter how trapped she felt, no matter what his diagnosis, she wouldn't have left him.

You look up. Tim's watching you intently.

'You feel it, don't you?' he asks softly. 'You feel what you felt when you were painting that.'

'I think anyone would. Any mother, anyway. It doesn't mean I'm a mind reader.' Something makes you add, 'Tim ... those articles I read earlier. *Were* you checking my emails?'

'Of course not,' he says, clearly offended. 'Why would I want to? We never had secrets from each other.'

You lie down in a bedroom and he hooks you up to a laptop. 'It might take a while,' he warns. 'The cable speeds out here are terrible.'

'That's all right ... And Tim?'

'Yes?'

'Would you kiss me before you go?'

'Of course.' He bends down and tenderly plants a kiss on your forehead. 'Goodnight, my love. Enjoy the upload.'

''Night.'

You close your eyes and let the elixir of memory flood your system, like an addict's fix of heroin.

23

You dream it, and you don't dream it. These uploaded memories are more vivid, and more painful, than any dream. For a few precious minutes you're yourself again – seeing the world through your own eyes, thinking with your own mind. Complete, once more.

Your wedding was beautiful, but somewhat unconventional. That was one of the things you loved about Tim – he never did things a certain way just because everyone else did. This house, for example. It's extraordinary – not just the location, but the building itself, surrounded by wild grass and rock in every direction, and screened from the highway by a gentle bluff. You could hardly believe it was his wedding gift to you.

For the day itself, the architects built a wooden deck between the house and the edge of the cliff, and erected an open-sided marquee on it. Tim had let you plan everything except the venue. The tent was decorated with sprigs of wild flowers mixed with eagle feathers, and the guests sat on hay bales instead of chairs. Your dress was white and simple, like a Roman toga. Instead of a veil, you wore a diamond head-circlet from India, another gift from Tim, along with a crown of braided cornflowers. The whole ceremony was presided over by a humanist priestess.

Your vows. *I give myself to you for all eternity* . . . Yes, you really had said those words to each other. You hadn't meant them literally, of course.

But, even in the dream, you realise Tim did. That's why you're here.

And finally, reading Sonnet 116 together:

> *Love alters not with his brief hours and weeks,*
> *But bears it out even to the edge of doom . . .*

That was *doom* in the old sense of the word, you remember telling Tim the first time you read the poem to him. Judgement Day. Eternity. Not the moment in a horror movie when someone meets the baddie.

In your dream you can even smell everything. The rich, savoury aroma of warm hay. The sweet, drifting scent of the patchouli sticks you'd placed on the tables. The salty tang of the ocean. The occasional whiff of weed from behind the house, where some of your artist friends had slipped away for a spliff . . .

Then, abruptly, you're going back – back to a few days before the wedding, and your last-minute jitters. The more you thought about it – really *thought* about it – the more you loathed the whole idea of marriage. What a brilliant way, historically, of controlling women! The woman gave herself to the man – or was given by her father – as his personal property. Her rights and feelings remained subservient to his, while at the same time power over reproduction – the only thing naturally controlled by her – got transferred to her husband as well. That's the reason they called it wedlock! How could any woman who called herself a feminist agree to such a medieval set-up?

You phoned Tim at work and spilled your worries. He waited patiently until you were done, then said, 'Fine. Let's not get married then, Abs. Let's just make our vows to each other someplace quiet, and go on as we are.'

'I don't think I want that, either.'

'Well, whatever you do want is fine by me. Give me a minute,' you heard him say to someone at the other end.

'It's just marriage itself, I think – the whole institution. I feel better now we've talked it through. I know *our* marriage would never be like that.'

'Good. Speaking of which, how's my wedding gift coming along?'

'Nearly finished. How's mine?'

He laughed. 'Also nearly finished.'

'When are you going to tell me what it is?' He'd been teasing you with this gift for months.

'When you see it on our wedding day.'

'Will I get to unwrap it?'

'Hmm – might be a bit large for that. Gotta go now, Abs. There are people standing outside my office.'

'Let them stand.'

'I already did. You wouldn't want me to be a tyrannical boss, would you?'

'They know you're not, really.'

He laughed again. 'I sincerely hope they don't.'

'Oh, and Tim—'

24

You open your eyes. The memory has stalled, somehow, the images frozen in your head. You search for the reason. And then – *clunk* – it comes to you.

Not enough bandwidth.

You wait, hoping the connection might resume, but nothing happens. It must be that dodgy internet Tim mentioned.

You unplug yourself and swing your legs onto the floor. You'll go downstairs and find something else to do until the connection improves.

Quietly, so as not to wake anyone, you pad along the landing. There are sounds coming from Sian's bedroom – grunts and moans. With a flash of surprise, mixed with amusement, you realise she's watching porn. Not such a prim little thing after all.

And then you remember the broken internet connection and realise she can't be. The thought has barely formed in your mind before the truth falls there instead, so stark and horrible that you gasp out loud.

You turn and look down the landing. The door to Tim's room is open. The bed is empty.

'Yes!' Sian groans. 'Yes!'

'Yes,' Tim agrees.

The door to her room is also ajar. You don't want to look but you can't help yourself. She's astride him, her back to you. There's something repulsively triumphant about the way she grinds herself into him, luxuriating in her own pleasure, sweeping her hair back with one hand, then immediately leaning forward again so it curtains her face, resting her palms on his chest like someone doing CPR.

'Yes,' she moans again.

Yes, you think, pain and anguish battering you, toppling you off-balance so that you actually have to put one hand to the wall to stop yourself falling. Yes, of course. Of course something like this would happen.

'Yes,' Sian groans.

No.

No. No. No.

EIGHT

For a couple of weeks after the firebot, things pretty much went back to the way they'd been before. We thought about new and exciting ways to make the shopbots sell people stuff. ('Like, how awesome would it be if they could spot when you were wearing last year's fashions, and call you out?' 'Pretty awesome, actually.') Abbie turned up in the mornings with her braids still wet and her surfboard strapped to the roof of her old Volvo. Tim, we thought, seemed unusually quiet – 'Dormant. Like Vesuvius,' someone commented. He was often closeted in meetings with the money guys. Apparently our backers thought the shopbots were turning out too expensive. That made some of us worry about cost-cutting, which might mean layoffs.

Then, one day, Megan Meyer turned up in her convertible Jaguar, closely followed by a couple of employees in a white van. From the back of the van, they – the employees, anyway – unloaded a rack of clothes. Men's clothes, we noticed, as they wheeled it behind Megan's elegant kitten heels to Tim's office: sports jackets, merino knitwear, tan slacks.

So we gathered that Tim was having a style consult. That was something Megan regularly did for her clients. It wasn't just about finding them dates: in Silicon Valley, where some of the wealthiest individuals were also the most socially dysfunctional, it was about teaching them *how* to date.

Later, after Megan had gone, Tim came out of his office. He was wearing a navy-blue Ralph Lauren polo shirt, chinos and brogues. No one said anything, of course. But, for those of us who'd never seen him in anything except black jeans, a grey T-shirt and a white baseball cap, the effect was strange, almost startling.

We noted that, by the end of the day, he'd put the baseball cap back on.

The following morning, he came into work wearing black jeans and a grey T-shirt again. We breathed a collective sigh of relief.

Mike, ever loyal, told us the style consult had been because Tim wanted to smarten himself up for an important meet-and-greet with some potential investors. Nobody really bought that, of course. But, out of respect for Mike, we pretended we did.

That day, Tim left the office at five o'clock. No one knew where he was. He'd stopped work early, Morag explained.

Again, we were confused. The whole idea that Tim might actually 'stop work' was problematic. Tim sent us emails at three, four in the morning. He would call us on Sundays to yell at us for some tiny glitch he'd just spotted in our coding. He once famously phoned Gabriella Pisano to locate a file he needed while she was in the early stages of labour, having forgotten she was on maternity. Even when she told him that's what she was doing, he didn't hang up.

Abbie, meanwhile, was working on a new art piece. But we noticed she was also talking a lot to Rajesh. Rajesh was one of the developers, a quiet vegetarian in his mid-twenties who no one knew a lot about. But when we saw the warmth blossoming between him and Abbie, we realised something we hadn't noticed before: Rajesh was a very beautiful young man. And *cool*. Rajesh was one of those people whose quietness masked a deep inner confidence. Someone looked up his personnel record and discovered he'd received the Dean's Award at Stanford.

Abbie's new piece, when she unveiled it, was an installation of three leather punchbags suspended by thick ropes from the ceiling of one of the conference rooms. At first, no one knew what to make of it. Unlike the firebot, she didn't present it to us. She simply left it there, along with three beaten-up pairs of boxing gloves. A small card on the wall said: *Goldilocks. Leather, rope, electronic circuits.*

It wasn't long before someone pulled on the gloves and started hitting the larger of the punchbags. Then they stopped, surprised. The punchbag had cried out, as if in pain.

The puncher hit the punchbag again. *'Ow!'* the punchbag yelled. The puncher laughed, and rained a series of blows, Rocky style, left-right-left. Each time, the punchbag yelled and hollered.

Someone else joined in on the next punchbag along. But they only landed one blow before they stopped, embarrassed. The second punchbag had also yelled out, but in a woman's voice.

So we tried the third punchbag. This time it was a child who screamed.

No one wanted to go near the punchbags after that. We all agreed it was a much less successful art piece than the firebot. That had been fun, we decided. This one was making some kind of statement. It felt naive and mean-spirited and a little bit obvious.

25

You stumble out of the beach house blindly, almost tripping over yourself in your haste to get away. You have no idea where you're going. You just know you can't stay there, in *your* house – the place where you got married – while your husband has sex with another woman.

Questions tumble through your mind. When did this start? Is Sian his girlfriend? His mistress? Have there been others?

How long was he even celibate for, after your death?

When you get to the security barrier and the fork in the drive, there's only one way you can go. Turning right would take you to the highway. You have to go left, down towards the ocean.

Unlike the drive leading to your house, this road is old and potholed, zigzagging down a steep incline. You pass houses – not grand, ultra-modern properties like yours, but smaller, older holiday homes. Most are in darkness. At the bottom, overlooking a rocky beach, is a ramshackle old diner. The windows are boarded up, their metal frames corroded from salt water.

You go and stand on the boardwalk, holding on to the rusty rail for support, staring miserably out to sea. Not for the first time, you find yourself wishing you could cry: anything to release these pent-up emotions. Instead, you yell, something shapeless and wordless, your agony and despair flung out at the endless ocean, the wind ripping the sound from your mouth almost before it's formed.

The waves churn and roil, their crests collapsing onto the sand in a crash of phosphorescence, only for that to be swept away in turn. Even through your misery – perhaps *because* of your misery – you can appreciate how beautiful that motion is. It feels like the waves must have a pattern to their endless movement, something almost unfathomable but deeply harmonious . . .

$$V = f \bullet \lambda$$

The wave equation. You don't know how you know, but it comes to you with yet another *clunk.*

'Danny used to stand right there and watch the sea like that,' a voice says behind you.

You whirl around, startled. A man of about sixty is standing a few yards off, watching you, his hands buried deep in the pockets of his waxed canvas jacket.

'I hope I didn't scare you,' he says conversationally. He nods towards a house a little way up the hill. 'I saw there was someone down here and thought I'd take a look. We don't get many night visitors. Not since your husband installed the electric gates.'

'You know who I am, then.' You almost stumble over that 'who'. But the stranger only nods.

'I saw you on the news. Don't worry. I won't tell any journalists you're here.' He holds out a hand. 'Charles Carter.'

'I'm Abbie,' you say as you shake it. You can't help adding miserably, 'At least, I *was*. I don't know what I am, now.'

He nods calmly. 'The news item mentioned that, too.' He turns, putting his own hands on the rail as well, so you're both looking out to sea. 'You used to surf out there,' he observes. 'All hours of the day. Nights, too, sometimes. It cleared your brain, you said.'

'I know. That was what I was doing the night I disappeared. Surfing.'

'So they say.' His tone is still conversational, but something makes you turn your head and look at him. He's a handsome man, you realise: his hair may be silver, but his jaw is rugged and the skin creases attractively around the corners of his eyes.

'What do you mean?' you ask.

'Oh, I didn't mean to imply anything. Just a lawyer's natural caution of speech.'

With a sudden flash of insight – not like the way the wave equation came to you, but equally sure and certain – you think, *There's something he's not telling me.*

He probably thinks you're Tim's creature, you realise. He thinks you'll report back anything he says.

'So you're a lawyer?' you say, to break the tension. 'What kind?'

'Large-scale corporate mergers and acquisitions, mostly.' You must look surprised, because he adds, 'We used to have a big house in the city as well. But after my wife passed, I decided to relocate here. I can work from home, mostly.'

'I'm sorry about your wife.'

He shrugs. 'It was eight years ago.' His eyes drift towards a boat, a thirty-foot sloop standing on the slipway below his house. There's a name painted on its prow: *Maggie*. 'You don't forget, but you do come to terms with it, eventually.'

You don't say anything. You suspect he's thinking the same thing you are: Tim never came to terms with it.

You realise something else. You feel strangely comfortable around this man, almost as if you're resuming a conversation you started a long time ago.

'Did I . . . Did I know you well?' you ask bluntly. 'Before, I mean.'

Again you get the sense that Charles Carter weighs his words carefully before answering.

'After your husband bought the land here and built his own house, he wanted rid of all these other properties just as soon as our leases expired, to increase his privacy. Naturally, some of us weren't too happy about that. Things got a little heated . . . It was you who persuaded him to let us stay. Beaches shouldn't be private, you said.' He nods at the building behind you. 'It was too late for Sally and Joe's diner. But the rest of us were grateful to you. It's a small community here, but we treasure it.'

'I'm glad I could help.' Once again, you feel like an imposter using that 'I', taking credit for something your former self did.

'Well, if there's ever anything I can do in return.' He pauses. 'Even if you just want to talk.' Again he gives you an appraising look.

There's a shout from the beach. 'Abbie! Abbie!' It's Tim, gesturing up at you from the shoreline. 'Abbie, stay there!' he calls. 'I'll come up.'

'I'd better go.' Charles Carter nods at you. 'Goodnight.'

Tim runs along the boardwalk. 'Abbie,' he says breathlessly. 'Thank God. I thought . . .' He throws an anguished glance at the ocean.

He thought you were going to walk into the sea, you realise. Having told you last night that it could destroy your fragile electronics, he was frightened you might have come down here in despair to let it do just that.

Yet, strangely, it never even crossed your mind. Because no mother, surely, could abandon her child like that.

Charles Carter has walked off without speaking to Tim. Tim casts a hostile glance after him, but says only, 'Come on. Let's get you back.'

'Tim, I know about Sian,' you say miserably. 'I saw you together.'

'Yes, I realised,' he says quietly. 'I saw you were gone when I went back to my room. We'll talk about it back at the house.'

26

Sian's in the kitchen, dressed and drinking coffee. She looks at you, but it's Tim she speaks to. 'You found her, then.'

'Yes. Go back to bed,' Tim says curtly.

'Wait . . .' you say. 'Tim, I need to know . . . Is Sian your *girlfriend*?'

Sian looks at Tim expectantly, and you realise she wants to hear the answer to this, too.

'No,' Tim says after a moment. 'She's someone I had sex with, that's all.'

You note that 'had'.

'Thanks, Tim,' Sian says sarcastically. 'Nicely done.'

'Abbie's upset,' he says tersely. 'Right now, that's my priority.'

'*Abbie's* upset?' she says incredulously. 'The *robot's* upset?'

'She's my wife,' he snarls.

Sian must know the warning signs by now, but she doesn't back off. 'So, if she's your wife, then what am *I*, exactly?'

'I could give you a word,' he says curtly. 'But you might not like it. Why don't you go upstairs and pack?'

She stares at him. 'Are you *firing* me?'

'Restructuring. Your services are no longer required.'

'Because I *slept* with you?'

'No,' he says calmly. 'Because Abbie can take over your

duties with Danny.' He turns to you. 'If that's acceptable to you, Abbie.'

'You *cannot* fire someone just because you slept with them,' Sian snaps, at the same time as you say, 'Tim, wait a minute. We need to think what's best for Danny, here.'

'There'll be a generous pay-off,' he tells Sian. 'I suggest you go and think about just how generous you'd like that to be.'

She doesn't reply. You can almost see the numbers turning in her brain.

Turning back to you, he says in a quieter tone, 'What do you mean, about Danny?'

'I can't replace her. Not yet, anyway. I know some of what she knows about Danny's therapy, but not nearly enough. She should stay. At least for the time being.' You hate saying it, but you really have no choice.

Tim nods. 'All right. Sian, you've got two more weeks, for which you'll also be well recompensed. And now I suggest we all go back to bed.'

27

'The point is, we can't go on like this,' Mike Austin says tentatively. 'Scott Robotics is under siege. Reporters have been harassing our employees. And John Renton's asked for an urgent meeting.'

It's the next morning. There are five of you sitting around the beach house's big outdoor table: Mike, Tim, a man called Elijah who's their chief financial officer, and Katrina Gooding, their PR consultant. Tim's insisted you join them – 'Abbie has as much right to be part of this as anyone –' but the truth is, you have nothing to contribute and the debate simply goes back and forth around you.

You still haven't had a chance to talk to Tim about Sian. You thought maybe he'd come to your room last night to explain, even apologise, but it's almost as if he regards the matter as closed now.

Compared with that, the problems at his company seem unimportant.

'What does Renton want?' Tim asks.

'We don't know exactly,' Mike answers. 'But it's a fair bet he's getting anxious about the return on his thirty million. We haven't exactly carried our investors with us on this journey.'

'Abbie should do an interview,' Katrina suggests.

Tim doesn't hesitate. 'She's not doing an interview.'

'What's the mortgage like on this place?' Elijah gestures at the beach house's stunning exterior. 'If Renton wobbles, you'll be the one whose loans are called in.'

'Yes,' Tim agrees icily. 'Those are *my* loans, *my* guarantees. I put *my* neck on the line to achieve this. And that's why it's *my* decision. When *you* have the balls to start your own company and do what it takes to keep it afloat, *then* you'll be entitled to an opinion.'

Elijah shrugs, apparently unoffended. No doubt he's heard similar things from Tim many times before. 'I see this differently from you, that's all. An interview could be a great opportunity – a chance to put our own, positive message out there. We've built something incredible. The more people become aware of that, the less our investors are going to be worried about short-term returns. We'll sell it as a deliberate strategy – first disrupt the existing paradigm, then figure out how to monetise it later.'

Tim shakes his head. 'I told you. Abbie doesn't want to do an interview.' But you can hear from his tone that he's taken Elijah's point.

As one, Elijah, Mike and Katrina all turn to look at you.

'Well,' you hear yourself say. 'Of course I'll do it. If you think it'll help.'

'It really is your decision, Abbie,' Tim says.

'It's fine. I want to be useful.' *A really useful engine.*

'Don't worry, we'll coach you in what to say – give you some lines to hit,' Katrina says reassuringly.

'When should we do it?' Tim asks.

She's already pulled out her phone. 'I'll start making some calls.'

While Katrina speaks to the TV networks, the discussion moves on. Tim makes all the decisions – the others seem to take that as a given. He's been away from Scott Robotics less than twenty-four hours, and already there's a long list of matters requiring his attention.

Leaving them to it, you go to explore outside the house. It's even more stunning in the daytime. The architects have cleverly positioned it in such a way that the other houses, the ones down by the beach, are completely hidden: up here, all you can see is ocean. The red cedar panelling of the walls is the same colour as the decking around the pool, so that it all feels like one harmonious composition, a sculptural object dropped onto the rocky scrubland. The early-morning fog has burnt off now, and the pool shimmers invitingly in the sunshine, its surface rippling as the pumps and filters do their work.

But, of course, you'll never swim in it again, you realise.

Just for a moment, as you look longingly at the pool, you have a kind of flash-memory: you, diving in, the water churning milky-grey as you arc your body up towards the surface, reaching out with a sure right arm in preparation for that first long stroke . . . Like your moment of insight about Charles Carter last night on the beach, it feels different from your other memories, somehow: more organic, not just retrieved from a data bank, but *found*.

You pause, willing more memories, but nothing comes, so you continue around the deck to the garage. There are two big double doors and a smaller one at the side. You pull open the smaller one and step inside.

Tim said this was where you worked on your art projects. If you hadn't been told that, you'd have taken this for construction junk: welding equipment, gas tanks, coils of tubing and compressed air pumps, power tools, tins of household paint. And, casually propped in a corner, three surfboards of differing lengths. Their names come to you smoothly: the first is a Malibu, the second a longboard, and the third, the largest, is the type surfers call an elephant gun.

You suppose there must have been a fourth, once. The one you took the night you died.

Looking around, something else strikes you. Tim said you'd been spending time out here in the run-up to that night, working on a big new project. But, if so, where is it? There are bits and pieces scattered around, but they look more like abandoned fragments than a major new artwork.

You weren't working on anything. You just wanted to get away. With your lover, probably.

Once again, the thought comes to you, unbidden but fully formed.

You have no proof of that, you tell yourself firmly. After all, you might have tried to make something and, dissatisfied, taken it apart again.

You spot something in the far corner and go over to look. It's a pair of blue overalls, casually discarded on the floor. When you pick them up, you see they're streaked with paint and oil. The contrast with the stylish, expensive dresses in your closet in San

Francisco couldn't be greater. Yet they were both aspects of who you were.

Did Abbie Cullen-Scott have other identities too, some of them kept hidden from the world? You stare at the overalls as if they'll somehow tell you.

'You used to spend a lot of time in those.'

You turn. It's Tim, coming in from outside. He adds, 'We used to joke you'd wear them to galas and openings if you could. But you could get changed faster than anyone I've ever known. I'd come down here when it was time to leave and you'd still be working, caught up in whatever you were doing. "I'm not late. Give me five minutes," you'd say, and in four minutes flat you'd be showered, changed and looking like a million dollars.' He smiles. 'Speaking of which, we have to leave in a couple of minutes. Katrina's arranged an interview on ABC7. If you're really OK with that.'

'Of course,' you say, although the truth is, you're dreading it.

As you leave the garage together, you add, 'Tim . . . Can I have memories that *haven't* been uploaded?'

He stops dead, then turns and studies you intently. 'What do you mean?' His voice is forceful, urgent. It's the way he speaks to his employees when something important is brought to him, you recall, his whole attention suddenly focused on them like a laser.

'I'm not sure, exactly,' you say, quailing under the ferocity of his gaze. 'It's just that several times in the last few days I've had a kind of . . .'

'Intuition?' he says softly.

'Yes. Yes, *intuition* is exactly right. But that's not possible, is it?'

'On the contrary.' You can hear the excitement in his voice. 'Have you heard of a game called Go?'

'It's the Chinese version of chess, isn't it? But played on a much bigger board.'

He nods. 'An artificial intelligence beating a human at Go was always going to be a milestone. Many people thought it could never be done. Then, in 2016, an AI built by a company called DeepMind beat the world's top human player. But what was really remarkable was the *way* it beat him. During the match, it played one particular move that was so reckless, so apparently random, no human player would ever think to try it. It turned out to be the decisive moment of the game.' He pauses. 'These memories you're talking about – they may be the first sign your brain's starting to make creative leaps. Filling the gaps in your knowledge with deductions and educated guesses.'

'But I can't necessarily trust those guesses? They might be wrong?'

He takes you by the shoulders. 'Why, Abbie?' he says urgently. 'What are these thoughts you've been having?' His energy is overwhelming, sucking the truth out of you, the way the slipstream of an express train pulls leaves into its wake.

You open your mouth to tell him. That, before you died, you might have been having an affair. That something feels wrong about the manner of your death. That you were lying to him about working on a new art project –

'It was nothing specific,' you hear yourself say. 'Just a moment where I remembered diving into the pool. But I'll tell you if there are any more.'

NINE

Next morning, Abbie's wasn't the only vehicle in the parking lot with a surfboard strapped to the roof. Alongside her beat-up Volvo was a Volkswagen SUV with a blue-and-yellow foamie strapped to the top – a beginner's board.

'It's Tim's,' Morag confirmed. 'He's taking lessons.'

The thought of Tim trying to act like some laid-back surfer dude was almost comical. But it made sense that, if he was, he'd be having lessons. Once Tim set his mind to something, he always achieved it. He once gave himself the challenge of learning Hindi in six months – although, to the best of our knowledge, he'd never visited India to use it.

Later, Darren overheard Abbie and Rajesh in the kitchen area, discussing the shopbots. Abbie was dissing them, and Rajesh – well, Rajesh wasn't exactly making much of a case in their defence.

'Of all the things robots could potentially do,' she was saying, 'is selling people shit they don't need really the best you could come up with?'

Rajesh's reply wasn't audible to Darren – he was softly spoken and gentle – but neither was it long. And, whatever it was, it clearly didn't convince Abbie.

'Oh, sure. And people like innovation, I get that. I'm just saying – wouldn't it be better if all this tech was actually doing something *useful*?'

And then Darren heard Tim's voice. That's right: Tim was in the kitchen too, unseen by either Rajesh or Abbie, listening.

'You think shopbots are the *end goal*?' he interrupted disbelievingly, in his quick, piercing voice. 'You think this is the *destination*? Commerce isn't the objective – commerce is the *means*. What do *you* think the world will look like a generation from now, if current trends continue? We already have 800 million people living in hunger – and the population is growing by eighty million a year. Over a billion people are in poverty – and present industrial strategies are making them poorer, not richer. The percentage of old people will double by 2050 – and already there aren't enough young people to care for them. Cancer rates are projected to increase by *seventy per cent* in the next fifteen years. Within two decades our oceans will contain more microplastics than fish. Oh, and fossil fuels will run out before the end of the century. Do you have an answer to those problems? *Because I do.* Robot farmers will increase food production twentyfold. Robot carers will give our seniors a dignified old age. Robot divers will clear up the mess humans have made of our seas. And so on, and so on – but every single step has to be costed and paid for by the profits of the last.'

He paused for breath, then went on, 'My vision is a society where autonomous, intelligent bots are as commonplace as computers are now. Think about that – how different our world could be. A world where disease, hunger, manufacturing, design – all are taken care of by AI. *That's* the revolution we're shooting for. The shopbots get us to the next level, that's all. And you know what? This is not some binary choice between idealism or realism, because for some of us idealism is just long-range realism. *This shit has to happen.* And you need to ask yourself, do you want to be part of that change? Or do you want to stand on the sidelines and bitch about the details?'

We had all heard this speech, or some version of it, either in our job interviews, or at company events, or in passionate late-night tirades. And on every single one of us it had had a deep and transformative effect. Most of us had come to Silicon Valley back in those heady days when it seemed a new generation finally had the tools and the intelligence to change the world. The hippies had tried and failed; the yuppies and bankers had had their turn. Now it was down to us techies. We were fired up, we were zealous, we felt the nobility of our calling . . . Only to discover that the general public, and our backers along with them, were more interested in 140 characters, fitness trackers and Grumpy Cat videos. The greatest, most powerful deep-learning computers in humanity's existence were inside Google and Facebook – and all humanity had to show for it were AdWords, sponsored links and teenagers hooked on sending each other pictures of their genitals.

Of all the tech titans, only Tim Scott still kept the faith. He offered us more than a job. He gave us a cause, a calling, that rekindled the burning flames of our youth.

This was why we loved him. This was why we bore the Tim-lashings, the impossible hours, the sudden mercurial changes of direction. We saw the shining path, and we knew we needed a prophet to lead us down it.

And that was why, years later, when he was accused on social media and beyond of so many terrible things – of which murder may have been the most serious, but was not the only one with the potential to stain his reputation – we stood by him. When all was said and done, we knew the man, and his accusers did not. We knew that, deep down, he was *moral*.

There was a long silence, Darren said, as the two of them, Abbie and Tim, stared at each other. Darren had manoeuvred himself by now so that he could see both their faces. It was as if Abbie was fascinated, he reported.

Mesmerised, even.

Then she said, 'OK, I get that.'

She said it a little distractedly, Darren told us, her eyes wide, as if a part of her mind was still gazing out over the endless, wheat-filled, well-irrigated future of Tim's imagination.

There were three things, we agreed later, that came out of that conversation. The first was that, towards the end of the day, Abbie went up to Tim and said casually, 'So you surf now?'

He shrugged. 'Just started. What you guys call a barney, I guess.'

'I'm heading over to Mavericks this weekend with some friends. Titans is on. Want to come along?'

Now, Titans of Mavericks was this semi-legendary surf competition over at Half Moon Bay that only took place when certain very specific conditions whipped the waves up into breaks the height of four-storey houses. Even to be on the email list so you knew when it was happening marked you out as a real surf insider.

'OK,' Tim said. 'Why not?'

The second was that, a few weeks later, Rajesh got a really good job at another company. No one ever knew quite how or why, but people said a headhunter had called him up out of the blue and

149

offered him a massive stock option in this hot new start-up, but only if he was available to interview immediately.

And the third was that Abbie painted the mural behind reception, the street-art-style one that says, *IDEALISM IS SIMPLY LONG-RANGE REALISM!* Which we took to be both a thank-you to Scott Robotics, for having her to stay, and a peace offering to its founder.

28

ABC7's studios are by Pier 15, between the financial district and North Beach. The interviewer is a woman called Judy Hersch. You've seen her on TV – immaculately coiffed blond hair, perfect white teeth, flawless skin – but you have no sense of what she's *like*, whether she'll be kind or not. She cried on air recently while doing an item about a puppy rescued from a collapsed building. So perhaps she'll be sympathetic.

She usually presents along with a co-anchor, an older man named Greg Kulvernan. But this is for an occasional series called *Judy Asks* . . . , which she presents from a sofa, rather than from behind her usual desk. Katrina thinks this is good. Less formal, more woman-to-woman.

You're whisked straight into Hair and Make-up. Two assistants work on you, applying layer after layer of foundations and creams. One of them is standing in front of you, blocking your view of the mirror, and it's only when they're done and she takes a step back that you finally see yourself. You look dreadful – as bad as that first day at Tim's office. You protest that you could have done it much better on your own.

'Take it off,' you say. 'All of it, and we'll start again. I'll tell you what to do this time.'

They look astonished. 'But you look great!' one cries, offended. 'Doesn't she, Trish?'

Trish agrees that you do indeed look a million dollars after your 'makeover', and explains that the bright lights of the studio make people seem, like, really washed out if they don't use a little more make-up than usual. At that moment, a very young production assistant with a headset and a clipboard appears and says Judy's ready for you. Reluctantly, you allow yourself to be escorted down a long airless corridor to the studio.

'We'll take you in during the commercial break, then Judy will introduce you as soon as we're live. There's nothing to it,' the PA explains with a bright, mechanical smile. 'Oh, and this is a family-friendly show. Please remember not to swear or reference any sexual acts.'

'I wasn't planning to.'

The studio is hot and bright. Behind a glass wall is the production booth, crowded with more people in headsets. You see Tim and Katrina standing at the back. On the far side of the studio, Judy is already ensconced on the famous cream sofa, being attended to by another assistant with electric hair tongs. Only when the assistant is done and Judy has checked herself in a hand mirror does she turn to you with a smile and say, 'Hi!'

'Hi,' you reply nervously.

'There's nothing to worry about,' she says reassuringly. 'I'll introduce you, and then the camera will be on you and you can answer my first question.'

'What will that be?'

She doesn't reply. Already a shadowy figure beyond the lights is counting down, using his fingers to sign the last few seconds: *Three – two – one. Zero.*

Judy smiles at the camera. 'From the *Bride of Frankenstein* to *Austin Powers*' sex-hungry fembots, by way of Ira Levin's *Stepford Wives*, humanity – or at least a certain geeky, male portion of it – has long dreamt of creating the ultimate subservient female,' she says conversationally. 'Now, a controversial Silicon Valley technologist has succeeded in doing just that, by building a robotic replica of his own wife. It's claimed to be the world's first emotionally intelligent companion robot, or "cobot", and, in a scoop for this show, I'm going to interview it.' She turns to you, still smiling. 'First of all, what do I call you?'

You stare at her. You've just realised what's happening here – that the awful make-up was entirely deliberate, and that this interview is going to be the very opposite of sympathetic.

'You can call me Abbie.' Something makes you add, 'And I'll call you Judy, shall I?'

Steel glints in her eyes. 'Abbie . . . That was the name of your creator's wife, wasn't it?'

'Yes.'

She looks into the camera. 'Viewers may recall Tim Scott, who four years ago was put on trial for his vanished wife's murder – a trial that dramatically collapsed when the judge dismissed all charges.' She turns back to you. 'It's been claimed you have feelings. How do you feel about replacing the *real* Abbie Cullen-Scott?'

'I'm not trying to replace her—'

'So you *don't* have feelings about that?'

'Well – it's complicated, obviously . . .' you say, trying to plot a path through all the verbal traps.

'How about Tim Scott? What are your feelings about him?'

'I love him,' you say defiantly. 'That hasn't changed. And by the way—'

'You *think* you love him,' she interrupts. 'But that's just the way you've been programmed, isn't it?'

'No,' you insist. 'Look, you've got this all wrong. What you said in your introduction just now – this isn't about creating a subservient little wife at all. Tim would hate that. He wants me to make my own decisions – to be autonomous—'

'But ultimately you are just a highly sophisticated, shall we say, pleasure machine—'

'No!' you say angrily. 'That's not what this is. I don't even have *genitals*. I'm here because Tim loved me so much he couldn't bear to lose me.'

The floor manager is holding up a printed board saying, *CAUTION! USE FAMILY-FRIENDLY LANGUAGE!* You ignore him. 'This isn't about some sad loner who couldn't get a girlfriend. This is about a man motivated by his own personal tragedy to create a completely new kind of companion.' At last you're hitting the points Katrina hammered out with you, and you start to feel better. 'One day, cobots will help out in care homes, retirement communities, hospitals—'

'Destroying American jobs?' Judy interrupts.

'Creating new jobs by stimulating economic growth,' you correct her.

'Perhaps, one day, you even see robots replacing news anchors,' she says, directing her smile, not to you, but to the camera and the viewers at home.

'Well, why not?' you say wearily. 'You're already three-quarters artificial.'

Her smile doesn't slip. 'He hasn't programmed you to be polite, I see!' Again, she turns to the camera. 'Earlier, we spoke to Abbie Cullen-Scott's sister, Lisa, to invite her on this show. She was too upset to take part, but confirmed the family *will* investigate whether data-protection or identity-theft laws have been breached.' She turns back to you. 'That's a problem, isn't it? If you have feelings, how do you square them with the pain and suffering you're causing others?'

For a moment you can't think of an answer. You're too distracted by thoughts of Lisa. Lisa, upset.

'No one wants to hurt other people,' you manage to say. 'But sometimes in life you can't help it.'

'Hmm,' Judy says, as if you've just proved her point. 'Other *people*, indeed. After these messages – can San Francisco afford the growing cost of crime?'

The monitors in the production booth cut to commercials. Judy looks up. 'Nancy, could I get a wipe?'

The assistant is already at your side, waiting to guide you away. 'That's it?' you say disbelievingly.

Judy glances in your direction. 'That's it,' she says lightly. You both stand up. 'I still don't get it, though. If you can't have sex with him, what's the point of you?'

You can't help it. You slap her. You do it instantly, without thought – although, as your palm lands on her flawless, botoxed skin, you find yourself thinking, *Bet that'll show.*

The floor manager and production assistant have already leapt forward and pinned your arms to your sides. Judy gapes at you, shocked. Then she raises her own hand and slaps you back, hard.

A knot of production people grab you and bundle you out of the studio. 'All right,' you say angrily, freeing yourself. 'You can let me go now.'

'Abbie . . .' Tim rushes up. 'Abbie, I'm so sorry you had to go through that. They promised us . . . But you were brilliant, Abs. Thank you.'

'I'm sorry about the slap.' The make-up team elbow you out of the way as they rush into the studio. To work on Judy's reddened skin, presumably.

'It doesn't matter. They were already into the commercials. And she slapped you back.'

'She provoked me,' you say. 'The whole time. It was deliberate.'

'It doesn't matter,' Tim repeats. He looks at Katrina, the PR advisor. 'It was fine, wasn't it?'

Katrina only shrugs.

29

You don't want to go back to the beach house, so Tim takes you to Dolores Street instead, arriving just as Sian brings Danny home from school. She doesn't stay, for which you're thankful. You want to talk to Tim about everything that's happened – her, the interview, the slap – but almost immediately, for no discernible reason, Danny has a meltdown, his body arcing in pain and terror as he screams, on and on. You sit with him, trying to soothe him by holding him, but he's too far gone. Even putting on one of his beloved Thomas videos makes no difference.

Eventually Tim takes your place, saying Danny's more used to him now. It does seem to help, a little. Even so, it's another hour before Danny calms down.

Tim comes downstairs, his face tired and drawn. 'That was the worst in a while.'

'What caused it, do you think?'

He grimaces. 'We used to think it was stomach pains, but we had all the tests and there was nothing conclusive. More likely it was some tiny, random thing – a fly, or a car alarm going off somewhere.'

'Perhaps he picked up some stress from Sian. Or me, for that matter.'

'Possibly. But I doubt it. People with autism have very low

empathy – they find it hard even to identify emotions, much less understand them.'

You're struck by something. 'It's odd, isn't it, how what Danny suffers from is the exact opposite of what you've achieved with me. He's a human with impaired empathy, and I'm . . . Well, I'm an empathetic machine.'

'Yes.' He glances at you. 'But it's not entirely coincidence. It was thinking about Danny's brain – wanting to *understand* him – that got me thinking about emotional intelligence. I thought . . .' His voice tails off. 'I thought, maybe if I could get an artificial brain to become more empathetic, I might get some insights into how to help him.'

'And did you?'

Tim shakes his head. 'The autistic brain simply doesn't have the same capacity to learn that an AI does. With autism, you have to use much more simplistic teaching methods.'

'Like the ABA programme.'

'Like the ABA,' he agrees.

You're both silent. 'Tim, we need to talk about Sian,' you say at last.

'Yes.' Even though you're indoors, he reaches for a baseball cap and pulls it firmly onto his head, bending the visor with both hands to get the shape just right. He takes a deep breath. 'It was a mistake – a terrible mistake. I know that. It started a while back, when I was going through . . . It was a difficult time. I thought she understood that it was simply a physical thing, a couple of quick hook-ups that meant nothing. But I . . . Well, I guess it became a habit. A habit I was too weak to break. And

I was working so hard. Once *you* were on the scene, I assumed she'd realise that she and I were done. But instead she seemed almost jealous of you.'

You think back to last night – the strained atmosphere at the dinner table. And then there'd been that jibe about the salt, and how there were still some things a robot couldn't do as well as a human. She'd been flirting with him, you realise.

And Tim – you recall the dark look he gave the TV when the reporter talked about you being creepy. Had he been having doubts about you? Was that why he didn't say no to Sian more firmly?

'This is so new, isn't it?' you say softly. 'No one's ever been in this position before. No one in all of history. We're going to have to figure it out as we go along.'

'Thank you for being so reasonable. I don't deserve it—'

'But the fact is, you *do*. You're not even middle-aged yet. You can't plan on being celibate for the rest of your life.' You hesitate. 'Isn't there *anything* we can do to make a physical relationship possible?'

He scowls. 'You heard that bitch this afternoon. It's the narrative people will always want to believe – that cobots are just million-dollar sex toys. Electronic Stepford Wives. I won't let that happen. I *can't*. I built you this way for a reason. So people couldn't ever say my love for you is anything but pure. So they'd understand that you're a *person*. Not some pathetic pleasure machine.'

'OK. I get that. But if you need . . . If there are times when it gets too much . . .' You stop, not quite believing you're actually saying these words out loud, that it's come to this. 'Just be discreet, all right? Don't do it so I'll know.'

'*You're* what I need, Abbie. I love you just the way you are.'

But you notice he stops short of saying he'll never need more.

30

Soon after, Tim goes up to bed. Before you do the same, you check the news channels to see how the interview went down. It isn't good. The slap might have happened during the commercial break, but the cameras were still recording. The cropping is slightly off – you're both standing, your heads out of shot – but you can clearly see your arm whip up and Judy Hersch recoiling, especially when they play it in slow motion. *AGGRESSIVE ROBOT ASSAULTS REPORTER*, the caption says. You turn to another channel, but the same words are scrolling along the bottom of the screen.

And suddenly there's Lisa, your sister, talking to a journalist's microphone. You turn the sound up.

'. . . *Nothing will bring Abbie back, but this is making an already painful situation even more difficult,*' she's saying. '*We will be challenging Tim Scott to prove he gained my sister's specific consent to have her data and personality used in this way.*' The crawl at the bottom now reads, *CULLEN FAMILY: WE'LL FIGHT 'COBOT'*.

You feel sick. Somehow this has all gone hopelessly wrong. You turn the TV off and toss the remote onto the sofa. It's a fair bet the news vans will be back outside the house tomorrow.

You go upstairs and lie down, but there are too many thoughts churning through your head to relax. Judy Hersch's words come back to you: *How do you feel about replacing the real Abbie Cullen-Scott?*

But I haven't, you think miserably. Nobody treats you the way they did before. And despite what Tim says, how can this be a real marriage if you can't make love? You get that he doesn't want people to look at him and think he's having sex with a machine, but why hasn't he considered *your* emotional needs in all this?

Something else occurs to you. Tim effectively said Sian came on to him last night. But if that was the case, wouldn't she have gone to *his* room? When you heard the two of them, they were in hers. Meaning it was much more likely that he went to *her.*

For all that Tim keeps saying he adores you – is it really *you* he loves? Or is it the idea of you – his creation, this amazing achievement? This extraordinary monument to his pure, enduring love?

If you were better off dead, would he let you go?

And you shiver in the darkness, because you're fairly sure the answer to that is *No.*

TEN

Of course, we were all eager to find out how the date at Mavericks had gone. 'I am agog,' Alexis declared, first thing Monday morning. 'I am literally *agog*,' and she was not alone.

In the end, it was one of the girls who asked Abbie, then reported back to us. 'Oh, it was nice,' Abbie had replied. 'But it wasn't really a date. We just hung out and watched the surfing with my friends, then we all went to Jersey Joe's for some beers . . . where we had this, like, massive disagreement,' she added, almost as an afterthought. 'Someone was talking about how homeo-pathy had cured their dermatitis, and Tim was kind of dismissive, so – just so my friends didn't think I was with a total jerk – I said, "But there's got to be something in it, right?"' She sighed. 'And then Tim started listing all these scientific studies that proved homeopathy was a waste of time. And I told him he was being boring.'

Our admiration for Abbie – which, if we were honest, had taken a knock when she asked Tim out on a date; it seemed a bit obvious somehow, a bit conventional, that she too should be so smitten with our charismatic leader – was instantly restored. She had told him he was boring! She was fearless as well as cool!

No one dared ask Tim for his side of the story. But Tim spoke to Mike, and Mike spoke to Jenny, who reported back that Tim had had a great time.

'She's amazing,' he'd told Mike, apparently. 'Smart, stimulating, and she likes to debate. She won't let me get away with anything. And she's drop-dead gorgeous, too. What's not to like?'

'He's asked me to go skydiving with him next week,' Abbie told us later. 'I've always wanted to skydive.'

Someone remembered that, a few years back, one of the psychology journals had published the results of a study into dating: what kind of activity you should schedule for a second and third date and so on. Something physically dangerous is ideal for a second date, apparently, because adrenalin boosts feelings of sexual attraction. The third date should be something like a salsa class – getting close and physical in a non-threatening environment. The fourth should be something intimate and nurturing, like feeding baby animals at the children's zoo. That was the best time for the relationship to become sexual, the study suggested – when both parties still had the excitement of novelty, but had acquired the safety of the familiar.

Yes, Tim had researched optimal dating methodology with the same rigour he applied to every other aspect of his life.

He didn't merely take Abbie skydiving for their next date, we discovered later. He booked a private flight with the Zero-G Corporation on their specially converted Boeing. During the three-hour flight, he and Abbie did fifteen parabolas out of the earth's atmosphere, experiencing weightlessness each time. Pictures on Abbie's Facebook page showed them floating about in the cabin, catching globules of champagne in their mouths. Then, when the plane was on its way back to base, they stepped out of the door for a parachute descent to earth.

Chartering the entire jumbo for a private trip like that cost around $200,000, according to Zero-G's website.

Rather than a salsa class, the up-close-and-physical date was at House of Air, the giant trampoline centre near the Golden Gate Bridge. Again, Tim rented out the whole place.

We waited with bated breath for the fourth date. It wasn't long in coming – just two weeks after that first outing to Mavericks. The next day, we scrutinised their faces for any signs as to how the sex had gone.

Nothing.

Tim had taken her to feed the ducks at Stow Lake, Abbie reported. He'd pulled out a loaf of bread and started tearing it into small pellets, before she'd stopped him.

'You do know that'll kill them, right?'

He'd blinked, astonished. 'But everyone feeds bread to ducks.'

'Everyone except smart people.'

She explained that, to wild ducks, bread was like junk food – it made their organs engorged and fatty, causing them to die of malnutrition or heart disease. It also made them too weak and bloated to take part in normal migrations.

'Domestic ducks, though, can't fly in the first place. So sometimes people release them into parks thinking that'll be a good environment for them. But, quite apart from the fact they've got no protection against predators, they'll die of digestive complications if they're fed on bread. And if there's so much bread they *don't* eat it, that's even worse. Bread left in water spreads salmonella and botulism, not to mention enteritis and a parasite called swimmer's itch.'

'Wow,' Tim said, considering. He put the bread away. 'You know, sometimes you remind me a little bit of me,' he added.

So would it be the fifth date when things finally turned intimate? It seemed not. The fifth date was a cooking lesson at a high-end restaurant. But there was no indication the next day of the two of them having consummated the relationship.

Eventually someone made a comment to Abbie, who was quite open about it.

'I guess we're taking things kind of slow. Slow and steady.' She paused. 'My last relationship was a bit wild. *Too* wild, actually. It's nice to be with a guy who respects me.'

It was at least six weeks before someone – summoned to Tim's office to discuss a new proposal that, just yesterday, had been judged *astounding* but was now terrible, *idiotic*, the dumbest idea *ever* – noticed a hand-painted mouse pad on Tim's otherwise fastidiously bare desk. It was a colourful piece of graffiti framing the words *ENGINEERS DO IT BETTER!* We recognised Abbie's street-art style.

Of course, we didn't tell her that it was ten years since anyone in our line of work had used a mouse pad.

But it was sweet to see Abbie and Tim reaching for each other's hands as they passed each other by the coffee machine, lacing their fingers together briefly when they thought no one was looking.

31

You wake up feeling more positive. It's a beautiful day and everything looks better in the sunlight, even the TV vans parked beyond the gates. Of course your relationship can survive without sex. You had a *marriage*, with all that entails. The physical side was nice, but you were so much more than that.

You feel almost ashamed for doubting it, when Tim so clearly doesn't. Somehow, together, you'll make this work.

Tim's cheerful, too. Mike called first thing to tell him that John Renton, Scott Robotics' biggest investor, saw the TV interview and wants you to come along to the meeting Tim's arranged with him.

'Mike said he sounded impressed,' Tim reports over breakfast. 'That's good.'

'Where's the meeting?'

'We haven't set that yet.'

'What about having it here? I could cook.' Tim frowns, but you forestall him. 'I know, I know – I don't have to. But I *like* cooking, remember? And we have all this great equipment.' An idea occurs to you. 'I'll make a bouillabaisse, like I used to before. I'll call Sea Forager and get everything delivered.'

'Well, if you're sure.' He gets up from the table. 'I'll see how Danny's doing with dressing.'

Danny has an idiosyncratic approach to breakfast. Even on a good day, the only thing he'll usually eat is dry Cheerios without milk, and even then he's as likely to comb his fingers through the bowl, transfixed, as eat them. Toast is a no-no, unless cut into precise one-inch squares. And, on a bad day, you're happy if you can get him to eat a few red M&Ms.

Today you're trying something you read about on an ABA website: instead of asking what he wants, you offer Danny a picture menu. The theory is that, if you say, 'Apples or grapes?' the person with autism will generally repeat, 'Grapes,' even though they don't actually want them. By letting Danny point, you're giving him time to process the information.

Sure enough, Danny points to fish fingers, then jelly. The fish fingers, you know, will have to be cut up into one-inch squares before having the jelly smeared over them. But that's OK – the main thing is, he made a choice, and one you'd never have thought to offer him yourself. There'll be time for improving the healthiness of his choices later.

After Danny and Tim have left the house, for school and the office respectively, you organise the shopping for tonight's dinner. Your voice is now almost indistinguishable from your old one; the man who takes the order clearly has no idea you're not just another customer. It'll be delivered by lunchtime, he promises. Persuading him to give you spare fish bones for the stock is trickier. He only agrees to throw some in when he decides you want them for a cat.

Capitalising on your good mood, you decide to change your hair – from cornrows to French braids, in honour of your menu tonight.

You go upstairs to look for some hair ties. Tim said he kept all your things, so they must be here somewhere. But where?

In the drawers beside your bed, you guess.

At the door to the master bedroom – Tim's bedroom, now – you hesitate. You haven't been in here since that first day. Your self-portrait stares down at you from the wall, an imperious, commanding presence, making you feel like an intruder.

Which is ridiculous. That portrait is of you. And this was your room, too.

You crouch down by what used to be your side of the bed and pull open the bottom drawer of the nightstand. It sticks a little, and you have to ease it upward to get it open. Inside are a jumble of old creams and bottles. And, at the bottom, some hair ties.

As you scrabble for them, your fingers encounter something else. Batteries. They're very old – leaking, now. You take them out to throw away.

Another flash of memory. A glimpse – an organic one, like when you remembered swimming in the pool. You, standing in this very room. And Tim, something in his hand.

Your vibrator. He's holding it at arm's length, distastefully, the way someone might hold an empty vodka bottle they'd just found hidden under a pile of laundry.

I'm not threatened, he's saying. *I'm disappointed, that's all.* He unscrews the end and shakes the batteries out, like someone shaking bullets out of a gun.

You blink, and the memory's gone.

Strange, you think. But, without more context, it could mean almost anything.

Your iPhone, charging on the kitchen counter, has a new message. You pick it up, thinking it'll be from Tim.

It's not. It's from Friend. And the message is the same as before:

This phone isn't safe.

You relax. The fact the message is identical proves, surely, that you were right last time, and it's just some kind of automated spam. Nothing to get worked up about.

Then a second message appears:

Buy another.

Followed, in swift succession, by:

A burner.

When you have it, reply with a BLANK message.

And finally:

TIM LIES.

You stare at it. It seems certain from the use of Tim's name that it's not spam, after all.

Quickly, you type a reply:

Who is this? Lies about what? What do you want?

There's no response.

32

'I have good news and I have bad news,' phone-shop guy says.

'What's the good news?'

'I can get some of the wiped data from the iPad back.'

'So what's the bad news?'

'It's heavily corrupted. I'll have to unscramble it.'

'That doesn't sound so terrible. If you can fix it, I mean.'

'No, but it's time-consuming. The question is, *why* would I fix it? Given how long it'll take me?' He tips his stool back and looks at you steadily. Something about the way he does it unnerves you.

'I'll pay you, obviously.' You've brought cash anyway, to buy a burner phone. Not that you believe Tim's been lying to you, but you can't help being curious about Friend's mysterious message.

The young man shakes his head. 'I don't want your money.'

'What, then?'

He smiles hungrily. 'The other day, after you left, I realised who you were. And I saw you on the news.' He nods at the dis-assembled laptop on the counter. 'I don't only fix these as a job, you know. Technology is my passion.'

'Terrific,' you say unenthusiastically. 'Good for you.'

'What Tim Scott's achieved with you is amazing. Like, *incredible*.'

He leans forward and gestures at your stomach. 'I want to take a look. Inside. At your code.'

You recoil. 'No way. Tim would never allow it. And even if he did, I wouldn't.'

'Well, that's the thing, isn't it?' the young man says. 'I started to ask myself, Where *did* she get that iPad? I mean, it clearly isn't yours. And then I thought, Why didn't she just give it to Tim's people to deal with? That's when I thought, *Ah*. As in, *Ah*, maybe it's actually Tim's, and she wants to see what's on it without him knowing.' He smiles again.

You can't be bothered to explain that the iPad has nothing to do with Tim. 'What are you suggesting, exactly?' you ask, although you suspect you already know.

'A trade. I'll give you the contents of the iPad as I unscramble them. In return, you let me look at your coding.'

You shake your head. 'That isn't going to happen.'

He holds up an Ethernet cable. 'You won't even notice I'm in there.'

The idea is faintly gross. 'No,' you repeat firmly.

He tosses the cable onto a shelf. 'Your choice. Too bad.'

'Give me back the iPad. I'll take it somewhere else.'

He folds his arms. 'Uh-uh. No deal, no iPad. In case you hadn't noticed, nothing gets nothing in this world.'

'You're pathetic, you know that?' you snap.

'I just want to see how you work,' he says plaintively. 'It's no different from a gearhead looking at an engine.'

'Excuse *me*,' you say sarcastically. 'From my perspective, it's really not very similar at all.'

He shrugs. 'Come back when you're ready to make a deal.'

'That iPad isn't yours. I'll go to the police.'

'Yeah, right. Be my guest.'

'Prick.'

'See you soon,' he says as you march furiously to the shop door.

'I'm Nathan, by the way.'

ELEVEN

A couple of days after the mouse pad appeared, Tim asked Abbie to join him in his office. Naturally, we all kept an eye on what was going on in there.

On one wall, there was a big flat-screen monitor – if you wanted to show Tim something, you'd hook your laptop up to it and present that way. It looked as if he was showing Abbie a presentation on it now.

Someone who had an excuse to walk past told us Tim was taking Abbie through a PowerPoint titled, 'Why Homeopathy Is Dumb'.

The presentation, we learnt later, dealt with many of the key elements of designing good scientific trials, from selection bias through to the placebo effect.

Perhaps remarkably, Abbie seemed fascinated.

'But if I take a homeopathic pill, all I know is, I feel better,' she was overheard to say. And Tim was heard to reply – not arrogantly or dismissively, but as if he was genuinely interested in explaining it to her – that this was indeed perfectly possible, and might well be due to the statistical effect known as 'regression to the mean'.

Now, it's fair to say that some of us were surprised by the

growing romance between Abbie and Tim. A few people even made disparaging remarks about Abbie's possible motives.

Those who took that position felt vindicated when, a week or so later, Abbie didn't turn up one day until way after noon. Someone spotted her striding across the parking lot, backpack dangling from one shoulder.

'Hey,' Tim said, when he saw her at her desk.

'Hey,' she replied.

'Thought you and I were going to have breakfast.'

'I know. I'm really sorry. My car broke down at the beach.'

'It broke?'

She nodded. 'It's the head gasket, apparently. I had to leave it and catch a bus. And then I had to organise the tow and the garage and it just took forever.'

Tim went into his office. A moment later, he came back with something in his hand.

'Here,' he said, dropping a bunch of car keys on her desk. 'For you. Now you needn't ever be late again.'

We waited for Abbie to throw the keys back at him, or at the very least to say she didn't want to be placed in his debt like that.

But she didn't. She picked up the keys. She said, 'Wow. Thanks.'

33

Bouillabaisse is not the simplest dish to make, although the results can be spectacular. Your previous effort used Elizabeth David's recipe, but the most authentic one, the one favoured by restaurateurs in Marseille, is from Jean-Baptiste Reboul's 1897 *La Cuisinière Provençale*, which stipulates half a dozen different rock fish, including grouper and striped bass. Since some of them are unavailable in North America, you decide to amalgamate that recipe with one from Chez Panisse.

Step one: make a fumet, or broth, of chopped vegetables, fish bones, fennel seeds and thyme.

Step two: add two cups of white wine, twelve mussels, the peel of an orange, two tablespoons of a French liqueur called Pernod, and an ounce of Spanish saffron. The saffron alone cost over a hundred dollars. Simmer for two hours, then strain and set aside.

Step three: make the rouille, the spicy paste you will serve on bread to accompany the bouillabaisse. Take half a cup of your fish stock and soak some breadcrumbs in it. Add more saffron and cayenne pepper. Chop a whole bulb of garlic very finely. (When tempted to use a garlic press, reread Elizabeth David's comment on the matter: *I regard garlic presses as both ridiculous and pathetic, their effect being precisely the reverse of what people who buy them believe . . . I have often wondered how it is that people who have once used one of these diabolical instruments don't notice this and forthwith throw the thing into the dustbin.* Decide to keep chopping.)

Add six egg yolks and whisk slowly together, adding a mixture of half olive and half grapeseed oil, drop by drop, in the manner of mayonnaise. Char two red peppers and two tomatoes over an open flame, then remove the skins and deseed. Pulverise in a mortar, and combine.

By the time you've finished chopping the garlic, it's late afternoon and Sian's brought Danny home. He seems fascinated by the charring of the peppers directly on the gas burner.

'How was your day, Danny?' you ask. He doesn't answer. Suddenly his hand darts out and he drags his fingers through the naked flame. Grabbing his wrist, you pull him straight over to the tap and run cold water on them, but it's too late. Two of his fingers are blistered.

There's no point in scolding him – he simply didn't understand; not because he hasn't encountered flames before, but because he has trouble extrapolating from those previous experiences that flames are always going to be hot.

'You have to be careful with him around fire,' Sian says unnecessarily.

'So I gather,' you say tartly. They're the first words you've exchanged since that night at the beach house.

Danny doesn't seem to feel pain as much as neurotypical children, but he is bothered by the blisters.

'When?' he says, flapping his hand in agitation. 'When?'

'They'll be better in a few days.' You know he won't let you put petroleum jelly on, let alone a bandage, so you don't even try.

'When?' he insists.

You give in to his need for an exact schedule. 'The blisters will be gone by Friday morning at ten o'clock.' You have no idea if this is true, but saying it may calm him.

It does, somewhat. Humming nervously, he goes off to check that his Thomas trains are still precisely lined up, just as he left them this morning. You get out the pestle and mortar and start pounding, glad you've got something to focus on other than Sian.

To your surprise, she suddenly says, 'Hey . . . I'm sorry.'

You look over at her.

'I saw that interview you did,' she adds. 'I hadn't realised . . . It can't be easy, being you.'

'How often did you and Tim sleep together?' You hate yourself for asking, but you have to know.

She hesitates. 'He's made me sign a non-disclosure agreement as part of my severance package. I can't discuss any of it.'

'He's just worried you'll speak to a reporter,' you say, though you can't help wondering if it's you Tim doesn't want Sian talking to. 'That doesn't apply to me, obviously.'

'I guess not. But I still can't take the risk. It's a lot of money.'

'Tell me this, then. Just this one thing, and I promise I won't repeat it to Tim. The other night, who initiated it? Did you go to his room, or did he come to yours?'

'I can't . . .' she begins, but then she sees your face. 'I guess he came to mine.'

You don't say anything.

'And it was him who got careless with the bedroom door.'

She stops, then says in a rush, 'Have you considered – maybe he *wanted* you to find us?'

'Why would he do that?' you say, mystified.

She shrugs. 'Jesus, I don't know. Guilt, maybe. Subconscious confession. He's pretty strange in bed anyway, right? All that tantric stuff.'

'Right,' you say, although you have no idea what she's talking about. 'I think you should go and check on Danny now.'

'OK.' At the door, she stops and turns back. 'Like I said, I'm sorry about what happened. I won't be sorry to leave, though. I mean, I'm getting a good pay-off and everything, but it's not about that. The whole set-up here, with Danny and you . . . I just can't figure out what he wants. From you. From any of us. And that freaks me out, y'know?'

'No,' you say firmly. 'I really don't.'

34

Two hours before John Renton and the other guests arrive, you make the marinade for the fish. Olive oil, white wine, fennel, peeled garlic cloves, Pernod and yet more saffron. You cube the fish into chunks and remove the bones with tweezers.

Step six: cut baguettes into slices, each three-eighths of an inch thick. Drizzle with olive oil and bake at 400 degrees Fahrenheit until crisp, then rub with a sliced clove of garlic and spread with the rouille.

Step seven: make the bouillabaisse.

Chop a dozen leeks and a dozen onions very finely, and sweat in an open pan along with a bay leaf and another pinch of saffron. Dice and deseed ten tomatoes, and whisk in a bowl along with yet more finely chopped garlic, more orange peel, and a glass of white wine. Add to the softened onions and pour in the fumet. Then add the chunks of seafood and poach for three to five minutes, until just done. Remove and keep warm.

The reason it's called a bouillabaisse is because of what happens next: you boil up the cooking liquid, very hard and fast, so everything emulsifies and acquires a soupy consistency.

Add more Pernod to taste, more saffron and pepper to taste, and you're done.

Except, of course, you couldn't actually taste it.

35

By the time Tim comes home, the kitchen is tidy again and the table laid. White wine – three bottles of Bâtard-Montrachet – is chilling in the fridge, as per his texted instructions. It's his best wine, a mark of how important this evening is to him.

'You've changed your hair,' he says, kissing you as he passes.

'Yes. Do you like it?'

'You should wear it any way you choose,' he says, frowning. 'That's the whole point. You're autonomous, not some Stepford Wife. Whether *I* like it isn't the point.'

'You hate it.'

'No, I like it. I'll get used to it, anyway.'

While Tim's in the shower, Mike arrives with Jenny, his wife. She's geeky and boyish-looking in a T-shirt and jeans. 'I worked on your deep-learning capabilities,' she tells you earnestly when you're introduced. It's hard to think of an answer to that. You're rescued by Mike, who adds proudly, 'Jenny has a PhD from Stanford in logistic neurons.' You nod as if you know what on earth that means. But, after a moment, of course, *clunk*, you do. *An antisymmetric sigmoidal function that can be trained from real-life examples rather than explicitly programmed.*

'You mean you built my brain,' you paraphrase.

She nods. 'I guess.'

Elijah brings his husband, Robert. A woman called Alicia Wright arrives on her own – late thirties, toned, her blond hair glossily smooth. 'Hi! I'm Scott Robotics' PR consultant,' she says brightly, holding out her hand. 'Pleased to meet you.'

'I thought Katrina was the PR consultant,' you say.

'Tim fired her this morning,' Elijah says. 'Alicia is new.'

'But fully up to speed, and super excited to be working with the famous Abbie!' she assures you.

Tim comes down from his shower. He's changed from the black jeans and grey James Perse T-shirt he came home in, into fresh black jeans and another grey T-shirt. While you open the wine, the others brief him.

'Try to behave,' Mike suggests. 'Renton's an idiot, but he's a smart idiot. He'll want to test you. Stand your ground, but don't let him rile you.'

'I always behave,' Tim says, bristling.

'Just not always well,' Elijah mutters.

As if on cue, John Renton arrives. To your surprise, given their descriptions of him, he's much younger than Tim and Mike. But his manner is of someone older – brash, confident, dominating the room. You see Tim stiffen as Renton slaps him on the shoulder, and know instantly that your husband dislikes this man.

When Renton's introduced to Alicia, he interrogates her about who else she's worked with. Each person she names, he tells her about his own last interaction with them: 'You PR for Shaun? He called me the other day, trying to get me to invest in that lame app he's building.' 'Oh, Catherine? Smart lady. We just shared a platform at TED.' You see her responding to his attention, how her body moves just a little more sensuously, how she touches her hair when he speaks. He has the opposite of good looks or charm – indeed, he's almost ugly – but you can see how some women might be charmed by him.

At last, he turns to you. 'So this is her!' he exclaims, holding out his hand.

You shake it. 'Pleased to meet you.'

He laughs delightedly. 'An AI with feelings. Get that! What are you feeling right now?'

You think. 'Happy. And a little nervous.'

'Do *I* make you nervous?' he says eagerly.

You shake your head. 'I'm just worried about how my bouillabaisse will turn out.'

'Anything else?'

'Well, I do feel a certain amount of monachopsis.'

Renton frowns. 'Monachopsis?'

'It's a persistent feeling of being out of place.'

His eyes widen. 'Monachopsis. I never even heard of that.' He turns to Tim. 'Impressive.'

Tim rolls his eyes. He clearly thinks that someone who's impressed by your use of a long word to describe a feeling – as opposed to the fact you can *have* a feeling in the first place – has missed the point of you completely.

'I'll get the wine,' you say hastily.

Half an hour later, you're opening a second bottle, and Renton's in full flow.

'I gotta tell you, Tim, when I first heard about this I thought you were nuts. I mean, *feelings*? Feelings are what made my wife my ex-wife, for Chrissake. Sure, I can see some possibilities.

Healthcare, maybe. The sex industry.' I see Tim wince. 'But fundamentally, there's an acceptability issue. People don't *want* their robots to have feelings. Because, if machines feel like humans, pretty soon some bleeding heart will decide we should *treat* them like humans. And then the whole economic argument for AI vanishes. Instead of being mechanical servants, tilling our fields and toiling in our sweatshops, suddenly they're indistinguishable from people. But making people is cheap, right? It's running them that's expensive. With AI, it should be the other way around. We start giving robots the same rights, the same consideration, maybe even the same pay, then where's the viability in that?'

'If you prick us, do we not bleed?' Mike says, nodding.

'Bleed?' Renton repeats, clearly puzzled.

'*The Merchant of Venice.* I forget how it goes on.'

'If you prick us, do we not bleed?' you say. *'If you tickle us, do we not laugh? If you poison us, do we not die? And if you wrong us, shall we not revenge?'*

There's a silence. 'My point exactly,' Renton says, frowning. 'You're not ticklish, right?'

You shake your head.

'The Shylock question is an interesting one, actually,' Jenny says thoughtfully. 'If the capacity to feel emotion means experiencing pain as well as pleasure, by what right do we inflict that on other intelligences?'

Tim's eyes flash. 'You're both missing the point. Cobots aren't slaves or pets. They're people. Just in another form.'

'Whatever they are, they're an expensive luxury item,' Renton says dismissively. 'An economic dead end. Your problem, Tim, is that you've invented this thing but you have no real vision for what to do with it.'

You stand up. 'I'll get the bouillabaisse.'

The debate – which is not quite an argument, but at times is so fierce it almost sounds like one – only pauses when you bring the soup to the table. You sit back and watch as they lift the first spoonful to their mouths.

Tim frowns. But it's Renton who speaks first.

'Whoa!' he says, staring at his bowl. 'What happened *here*?'

Mike sniffs his spoonful. 'That's rank,' he says quietly.

'What's wrong?' you ask anxiously.

'I think some of your fish may have been off,' Jenny says nervously.

'That's not possible . . .' you begin, but then you remember. The employee who thought the fish bones were for your cat. Clearly, he'd simply tossed a bag from the trash in with the order, assuming your pet would sort out the edible ones.

Your stock – your beautiful, elaborate, saffron-infused fumet – was poisoned from the start.

'I'm so sorry,' you say helplessly.

Tim pulls out his phone. 'Basilico can have pizza here in thirty minutes. That good for everyone?'

Numbly, you collect the bowls and carry them back to the kitchen. Jenny gets up to help.

'I feel such an idiot,' you say miserably when you're alone.

'It isn't your fault.'

'I've let Tim down. John Renton came here convinced I'm an expensive white elephant and I've just proved him right. Of course I can't smell anything. I'm a *robot*.'

'I wouldn't necessarily assume that's Renton's view,' Jenny says cautiously. 'He wouldn't be here if it was. He's just sparring. He's like that. All those tech guys are.'

You glance at her. 'Mike's not, though.'

'Mike's not,' she agrees. 'Or not so much. Which is why I married him.' She gives you a sideways look. 'Why do you say, of course you can't smell?'

'I can't, can I?'

She shrugs. 'The food industry already uses artificial taste buds. The deep learning for an artificial nose has existed for years.'

'So why . . .' You stop, thinking through the implications. 'Tim wanted to build me as quickly as he could,' you realise. 'To get me back. Even if it meant having to cut a few corners.'

'Well, I guess that's men for you. Their priorities come first.'

'He loves me,' you say defensively. 'He couldn't wait a day longer than he absolutely had to.'

You say it, but once again you have that uneasy feeling about Tim's love for you – that it's as driven and uncompromising as everything else he does. There could be something claustrophobic, even frightening, about being loved so much and so inflexibly.

'Yes,' Jenny says. 'Tim turned out quite the romantic, in the end.' And again you have a sense of hidden history, of backstories and shared memories and past events that are still unknown to you.

36

While they wait for the pizza to arrive, they finish the Batard-Montrachet and start on the Pernod, which is eighty-six degrees proof. Only Alicia refuses – she's still barely touched her wine. Jenny fills a shot glass along with the rest, but sips it slowly. The others down theirs in one, then reach for refills.

John Renton keeps coming back to the same issue.

'There are only two drivers for emerging technology.' He taps the table in time with his words. 'Productivity and sex. You've already ruled out the first. So that just leaves sex. Everyone knows VCR beat Betamax because the porn industry adopted VCR. Snapchat beat messaging apps like Slingshot because it made sexting possible. You make your robots – how shall I put it? – *fully functional*, maybe you have a chance.'

'Cobots are completely sentient,' Mike says. 'That implies they could withhold consent.'

'I don't see how that would stack up, legally. Can't rape a robot, am I right?' Renton thinks for a moment. 'Slutbots. Now *there's* a product.'

'Sexting and watching porn are private activities.' Tim speaks calmly, but you can tell how angry he's getting. 'Having a relationship with a cobot is very public, as I've already proved.

No one's going to pay millions of dollars for people to laugh at them.'

'Then, my friend, I don't think you have a market,' Renton says with finality.

'You don't get it, do you, you stupid prick,' Tim says. Renton laughs, a short, happy bark, and you realise this is what he's been working towards all along, that he's been deliberately goading Tim into losing his temper.

'This isn't about millennial self-gratification. Look at the fucking *bigger picture*. Forget the robot for one second – that's just the delivery mechanism. Abbie's *mind* now exists as something purely digital. And therefore *transferable*. Don't you see the potential of that?' Tim gestures at you. 'She's not some fucking *toy*. Effectively, she's *immortal*.'

There's silence. Mike looks at Elijah, as if to ask whether he's heard any of this before. Elijah gives a slight, mystified shake of his head.

John Renton laughs again. 'Immortal? Are you fucking kidding me?'

'I don't kid,' Tim says coldly. 'Abbie's mind will go on growing and learning forever. Her body – the shell – is replaceable, and therefore upgradeable. Everything else can be transferred. Effectively, our bodies – our *original* bodies – are now just the boot program for something better. For version 2.0, if you like.'

'That's *insane*,' Renton says. But he says it with delight, as if the idea is a shiny new present he's just been handed.

'Most people think death is inevitable,' Tim goes on. 'But what if that's just a failure of our collective imagination? What if death is just another problem to be hacked? Right now, it's a massacre out there – fifty million human beings mown down every year. If that resulted from any cause other than old age, don't you think we'd have done something about it?' He looks slowly around the table, then back at Renton. 'Robots aren't just the potential saviours of humanity. Robots are the *future* of humanity. And once you start to see it like that, you realise they're way, way more important than some stupid texting app. Peter Theil, Sergey Brin, Larry Ellison – they're all investing billions in this area. I'm meeting Larry in a couple of days to see if he wants to come on board.'

'Whoa. Now *this* is big,' Renton says, drumming his fingers. '*This* is visionary.'

He stares at you hungrily. Something has changed, something you can't altogether get your head around. 'How much?' he says abruptly.

Elijah opens his mouth but it's Tim who answers. 'Eighty million. Initially. If you want exclusivity.'

'For a company that doesn't even have a business plan? You're shitting me.'

Tim shrugs. Renton continues to drum his fingers. 'And you can do this for anyone? You can do it for *me*?'

'Of course,' Tim says evenly. 'There are some issues to iron out, but nothing that can't be fixed. Forget cutting your head off and sticking it in some scummy tub of liquid nitrogen. Living forever will become as simple as making an upload. It'll be expensive, of course. But we see that as a good thing. By restricting it to a select few founder investors, we'll avoid putting additional pressure on the earth's resources.'

There's something creepy about the expression in Renton's

eyes as he looks at you. It was bad enough when he was talking about slutbots, but now he's almost salivating.

'I want to see her without her skin,' he says abruptly. 'I want to see what . . . what I'll end up like.'

You wait for Tim to tell him to get lost, but he only says calmly, 'That's up to Abbie.'

Renton turns to you. 'Well?'

You freeze as you realise he's serious. You try to think how to say no without giving offence.

But then you think of Tim, who against all the odds has turned this evening around.

'Of course,' you hear yourself say. You look over at Jenny. 'Could you give me a hand?'

Together, you get up from the table and go upstairs, where you take a robe from the bathroom door before removing your clothes.

'I know what to do,' Jenny assures you. 'It's pretty straight-forward, actually.'

She fiddles with the back of your neck, looking for the seam. As she peels your face off, you close your eyes. You can feel the seam opening all the way down your back.

You step out of your skin as if from a wetsuit, Jenny's hands gently tugging it away from your torso. You try not to look, but when it catches on your knees you can't help glancing down at the hard white plastic you're made of, perfectly smooth, your contours sleek and elegantly moulded.

You think how typical it is of Tim that he made even this aspect of you, a part not intended to be seen, as perfect as it possibly could be.

You put the robe on. Silently, you go back downstairs, Jenny behind you. You feel like a prisoner being escorted to the scaffold.

But you feel something else, too. Without the heavy rubber skin, your movements feel lighter, less constrained. You feel strangely . . . *liberated.*

Outside the dining room, you take off the robe and hand it to Jenny. You pause for a moment, summoning your resolve, then step inside.

As you enter, there's complete silence. All of them, to varying degrees, have the same expression on their faces.

They look *awestruck.*

'Well, here I am,' you say. No one replies. Renton swallows, his Adam's apple bobbing nervously.

You turn around. You walk out, a little taller than before.

'Holy shit,' you hear Renton say wistfully behind you. 'She's *beautiful.*'

37

The evening breaks up as soon as the pizzas are eaten. Renton leaves first, promising he'll get straight on to his money people. When he's gone, the rest of you look at each other, not quite sure what just happened.

It's Tim who speaks first. 'Well done,' he says to you. 'That made a huge difference.'

'Immortality, Tim?' Mike says suddenly. 'Really? *That's* your vision? That's our business, now?'

'In the early twentieth century,' Tim says thoughtfully, 'rich men from all over the world travelled to the French Riviera to have monkey glands injected into their ball-sacks. It was painful and expensive and there was absolutely no evidence it worked. But thousands of people thought it was a price worth paying for a second chance at youth.'

Mike frowns. 'What's your point?'

'And in the fifteenth century, when Pope Innocent the Eighth was close to death, the Church paid ten-year-old boys a ducat each to give him their blood. The boys all died. So did the pope, of course. You might have supposed an organisation that already believed in eternal life wouldn't have been quite so desperate.' Tim gets up and stretches. 'My point is, Renton's an idiot. Someone who's just rational enough not to have faith in religion, but not nearly rational enough to accept his own mortality. But if he chooses to believe I can make him live forever, great. We'll take his cash.'

'So you *don't* have a vision,' Elijah says.

'Oh, I have a vision,' Tim says. 'Just not the one Renton thinks.'

TWELVE

The gift of Tim's Volkswagen marked a new phase in the relationship between Tim and Abbie. Ironically, she soon stopped
using it – she'd get a ride to the office with him instead, which
we took to mean she was staying over. He was busy around that
time, raising more funding for the shopbots. Most nights, he'd be
out at events in Silicon Valley, endlessly networking in window-
less convention rooms, eating self-serve food from tables with
green tablecloths and two kinds of strip steak piled high in metal
warming trays. Abbie went along too, though she must have
found those evenings dull by comparison with the festivals and
gallery openings she was used to.

But there was no doubt it was beneficial to Tim to have a tall,
strikingly beautiful artist by his side. It did more than just get
him noticed. The people who ran these venture-capital companies tended to be competitive, alpha-male types. Abbie got Tim
respect. And respect soon turned into a flow of funds. It was said
one billionaire put in forty million after a five-minute conversation with her.

Abbie started baking cakes and bringing them into the break
room for us. They were really good. You had to get there early

if you wanted some; by nine a.m., there was never anything left but crumbs.

The girls, of course, all tried to get Abbie to open up about what Tim was like in bed. Abbie wasn't a gossip, but neither did she show the faintest trace of embarrassment. One day, for example, she casually mentioned that Tim preferred not to ejaculate.

'It's a tantric thing. Athletes do it too. He says it conserves his energies for work.'

It was downright weird, if you asked us. But we looked it up and, sure enough, ejaculatory control was right there in the Buddhist texts. It seemed particularly strange in a man who generally scoffed at mysticism of any kind. But it fed our wish to believe that Tim was fundamentally different from the rest of us. And we all got it. The desire to hack our own health was not uncommon among us. Whether it was chugging micronutrients or replacing dairy with almond milk, we all experimented con-stantly with our own biology.

38

The morning after the dinner with Renton is like waking up after a party at which you got very drunk. Did all that really happen? Or did you just imagine it?

But Tim comes down to breakfast humming. 'Last night went well.'

'I nearly poisoned your biggest investor.'

'An even bigger investor now, thanks to you.' He kisses the top of your head. 'You've changed your hair back,' he notes.

'I decided French braids aren't really my style. Or anything French, actually.'

He laughs. 'You know, I've been thinking. We should really be getting you out there more. You should be doing TED Talks and neuroscience conferences – serious stuff, not like that trashy day-time TV Katrina got you on. The sooner people see what you're really like, the sooner this whole ridiculous media circus will blow over.'

'Tim . . .' you say.

'Yes, Abs?'

'Is this working for you? I mean *really* working? Am I really what you longed for, all those years?'

He looks surprised. 'Of course. Why do you ask?'

'It's just that . . . I feel like an imposter most of the time.'

'You're Abbie. And I love you. That's all that matters.' He frowns. 'Are you saying you aren't happy?'

He sounds so upset that you back off.

'You're right,' you say, managing a smile. 'Loving each other is what really matters. And I *am* happy.'

You wonder if there was ever a time when Tim and you could actually talk about your relationship, or if you were always met with this blank wall of adoration.

THIRTEEN

One day, we overheard Tim asking Morag, his then assistant, how many people from Google would be at a function he and Abbie were scheduled to attend that evening.

'Thirty-six,' Morag replied.

'Thirty-six?' Abbie interjected happily. 'But there were thirty-seven last year!'

Tim looked at her, clearly confused.

'*Harry Potter*,' she explained, as if it were obvious. 'Dudley Dursley wasn't happy with thirty-six presents, remember?'

'I never read those books,' he said dismissively.

'You *never read Harry Potter*?' She sounded amazed. 'But you've seen the movies, right?'

'I don't really go to movies. They're too long. I watched *South Park*, as a kid.'

'Jesus,' she said disbelievingly. 'I'll get the first book delivered.'

So then Tim was observed to be reading *Harry Potter and the Philosopher's Stone* between meetings. Being Tim, he finished it in two days, then immediately ordered the next one.

Abbie got up the Pottermore website, and they did the Sorting Hat quiz together.

'That's amazing,' Abbie was heard to say. 'We're both Hufflepuff!'

Now, of course, the whole point of the Sorting Hat was that it could see things about you that you didn't even know yourself. But Hufflepuff? House of kindness and loyalty? *Tim?* Really?

We guessed he'd gone online and found a site that told you what answers to give to get sorted into specific houses. It was endearing, in a way – that even a multimillionaire like him felt the need to impress a girl. But still. Nerds that we were, we all knew you should never, ever try to get yourself put into the wrong house at Hogwarts.

The time we realised this relationship was *really* serious, though, was when Darren screwed up the runway walking. Human sales assistants spent a lot of time standing around waiting for customers – that was one of the things we didn't like about them, we agreed, the way they always seemed to be hanging by the register, looking bored out of their minds. Tim decided it would be cool if, instead, when you walked into the store, the shopbots were already walking up and down like models on a runway, showing off the store's new lines. Then one would peel off to come and talk to you.

We spent a bit of time analysing video of real models on runways, and Darren turned the distinctive hand-on-hip stride into code. Eventually he was ready to demonstrate his handiwork. He activated a shopbot, which sashayed up and down the demonstration area. It looked impressive – exactly like a model at a Victoria's Secret show.

'Great!' Tim said. 'Now show me what it's like with more!'

Darren looked confused. 'More?'

'There should be half a dozen, all parading at once,' Tim said. 'That's the whole *point*. That's what makes it cool.'

Darren nodded, which was his first big mistake. Well, actually it was his second – his first mistake was that he'd neglected to think through what would happen when half a dozen shopbots paraded up and down a narrow runway at once. Being a geek, he'd never actually been to a fashion show. But, whatever the reason, he should have immediately told Tim he hadn't got around to that part yet, instead of trying to wing it.

He activated another shopbot, then another, then two more. For a moment, it looked amazing – five identical robotic mannequins, tall, elegant and impeccably engineered, striding up and down an imaginary runway in a variety of imaginary outfits.

'They do it to music, too,' Darren said proudly, and turned on a speaker. The Red Hot Chili Peppers' 'Snow (Hey Oh)' blasted around the room, and, without breaking stride, the shopbots started swaying their shoulders and heads in time to the beat. One of them even twirled her hand. (Yes, *her* hand – it was impossible to think of the shopbot as *it* when it was dancing like that.) People around the office started clapping along and whooping – Abbie, too; her face lit up as she hollered and whistled. (She had a hell of a whistle, we learnt: the full two-finger Texan cattle-whistle.) For a brief moment, our office felt like a party.

Then the inevitable happened. The twirling-hand shopbot reached the end of the runway and turned – straight into the shopbot immediately behind. Both crashed to the floor. A third tripped over them. Within seconds, the parade had turned into a pile of mechatronic limbs, still attempting to stride but succeeding only in kicking one another. They looked like something from a war zone, a pile of plastic bodies twitching in exaggerated death throes.

'Jesus,' Tim muttered under his breath. 'We can't even copy the dumbest humans on the planet.'

Someone turned the music off. The sudden silence was deafening.

'That's solvable,' Mike said nervously. 'We just need to port in some driverless-car sensors, so they swerve around each other. It would look pretty neat, actually.'

'Exactly,' Tim said. 'Solvable. And therefore predictable.'

We all waited for the inevitable Tim-lashing that would follow. Darren's head drooped, like a dog that knows it's about to get whipped.

Then Tim looked across at Abbie. 'Still, not bad, huh?' he said to her with a smile. 'For a first attempt.'

A few days after that, someone glanced into Tim's office and said, 'Wow.'

Abbie was in there. She was wearing a wetsuit. On every limb were small green stickers – for motion capture, someone said. Tim was videoing her. She was sashaying up and down like a model.

Clearly, Tim was refining the runway tech, and Abbie had offered to help out. In her figure-hugging wetsuit, she looked incredible. But some of us felt uneasy. Abbie had been employed as an artist, yet here she was doing a task that could not, by any stretch, be considered art. It was blurring the lines, somehow.

On the other hand, someone pointed out, maybe Tim didn't

want to ask one of his female employees to parade up and down in a wetsuit for him.

There was a long silence as we thought about that. The person who made the comment was new, and didn't understand the ramifications.

But it was great to see Tim so happy, we agreed. Abbie was really good for him. It was a story old as time: hard-ass falls in love, stops being such a hard-ass.

At one of the boring investment functions, Abbie and John Renton's ex-wife got drunk and danced on a table. Some of the men gathered around them, whooping, and tucked hundred-dollar bills into their shoes, like they were strippers.

Tim watched this with a strange expression on his face, Elijah reported. It was as if he was half proud of Abbie, half worried she was going too far.

Elijah heard him say to her later, as they were walking out to the parking desk, '*I* know you're not a slut. It's just that none of *them* know that.'

She linked her arm through his. 'And every single one of them was jealous of you,' she teased, 'thinking you might have a slutty girlfriend ... Which I am most definitely not, by the way,' she added.

'I know,' Tim said. 'It's one of the things I love about you.' And he laughed, that high, goofy giggle that always seemed so unlikely, coming from his mouth.

The next day, someone glimpsed a PowerPoint Tim was working on in his office. It was titled, 'Why Polyamory Is Dumb'.

*

203

Someone who went to Maker Faire saw Abbie's name on the exhibitors' list and went to see what she was showing. It was a sculpture made out of six pairs of shopbot legs, walking on a treadmill. It wasn't her best work, he reported. It was basically just the runway incident, rehashed.

What was more noteworthy was that Abbie was hanging out with a bunch of people who looked like rock musicians – tattooed, long haired, bearded. They all seemed wasted. Not on alcohol, either, our informant said – it was more like they were on speed or coke. He spoke to Abbie, or tried to, but she too was gabbling nonsense, her eyes popping and her forehead shiny with sweat.

We were surprised, and also disappointed. Sure, Abbie had to let off steam occasionally. And sure, she was an artist. She'd probably been around people who were doing drugs for years. But still . . . She herself had seemed so clean-living, so wholesome. It was hard to reconcile those clear eyes, that fresh, unspoilt beauty, with any kind of substance abuse.

We all wondered who was going to be the one to tell Tim his girlfriend was a cokehead. Well, perhaps *cokehead* was a bit strong; *recreational user* was probably more accurate, but that was not a distinction we imagined Tim would take much notice of. He had a zero-tolerance policy for drugs in the office, with testing a mandatory part of the recruitment process. Even outside of work, he rarely touched anything stronger than a glass of wine.

Of course, we told each other wisely, that had been part of Abbie's appeal for him – her otherness, the fact that she came from a different, more creative milieu. But even so, we predicted the relationship was now headed for the rocks. Tim was not someone who could compromise over a matter like drugs. Or, indeed, any matter. And we felt sad about that, because we'd really liked Abbie. And we'd really, really liked what she did to Tim.

39

When Danny comes to the table for breakfast, you show him the picture menu you made. But today it isn't working. He gives it a cursory glance, then ignores it.

'Come on, Danny,' you say at last. 'There must be something you want to eat.'

Scrambling down from his chair, he goes and fetches one of his *Thomas the Tank Engine* books. You see him considering. Then, quickly, he slips the book into the toaster and pushes down the handle.

'Hmm. Maybe not such a good idea,' you say, retrieving it and handing it back to him. Immediately, he tries to take a bite from it.

'Bother that telephone!' he says distinctly.

You look at him, thinking hard. Those words he just said – you recognise them. They're from *Toby the Tram Engine* – the same book he's just tried to eat.

Coaxing the book from him, you find the page where the Fat Controller is being served toast and marmalade by his butler when the telephone rings, interrupting his breakfast.

'Is that what you want, Danny?' you ask. 'Toast and marmalade?'

'Well, blister my buffers,' Danny says. He seems almost

startled that you've been able to follow his circuitous thought processes.

Startled, and also pleased.

After Sian's collected Danny to take him to school, you get out your phone. You don't know exactly when you made the decision to call Lisa, but having made it, it feels right.

You find her name in your contacts and press *call*. So simple. You imagine your sister picking up her own phone, staring at the caller ID. There'll be a few moments of shock, you imagine. But, after all, she's seen you on TV now. At some point, she'll answer.

But she doesn't. After a few rings, the call goes to voicemail. You can't bring yourself to leave a message. Your first contact with her after so long shouldn't be a recording.

A few minutes later, you try again. This time it cuts out after one ring. You imagine her holding the phone, waiting for your name to appear, her finger jabbing down at the button to cut you off. To get *Abbie* off her screen as quickly as possible.

Sighing, you send a text.

Lisa, it's me. It's REALLY me, whatever you may have read or heard. I'm going to call again. Pick up this time, will you?

Delivered, the phone tells you. Then: *Read*. Three dots appear, meaning she's typing. But no reply comes. She must have deleted her answer before sending it.

Encouraged, you try dialling again. And this time it's answered. She doesn't say anything, but you can hear her breathing.

'Leese, we need to meet,' you say into the silence. 'I know you think this is weird – I do too. But it's not like I had any say in the matter.'

'Jesus,' she whispers disbelievingly. 'Jesus. It sounds . . . It sounds . . .' She starts to cry.

'Why don't I come to Spike's?' you say, naming the coffee bar where you used to meet up sometimes, halfway between your houses. 'Say, at eleven?'

She doesn't reply, just sniffs back tears.

'Look, I'm going to be there anyway,' you say, after a while. 'Please come. I need to see you.'

FOURTEEN

It has to be said, we couldn't spot any signs of Abbie's alleged drug use at work, no matter how closely we looked. What we saw instead was someone immersing herself in a new creative project. There was a full-sized 3-D printer in the workshop, a very expensive piece of machinery for making prototypes. At Abbie's request, Darren showed her how it could be used to make perfect replicas of almost anything.

She ordered in a load of Newplast, a soft modelling putty favoured by stop-motion animators. Then, for a whole week, she took over the printer booth. We didn't know what she was doing in there, but she started arriving late and working through the night. Tim was cool with that, we gathered.

As with the punchbags, she made no fanfare about this new artwork when it was finished. We simply came into work one day and found Sol, who usually got in earliest, in a state of high excitement.

'You have *got* to come and see what she's done this time,' he told us.

He led us to one of the meeting rooms. And there it was – a life-sized, 3-D replica of Abbie, fashioned out of flesh-coloured putty. Apart from the briefest of thongs, she was nude. She stood with her hands on her hips, her torso turned slightly sideways, as if looking at herself in a mirror.

'Holy fuck,' someone breathed, and indeed it was a remarkable sight. Nobody wanted to look uncool by commenting on it directly, but Abbie really did have an awesome body. It was more than that, though. It might only have been a 3-D printout, but you really got a sense of what kind of person she was: vibrant, optimistic, even somewhat innocent.

It was only after we'd been staring for several minutes that someone spotted the printed card fixed to the nearby wall.

DO AS YOU PLEASE (FEEL FREE!)
3D-printed modelling putty and wireframe

Interactive installation

Dimensions variable

'How is it interactive?' someone else wondered. 'It doesn't do anything, does it?'

'And why "dimensions variable"?' asked one of the girls.

'Maybe,' Kenneth suggested, 'we're meant to – you know – play with it?'

There was silence while we digested this. Someone bent down and gave the sculpture's foot a tentative squeeze, just above the toes. 'It's soft, all right,' he reported.

'Hey, don't ruin it!' Marie Necker protested.

'But I think that's the whole idea. I think we're supposed to – *refashion* it.'

Sol placed his thumb on the sculpture's right hip and pressed.

When he took his hand away, it left a small dish-shaped dimple containing his thumbprint.

'I don't think you should have done that,' Marie said nervously.

'Why not?' Sol retorted.

'Has Tim seen it yet?' someone else wondered aloud. That brought us all up short. Whatever we were meant to do with the sculpture, no one wanted to be the one who did it before Tim had had a chance to decide what the right reaction was.

40

You get to Spike's early. Lisa's late – so late, you start to wonder if she's coming at all. But you're confident she'll show in the end. Somehow, it's just one of the things you know about her.

While you wait, you look through the video clips stored in your phone. They're of Danny, mostly. In one, taken the morning of his fourth birthday – just a few months before his regression – he's singing 'Happy Birthday' to himself in his excitement. His face is almost broken in two by his toothy smile as he reaches the end: 'Happy BURFDAY dear Danneeeee . . . Happity burfday to MEEEEE!'

Your voice, behind the camera, can be heard correcting gently, 'Not *burfday*, Danny. *Birthday*.'

'Burfday!' he repeats eagerly. 'Vat's what I *said*.' He had a slight lisp – a result of hooking his front teeth over his bottom lip, the speech therapist told you. She said he'd almost certainly grow out of it, but you could help by modelling correct pronunciation.

You sigh at the memory. But then you remember that tiny moment of connection at breakfast over the toast this morning, and you can't help smiling. Danny might have changed almost beyond recognition, but he's still your child.

*

Lisa eventually turns up at half past, staring at you through the window. You give her a tentative wave and a rueful smile that says, *I didn't mean for it to be like this.*

She doesn't get coffee, just comes straight over and sits down. Physically, she's not like you – you somehow got her share of good looks as well as your own, she used to say, wryly – but you have exactly the same eyes. Most people wouldn't even notice, but looking at that one part of her is like looking into a mirror. Of course, she's five years older than when you last saw her, but Lisa always dressed middle-aged anyway.

'I saw you on TV,' she says abruptly. 'But somehow, in the flesh . . .' She swallows. 'Christ, what am I even saying? There's no *flesh* involved.'

'They deliberately made me look terrible on TV. But at least it means I don't get recognised in places like this.'

She gives herself a little shake. 'It *sounds* like you. Like her, I mean.'

'It *is* me. At least, I think it is. It's *my* mind, Leese. A very small sliver of it, I gather, but enough to feel like me. You can debate whether that makes me AI or trans-human – and, believe me, Tim's friends debated it for an hour over dinner only last night – but the point is, I'm not just some electromechanical lookalike.'

'What was the name of your first doll?' she demands.

'Trick question. Grafton. Our parents insisted all our toys were gender neutral. They were pretty advanced like that.'

She stares at you.

'But, to be fair, my memories are patchy,' you add. 'You'd be amazed how few you actually need to retain a sense of self. I'm like an Alzheimer's sufferer in reverse – slowly filling in the gaps.'

213

She shakes her head. 'This is so weird.'

'Tell me about it.' You reach forward and take her hand. 'I've missed you.'

She snatches her hand away. 'Oh God,' she whispers. '*God.*' She starts to cry. 'This is all his fault,' she adds through her tears. 'That *bastard.*'

'Tim? He's given me a second chance at life. He loves me. How does that make him a bastard?'

'This isn't love. This is – this is *necrophilia.*'

'Hardly,' you say drily. 'He hasn't given me any genitals.'

Lisa snorts. 'That doesn't surprise me.'

'What do you mean?'

'He's a control freak,' she says bluntly. 'Always was. One of the ways he liked to control you was by withholding sex.'

You frown. '*I* told you that?'

She swipes at her tears. 'Not in so many words. That is, you defended him. It was a sign he respected you, you said. Personally, I always thought it was a sign he didn't care about your needs at all. Just this grand, narcissistic passion of his. Loving you was all about *him* – how romantic he was, how forgiving, how much adoration he was capable of. But God help you if you ever stepped off your pedestal.'

'Did I ever try?'

'Sometimes. But never particularly hard, it seemed to me.' She looks at you for a moment, thinking. 'OK – here's an example, off the top of my head. This one time, you were really, really tired – Danny hadn't been sleeping. But Tim wanted sex. Since he wasn't actually going to come – too messy, too out of control – sex usually went on until *you* came. So, on this occasion, you faked it. But you obviously didn't do it too well, because he picked up on it. He went on at you about it for days. If Jack had done that to me, I'd have given him his marching orders. But you were always so damn *understanding*. Anyway, I told you Tim's attitude was outrageous – I couldn't understand why you'd felt obligated to have sex in the first place, let alone fake an orgasm, but since you had, it was none of his business. I must have convinced you I was right, because that's what you eventually told him.' She shrugs. 'Hardly a big deal, right? But Tim didn't talk to you for weeks. Just cut you off. Then, when he *did* start talking, and you told him it had come from me, he wouldn't have me in the house. He got mad if you even spoke to me on the phone.'

You wait to see if the memory of what Lisa's describing comes back to you. But there's nothing. 'How *are* you and Jack these days?'

She gives a short, bitter bark of laughter. 'Well, there's the thing. We separated a few years back.'

'Tim and I must have been doing something right, then.'

'I guess.' She gives you a glance. 'Or you were too scared to leave him.'

You frown at her. 'What makes you say that?'

'You always tiptoed round him. Everyone did. The brilliant Tim Scott, the boy wonder who was going to change the world. He didn't have employees – he had *acolytes*. Like a cult. I always thought it was a shame you met him in that environment – all those yes-kids falling to their knees whenever he so much as walked past their desks. Personally, I can't imagine anything worse than living with someone like that. There was something creepy about the way you always had to live up to this perfect image of yourself he'd created in his head.' She shudders. 'But if you *were* having second thoughts, you probably wouldn't have told me. You'd have hated me to have been right about him.'

You think of that book hidden in the bookcase, *Overcoming Infatuation*. Perhaps it wasn't you who was the infatuated one, after all. Perhaps you were simply trying to understand the man you were married to.

You push the thought away. Lisa always did this. She enjoyed being the all-knowing, sensible older sister. It was one of the things that, growing up, made you delight in being reckless. Whenever she said something was too dangerous, you just went ahead and did it anyway.

'And do you remember how you cut off all your hair that time?' she's saying. 'You decided braids were impractical now you were a mother. Plus, there'd been some stuff on social media about it being cultural appropriation or something. So you took a pair of scissors to them. It looked stunning, actually – everything looked stunning on you. But you hadn't consulted Tim. He was furious. You had to get extensions and braid them exactly the way they'd been before.'

You shake your head. 'I don't remember that, no. Are you sure that really happened? Perhaps I was exaggerating.'

'You didn't exaggerate. If anything, you had – what do they call it? – Pangloss syndrome. Everything was always beautiful and brilliant and so damn *perfect* in this amazing new world you and Tim were building together. *Arrgh*.' She mimes sticking her fingers down her throat.

You think how, just the other day, you'd asked Tim whether he liked your French braids, and he'd said it was up to you how you wore your hair. And yet, after the poisoned fish debacle, you'd changed it back again. Unconsciously trying to please him, perhaps?

Such tiny, tiny things. And, after all, there are little glitches in any relationship, tiny creases in the carpet. Faking an orgasm – in the great scheme of things, it was nothing. Every wife has done it, and every husband's suspected her of it. OK, maybe Lisa wouldn't, out of some kind of feminist principle, but Lisa always ended up with quiet, downtrodden partners who eventually ran off with someone more fun anyway.

Nothing she's said makes you believe that Tim ever did anything to frighten you.

Unless I was having an affair, you think. Being unfaithful would change everything. Because one thing you definitely know about Tim is that he demands absolute loyalty.

'Was I . . .' you begin, then stop, unsure how to put this.

'What?' Lisa says quietly, and you get the sense that, somehow, she knows what you're trying to ask.

'Was our marriage in any difficulty? Anything specific, I mean?'

'You mean, did Tim have any reason to kill you?' she says baldly.

Even though it's exactly what you mean, hearing the words spoken out loud makes it sound so much worse.

After a moment, she shrugs. 'As you can imagine, I asked myself that question a thousand times after you disappeared. Because there's one thing I *am* sure of. Whatever happened that night, it wasn't a surfing accident.'

'Why do you say that?'

'You and I grew up in the ocean. Sure, you were a risk-taker – you might have gone out in bad weather, particularly if the waves were breaking well. But you'd have taken the right board. You'd have taken the gun.'

For a second, you have to think what she means. Then it comes to you. The elephant gun. The biggest, heaviest board, originally designed for paddleboarding but used by experienced surfers for stability in the largest waves. Your gun was still in the garage at the beach house.

'What board *did* I take?'

'Supposedly, your regular shortie – at least, that's what was missing from your garage. To anyone who didn't know you, or who didn't really know surfing, that would have made sense – it was the board you used most often. It just wasn't right for those conditions.'

'Did you tell the police?'

'Of course. They said it didn't prove anything. Surfers experiment with different boards sometimes. They seemed disappointed that was all I had.'

'Well, they're right. About it not being conclusive, I mean.'

'I know you,' Lisa insists. 'I know the way you surf.' Her eyes fill with tears again. 'You know, I didn't expect meeting you to be like this. I thought I'd be sitting down with some kind of *doll*. Something that might look like you, sound like you, that might even parrot things you'd said. I never expected to meet . . . to meet . . .'

'To meet your sister,' you finish.

She nods, swallowing hard. Then she reaches out and puts her hand on yours.

'And that's why I'm saying, please be careful,' she says softly. 'Whatever happened to you before, don't assume it couldn't happen again.'

FIFTEEN

Tim studied *DO AS YOU PLEASE (FEEL FREE!)* for several minutes, walking around to inspect it from every angle. He was always a hard person to read – we never knew what he was thinking until his thoughts burst over us in a cascade of invective, or, more rarely, praise.

'This is fucking *genius*,' he said at last.

We nodded. We thought so, too.

'It's her best yet,' he added. 'It's totally *awesome*.'

'I really like the way she's standing,' someone suggested. 'She's got so much *attitude*.'

We all ignored him. The statue's attitude was completely missing the point.

'Where is she?' Tim demanded, looking around eagerly. 'Where's Abbie?'

We shrugged. We didn't know.

He pulled out a phone and dialled. 'Hey, you,' he said, and we were struck by the tenderness in his tone. 'Yes, I'm by it now. You look *amazing*, by the way. No, nobody has yet. Shall I . . . ?'

He reached out and, gently, squeezed the sculpture's right shoulder. His fingers left small dimples in the flesh-coloured putty.

'Are you sure?' he said, still into the phone. 'It seems a shame to.'

Whatever Abbie said, it must have reassured him, because he reached out and squeezed the sculpture's other shoulder too, harder this time.

'Amazing,' he said again. Then he walked away, still on the phone, so he could talk to her privately.

A few of us followed his lead, laying our hands on the sculpture and squeezing. But despite the instruction in the piece's title, we held back. A few indentations from the tips of our fingers, a very slight deformation of an arm or elbow, was the most we felt entitled to do.

So how did it happen, then, that *DO AS YOU PLEASE (FEEL FREE!)* got so thoroughly trashed over the days and weeks that followed? For one thing, it became apparent that people felt less restrained in their remoulding when they were alone, or in small groups of two or three. It was less than a day before the first fingermarks began to appear in the sculpture's breasts. The soft modelling putty recorded each one; with a little fingerprint powder, someone joked, Tim could easily identify who among us had been groping his girlfriend. Some clown left a big five-fingered handprint across the left buttock, as clear as the fossil outline of a leaf. But that, too, was soon obliterated by other fingerprints and indentations, sly squeezings and strokes and pinches that left the once-smooth surface pocked and pitted as if by cellulite. Someone used the sharp point of a pencil to gouge a long, wavy incision down the back of the right calf that, had it been the real Abbie and not simply her likeness, would have required a trip to the ER. (We knew it was a pencil because he, or possibly she, left it impaled in Abbie's right foot.) The nipples, perhaps not surprisingly, came in for a lot of attention, and were soon twisted off altogether – one lay discarded nearby, carefully placed on a table, as if the person who'd done it thought maybe it could be repaired. The right breast bulged from the impression of so many kneading fingers that it, too, fell off in the end. On first seeing the piece, some of us had called to mind votive statues, their bronze surfaces worn smooth by praying hands and kisses, but it soon became clear that this was something altogether more savage, like those gruesome medieval depictions of martyrs fingering their open wounds. Pretty soon the statue resembled a carcass on which wolves had feasted, a slow-motion explosion of modelling putty and body parts.

Far from being annoyed by the artwork's disintegration, Tim seemed fascinated. He came to inspect it at least twice a day, pointing out the latest changes, however small, to whoever happened to be in there. He took no part in the remoulding himself, or none we ever saw, but it was as if his fascination egged us on. The sculpture lost both hands – vanished, presumed stolen – and its head began to loll drunkenly. Many people simply tugged a small lump of putty from one part of the body, rolled it into a cylinder between their palms, and stuck it back on somewhere else, so eventually it looked as if the statue was covered with fat little worms. And finally there was a kind of tipping point, a moment when *DO AS YOU PLEASE (FEEL FREE!)* no longer even resembled a human form, but simply became a big block of malleable graffiti. What had once been the shoulder was fashioned into a rough approximation of a gurning second head. Someone broke off part of the arm and used it to make a crude penis that jutted, for a while, from the statue's crotch – until that, too, fell off, and lay with all the other handfuls and scrapings of Newplast trodden into the floor like lumps of chewed gum. And then the head itself was gone, ripped off and torn in two, as if the unknown perpetrator had tried to peer inside it. 'Like a Greek Aphrodite,' someone said pretentiously of the malformed torso that remained, but we all knew this was quite different from those graceful effigies.

Next morning, the sculpture – what was left of it – had disappeared. Abbie had even cleaned up after it. The meeting room was spotless.

We felt slightly ashamed, the way we might feel after a night that had involved tequila, a night when we hadn't behaved quite as well as we should. Some people even went so far as to suggest that, if there was another opportunity, they'd do things differently next time. Like, maybe take turns to act as security guards. A roster could be drawn up, CCTV installed.

But most of us felt that was missing the point. There wouldn't be another time. What had happened to the sculpture had happened. That was the whole purpose of it.

A few days later, our office walls were taken over by a display of photographs. Giant black-and-white prints, three feet square, starkly lit, taken at twenty-four-hour intervals, documenting the gradual disintegration of *DO AS YOU PLEASE (FEEL FREE!)*. Abbie had come in each night to photograph our handiwork.

We were pleased there was a record of the project. We hadn't liked to think of it just vanishing into the ether. But now that we studied it in time-lapse, as it were, frozen mercilessly in those big, stark photographs, we could see just how quickly the sculpture had been reduced from graceful humanity to primordial sludge. It made us uneasy to think about it.

Those pictures, digital copies of which were sent – by Abbie? Or one of us? – to several art blogs and Instagram feeds, eventually found their way on to the *Chronicle*'s website, and from there to several Bay Area TV stations. As a result, Abbie became quite well known for a time, a minor local celebrity. The news stations' angle was that what we'd done to the sculpture showed tech workers in a bad light, that we'd been creepy and destructive, like the antisocial nerds we were. We thought that was unfair. We were hardly vandals. Anyone would have reacted to the installation, and its deliberately provocative title, the way we did.

Luckily for us, Tim didn't think it reflected badly on the company at all. He was immensely proud, particularly when Abbie started getting interviews and profiles. He even had one of her black-and-whites, the first one in the series, hung in his office, opposite the Muhammad Ali quote. And Katrina Gooding, the PR consultant, placed pieces in several tech blogs about how visionary and radical Tim was, to have thought of employing an artist-in-residence in the first place.

41

After Lisa leaves, you stay in the café, thinking. You're pleased with how the conversation went, given what she'd previously said to the TV station. But then, you of all people know how those reporters can get someone to say whatever they want.

But you still have a sense – an intuition, if you like – that your sister was holding something back, not quite telling you everything.

Does *she* know your secret? Is she another one who's afraid you'll pass whatever she tells you straight back to Tim?

Before Lisa left, she asked if you remembered the *Twilight Zone* episode where a small-time thief wakes up in the afterlife. He finds himself living in a beautiful apartment, he never loses at the casino and he's surrounded by beautiful women. Eventually, he becomes bored and tells his guide he'd like a break from being in heaven – he likes the idea of visiting the other place. To which his guide retorts, 'What gave you the idea you were in heaven? This *is* the other place.'

'Or, to put it another way,' Lisa concluded, 'be careful what you wish for.' And she'd given you a look you couldn't decipher.

Even now, you can't puzzle out what she meant.

You really have no choice, you realise. However unsavoury

the guy in the phone shop might be, you have to know what's on that iPad.

When you get there, Nerdy Nathan's leaning against the counter, doing something to the insides of a phone. Seeing you, he grins and pushes it to one side. Then he comes out from behind the counter and turns the sign on the back of the shop door to *Closed*, flipping the deadlock for good measure.

'Come in the back,' he says.

He leads you to a tiny storeroom, piled high with boxes. There's a workbench, almost hidden by tangles of leads and bits of equipment, with a laptop open on it. You can feel the excitement radiating off him. Or is that just your own nerves?

'There'll be a port,' he says impatiently. 'Somewhere I can plug into.'

'On my hip. But I want the iPad first.'

'It's still scanning. I can show you what I've got, though. I printed it out. I knew you'd be back.' He takes some sheets of paper from a shelf. 'It's part of someone's internet history. It's garbled, but it makes pretty interesting reading.'

You hold out your hand for it, but he shakes his head. 'Uh-uh. When you're hooked up.'

'Get on with it, then.' You give him a hostile stare.

You could help him by undoing your jeans, but you don't want to make this easy for him. You *want* him to feel awkward, to realise what a violation it is. You look on with what you hope is a withering expression as he pushes down your waistband.

'That's nice,' he says, oblivious, studying the neat row of ports. 'Options. We'll go for FireWire.'

You hear the click as he plugs in a cable. Then he turns back to his laptop.

'The printout,' you remind him. Distractedly, he puts the pages in your hand.

'Incredible,' he breathes, tracing the numbers flickering across the screen with his finger. You ignore him and look at the first page.

And what you see there brings you up short.

42

€€˜ ˜ ˜

WWW.Undertheradar.com How to go off grid and
disappear completely 0===== €€

˜ XÿŒ 0

STEP ONE Plan carefully. About a month before
you intend to disappear, show signs of depression. Ask your doctor for medication and remove
the correct number of pills from the bottle
each day.

€˜ 0€

STEP TWO Delete your computer history. Remove
your laptop hard drive and boil it, then smash
it with a hammer. Finally, run a degausser
(electromagnetic wand) over it to obliterate
information that may give you away (such as
visiting this web page).

€Üàšª#

e   g   ¼   À   ðE

STEP THREE Erase all information from your
phone, then leave it on public transport.

Someone will take it and start using it, providing a false trail which will help frustrate
those looking for you later.

ÿÿÿÿÿÿÿÿ
   Ë

STEP FOUR Purchase a vehicle for cash. Provide
a false name. Remove all tracking devices (toll
passes with RFID chips, satnav, OnStar car
system, etc.).
   Root
   STEP FIVE Practise your new lifestyle. Get
food to go. Never order from chain restaurants.
Change your eating habits, e.g. if you are a
vegetarian, consider eating meat. Use alcohol
wipes on glasses and cutlery to avoid leaving
fingerprints/DNA which can be read with an
easily purchased BPac machine. Use a sleeping
bag in (non-chain) motels. Always pay cash.
   ÿÿÿÿÿÿÿÿ
   STEP SIX Reduce social-media activity. Create
a new, offline-only identity. (Do not make the
common mistake of trying to obtain false papers
in the name of a dead person.)
   X0X0X0~~STEP SEVEN Accumulate large amounts
of cash. Getting into debt with a loan shark
or drug dealer is a risky but effective ploy.
They will come looking for you after your

disappearance, which can help divert attention.

%%%%%0x0

STEP EIGHT Tell people close to you you're worried about being followed. Alternatively, tell them you've started hiking in remote locations. (Hiking is preferable to drowning, as fewer bodies are recovered from hiking accidents.) Tell no one what you plan to do, not even those you trust the most.

#&

Purchase a baseball cap with LED lights under the flap. This will make your face a blur to infrared CCTV cameras when travelling.

#&

#&

Entry

%%%%%0xx0

STEP NINE Create a corporation under a name not connected to you. This will be a legal entity able to lease an apartment, pay bills, run a bank account etc. Use the corporation account rather than your personal account to pay whoever set it up for you.

Entr%%

#&

STEP TEN Ditch all your credit cards, personal possessions etc. Then leave.

43

You stare at the pages. Whatever you'd been expecting, it certainly hadn't been this.

Not an affair, after all. Not a suicide. A secret of a totally different kind.

You ran away.

True, not all the details match – the web page specifically said not to fake being drowned, for example, and the iPad clearly hasn't been hit with a hammer or boiled. But you must have decided your well-known love of surfing made the ocean more believable than a hiking accident. As for the iPad, perhaps you meant to take it with you. All the other details, such as the pills, are too close to be a coincidence.

You're still alive.

The thought is shocking. Everything Tim believes – everything he's *done*, from raising Danny on his own to reconstructing you – has been built on a monstrous deception. A lie, perpetrated by the woman he loved. The woman who always said she loved him in return.

Ironically, by finding the information that finally clears Tim of your murder, you've discovered something that will completely destroy him.

But – *why?* That's what you still can't get your head around. You had a good life, an adoring husband. OK, so he preferred you with braids and didn't like it when you faked an orgasm. Hardly reasons to fake your own death.

And if you *had* stopped loving Tim for whatever reason, it would have been a shame – but there would always have been the option of divorce. This was a man who gave you a beach house as a wedding gift. You could have separated and both still been ridiculously wealthy.

Most of all, though, you can't understand how you could ever have abandoned Danny. No mother, surely, would walk out on her child like that – especially not a child as heart-achingly vulnerable as him.

People do, an internal voice reminds you. *It happens.*

But not people like you and Tim. Not strong, unselfish, principled people. *Good* people.

If that's what you are.

'Awesome,' Nathan breathes. He's looking at the numbers flying across the screen. 'I can literally see your mind working.'

'What do you mean?' you say sharply.

'Don't worry – I can't read your thoughts. Just see you're thinking hard.' He glances at the printout you're still holding. 'Going to take that to the police?'

'I haven't decided.' But already you can see how tricky that would be. The police will reopen the investigation. You don't know if it's legal to fake your own death, but you suspect that, if they do end up finding Abigail Cullen-Scott alive and well, at the very least there'd be a charge of wasting police time.

More to the point, Tim will know what you did. That you walked out on your marriage. Your disabled son. And him.

You remember what Mike said, that time he came to see you. *Remember how fragile he still is, would you?*

You can't hurt Tim like that. At least, not yet.

'If you take that printout to the cops,' Nathan says slyly, 'they'll confiscate the iPad. And there's more on it, I reckon.'

Abruptly, you reach down and pull the cable out of your hip. 'Hey!' he protests. 'That should be properly ejected—'

'How much more?'

'I'm not sure.' He gestures hungrily at the cable, now dangling from his laptop. 'Hook me up again, and I'll start another batch tonight.'

'No,' you say, taking a step back. 'Unscramble some more, and then I'll see about letting you plug it in again. Nothing gets nothing in this world – remember?'

SIXTEEN

(FEEL FREE!) was probably the highlight of Abbie's work as our artist-in-residence. People would say to her, 'How're you going to top *that*?' and she'd just smile and shrug. 'Something'll come,' she'd reply. 'It always does.'

But as the weeks, then months, went by, the smile faded. Someone suggested she could do a whole series of putty statues, and she just sighed and said, 'Maybe I should,' as if they'd suggested she get a job in an insurance company or something. There was talk of a project making 3-D busts of our heads that came to nothing. It was ironic that, because of the time lag with social media, the height of her viral success with the pictures of *(FEEL FREE!)* coincided almost exactly with Abbie herself going through a lean period.

We felt disappointed, initially – we'd gotten used to the regular entertainment of her artworks; they lightened the mechanical drudgery of our lives – but we also felt protective of her. Why should she feel obliged to amuse us, like a magician pulling yet another balloon out of his pocket at a party, or a musician playing his greatest hit for the thousandth time? She was an artist, *our* artist, and her function was lofty and holy.

Plus, she was the founder's girlfriend. Their romance had started to make headlines, at least on local websites devoted to tech-valley gossip. For her twenty-fifth birthday, Tim hired the San Francisco Gay Men's Chorus to sing 'Happy Birthday' outside her bedroom window. Then he took her wing-walking, followed by a trip in a private jet to Lanai, Larry Ellison's Hawaiian island, for a couple of days' surfing.

But he was still the founder, and work came first. Most nights, he'd still be in the office until ten p.m. or even later. And along with the amazing shots on social media of the two of them standing by the edge of a live volcano on Hawaii, there were also darker, more disturbing whispers. Someone spotted Abbie in Slim's late one night with a bunch of musos, clearly wasted. Somebody relayed an incoherent conversation they'd had with her in Mezzanine, covered in sweat. She showed up to the office less frequently. And if she did put in an appearance, it was generally in the afternoon, while Tim was always in by seven.

So when she stopped turning up altogether, we all jumped to the same conclusion. We assumed she'd dropped us, and probably Tim too. 'Seen Abbie recently?' became a question we no longer even asked each other, because the answer was always the same. It was as if she'd vanished.

Her six-month-residency end date came and went without being marked, or even mentioned.

It was about three weeks after that that the news flashed round the office. Abbie was coming back! The residency had been extended! No – not extended: *resumed*. Unbeknownst to us, Abbie had been on sick leave. After that was taken into account, she had twelve weeks left to run in her contract, and would be back with us for at least that length of time.

We did the math: she'd been off sick for just over ninety days. We quickly turned to the internet. A link went around to an article headed: 'Study Shows Optimal Time for Residential Rehab Is 90 Days or Longer'. Someone else checked the company's health insurance. Rehab was a co-pay, which meant hefty bills for the individual. But somehow we doubted Abbie had picked up the bill herself.

And then, a few days later, in she strolled, her old self again, the very picture of sun-kissed Californian health – the facility she'd been in had encouraged outdoor work, she explained; the way she told it, it was like a cross between a mental asylum and a kibbutz. She was quite open about having been in rehab. 'I had a problem and, when Tim realised, he sorted it,' she said gratefully. It turned out she'd crashed his Volkswagen, and the cops had taken a blood test at the scene. As part of her plea bargain, her lawyer told the court she was checking into rehab. Meanwhile, Tim simply identified which rehab facility had the highest documented long-term abstinence rate, and that's where he sent her. Of course.

So then it was just a matter of following in Tim's footsteps. We put *rehab California best long-term* into a search engine and came up with Moving On, a small treatment centre in Napa Valley that looked, from the pictures, more like a boutique hotel than a detox facility. There was a kidney-shaped swimming pool surrounded by sun loungers and parasols, a restaurant with a vegetarian chef, a gym . . . The place even had its own vineyard, although the version of its flagship Cabernet served to guests was alcohol free. The website was coy about charges, but elsewhere on the net they were described as $2,500 a day, plus extras.

Some of us had a preconceived notion places like that were little more than fancy spas. But then we dug a little deeper. The reason Moving On had such high success rates was not the pool, or the gym, and certainly not the alcohol-free wine. Moving On treated addiction with chemical aversives – specifically, apomorphine and succinylcholine. Apomorphine, we read, was administered by injection as the patient prepared to ingest a small quantity of recreational drugs, such as a line of coke. It produced overwhelming nausea followed by involuntary vomiting; over time, the two became inextricably linked in the patient's mind, so that even looking at cocaine induced a feeling of nausea. Succinylcholine was similar, but different: it caused immediate paralysis to every muscle in the body, including the muscles of respiration. The subject believed themselves to be asphyxiating – indeed, they *were* asphyxiating. The drug wore off in under a minute, but the terror it induced was so severe that its use in CIA interrogations had been banned, even during the Bush era. That rehab had been no vacation for Abbie. And indeed, when we looked at her a little more closely, we realised she *wasn't* quite her old self: there was something brittle, something forced about her cheerfulness now. Nor did she dance on tables, or even slip outside for roll-your-owns and gossip in the parking lot. She was as clean as the day she was born.

'I owe Tim everything for helping me sort myself out,' she told Morag in the break room. 'I've even stopped craving nicotine.'

'I made her better. I fixed her,' Tim told Mike in the same location, a couple of days later. 'Anyone would do the same for someone they really loved.'

44

You're still in shock when Tim gets home that evening, tired but triumphant. Renton's money has come through. Although he doesn't actually say the company is saved, it's apparent from the relief written across his face.

In the circumstances, it's easy to pretend your own day has been uneventful. You don't tell him what Nathan found on the iPad. Instead, you mention you met Lisa.

He frowns. 'Not my biggest fan.'

'She was OK. She was just upset about seeing me on TV like that, with no warning. But I think we're good now.'

'That's nice,' he says, a little absently. He's flicking through emails on his phone. Sometimes there are over a hundred he hasn't had time to look at in the office.

Is that why you did it? Did you feel ignored?

Everything Tim says or does now is going to prompt the same question, you realise. Is *that* the reason you ran away? Was *that* what you found unbearable?

He looks up and sees you staring. 'Sorry, babe. I'm being rude.' He puts the phone down.

'No, it's fine,' you say hastily. 'I'll cook, and we can talk over dinner.' But you can't help adding, 'Did I mind . . . before? Was how hard you worked ever a problem for us?'

He thinks. 'Sometimes,' he admits. 'But when it was, you'd say so, and we'd make time for each other. We always put our marriage first. Even after Danny's diagnosis, we made sure we got away occasionally, even if it was just for a weekend. His school does residential respite, so sometimes we'd pack him off on a Friday, then head out to the beach house, or take a private jet to Lake Tahoe for a couple of days' snowboarding. Then he'd come home as usual on Monday, and we'd resume family life.'

You think of the life you must be leading now. You're pretty sure it doesn't involve beach houses or snowboarding, let alone private jets. What had that website said? *Use a sleeping bag in (non-chain) motels . . . Never order from chain restaurants . . . Use alcohol wipes on glasses and cutlery to avoid leaving fingerprints / DNA.*

Suddenly there's a sharp, stabbing sensation in your head. Involuntarily, you wince.

'Are you all right?' Tim says, concerned.

'I feel . . .' Abruptly, you stumble against the stove. 'Perhaps I'd better sit down.'

'Of course.' Instantly, he's at your side, helping you into a chair. 'What is it?'

'It's nothing. I felt dizzy for a second, that's all.'

But you know it was more than just dizziness. For a moment, you'd felt a terrifying, nauseous rush of panic. It was as if you were being split apart and your brain was floating away from you, like a bubble of air underwater. A feeling that you were simultaneously *you* and *not you*, that you were something impossible, something that didn't add up . . .

'That's not supposed to happen.' Tim is looking concerned. 'Will you tell me if it happens again?'

You nod. Perhaps you should have let Nathan eject that connection properly, you think.

Or maybe it's something more fundamental, something to do with what you read on that printout.

Eventually you persuade Tim to go back to his emails. You open some wine, then make a salad.

'Bastards,' he snaps suddenly.

'Who?'

'I thought you said Lisa was onside.' His fingers stab at the screen as he types a response.

'She is,' you say, mystified. 'At least, she seemed to be.'

Silently, Tim holds out his phone so you can read it. The email is from a law firm called Stanton Flowers LLP. The first section seems to consist mainly of impenetrable definitions. (*'The entity' shall hereinafter be taken to encompass all personal information, computational networks and other input/outputs as may be said to form a data file or files . . .*)

'What does it mean?' you say, looking up.

'It means your so-called family wants you destroyed,' Tim says grimly.

'What?'

'And they're trying to get custody of Danny, too.' He resumes his jabbing.

You stare at him, appalled. 'On what grounds?'

'The Danny part? They're claiming you're unpredictable and could be a danger to him – that slap you gave the news anchor.

The destroying part is because you never gave explicit consent for what I did.' His face is a mask of fury. 'Those jokers. Insignificant, small-minded people who can't see further than their noses. Of *course* existing data laws can't apply to you. You're fucking *unique*.' He jumps up, too angry to sit, and paces round the kitchen.

'She lied to me,' you say slowly. 'Lisa. She told me it was like meeting her sister again. But all the time she must have known about *this*.'

'I told you she was a bitch. I need to call my lawyer.'

'Now?' you say, meaning, *Can't it wait until after dinner?* But Tim misunderstands.

'Don't worry, he'll take my call. I'm paying him a fortune. And there's no way I'm letting those ignorant bastards destroy my family.'

45

That night, sleep mode eludes you. You lie down, but your mind is churning, questions tumbling through your head.

Your disappearance. Lisa's betrayal. That strange, hidden book. The website Nathan found . . . So many things that refuse to join up, to make a pattern. You can feel your brain reaching for connections, jumping from possibility to possibility. But nothing clicks.

When you do doze off, you dream about your engagement again, that wonderful night in Jaipur. But it feels different now. Instead of reliving a memory, it feels as if you're watching someone else. Seeing through her eyes, sharing her thoughts, but somehow an observer, inside the head of someone you simply don't understand.

Before I do anything else, you think drowsily, *I have to find her. I have to know where Abbie's gone, and why. Only then do I tell Tim—*

Suddenly, you feel it again – that random, vertiginous panic, so piercing it jolts you fully awake.

You stare into the darkness, aware something important just happened. But what?

Then it hits you. In the dream, you thought about Abbie as 'her'. As someone separate from you.

If Abbie isn't dead, everything's changed. Because if she's alive, then what are you? You can't be who you thought you were. That person – Abbie – already exists.

You're a copy. A doppelgänger. No, not even that: something indescribable, a kind of abomination, something that shouldn't even be possible. But definitely not Abbie Cullen-Scott, brought back from the dead, as Tim believed when he created you.

Yes, you have some of her memories – you may even have some of her personality – but with different thoughts, different aims, a different identity.

A creature with no name. A thing.

The terror returns – a sense of being split apart – but with it comes clarity.

You are not Abbie.

What are you, then?

~~Abbie~~. *Not-Abbie. Abbie-negative* . . . A burst of symbols cascades through your head as your mind tries to find an answer to that and fails.

Are you ≠? ≈? A? 0? None of them fits.

Another stab of terror, squeezing your brain. Blackness rushing towards you—

And then you know what this feels like.

It feels like being born.

46

'On the face of it,' the lawyer says carefully, 'they do have a pretty good case.'

Tim's features twist into a snarl of anger, and the lawyer – whose name is Pete Maines – holds up his hand placatingly. 'Which is not to say they'll succeed. I just want us to be clear about the scale of the task.'

And the size of the bill, you think cynically.

There are five people gathered around the glass-topped table in the lawyer's plush office. As well as Maines, Tim and you, there's Mike and Elijah, though you can't actually see what this has to do with them.

Maines ticks off points on his fingers. 'First, they're claiming emotional distress. We can pretty much discount that – it's the usual chaff, to bulk out their other arguments. Second, data protection. That looks scary, but actually data laws are riddled with loopholes, as Google and Facebook know only too well. It's the remaining three points that concern me more.'

'Go on,' Tim snaps.

'Their third contention is over "rights of publicity". Unauthorised appropriation of name and likeness for a commercial endeavour, such as the creation of merchandise, is always a no-go.'

'She isn't *merchandise*,' Tim says with quiet fury. 'She's my *wife*.'

Pete Maines continues as though he hasn't spoken. 'The concept of "likeness", incidentally, has evolved through case law, and can include features such as mannerisms, speech and personal style.'

'Wait a minute,' Elijah interjects. 'I know something about this. Don't a person's image rights automatically pass to their estate after their death?'

Maines nods. 'That's correct.'

Elijah looks around the room with a grin. 'Well, then, we're in the clear. Abbie's image rights are now Tim's.'

There's a long silence. Tim shakes his head.

'Why not?' Elijah demands, puzzled.

'Abbie isn't legally dead,' the lawyer replies. 'She's missing, certainly, and her death has been presumed. But in the absence of a body or a conviction for her murder, she won't be declared dead until five years from the date of the inquest. In three months' time, in other words.'

'So we stall,' Elijah says immediately.

'We can try. But, for the same reason, they'll be pressing to get this in front of a judge as fast as possible.' Maines ticks off his fingers again. 'Point four is consent. Did your wife ever explicitly or implicitly give her permission to be recreated in this way?'

Tim's face is dark. 'She didn't need to. It was understood between us.'

'But nothing in writing. Or in front of witnesses.'

He shakes his head.

'That's not true,' you say slowly.

They all look at you.

'Our wedding vows. *I give myself to you for all eternity.* Remember?'

'Very moving,' Maines says. 'But, sadly, wedding vows have no actual weight in law. I don't suppose anything was mentioned in the prenup?'

Tim shakes his head.

'Well, that does bring us to another point. Who actually owns this remarkable creation?' Maines gestures casually at you with the same hand that's counting off points.

You stare at him, shocked. Tim flinches. '*Owns?* She's not *property*, for Christ's sake.'

'You may not like to think of her that way, but the courts will view it differently. She was constructed by Scott Robotics, I take it? Have you purchased her from the company? Or is she still the company's asset?'

Tim bangs a fist on the table. 'Don't be ridiculous. It's *my* company.'

'It's the *shareholders'* company. Remind me who the majority investors are?'

'As of yesterday,' Mike answers quietly, 'John Renton.'

Maines whistles. 'Well, the good news is, it'll be the company, rather than you personally, that bears the costs of fighting this.' He pauses. 'Or makes some kind of settlement.'

'We're not settling,' Tim says through gritted teeth. You can tell it's costing him an effort not to explode.

'You should really hear me out before you make that call.' Maines holds up his hand again, the thumb extended. 'The fifth and final point relates to moral rights. And that's the one I think we're going to find hardest to win.'

Elijah frowns. '*Moral* rights? What are those?'

'The rights of an artist to control his or her creation. California's the only state to recognise them.'

'I don't understand,' you say. 'How am I Abbie's creation?' Too late, you realise you've just said 'Abbie' instead of 'my'. You'll need to be careful about that. But no one else appears to have noticed.

It's Tim who answers. 'The very first version of you – the beta, if you like. It was your idea.'

SEVENTEEN

'I'd love to make a robot of you.'

Later, several of us would swear we'd heard Tim say those words, or some variation of them, to Abbie as they walked through reception. (Since she'd gotten back from rehab, they'd started coming in together again, hand in hand, their other hands clasping matching lattes from Urban Beans.) And while it was, on the face of it, an unusual thing to say, we all got it. We were roboticists, after all. We had long ago stopped thinking of robots as something freaky or weird.

What Abbie said in reply was the subject of greater debate. Some of us thought she laughed and said, 'Sure.' As in, *Sure you would, but that isn't going to happen.* Others thought she might have said 'Sure' – as in, *Sure, why not?* And many of us thought she said, 'Sure?' As in, *Really? Because I'm up for it, if you are.*

What was not in dispute, because Tim said it as they stood by the open door of his office, a few minutes later, was that he also told her, 'I could teach *anyone* basic coding in about two weeks.'

'Not me.' Abbie shook her head. 'Love tech, terrible at math.'

'Coding isn't math. You cook, don't you? Coding is like writing down a recipe. Or giving someone directions to your house. Just in a very unambiguous way.'

What happened after that was almost inevitable. Tim cancelled his meetings. Within an hour, he'd taught Abbie to write her first line of code, and a simple program by lunchtime. Before the end of the day, she'd sent him the following –

```
int main( ) {
            while(1) {
                    doesLove(you);
            }
    {
    doesLove(String str {
            printf("I love %s!", str);
    }
```

– which, while it might not look like much of a love poem, had the effect of printing the words *I love you* on his computer screen, over and over again.

She also sent him a program in ASCII which caused his printer to spew out:

```
_____00000000000_____000000000000_____
_____00000000_____00000___000000_____0000000_____
____0000000_____000_____00000_____
___0000000_____0_____0000_____
__000000_____0000___
__00000_____0000__
_00000_____00000__
_00000_____TIM_____ABBIE_____000000__
_000000_____0000000___
__0000000_____0000000____
___000000_____000000_____
_____000000_____000000_____
_____00000_____0000_____
_____0000_____0000_____
_____0000_____000_____
_____000_____000_____
_____000_____00_____
_____00___00_____
_____00_____
```

250

But, since the printer was actually by someone else's desk, he missed it.

By the end of the second day, they were working on hello-world programs. And at the end of two weeks, we were introduced to the first bot version of Abbie. All the components were to hand, after all. The 3-D full-body scan she'd used to make *DO AS YOU PLEASE (FEEL FREE!)* just needed to be reprinted in a new, hard-setting material. The mechanics, sensors and motors of the shopbots were all ready to be incorporated, along with a simple voice function. Of course, it was slung together – what developers call a 'quick-and-dirty'. But it was good enough for Bot Abbie to go around our desks with a plate of cookies, offering them to each of us by name, while Tim and the real Abbie stood back, watching, like proud parents.

'That is *so* incredible,' Abbie said. She looked better, we thought. More energised. Excited, even.

'Really, it's just the beginning,' Tim told her. 'I've already thought of some improvements.'

47

You get home from the lawyer's feeling despondent. It's become apparent that, even though you have your own thoughts and personality, where the law's concerned, you're nothing more than a machine that can be switched off or transferred to a new owner at any time.

You still haven't told anyone else about Abbie being alive. As far as you can see, it just makes your own situation more precarious. Pete Maines' strategy depends on convincing a judge that your sentience, as he calls it, is so unique it shouldn't be destroyed until questions of ownership have been resolved beyond all possibility of appeal. If you reveal that, far from being a unique backup of a dead woman's mind, you're actually a kind of distorted partial clone of someone still living, you suspect your own life expectancy will be very short indeed.

Besides, you still can't bring yourself to tell Tim that his beloved wife faked her own death.

For his part, he's come back from the meeting furious, his anger now directed at his lawyer. That's how Tim drives people. If he can, he'll inspire them, but if he can't, he'll beat them down through sheer determination. He'd demanded to know *why* Pete

Maines didn't have all the answers, *why* he couldn't guarantee he could make this go away, why he was such a dumb waste of time and money.

'I can't rewrite the law,' Maines had answered patiently. 'All I can do is put together the strongest case possible. And advise you what to do when it's a weak one.'

Basically, he thinks Scott Robotics should pay Lisa and the rest of Abbie's family whatever it takes to withdraw their suit. That was the course of action everyone was agreed on as the meeting broke up. But you know that, at best, it will only buy you a little time. Lisa isn't motivated by money.

Who actually owns this remarkable creation?

Just because you feel like you, think like you, it's been so easy to forget that you're actually nothing more than an assembly of processors and logic boards. Just intellectual property and patents, to be fought over by competing parties like a valuable car in a divorce battle.

At least Tim still loves you. Tim will protect you. A wave of relief and love for him washes over you as you realise that, yes, *Tim will make this all right.* Just like he always has. He's a fighter. And he's in your corner.

'I'm going to bed,' he says now. 'I need to be up early, get on top of this thing before those bastards come up with any more ways to fuck us over.'

He bends to kiss the top of your forehead, just as he always does before he goes to bed. Tonight, though, you lift your head so his lips land on yours. It feels so good, so *right*, that you find yourself kissing him more deeply. You put your hands around his head, pulling him to you. And then you're pressing yourself against him, desperate for his touch, running your hands down his back –

'Whoa,' he says, pulling away. 'What's this, Abs?'

'I want to sleep with you,' you say urgently. You feel a desperate need to be held. But more than that. You need reassurance that you're *alive*, not just some irrelevant mechatronic construction. You need, very badly, to feel his desire for you, to be wanted. 'To make love. I want you—'

'You know that's not possible,' he says gently. 'Physically, I mean. You're just not built that way.'

'We'll figure something out. Even if I can't feel anything myself, it would give *me* pleasure to give *you* pleasure. That's what love is, when it comes right down to it, isn't it? Wanting the other person to be happy. And I *need* us to be intimate. To have a physical relationship. Otherwise, how am I even your wife?'

He's silent a moment. 'I'd like that too, Abbie. Very much.'

'Then let's—'

'But it would be wrong,' he interrupts. 'I'm sorry. I just can't get around that.'

'But *why*?' you plead. 'Why would it be so terrible to have a sexual relationship with me?'

'Because it would feel as if I were being unfaithful,' he answers quietly. 'You see, in my heart of hearts, I know you didn't die.'

48

You stare at him.

So he's known all along. About what's on the iPad. What Abbie did. You start to say something—

'I can't put my finger on it,' he adds. 'And I don't have any proof. I just know you weren't the sort to leave me and Danny all alone.'

'What, then?' You force yourself to sound casual. 'You think I just upped and left?'

He shakes his head. 'God, no. Something must have happened during those last few days, when you were at the beach house on your own – something catastrophic. We didn't communicate much during that time. That was deliberate on my part; I was trying to give you space to work. But what if you were going through some kind of crisis? What if you had a breakdown? I've imagined so many different scenarios. Maybe you were abducted. You were – are – a beautiful woman, and I left you there on your own, without any kind of protection. I've tortured myself over that. There's that lawyer who lives down at the beach – Charles Carter. I always got the impression he had a thing for you. What if he's got you locked up in a basement somewhere? But the police refused to even consider it. They followed the evidence, they said, and there was no sign of a break-in or a struggle that would implicate anyone, let alone Carter. It was sheer laziness on their part. How could they follow the evidence if they never got off their backsides and went looking for any?'

He has no idea, you realise. You feel relieved and sad at the same time. Because you know, one day, Tim will have to learn the truth about how his wife abandoned him, and this time you think it'll crush him completely.

'Of course, it didn't stop me grieving for you,' he adds. 'In some ways, it made it even harder. I kept see-sawing between hope and despair – one day convinced you were dead, the next expecting you to walk through that door as if nothing had happened. I even prepared a little speech, telling you how sorry I was if I'd neglected you, how much I loved and needed you. And when the judge confirmed what we all knew – that my arrest had been a travesty – but the cops still refused to investigate any other possibilities, I realised it was up to me now. That was when I saw the potential of making something that could train itself to become self-aware. To become *you*.'

'But it hasn't worked, has it?' you say sadly. 'When all's said and done, I'm no replacement for the woman you love. You just said so – you still grieve for *her*, obsess about finding *her*—'

'I never thought you'd be a replacement for the real Abbie,' he interrupts. 'I'm sorry if I gave you that impression. But that wasn't the reason I created you, not at all.'

'What, then?' you say, confused.

'Do you remember what an algorithm is?'

'Of course.' You could hardly be married to Tim Scott and not know what an algorithm is. 'It's a kind of equation. A formula for working something out.'

'That's right. Like when you did long multiplication at school. It's just a tool, really. A process to bring about a certain result.'

'But what does that have to do with me?'

He says calmly, 'You see, you're a kind of algorithm, too. An algorithm to help me find her.'

49

'I don't get it,' you say, bewildered. 'You told me I was a cobot – a companion—'

'I said you were *special*,' he cuts in. 'I just didn't tell you why.'

'But how can *I* find her? If the police couldn't—'

'The police didn't *try*. Like I said, I realised it was up to me now. But I didn't have the right tools.' He gestures at you with both hands. *Voila.* 'I had to *build* the right tools. That was the first step. Then I had to let you run in. If I'd told you all this right at the beginning, it would have been way too much for you to handle.'

It still is, you think numbly. 'But I still don't see what makes you think *I* can succeed in finding her. Given that no one else has.'

Tim begins to pace the width of the kitchen, his face rigid with concentration. 'You remember we talked about how deep-learning machines may be capable of intuition? How they can see things even their programmers can't? That's what I'm hoping for here. That you'll be able to . . . walk in her footsteps, as it were. Make the same decisions she'd have made. And then make the leap to working out where she is.'

You're shocked. Hurt, too. So this is the reason he breathed life into you. OK, it's because he loves you so very much. It's just that he wants the real you. The original. *Her.* Not this hideous plastic-and-electronic simulacrum.

The one thing that's been keeping your self-loathing at bay is believing that Tim adores you now, in electronic form, just as much as he ever did. *Love is not love which alters when it alteration finds.*

But it was all a lie.

Of course he doesn't love *you.* Who could? You disgust him.

You feel numb. And more: you feel *betrayed.* Screwing Sian was nothing compared to the way he's been manipulating you.

'And what if you do find her?' you hear yourself say. 'What if you find her and she doesn't want to come back? Have you thought of that?'

'I can't believe that would be the case. But if it is, at least I'll have done everything I could. And if the worst comes to the worst . . .'

He stops. But you know exactly what he was going to say. Call it your deep-learning intuition.

If the worst comes to the worst, I'll still have you.

I'll still have this pathetic, second-best version of my wife I threw together in my company's workshop.

Just for a moment, you experience an unfamiliar emotion.

Just for a moment, you hate them both.

You hate Abbie Cullen-Scott, the object of Tim's devotion. And you hate him for worshipping her.

You open your mouth to tell him everything. About what his adored Abbie was really like. About the hidden iPad. About the artwork she never made, the pills she never took, the website advising her to fake depression as a prelude to faking her own death.

But you don't.

Once you give him that information, you can't take it back. And, from what you know of Tim, it still may not be enough. He's so willing to think the best of her, he'll probably convince himself there's some perfectly innocent explanation for why she ran away.

No; better to say nothing, at least for now. You need to think this through.

Because there's a part of you that's already hoping Abbie isn't alive, after all. Or that Tim never finds her.

Because if he *does* find her, and she wants to come back, what's going to happen to *you*?

EIGHTEEN

Seeing Tim and Abbie collaborate on the evolution of the A-bot, as we soon dubbed it, illuminated for us just how their relationship really functioned. Superficially so different – one hyperlogical, strategic, impatient; the other cool, impassioned, creative – they were, at heart, simply two geeks. There was something almost childlike in the way they took to the task. When we peeked into Tim's office, we'd see the two of them cross-legged on the floor, either side of the A-bot's disassembled frame: Tim with his laptop, frowning intently at some code, Abbie filing away at some old shopbot part. (Despite what he'd said about teaching her to code, pretty soon they reverted to their existing skill-sets. As Kenneth explained loftily to Caitlin, 'That's why there are so few top-rank female mathematicians. It's Darwinian. Men are housebuilders, women are homemakers.' Jenny, who happened to be standing nearby, merely rolled her eyes.) We heard laughter – Abbie's musical chuckle, Tim's goofy giggle. Often, they'd be there when we arrived in the morning, and still be at it when we left for the night. The pool table, on which Abbie had so memorably beaten Rajesh on her first day, was now only used to hold late-night pizza deliveries from Zume. Sometimes the boxes were still there the next morning, unopened: a Veggie Zupreme for him, a low-fat Chick-en-Chill for her, forgotten in the fascination of their enterprise.

Right from the start, it was clear they had ambitions for the A-bot that went far beyond what the shopbots were capable of. When all was said and done, the shopbots were chatbots in a fancy animatronic shell. They could walk, do a rudimentary dance and identify clothing, but that was about it. They worked a script, without much by way of genuine personality or character. The A-bot was a chance to move the concept on. It had the potential to open up massive new revenue streams for the company – but we all knew that wasn't why they were doing it.

It was in the third week that the project really started to come alive, in both senses of the word. In one experiment, Abbie operated the A-bot remotely, taking care to react to whatever it encountered. If she saw something through the robot's eyes that was funny, she laughed; if she saw something to startle her, she gasped; if someone made a remark to the robot, she responded, just as if it had been addressed to her. From these sessions, Tim created a simple form of machine learning. After that it was a relatively simple matter to add additional sources, such as Abbie's Facebook profile. The A-bot was starting to take on her personality.

Over one marathon programming session, Tim inputted every single text message they'd ever sent each other. On another occasion, he had it sample her voicemails. After that, he could have the A-bot say anything, literally anything he wanted, in Abbie's voice. Apparently, the first thing he made it say was, 'Tim Scott, you are the cutest man in the world.' To which Abbie added, 'Though you can also be a bit of a dork sometimes.'

We didn't even notice when they started calling it 'her'. To be honest, we didn't notice when we did, either.

50

You spend another miserable night. Tim might not have told you a direct lie, but he certainly allowed you to believe that he built you out of love, his own personal Taj Mahal. To discover that his adoration is actually directed at another, better version of yourself is crushing.

The worst of it is, you can't even blame him for it. From every perspective except your own, he's done a remarkable, wonderful, romantic thing. It's just that he's done it without any regard for *your* feelings.

You wonder if that blinkered vision of his could have been part of the reason Abbie left. It would be an extreme way to escape a marriage, but then it was an extraordinary marriage. And Tim was no ordinary husband.

You're so busy thinking about Abbie that it's a while before something else strikes you. *It would feel as if I were being unfaithful,* Tim had said earlier about sleeping with you. Yet this was the same man who'd screwed the nanny without a second thought.

For such a brilliant man, your husband can be remarkably thoughtless sometimes.

*

The next morning, Danny's up early. He's cheerful, though, and eager to come to the table for breakfast. But when you give him the picture menu to choose from, he bats it into the air with a 'Wheesh!'

'OK, Danny. Let's have another try, shall we?' You hand him the menu again, and again he knocks it flying, making the same *wheesh* sound.

It's some kind of game, you realise. 'Danny, we're not playing now. Choose something for breakfast, then we'll play later.'

'The stationmaster was furious,' he mumbles shyly.

'Of course I'm not furious. It's just . . .' You stop. The line he's just spoken comes from *Thomas Comes to Breakfast*, a story in which Thomas crashes into the stationmaster's house. The children's breakfast goes flying, and the stationmaster's wife has to make it all over again.

Could this be like the toast – a way of communicating what he wants, but in a kind of Danny code? You try to think. When Thomas came through the wall, what was the stationmaster's family eating? Eggs? Toast? Cereal?

Boiled eggs?

'Are you saying you want boiled eggs, Danny?'

'Wheesh!' he agrees.

You know that Sian, if she were here, would say that giving him eggs right now would simply be rewarding an undesirable behaviour. If Danny starts throwing stuff in the air every time he wants an egg, you'll have created a monster.

But Sian isn't here. And you know your son. Throwing things was simply the only way his brain would allow him to tell you what he wanted. And that, surely, is the most important thing right now: letting Danny know you're listening to him, or trying to. That you understand how unbearably difficult the whole notion of communicating is for him, and you'll do whatever you can to make it easier.

'You miserable engine,' you say in the outraged Liverpudlian tones Ringo Starr adopted for the stationmaster's wife in the original version. 'Just look what you've done to our breakfast! Now I shall have to cook some more!'

'Thundering funnels!' Danny giggles happily as you get out the eggs.

Later, while Danny's getting dressed, you make Tim his own favourite breakfast, fruit salad.

'If I'm going to figure out where Abbie is, I need to know everything,' you tell him as he eats. 'Did anything happen in the run-up to her disappearance – anything out of the ordinary?'

He thinks. 'Well, she lost her phone. She thought she'd probably left it on a bus. Of course, I tried the GPS locator, but it was already out of battery. But then we had a piece of luck. Someone found it and handed it in to the transit authority. And that papier-mâché case was so distinctive that, when I contacted them, they were able to identify it.'

That must have annoyed Abbie, you think. The very first instruction she'd tried to follow from the website, and it had backfired.

'Weirdly, when I got it back, it had been wiped,' Tim adds. 'But, of course, I'd always been careful to make backups for her.'

'Anything else? Please, Tim – I need to know everything. Good and bad.'

'Well . . .' He lowers his voice. 'I had my suspicions she might have been using drugs again.'

'*Drugs?* What made you think that?'

'Nothing specific – no actual *proof*, I mean. But it was something I was very tuned into. After all, over fifty per cent of addicts do relapse at some point. So, if she seemed to have unexplained mood swings, or be a little too happy sometimes, I'd worry. So I got Megan to give her a drugs test—'

'Whoa,' you say. 'Back up: Megan Meyer, the dating coach? You had her administer a drugs test to Abbie?'

Tim nods. 'It was Megan who helped us draw up the prenup – that's one of the services she provides. Random drugs testing was a condition we both agreed to.'

'Is that . . . usual?'

'Megan's view is, if something's going to be an issue, you might as well discuss it *before* the wedding, right? And since we'd both agreed we were going to lead clean lifestyles, neither of us minded the drugs clause.'

'I think I'd better see this prenup.'

'Of course.' Tim gets up and fetches a document from his study. 'There.' He hands it to you and sits back down with his salad.

You flick through it. The document runs to about twenty pages. Some of the clauses are in legalese, but most are pretty straight-forward – at least, straightforward to understand. You imagine they might have been somewhat harder to live up to.

The first section is headed *Fitness, Weight and Lifestyle*.

The parties hereby contract not to gain more than three (3) pounds avoirdupois per annum (excepting in the year during which a confirmed pregnancy or delivery of a child takes place). After any such gain, the infringing party will book into a health spa or weight-loss clinic of the other party's choosing, at the infringing party's expense . . .

The parties hereby contract not to take illegal drugs, 'legal highs', or abuse prescription medication, and to submit to random drug-testing at a frequency to be determined by the other party . . .

The parties hereby contract to eat meat-free meals at least three (3) days a week . . .

'Wow,' you say, flicking on. 'This is pretty comprehensive.'
Tim shrugs. 'That was the point of it. Great fruit salad, by the way.'
Further on, your eye is caught by a section headed *Affection and Intimacy*.

The parties hereby contract to spend at least one (1) full day per week devoted to family, without work.

The parties hereby contract to take at least two (2) vacations each year, with at least two (2) additional long-weekend excursions.

The parties hereby contract to spend at least one hundred (100) minutes alone together each week . . .

Each clause is accompanied by a detailed list of the consequences for infringements, from a $10,000 fine for working too
hard to $100,000 for missing a vacation.

The section on finance is relatively brief.

The parties hereby relinquish all rights in the other's
pre-existing property, assets, stock options and intellectual
property. In the event of separation or divorce, spousal main-
tenance will be set at one fifth of the higher earner's net
income.

The final, and longest, section is headed *Childcare and Education*.

The parties hereby contract that their children will take the
name Cullen-Scott in perpetuity.

The parties hereby contract that their children will follow
an ambitious curriculum valuing arts and sciences in equal
measure . . .

And then Danny came along, you think. Turning all these carefully worked-out assumptions on their head.

'The point was, we agreed on pretty much all of this stuff
anyway,' Tim's saying. 'It really wasn't a big deal. And there's no
harm in being clear about what your expectations are, right?'

You flick back to the section on drugs tests to see what the
penalty for failing was.

The party at fault will immediately book into a substance-abuse rehabilitation clinic of the other party's choosing, for a duration of no less than ninety (90) days . . .

In addition, the second party hereby contracts with the first party to attend monthly drugs counselling sessions with an authorised representative of the Moving On rehabilitation clinic for a period of no less than ten (10) years from the date of the marriage, or until mutually agreed with the first party . . .

'What's this?' you ask. 'Abbie went to drugs counselling?'

Tim nods. 'It was part of her rehab programme. The most effective way to prevent a relapse is to go on seeing a counsellor regularly.'

You sit back, thinking. It seems to you that what Tim had taken for drug-induced mood swings – Abbie being *a little too happy sometimes* – might equally have been the highs and lows of a secret love affair. But you're not going to say so, at least not until you have proof.

And a plan, too: what to do with that information.

What were those words he spoke to you last night? *I had to build the right tools.* That's all you are to him, you realise. An appliance. Like a socket wrench or a motorised screwdriver.

Well, this tool has a mind of her own. And she's going to start using it.

51

'I must admit,' Megan Meyer says cheerfully, 'I never expected to see *you* here.'

The matchmaker's offices are in San Mateo, equidistant from San Francisco and Silicon Valley. You came in an Uber, summoned with a tap on your phone. You could even use the app to choose the playlist on the car's stereo, thus ensuring the driver didn't talk to you. As you crawled through the endless traffic, you found yourself reflecting that, really, no one needed robots or driverless cars, when human beings were already this automated.

Megan's offices are much as you expected. A water feature burbles in the reception area. There are fresh flowers in alcoves, tasteful art on the walls, and the magazines in the lobby range from *MIT Technology Review* to *The Economist*.

Megan herself, though, is a surprise. You'd been expecting someone like Judy Hersch, the news anchor, coiffed and brittle. But although Megan is equally well groomed and even more expensively dressed, her eyes are shrewd and humorous.

'I used to be a headhunter, filling leadership roles in start-ups,' she confides as she leads you into her office. 'But so many of my clients asked if I had any friends they could date, I realised there was no one catering to that side of their lives. Tech people might be able to write the code for a dating app, but they'd be the very worst at using it. They don't have the social skills to decode profiles, they tend to choose on appearance rather than personality, and, when they do date, they often have no clue how to behave. So, my pitch to them is, no swiping, just old-fashioned matchmaking. Besides, I'm good at it. I'm curious about people. And I genuinely believe that everyone, however strange they may seem, has a soulmate out there somewhere.'

You realise something else about Megan: she's one of the very few people who immediately talks to you like a person, rather than a machine.

'What about Abbie?' you say as you take a seat on one of Megan's two enormous sofas. 'Was she Tim Scott's soulmate?'

'Well, he thought so. And he's my client, so . . .' She smiles.

'But you weren't sure?'

She hesitates, then leans forward. 'Look, I probably shouldn't say this, but I knew two things the moment I met Abbie Cullen. First, that Tim was going to fall in love with her. Heck, he was already in love with her. That's why I made a point of going to talk to her that day. He'd just ignored every single one of the women I was trying to pitch him and gone on and on about this incredible artist he'd hired.' She sits back again. 'And second, I knew it would end in tears.'

'Why?'

'Do you know what I mean by Galatea syndrome?'

You shake your head.

'The men who start tech companies . . . they tend to be a

particular type. First, they have impossibly high standards. Second, they have a vision. Which is to say, a view of the world. Often, they like nothing better than to impart that view to some receptive, impressionable young person. If the young person is fresh and sweet and drop-dead gorgeous too, well, so much the better. And, to be fair, the younger person is often just as keen to learn as the older one is to teach.

'But fast-forward a few years and the dynamic has shifted. The older person still has the vision, but the younger one has heard it all before. And they're probably not so sweet and fresh anymore, either. So, inevitably, they move on.'

'Why's it called Galatea syndrome?'

'From an ancient Greek myth. About a sculptor called Pygmalion, who rejected all the women of Cyprus as frivolous and wanton. Until one day, he carved a statue of a woman so beautiful and pure, he couldn't help falling in love with it. At which point, the statue came to life and loved him right back. He called her Galatea. I guess today we'd say he fell in love with an ideal, rather than a person.'

'I think I know how that feels. On the receiving end, I mean.'

Megan nods. 'I did suggest to Tim that jumping into marriage with a woman a decade younger than him, who he'd only known for a few months at that, wasn't wise. But Tim believes in being decisive. The best I could do was get the two of them to sit down and talk through a prenup.'

'I did wonder about that. I read it this morning. It seemed quite . . . draconian.' You'd wondered if Megan even deliberately set the marriage up to fail, hoping for repeat business.

'The point of the prenup is never the prenup,' she says flatly.

'The point of the prenup is, first, to get two idealistic, loved-up individuals to be honest about what their expectations for this relationship are. And second, to provide some kind of road map for a healthy marriage.' She waves a hand in the direction of Silicon Valley. 'Most of my clients couldn't navigate a cocktail party without a list of step-by-step instructions, preferably written in JavaScript or Python. I like to think that, by incorporating things like date nights, vacations and non-work days into a prenup, I'm giving them some sort of blueprint for normality.'

'I think Tim may have taken it more literally than you intended. Getting Abbie to take a drugs test every time she seemed a bit too cheerful.'

'Yes. Well, I did what I could to get them both over that particular road bump.'

'What do you mean?'

Megan only lifts an eyebrow, but you immediately guess.

'Abbie failed the drugs test. She failed, but you told Tim she'd passed.'

Megan hesitates, as if deciding how much to tell you. 'Not exactly. According to the hair analysis, she was clean for coke and other class-A drugs. But it showed high levels of alcohol. That wasn't covered by the prenup, so officially it was none of my business. But I sat her down and read her the riot act anyway. Even though she wasn't the one who was my client, I felt responsible for her. Protective, even. She was always this sweet, optimistic person, and then her kid got that horrible condition . . . It can't have been easy.'

'What did she say when you did that?'

274

'She said she was talking to her drugs counsellor about it. That she was determined to make the marriage work – for Danny's sake, if nothing else.' Megan shrugs. 'She was probably lying. All addicts lie. Drinkers too – to themselves, mostly. I should know. I used to be one.'

You think. Megan assumed Abbie was lying because she was a drinker who wasn't going to stop. But what if Abbie had been planning to leave, even then? And what if the drinking wasn't the cause of the marriage breakdown, but a consequence of it?

'When was this?' you ask.

Megan pinches the bridge of her nose as she thinks. 'Roughly the middle of July.'

Three months before Abbie left. Perhaps it wasn't only Tim who'd been in love with an ideal, you reflect. Perhaps Abbie, too, had had a kind of fantasy of a perfect life: a perfect marriage, perfect children, a wealthy and successful husband. When that dream collapsed, had her first response been to dull the reality with alcohol, and her second to flee altogether?

You feel a flash of sympathy – sympathy you're careful to suppress. Abbie's flaws were human, certainly. But her flaws are also your strengths. You will never be addicted to alcohol or drugs. Your decisions will never be clouded by medication or idealism or lust.

'If you thought Abbie was wrong for Tim,' you say, 'who would have been right?'

Megan's eyes narrow. 'Pygmalion fell in love with his own creation. Because only his own creation could truly live up to the ideal inside his head. Not to mention, remain untainted by all the weakness and vanity he thought he perceived in flesh-and-blood women.' She points an elegantly manicured finger at you. 'Frankly, I'd say *you're* a far better match for Tim Scott than the real Abbie could ever be. He just hasn't realised it yet.'

52

You're heading back to the city in another Uber, thinking over what Megan told you, when Tim calls.

'Where are you?' he wants to know. 'Is that traffic I can hear?'

'Just doing some shopping.' An idea occurs to you. 'For tonight. I'm cooking something special. Can you be home by eight?'

'Hmm – sounds intriguing. I'll try.'

After he hangs up, you pop open the SIM holder and remove the card. You don't want Tim going on Find My Phone to check your whereabouts.

'Change of destination,' you tell the Uber driver.

There's a customer in the phone shop, so you wait for her to leave before entering. As soon as Nathan sees you, he comes out from behind the counter and locks the door.

'I was wondering when you'd show up again. I've unscrambled some more material.'

'First things first. I want a burner phone.' You'd meant to get one before, but the argument over whether Nathan could look at your code had distracted you.

He raises his eyebrows. 'Know all the lingo, don't we? What sort of burner?'

'What have you got?'

'That depends on whether you need international roaming.' He starts describing different models. But you're not listening.

You've had an intuition – a flashback, almost. You were here once before, buying a secret phone, just as you are now.

Which, when you think about it, makes perfect sense. This is the nearest phone shop to Dolores Street. It's only natural that this is where Abbie would have come.

'Well, you tell me,' you interrupt. 'Did I get international before?'

You stare him out.

'Yes,' he says, dropping his eyes. 'You got one of these.'

He passes you a blister pack containing a cheap flip phone. It would have looked dated even back then.

'It comes with data preloaded,' he adds. 'And you can use it any-where in the world. You were very insistent about needing that.'

So, is Abbie abroad now? Your instinct says not. Your instinct tells you she wouldn't have trusted this creep, just as you don't. She wouldn't have wanted to give him even the smallest clue of where she might be headed. So she chose the phone that nar-rowed it down the least.

Something else occurs to you. Not a memory this time, but a small leap of logic. 'I bought the iPad here as well, didn't I? And I bet, later, she asked you to wipe it for her. Only you didn't do it properly. Just like you never told anyone about the secret phone.'

'I respect my customers' privacy,' Nathan says uneasily. 'Some women, they buy a burner for dating, so they don't have to give out their real number. If they're married . . . well, discretion becomes even more important. So I don't ask questions. Just like I'm not asking you why you need *that*.' He points at the flip phone.

You think. You'd assumed Abbie had just been following the instructions on the website by getting the burner phone. But if she was having an affair, maybe she had one already. As Nathan said, a married woman had to be discreet. 'When was it that she bought the phone?'

'November. I remember because it wasn't long after I'd started working here. I don't get many customers who look like she did, believe me.'

Almost a year before she vanished. Yet another thing that suggests she was cheating on Tim.

'And the iPad?'

'A couple of months after that.'

'You'd better show me what else you've found on it.'

He takes you into the back room. Again, there's a printout waiting, tucked into a see-through plastic binder. His laptop and a cable, neatly coiled, lie ready on the workbench.

You think of him preparing for this, getting everything ready for you, like some disgusting parody of a date.

He hands you the printout. You start to read. After a moment's hesitation, his hands go to your waist, looking for the ports.

53

~

€€

www.discreetliaisons.com Meet like-minded mar-
rieds looking for adventure! µ Welcome back
AC89 You have 55 new messages µ Messages 1-10:
Hi. µ Hi, just saw your profile. Hi, what are
you looking for? µ Can we talk? Hey AC89, love
your pic µ Hiya sexy µ ˜ XÿŒ

€

www.illicitadventure.com Where married people
come to play [] You have 46 new messages µ
€˜ ¼•#
www.secretlover.com Rediscover the thrill.
Message 1 of 50. Hi beautiful, can we meet? µ µ
Thank you for your request. You are now unsubscribed from discreetliaisons.com
You are now unsubscribed from illicit adventure
Sorry to see you go [secretlover5589] Come back
soon . . .

54

After so many clues leading in this direction, you shouldn't be surprised. But you are. Quite apart from anything else, there's the sheer number of sites Abbie was active on – the printout runs to several pages. She'd clearly been inundated with replies, too. It makes you wonder how many of those men she actually met up with.

But, of course, it doesn't solve the mystery of why she left. Quite the reverse. Sites like these were explicitly aimed at married people looking for casual hook-ups – one was even called Brief Encounter. By definition, they were for people who want to have affairs undetected and stay married. Not people who wanted to disappear forever from their partners and their lives.

Unless, you think, someone she met online turned into more than just a casual liaison. Had sex turned to love, and love turned to plotting to run away together? In which case, perhaps it hadn't been Abbie who'd needed to take the nuclear option of faking death. Perhaps it was the man she met who pushed her into taking such a drastic step.

The more you learn, the more puzzling this gets. Call it snobbery on your part, but there's something seedy about a cheating site, something that seems tacky and furtive and at odds with everything you know about Abbie. What happened to turn the confident young artist who painted that self-portrait into SecretLover5589?

'Do that again,' Nathan says, smirking.

You'd almost forgotten he was there. 'Do what?'

'Whatever you were thinking – it made a kind of pattern. All the code just clustered together and stopped.'

You stare at him. 'Are you saying you can tell what I'm thinking about?'

'Not exactly. But there are shapes that seem to recur. I guess, with enough— Hey!'

You've reached down and unplugged the cable.

'That's enough,' you say sharply. The last thing you want right now is for Nathan, or anyone else for that matter, to have access to what's going through your mind.

55

Back home, you unpack the shopping – you stopped by Gus's to buy ingredients on the way. Then you go and get the book that was hidden behind a false cover, *Overcoming Infatuation*, and look up *Galatea syndrome*.

Sure enough, there's an entry. And when you turn to it, you find a whole section that's been highlighted in pencil.

Galatea syndrome is, at root, a manifestation of profound ambivalence towards female sexuality. For some men, the 'perfect' woman will always be their mother, a woman with whom they necessarily enjoyed an asexual relationship. Such men mentally assign all women to one of two categories, Madonna or Whore: the idealised 'good' woman they can put on a pedestal, or the disposable and despised object of their sexual urges.

'Where such men love,' Sigmund Freud wrote, 'they cannot desire, and where they desire, they cannot love.' This split may become more pronounced after the birth of a child: the woman he married is now no longer his girlfriend but a Mother, whom he refuses to dishonour with his baser desires.

For the woman, being idealised in this way may be a frustrating experience. She may feel inadequate in her sexuality, or that she cannot excite her man anymore. She may interpret his emotional distance and lack of intimacy as lack of love. She may feel she can't reveal the ways in which she doesn't live up to his grand expectations. Above all, she may feel confused. Society sends out many contradictory signals about women's sexuality – from pretending it doesn't exist, at one end of the spectrum, to 'slut shaming' at the other – while at the same time valuing women principally for their thinness, youth and overall sexual desirability. In such situations, some women will inevitably seek other ways to validate themselves as sexual beings.

So this is how Tim saw her, you think. This was the canker eating away at their marriage. You understand now why he was able to say with a straight face that sex with you would be betraying Abbie, when he'd screwed the nanny without a moment's thought. Women like Sian, women who wanted it, were just sluts. Abbie was the revered mother of his child.

Just for a moment, you feel another unfamiliar emotion. You feel superior. When all's said and done, humanity's a joke.

You push the thought aside. Abbie isn't the one facing extinction on some laboratory workbench. She isn't the one Tim only created as a means to an end.

The issue here isn't whether you're superior to her. It's whether you can convince Tim you are. And *Overcoming Infatuation*, you realise, may be a very good guide to doing exactly that.

*

As you put the book down, you remember the burner phone. You're going to have to hide it somewhere. You decide to take a leaf out of Abbie's book – literally.

Pulling a hardback from the bookshelves, you tear the cover off and toss away the contents. The phone fits neatly between the empty covers, the perfect hiding place.

But before you put it in the bookshelves, it's time to finally communicate with the mysterious Friend. You already put the SIM card back in your iPhone. Now you send a blank text in reply to Friend's last message, as per the instructions.

Nothing.

You'd been half-expecting that. It still seems to you that Friend is most likely either a journalist, or one of the many trolls and ill-wishers who pestered Tim after the trial.

Then, with a ping, there's a message. Not a text this time, but in Facebook Messenger. It's headed *Secret Conversation* and has a big padlock logo to show it's encrypted.

The message reads:

Open this app on your new phone.

Again, you follow the instruction. On the new phone, you immediately get another message. Again, the sender is Friend.

Store this contact.

You type back:

Why? Who are you?

The answer is instant.

You tell me.

And then, a little later:

When you've worked it out, we'll talk.

NINETEEN

Abbie's nine months' extended employment now had only a few weeks left to run. People were starting to ask her what she was going to do afterward. A few even wondered if she was thinking of staying on.

'Well, I'd love to,' she'd say. 'But it can't really work like that. Then you stop being an artist-in-residence and become a regular employee. And the art world wouldn't take you seriously anymore.'

Privately, we speculated whether the relationship with Tim would survive her departure. After all, his first love was the company. When Abbie was at the office, front of mind and there in beautiful person, we could just about see how it worked. A regular domestic boyfriend–girlfriend thing? That would be a whole lot different.

It was noteworthy, too, that the A-bot project had stalled, or at any rate reached its natural limitations. Tim had created a simple AI for it, so you could ask it any question and it would reply, not just with words or phrases Abbie had used in the past, but recombining phrases to make new sentences. That was pretty cool. For a while, the A-bot travelled round trade shows with the shopbots. It even got interviewed by a few journalists. But, really, there were only so many conversations you could have with it. Most times, you'd ask it a question and it would reply with something frustratingly random.

> **Person**: Hi, A-bot. How are you today?
> **A-bot**: I am good, thank you.
> **Person**: What are you thinking?
> **A-bot**: Why are you interested in what are you thinking?
> **Person**: Well, I want to judge how intelligent you are.
> **A-bot**: What makes you think it that I am not intelligent?
> **Person**: [Pause] I'm trying to come up with a question that will prove how smart you are.
> **A-bot**: What is the difficulty here?

It was, someone remarked, a bit like having a session with a very stoned therapist. Or, Darren added sadly, like being on a date with a beautiful girl who's messaging three other guys on Tinder at the same time.

One of the developers, a quiet but brilliant Russian called Grigory, wrote an interesting blog piece about the A-bot, saying it exposed the flaws in our current approach. He suggested that, if we wanted to make a bot that really talked like a human, we should have it learn from conversations in which the other party didn't know it was a bot. Since you could assume that the longer the conversation lasted, the more successful it was, the bot could train itself to become increasingly authentic. He even sketched out some details of the kind of code that would allow that to happen, via a new type of deep-learning engine called a convolutional neural network.

We could see his point, but no one was eager to spend their limited free time pursuing such a theoretical subject.

Then Tim took Abbie to India on vacation, and she came back with a big smile on her face and a giant diamond on her finger. Soon the A-bot joined the other prototypes and betas in the workshop, all but forgotten, while we started speculating about which of us would be invited to the wedding.

56

When Tim gets home, there are candles on the table and a dish of butter chicken on the stove. Danny's already been fed and is watching Thomas videos.

'What's this?' Tim says, coming into the kitchen.

'I wanted to make something special,' you tell him. 'Something to remind us of India. Ready in ten?'

'Sure. I'll just take a shower.'

By the time he comes down, everything's on the table and you've opened some wine.

'Can I ask you something?' you say as you hand him a glass.

'Of course.'

You fetch a bowl from the kitchen counter. 'I found a gap in my knowledge today. What are these?'

'These?' He takes the bowl from you gently. 'These are eggs. At least, that's what people call them, but that's actually imprecise. Specifically, they're hens' eggs.'

Within five minutes, he's explained all the marvellous properties of an egg. He's shown you how it's impossible to break one by squeezing, no matter how hard you try, whereas a sharp tap shatters it at once. He's demonstrated how the unique ellipsoid shape means an egg can't roll away on gentle slopes. And he's told you how, for thousands of years, humankind has been asking which came first, the chicken or the egg. 'Which sounds like kind of a dumb question, because of course there were egg-laying mammals long before chickens appeared on the scene. But it's more complex than it appears. It turns out the formation of the egg is only possible because of a specific protein, ovocledidin-17, in the hen's ovaries.'

'I think the chicken came first,' you say.

'Why's that?'

'The egg doesn't have legs. It would still be stuck on the starting line when the chicken was crossing the finish.'

He stares at you for a second, nonplussed, before he gets it. 'That's brilliant,' he says wonderingly. 'You took an age-old conundrum and turned it into wordplay. That's *fantastic*.' He looks at you with all the pride of a scientist who's just taught his favourite lab rat to juggle.

You know perfectly well what eggs are, of course, and you got the joke from the internet, but Tim isn't to know that. You're re-establishing yourself as the pupil to his teacher. Galatea to his Pygmalion.

Over dinner, he talks about his day. The company is still planning on making an offer of settlement to Lisa and the rest of the Cullen family. As for the issue of ownership, no one appears to be grasping that particular nettle right now. But it seems from what Tim's saying that this crisis has precipitated a kind of battle for the soul of Scott Robotics. It's hardly surprising. For years, Tim has surrounded himself with weak, easily led yes-men – not intentionally, but because those were the only kind who would stick with a boss like him. Now there's another domineering alpha around, in the form of John Renton, they're starting to wonder if they shouldn't get behind him instead.

'I'm talking too much,' he says at last. 'How was your day? Any ideas about where to look for Abbie yet?'

You shake your head. 'Just questions.'

'Any I can help with?'

'Well . . .' You make a point of hesitating, as if you're reluctant to even ask this. 'Would you say Abbie was hypersexual sometimes?'

Tim's eyes narrow. 'Why do you ask that?'

'Nothing,' you say quickly. Then: 'Just that, in some of the photos, she seems to be wearing clothes that aren't really suitable for a young mother. And I found what look like some vibrator batteries in her pantie drawer. I'm just wondering if there might be a clue to her disappearance in that aspect of her personality.'

He's silent for a moment. 'She had quite a sexual nature, it's true,' he admits. 'And sometimes it did seem to me she . . . indulged that side of herself a little too much. But she'd settled down since she had Danny.'

I note that *indulged*. 'But you never felt she was sexually dissatisfied?'

'Of course not,' he says uneasily. 'Why? Where's this going?'

'Just something I wanted to double-check, that's all.' You change the subject back to his work.

After dinner, getting up from the table, you say, 'Tim, I want to talk some more about Abbie. But would you mind if I made myself more comfortable first?'

'In what way?'

You touch your cheek. 'Now I know Abbie's alive, it feels weird to be wearing her skin. Would you mind if I took it off sometimes? Just while we're alone?'

'Well, OK.' He sounds bemused.

'I'll be right back.'

Upstairs, you feel for the seam at the back of your head. Then, carefully, you peel away the rubbery flesh, exposing the glossy white plastic underneath, and pull it off, all the way down to your feet.

As you step out of it, you catch sight of yourself in the mirror. You remember the disgust you felt the first time you saw these white limbs, this blank, glossy face. How much has changed since then.

You reach for a bottle of perfume, then think better of it. The less feminine artifice you use, the better. You content yourself with giving your face a polish with a towel, then carefully pick off some dust and lint attracted by the static.

When you're pristine, as shiny as a supermarket apple, you look at your reflection again.

Frankly, I'd say you're a far better match for Tim Scott than the real Abbie could ever be. He just hasn't realised it yet.

'Everything OK?' Tim's voice floats up the stairs.

'Of course. I'll be right there,' you call.

'Now, tell me all about Abbie and you,' you say when you're downstairs again, curling up beside him on the couch. 'I want to know everything.'

57

You'd been hoping Tim would talk to you. *Really* talk, that is. About the cracks in his marriage, about what he and Abbie were like when everyone else had left them and they were alone. And you'd thought, in that context of honesty and intimacy, you'd begin to forge your own intimate connection with him.

But all you get is more of this unrelenting, sappy drivel about how wonderful she was. You want to scream at him to wake up, that no one's *that* perfect, but of course you don't. You nod and smile and say, 'Uh-huh,' and, 'That's nice,' and, 'Oh, how sweet.'

Inevitably, he ends up talking mostly about himself, this grand vision for humanity's future that he and Abbie supposedly shared.

'And she *changed* me. There are plenty of people in Silicon Valley who think AIs will end up smarter than humans, so effectively we'll become their puppets. And there was a time when I'd say, "Well, they can hardly do a worse job of running the planet than we do, so bring it on." But Abbie made me see that a society of incredible technological brilliance but no richness of human experience would be like Disneyland without children. If it hadn't been for her, I'd never have started thinking about the whole area of machine empathy.'

'Wow,' you say. 'Amazing.'

It's a good thing you can't yawn.

Eventually, Tim says he needs to go to bed.

'Tonight reminded me so much of those early days with her,' he adds happily as he gets up. 'Talking into the small hours about the kind of world we were going to create. I've really enjoyed this evening. Thank you.'

As you lie down on your own bed, a quotation comes to you. *There is surely nothing finer than to educate a young thing for oneself: a lass of eighteen or twenty years old is as pliable as wax.*

Who said that?

You wait, and sure enough, that comes to you too. *Clunk.*

Adolf Hitler.

58

As you drift off, you find yourself thinking again about those websites Abbie signed up to. When you were fourteen and in junior high, the worst insult that could be directed at a girl was that she was a prude. Three years later, it was that she was a slut. The girls all called themselves feminists, but they also told each other not to sleep with a boy on the first date, not to admit how many sexual partners they'd had, not to make the first move. They claimed it was about earning a boy's 'respect', but, really, it was about proving they were respectable.

In some ways, you realise, those double standards have rubbed off on you. Confronted by evidence that Abbie had been unfaithful, your first thought was, *How tacky*. To blame her, in other words. Whereas, when you found out Tim had slept with Sian, your first instinct was to blame yourself.

Perhaps you'll never solve the mystery of why she left, you think. Perhaps you and Tim will just muddle along like this for-ever. After all, even if you do locate her, you don't necessarily have to share that information with Tim. You could just leave her be, and hope that, little by little, he'll come to fall in love with you instead.

But in your heart of hearts you suspect that's not really an option. Tim shows no sign of preferring you to her. And the whole situation with Lisa and the courts and John Renton feels like it must surely come to a head soon. Time is the one thing you don't have.

Next morning, you don't bother with the picture menu. Instead, you simply ask Danny what he'd like.

He thinks. 'My funnel's cold. I want a scarf.'

'We don't have scarves for . . .' you begin, then realise this is another of his oblique requests. 'You're talking about Percy, aren't you? That time he crashed into the trucks and got himself covered in jelly. You're saying you want jelly for breakfast.'

Danny starts to look stressed. 'Scarf! Scarf!' he shouts anxiously.

You think again. You'd been so sure you'd got it right. Then it comes to you why he's anxious. 'Oh – I get it. In the book, it's called jam. But their jam is actually our jelly. Just like their jelly is our Jell-O.'

Jell-O is called jelly! Danny laughs so hard, he almost falls off his chair.

You make some jelly sandwiches. Every time Danny stops laughing, you say, 'Jam! Jelly! Jell-O!' to him, and he erupts back into giggles, spluttering jelly – or jam, if you prefer – all down his shirt front. By the time you're done with breakfast, you're both almost as covered with the stuff as Percy was in the story. It's a good thing Tim's in his study, firing off emails. You've long since left the approved ABA protocols far, far behind.

But at least you and your little boy are having a good time.

*

'I'd like to take Danny to school,' you say to Tim later. 'It seems crazy that everyone's raving about what a brilliant place Meadowbank is, and I've never seen it.'

'Ah.' Tim looks wary. 'Actually, that might be tricky.'

'Why?'

'I should probably have told you last night. But I didn't want to spoil the mood.'

'Tell me what?'

'The Cullen family have got an injunction preventing you from being alone with Danny.'

'Oh, great,' you say bitterly. 'So how's that going to work, with Sian leaving?'

'Well, clearly it wouldn't. So I've asked her to stay and continue with what she's been doing. Just for the time being.' He catches your look. 'You said yourself, we need to think what's best for Danny, here.'

It's on the tip of your tongue to ask Tim why he bothered to give you feelings in the first place, since he seems so intent on riding roughshod over them. But, with an effort, you manage to contain yourself.

'I guess that'll be difficult for you,' you say sympathetically. 'Having her around, after the way she came on to you. But Danny knows her, and she knows his routine . . . So we'll just have to make it work.'

'Exactly,' he says, clearly relieved. 'I knew you'd understand.'

You tell Tim you want to see Meadowbank anyway, even if Sian's taking Danny. You're not surprised when he says, in that case, he'll come too.

He drives. You sit in the back, with Danny between you and Sian. To your satisfaction, you find you're now better at getting communication out of Danny than she is. You don't kid yourself it's because you look like his mother. It's because you're not human. Your facial expressions change less frequently, and within a narrower range, than a real person's do. Your gaze is steady, without the demanding ocular interaction others impose. Your body language is so muted, it's almost silent. You're as close to being Thomas the Tank Engine as a person can get, dammit.

Really, you're so right for this family, it's absurd.

When you get to the school, Danny's greeted by a support worker and led inside. Sian goes with them.

'Let me talk to the principal's office,' Tim says. 'There should be someone who can show us around.'

A few minutes later, he comes back with the principal himself. You're not surprised at that, either. Not many people pass up the chance to schmooze a tech millionaire.

'Rob Hadfield,' the principal says, introducing himself with an ingratiating smile. If he thinks it odd to be shaking a mechanical hand, he hides it well. Probably for the same reason he's showing you around, you think cynically.

The three of you stroll through a well-lit vestibule.

'Meadowbank is one of only two facilities for autistic learners in the whole of the US where the teaching methods are still based on B. F. Skinner's original studies,' Hadfield begins, launching into what's clearly a well-rehearsed patter. 'That's one reason our results are so good. Where most practitioners have watered down their practices to fit in with current trends, our approach is evidence based.' He leads the way into what looks like an amusement arcade. 'This is our Yellow Brick Road area. Students who earn points for good behaviour can spend them here. That's the positive-reinforcement side of what we do.'

There are Xboxes, a brightly coloured candy store, even a replica McDonald's. A single student is playing on an Xbox, his face rigid and expressionless. 'Jonathan,' the principal calls. 'Say good morning to our visitors.'

The student pauses the game. 'Good morning,' he echoes dully. His eyes don't meet yours, but he waits until you say, 'Good morning,' in return, before turning back to his game.

'B. F. Skinner,' you say. 'Wasn't he the rat man?'

'Some of Skinner's work originated with rat behaviours, yes. He moved on to examining the fundamental drivers of all animal learning. Including human learning.'

You're walking into an area of glass-walled classrooms now. The rooms are small, no more than half a dozen students in each. All the students are wearing black backpacks – not slung casually over a shoulder, as a normal student might, but fastened across their backs. Danny also has such a backpack, you realise. It accompanies him in the car each day, though you've never seen him wear it.

'Is that where they keep their things? Those backpacks?'

Hadfield nods. 'And the power supplies for their clickers.'

'Clickers?'

'It's what the students call their GEDs – their graduated electronic decelerators.'

It's not a term you're familiar with. You wait, in the hope it might come to you, but before anything does, the principal adds,

'The GED delivers a small contingent aversive whenever the student exhibits negative behaviours.'

You have to puzzle out the jargon. '"Contingent aversive" – you mean punishment? You're giving the students electric shocks when they misbehave?'

'"Misbehave" isn't really a word you can use of these learners,' Hadfield says with a smile. 'Or "punishment", for that matter. We don't assume they know the difference between right and wrong. We simply ask, what are the behaviours we want them to display less of? And then we provide a negative consequence every time it happens.'

Your eye is drawn through one of the classroom windows. A teenager has begun flapping his hands in front of his face, his elbows pumping up and down. A member of staff sitting at the back reaches out to a bank of controllers and taps one. Instantly, the student's body jumps, as if stung.

'We make no apology for using these techniques,' Hadfield adds. 'If you look at the studies that demonstrate the effectiveness of behavioural approaches, they all used similar methods.' He nods through the window. 'When Simeon came to us a year ago, he was biting his hands until they bled. His parents had taped boxing gloves to his hands to try to stop him, and he was deranged with stress from trying to rip the tape off with his teeth. Using the GED, we've reduced his hand biting to around three episodes a week.'

'And Danny?' you say, appalled. 'Does he get shocked too?'

'He has been. I'm glad to say that, in his case, the aversives had a very beneficial effect.'

'You mean, he no longer hurts himself as much, because he knows that, if he does, you'll hurt him even more.'

Hadfield shrugs. 'That's the basic idea, yes.'

You look at Tim. 'And Abbie agreed with all this?'

Throughout the principal's spiel, Tim hasn't said a word. But you've sensed the intensity with which he's been watching you.

'It took her a while,' he says. 'But eventually, yes. Because it *works*. We'd tried everything else. Vitamin shots, craniosacral head massages, sleeping in an oxygen tent, crazy diets . . . Abbie even took him to some guy who claimed to be able to identify the cause of Danny's autism by examining the irises of his eyes. None of those therapies made a shred of difference. This did.'

You're silent.

'We don't even have to shock him now,' he adds. 'Or very rarely. A clicker comes home with him in his backpack, and if he ever becomes uncontrollable, it's enough just to show it to him and he stops.'

'The threat alone terrifies him, you mean,' you say quietly.

'What we do here is highly regulated,' Hadfield insists. 'Only last year, at the FDA's request, we reduced the intensity of the shocks by five milliamps.'

'And Sian? She went along with this, I suppose?'

'Sian Fraser was one of our highest-rated interns,' the principal says. 'Your husband poached her from us.'

You snort. 'I bet he did.'

There's an awkward silence. Tim says patiently, 'Look, I know it takes a while to get your head around this. We both struggled with it, back then. But ultimately we came to the view that what matters is Danny. If something helps him, however unpalatable or unfashionable, it's worth a try. You wouldn't refuse to carry out a medical operation on a child because the surgery might be painful, would you? So why would you refuse to administer a small skin shock with no lasting side effects? When you've had time to think all this through again, I'm certain you'll come to the same conclusion as you did back then.'

TWENTY

We didn't see so much of Tim after he and Abbie got engaged. He started doing a four-day week. Even on the days he was supposed to be in the office, he either wasn't around or was closeted with a firm of architects. Those who sneaked a look at his desk reported that he was designing a house. We immediately guessed this was a wedding gift to Abbie – somewhere by the ocean, perhaps, where she could surf. When we heard he'd bought a house in the Mission, San Francisco's hippest district, and was installing a restaurant-grade kitchen, we assumed his plans had changed. But the meetings with the architects continued. It took us a while to work out that he intended the two of them to have the house in the Mission *and* a custom-built beach house as well.

Tim had never lived more than a mile from the office before. People who'd visited his home said he'd never even gotten around to plugging in his TV. Now he was almost an hour's commute away. What's more, he was immersing himself in a new lifestyle. Abbie knew lots of people in the city, and suddenly their evenings were busy with openings and exhibitions. Dragging themselves up and down Sand Hill Road, where the venture-capital firms were housed in identikit glass-and-chrome offices, didn't have quite the same glamour.

For our part, we loved that time. Tim was relaxed – happy, even. Occasionally, he hung out in the break room and chatted with us. It felt like we were in a golden period.

It took a while to sink in that, actually, the reverse was true. When Scott Robotics first announced the shopbot program, investors had fallen over themselves to get a piece of it. Tim was the chatbot genius, after all, with a proven track record. It was simply a question of being first to market.

And yet, and yet . . . There had been snags – some technical, some psychological. Every time we did a field trial to refine what the marketing guys called the UX, or user experience, we were surprised by the negativity of the feedback. It seemed many people, especially women, actually quite liked being able to chat to the assistants while they shopped, or to ask their opinion on a potential purchase. When the assistant was a robot, it made it much more obvious that it was only flattering you to make you buy stuff.

Tim came up with a solution to that one. 'Men hate shopping,' he pointed out, 'so let's target men's stores.' But by that time men were deserting bricks-and-mortar stores so fast, the economics of staffing a retail environment with million-dollar robots made no sense.

We had to find ways of bringing the costs down. And that, frankly, was a task Tim wasn't very good at. He was a visionary, not a bean counter. So the problem never really got solved, and the funding slowly drifted away. We were stagnating.

It was Mike who eventually called Tim on it, a couple of months before the wedding. He walked into Tim's office, shut the door, leaned his back against it and folded his arms. His whole posture shouted, *We have to talk.*

Someone reported that, through the glass, you could see his knees shaking.

The discussion was amicable at first. Tim got up from behind his desk and paced. Mike stayed with his back to the door, talking.

Then things started to get heated. There was yelling, although we couldn't make out the words. At one point, Tim picked up the framed picture of Abbie on his desk and waved it at Mike.

'Tim force four?' someone suggested, watching.

'Five,' someone else decided.

There were a couple of newbies around who had never seen a full Tim eruption before. 'Watch and learn,' we told them. 'This is what it used to be like all the time.'

But, actually, this was like nothing we'd ever seen before. It escalated beyond a five, to a six, a seven and even beyond. Eventually, the door of Tim's office crashed open. He was gesticulating at Mike. 'Get out!' he was shouting, amid a stream of profanities. 'You're fucking fired!'

'Fine,' Mike yelled back. 'But when you realise I was right, don't ask me back.'

From which we deduced that Mike's pep talk hadn't gone so well.

'Listen, you fucking creep,' Tim snapped. 'She's worth a dozen of you. *And* that sexless stick insect you married.'

It was only then we realised they hadn't only been arguing about the company. They'd been arguing about whether Tim was doing the right thing marrying Abbie.

59

After Tim drops you back at the house, you use the burner phone to do an online search for *graduated electronic decelerator*. The links take you to a news story about a mother who sued Meadowbank for assaulting her eighteen-year-old son. There's footage of him strapped to a board, being shocked thirty-one times. It's disturbing to watch him scream, 'No!' over and over, jerking in pain as the electricity hits his body.

That film was made five and a half years ago, you notice. Only a short time before Abbie's disappearance.

Did the footage spark a disagreement between her and Tim? Had she only then realised exactly what sending Danny to Meadowbank would entail? Could that have been another factor in what happened?

You find yourself thinking about the period of Danny's diagnosis. Your memories of that time are hazy – almost as if they happened to someone else. Which of course they did, in a sense. They happened to *her*, to Abbie, and, like all her most personal memories, left little trace on social media for Tim's algorithms to reconstruct.

Even so, the terror of that time is embedded deep in your brain.

You realised quite quickly something was wrong, of course. You just didn't know what.

'Danny?' you called one day. 'Lunchtime.'

Normally that would have been enough to bring him running to the table. But not that day. You knew he was in the playroom, playing with a dinosaur he'd got for his birthday. When he still didn't come after you called a second time, you put your head around the door.

'Danny!'

He didn't look up. The dinosaur was on the floor, and he was staring at it. Just staring.

'Lunch,' you repeated. Still he didn't look up.

You took a step forward, concerned. Then suddenly he turned to look at you, and his familiar toothy smile lit up his face.

'I think Danny might have glue ear,' you told Tim that evening. 'He seems to find it hard to hear me sometimes.'

Tim frowned. 'Danny?'

At the sound of his father's voice, Danny looked up. 'Yef?'

'Seems all right to me.' Tim turned back to his BlackBerry.

'It varies,' you said defensively. 'Anyway, I booked an appointment with the audiologist.'

'My grandpa used to have a saying,' Tim said mildly. *There's none so deaf as them who don't want to hear.'*

'I'm so sad I never met Grandpa Scott. He always sounds so much fun.'

'He was a miserable old bastard,' Tim agreed.

You pointed silently at Danny.

'Sorry – miserable old *person*,' Tim said. 'My point is, what was the consequence of Danny not paying attention to you? Did his lunch go in the trash?'

'Of course not.'

'Hmm.' Which was shorthand for a whole debate you and Tim had on a regular basis. For him, parenting was a subdivision of engineering, a collection of design processes that merely had to be applied with total consistency in order to produce a well-mannered, efficient outcome. For you, it was a relationship, and half the fun was seeing what happened when you threw the rule book out of the window.

You'd never have admitted it to Tim, but you secretly encouraged Danny to climb into bed with you at first light every morning. Feeling your son's warm, perfect body wriggling alongside yours was the best part of the day. Even his rare outbreaks of naughtiness seemed like cause for celebration, proof he was going to be an independent thinker, his own man – a creative, not a suit. Sometimes, when he got angry or defiant with you, it was all you could do not to cheer him on.

When, later that week, the very expensive audiologist diagnosed glue ear and told you it would most likely clear up over time, you felt quietly vindicated.

You'd managed to place Danny in the local Montessori. It was a compromise between Tim and you: you'd rather Danny stayed home, Tim wanted a 'proper' preschool.

'Research shows that children who start school earlier do better,' he told you more than once.

'Better at *what*, exactly?'

'Better at school.'

'But do we really care if he's academic?' you wondered aloud. 'I can teach him to paint better than any classroom assistant.'

'Better socially *and* academically,' Tim said patiently.

In the end, it was the fact the preschool was just a few blocks away that persuaded you. Plus, if you were honest, you were seduced by the sheer beauty of the Montessori teaching materials – handcrafted from pale Scandinavian oak, not a plastic toy among them.

As you picked Danny up one afternoon, the teacher came over. 'I'm a little concerned about Danny's language, Mrs Cullen-Scott. He seems to use a lot of nouns. Very few verbs.'

You looked at her, surprised. You hadn't known the ratio of nouns to verbs was even a thing. 'Do you want us to work on it?'

'Oh, no,' she said breezily. 'I'm sure it'll sort itself out.'

Needless to say, you spent the rest of the day randomly tossing verbs at him – 'Look, Danny, dancing! Look, Danny, jumping! Danny, waving!' He seemed puzzled, but bore it with his customary good humour.

A few days later, the same teacher said, 'I'm a little concerned about Danny's hearing. He doesn't always seem very . . . present.'

'Well, it's not glue ear,' you said. 'He had that, but the audiologist says it's cleared up.'

'Have you had him tested for a language processing disorder?'

'For a *what*?' you said, instantly concerned. You never knew parenthood was going to be such a minefield of disorders. It felt like every day there was a new one you should be worrying about.

'Sometimes it's like he's . . . tuned out for a few moments. It's probably nothing, but . . .'

'No,' you said. 'No, I've seen the exact same thing.' Because there had been four or five instances of this at home now, this *switching off* as you'd come to think of it. You hadn't wanted to mention it to Tim. You knew he'd ask what the consequences were, and raise his eyebrows when you told him the only consequence was that you got completely terrified.

You made an appointment with a paediatric neurologist. Her assistant told you that, for elective scans, there was a waiting time of about seven weeks. Her tone made it clear that *elective* meant *unnecessary*.

You went ahead and booked a full set anyway.

Having made the appointment, you felt better – you'd done *something*, after all. It was probably nothing, but it was going to be checked out.

The next day was a Saturday. Tim went to the office, as usual – he liked it when there were fewer people around, he said, though from what you knew of Tim's employees, they mostly spent weekends at the office, too.

In the night, you'd been woken by laughter coming from Danny's bedroom – a strange, eerie cackling. Not wanting to wake Tim, you'd crept to take a look. Danny's eyes were open, and he was staring at the ceiling. His eyelids were fluttering.

According to a site you found on the internet, twitching eyelids could be a sign of abnormal brain activity.

Or, admittedly, it could just have been a sign he was dreaming with his eyes open.

Tim, of course, was scathing about people who used the web to make diagnoses. But this looked like a proper site, run by doctors.

You had to get groceries, so you and Danny went to Whole Foods. In the car, he was unusually quiet. You kept twisting round to look at him, until you nearly caused an accident.

'They're bad animals,' he said in a quiet, slurred voice.

You pulled over then.

'They're bad animals,' he repeated. He was looking at the other cars. 'Bad animals! Bad animals! Kill them!' He was agitated now, wriggling in his booster seat, trying to bend his tiny body out of it. 'Take it off,' he screamed at you. 'Take it off! It hurts!'

He was pointing at his own head.

'What is it, Danny? What's wrong?'

Then, as fast as it had come, the agitation stopped. He slumped back in his seat.

'Danny, what happened?'

'I saw a red one,' he said faintly. 'Red ones are the baddest.'

At the store, he trotted around next to you as usual, one hand on the trolley. When you got to the checkout, there was a line. An old lady was paying with coins, very slowly, counting them out and chatting to the cashier.

You always tried not to mind things like that – if the woman needed to take more time, she should. It was just unfortunate she was there today, when you really wanted to get Danny home.

That's when you heard a low growling sound coming from his throat. He was staring at the people in front of you.

'It always takes longer at weekends,' you said, to distract him.

And then he started screaming.

It was so high pitched, so strained, it was hard to make out any words. But it sounded something like, 'They're doing it wrong!' His face was – there was no other word for it – *crazy*. Like he was hallucinating.

Then, abruptly, he turned and ran away. As he ran, he stuck his arms out, flailing as if at invisible bees, cannoning into the displays of fruit, the proud pyramids of organic grapefruit and oranges that collapsed in bouncing cascades of tumbling colours. Then he ran down the canned-foods aisle, headbanging the tins. Next it was the turn of the breakfast cereals. Then the Coke bottles. And, all the while, he screamed.

People stared. And then, even worse, they looked away and pretended nothing was happening. *Honey, there was a really badly behaved kid in the store today.*

When you caught up with him, he was lying on the floor, his body arcing in pain, bouncing off the ground like a landed fish. Was it a fit? It looked like a fit. But then he stuck his fingers in his mouth and bit them, hard enough to draw blood.

You managed to get his hands away from his mouth, then get your own hands between his fragile skull and the floor.

When Danny finally stopped crying, he babbled gibberish. You carried him back to the car and drove straight to the ER.

'It sounds like you have a child with a behavioural problem,' the doctor said.

They'd done some basic tests, checked his pulse. Meanwhile, Danny slowly came back to normal. No: not normal. He still wasn't himself. But convincing the doctors of that seemed impossible.

'Will you at least order an EEG?' you asked desperately.

The doctor shook his head. 'That really isn't indicated.'

'Please.' The thought of having to go home and tell Tim that Danny had been diagnosed with – essentially – extreme naughtiness terrified you. Because you knew that, however much he loved Danny and you, he would side with the doctors. In Tim's world, doctors were scientists, and therefore on the side of Truth. Mothers were emotional, irrational, and therefore on the side of False Intuition. He would smile that smile at you, the one that said, *Your lack of logic is so cute. But now it's time for the grown-ups to make a decision.*

'You could think about seeing a child psychologist,' the doctor suggested. 'For some tips on parenting.'

Then Danny started growling, deep in his throat.

'It's moving again,' your son said to you, looking at the ceiling. 'Make it stop. Please, make it stop.'

Those were the last coherent sentences he spoke. Two minutes later, he was on the floor, screaming.

The medical process did at least snap into action after that. X-rays, EEGs, MRIs and an ultrasound were ordered. Nightmare scenario after nightmare scenario was raised, *rat-a-tat-tat*, as possibilities to be investigated and eliminated. Schizophrenia. Brain abnormalities. Epilepsy. Tumour.

By the time Tim got to the ER, they were hypothesising that Danny might have taken something – found a pill on the floor, say, or down the back of a seat. Over and over, you denied such a thing could have happened. But you could see them sneaking glances at you, at your ear studs and tattoo, putting two and two together and making seven.

They did a blood test. You made them do one on you as well, just to prove to them that you weren't a junkie.

To them, but also to Tim.

For forty-eight hours, they ran more tests. Finally, you and Tim were called into a room to speak to a very senior doctor.

'Well, overall the test results are good,' he said, running his finger down a list. He was in his sixties, charming and white haired. 'The EEG is normal, which pretty much rules out epilepsy. All the scans are fine, ditto the blood work. There's no infection or any sign of toxins. And no tumour that we can detect.'

You heard that word *good* and fastened on it. *Good* was positive. *Good* was great news. Wasn't it?

It took you a while to work out that *good* actually meant the opposite. *Good* results didn't mean Danny was going to be fine. It just meant their previous theories about what was wrong hadn't stacked up.

'That really only leaves two possibilities,' the doctor added. 'Juvenile psychosis, or Heller's syndrome.'

At the time, *psychosis* sounded the scarier of the two. It was only later – after more researching on the internet – that you discovered how wrong you were. Psychosis is temporary, while Heller's syndrome – otherwise known as childhood disintegrative disorder, or late-onset autism – is a friend for life.

'If, as I suspect, it turns out to be Heller's,' the doctor said, 'please remember, he's still the same kid now that he was before the diagnosis. Having a label like autism can be hard for parents. But that's all it is – a label.'

And, with that, he sent you away. It was kind of him to try

to sweeten the pill. But, for all his well-meaning words, he was wrong. Danny *wasn't* the same person anymore. The Danny you knew and loved, your little boy, was gone. Autism had stolen him.

TWENTY-ONE

None of us took Mike's firing very seriously. Tim was always firing people. Often, his rage lasted no longer than it took them to clear their desk, by which time he would have gone over and said, 'Forget it. I didn't mean it.'

Mike, though, walked out and didn't come back. We waited for Tim to call him up and apologise, but it never happened.

It was because they had insulted each other's wives, we decided. They'd crossed a line. That was what made this argument different.

It was made even more awkward by the fact that Jenny had been sitting right there on the mathematicians' desk when it happened. We'd all heard what Tim had called her. The chances were, she had too. But she still showed up for work every day, just as if nothing had happened.

But then, we had all of us become adept at turning a blind eye and a deaf ear, working in that environment.

The stand-off went on for weeks. The weeks became months. Still there was no sign of Mike. Someone heard from a friend of a friend at another tech company that he was on his fourth round of interviews there.

It was Abbie who decided enough was enough. She booked a

table at Fuki Sushi for lunch. When Tim got there, he saw the table was set for three. Then Mike turned up. He looked just as surprised to see Tim as Tim was to see him.

According to legend, Abbie stood up and said, 'I'm leaving you guys to it. Bottom line is, it's my wedding in three weeks. And, right now, Tim doesn't have a best man.'

To Mike, she added, 'You don't have to like me, or think I'm the right partner for Tim. But we both care about him. So let's try to make this work, shall we?'

The next day, Mike was back at his desk. Three weeks later, he was Tim's best man. And when, a year later, Tim and Abbie celebrated the birth of their son, Mike was the godfather.

We heard Tim had promised Mike, during the lunch, that, once the honeymoon was over, he'd get right back to touring investors and raising more capital. And he did. We soon had enough funding to iron out the glitches and develop new, more cost-efficient ways of manufacturing the shopbots.

Throughout all this, Jenny kept her own counsel. We still had no idea whether she'd heard what Tim had said about her.

At least she and Mike got to go to the wedding. None of the rest of us did.

60

You're still thinking about Danny and what you saw at Meadowbank when the front-door intercom buzzes. 'Who is it?' you ask cautiously.

'Detective Tanner.'

The cop who was so unpleasant to you at the station house. You go and open the door part-way. His big, threatening body fills the frame, and you're reminded of the time he blocked you from leaving the interview room.

'Can I come in?' he says brusquely.

'I'd rather you didn't.'

He doesn't react to that. 'I hear there are legal moves to have you destroyed.'

You stare at him haughtily. 'We're fighting them.'

'Good luck with that.' He stares right back at you. 'You remember what I said to you, last time we spoke?'

'Of course. You told me you still had it in for Tim.'

He shakes his head. 'I said I wanted justice for Abbie. And that, if you could help me, you should. For her sake.'

You don't reply.

'Look,' he says urgently. 'Time may be running out for you. And, therefore, for *her*. If you know anything – if he's said *anything* that could help us get to the truth – you need to tell me now. Before it's too late.'

After a moment's thought, you pull the door all the way open. 'All right. Come in.'

You've no intention of telling Detective Tanner anything, of course. But it's occurred to you that this might be a good opportunity to find out what *he* knows.

'Here's the deal,' you say. 'I'll tell you what I discover, if you point me in the right direction.'

'What do you mean?' he asks warily.

'There was evidence that wasn't produced at the trial, wasn't there – you hinted as much, when you spoke to the media after the dismissal. And those articles speculating about Abbie having affairs – none of that stuff even got mentioned in court. There must have been a reason for that.'

'There was,' he says after a brief pause. 'A couple of reasons, in fact.'

You wait.

'First, the prosecutor wanted to avoid any suggestion of victim blaming. Juries hate that, particularly when the victim is an attractive young woman. Better to let them feel we're on the side of the deceased – the good wife, the saintly mother. Then they become angry on her behalf.'

'And the second reason?'

'The second reason was that Abbie's sex life didn't provide a motive to kill her.'

'Why not? If she was using those websites . . .' Then you realise what he must mean. 'Tim *knew*? They had an open marriage?'

Tanner's expression doesn't change. 'So his defence team claimed. She'd been in a polyamorous relationship before they met, apparently, and the two of them had agreed she could continue that lifestyle after the marriage, if she chose to.'

'I don't believe it,' you say immediately. You're quite certain Tim would have hated Abbie to have taken other lovers. Tim never shares anything. Besides, there had been nothing about it in the prenup. It seemed unlikely that a document detailed enough to determine the penalty for putting on three pounds in weight wouldn't cover something as unusual as polyamory.

'Me neither,' Tanner says. 'But it was enough to muddy the waters and make the prosecution wary of using it. And, while plenty of women came forward after his arrest to allege he'd tried it on with *them* over the years, we were never able to find a single man *she'd* actually hooked up with.' Tanner pauses. 'There was something else they didn't bring before the jury. Something that, in my view, was much more likely to be relevant.'

It takes a moment for what Tanner's just told you about the other women to sink in. So Sian wasn't the first. But of course she wouldn't be – not if Tim was conforming to the pattern described in that book. *Where they desire, they cannot love.* If all the women who weren't Madonnas were whores, that still left an awful lot of whores.

And you . . . Is that the real reason Tim didn't give you genitals? Not because it was too difficult, or because of what people might say, but out of some almost primeval, patriarchal obsession with female modesty? Are you simply the modern-day equivalent of all those untold millions of women throughout history, mutilated to disable their threatening sexuality? To shame them, control their desires, stop them from being fully human?

Tanner's looking at you expectantly. You drag your attention back to him. 'What?'

'I said, Abbie's drug counsellor had reported a child-protection issue.'

'What kind of issue?'

The detective grimaces. 'That was the frustrating thing. State law requires drugs counsellors to report any issue affecting the safety of a child. But it doesn't mandate that they have to be specific about it, or give any follow-up information. So, the way many of them balance the law with client confidentiality is to make an initial report, then clam up. Abbie's counsellor was no exception.'

You make a decision. 'Does this counsellor have a name?'

'Piers Boyd. Works out of his home, near Half Moon Bay. I guess that's why she chose him – he was close to their beach house.' Tanner shoots you a look. 'You thinking of speaking to him?'

'It can't hurt.'

'Well, if he says anything, be sure to share it with me. You bring me something about Abbie, I might be able to talk to Lisa Cullen. Get her to reconsider those proceedings.'

'I don't need your protection,' you say loftily. 'I've got Tim and his lawyer.'

But, despite your defiant words, you know it isn't true. As far as Tim's concerned, you're just an algorithm to find his wife. To his lawyer, you're a bargaining chip in the settlement deal he's probably hammering out right now. Having Detective Tanner on your side might turn out to be a lifesaver.

61

Piers Boyd's address is on his website, an amateur-looking affair that reveals he's a life coach and qualified reiki healer as well as a licensed drugs counsellor. But not, it seems, a particularly busy one. You call ahead to make an appointment, and there doesn't seem to be any difficulty fixing a time to see him today.

'What name?' he wants to know.

'Gail,' you say, after the briefest pause.

'How nice.' His voice is obscured briefly as he pulls the top off a pen with his teeth. 'Short for Abigail, presumably?'

'Kind of.' That's to say, *Abbie* is already taken, so you get the only bit of *Abigail* left over. Story of your life, you think ruefully.

Boyd lives on Balboa Boulevard, just across the street from the ocean. A wind chime tinkles gently by the gate, and down the side of the house you glimpse a couple of surfboards and a wetsuit, still dripping on to the concrete. The man who opens the door is in his late forties, his hair tied up in a man-bun. His feet are bare and he's wearing a leather necklace, a cotton shirt and baggy Indian trousers – *dhoti pants*, an inner voice identifies them as.

'Gail?' he says, and then, 'Oh. It's *you*.' He seems both startled and a little uneasy, which is exactly what you intended.

'Yes. The cobot of the woman you counselled. Can I come in?'

'I guess.' He opens the door, a little reluctantly.

'I read about you,' he says when you're both seated in a small consultation room that was clearly once a garage. 'I never thought I'd see you in my house, though.'

'That makes two of us.'

He regards you curiously. 'Do you think you have a soul?'

Now it's your turn to be surprised. 'Do you know, you're the first person who's asked me that.' You consider. 'Yes, I think I probably do. At least, for now. Because, after all, the whole point about a soul is that it's something separate from the body. So, not having a flesh-and-blood body can't be a reason for not having one.'

'Why "for now"?'

'A court may order me destroyed.'

You explain about the legal proceedings, careful to frame them not as something Lisa requested to spare her family pain, but rather as the machinations of a big corporation eager to control and monetise Tim's breakthrough.

'So that's why I'm here,' you conclude. 'If I can understand what prompted you to file that child-protection report, I may be able to use it to stop myself getting wiped.'

Piers Boyd fiddles nervously with his necklace. 'I guess the question is, are you Abbie? If you're not, I can't tell you. But if you are, confidentiality isn't an issue.'

'The lawyers would say I'm not,' you admit. 'But then, the lawyers would say I don't have a soul.'

'Yes.' He's clearly torn. 'It's a tricky one.'

'I *feel* like I'm Abbie, though,' you lie. 'I have Abbie's thoughts, Abbie's consciousness, Abbie's memories. What *is* identity, if not that?'

He hesitates. 'Why don't you tell me what you need to know? And then I'll tell you whether I can share it.'

Within ten minutes, you've got him talking. Piers Boyd would never have felt comfortable speaking to the police – he's way too alternative for that – but you're a different matter.

'I'd been her counsellor for a long time,' he explains. 'It was a condition of her prenup that she have one. But, gradually, we stopped talking about her so-called addiction and focused more on her other issues.'

'Why "so-called"?'

'Abbie was only ever a recreational abuser. Of course, there are plenty of people who do graduate from recreational use to full-blown addiction. So, you can either believe that Tim did her a favour by nipping it in the bud ... or that he massively over-reacted in the first place.'

Interesting. 'And what were these other issues you discussed?'

'Danny,' he answers quietly. 'We talked about Danny a lot. Abbie was ... Well, I'd say she was traumatised by what had happened to him. The outside world saw the beautiful, positive woman who just got on with it. The amazing mother who took everything in her stride. In this room, I saw a woman struggling to come to terms with heartbreak.'

'You helped her with that.'

'I tried.' Boyd looks troubled. 'That is, I listened. She was so used to not being listened to that, at first, it was hard for her. But, little by little, she opened up. I doubt anyone else had seen that side of her. Certainly not her husband.'

Piers Boyd had been a little bit in love with Abbie, you realise.

Did she use her beauty and her vulnerability to manipulate him? Or are you being too cynical about that?

'And what was the specific issue that made you file a child-protection report?' you ask. 'Was it to do with drugs? Drinking?'

Boyd shakes his head. 'Nothing like that. She was planning to abduct Danny.'

You sit back, reeling. 'Abduct him? How?'

'He'd been put in a special-ed school, one chosen by Tim. He'd shown Abbie all these studies proving it was the most effective placement, bullied her into going along with it . . . It was only after Danny started there that she realised just how bad it was.'

'I know. I saw it myself, this morning.'

Piers Boyd nods. 'Horrible, right? Abbie had been through something similar herself, back in the rehab unit Tim put her in. But, while she'd accepted it for herself, she couldn't bear the thought of Danny suffering like that. So she decided to take him away.'

'But . . .' You stop. In the last few hours, all your assumptions about Abbie have been turned upside down. Not a bad mother, but a devoted one. Not a party animal, but a parent caught in an impossible position.

'The thing is, I was torn,' Boyd adds. 'I could see why she hated that place. But it didn't seem to me she'd properly thought through the alternative. They were just going to take off and start a new life somewhere, she claimed, like it was easy. But, when I pressed her, she didn't know where or how, or what the arrangements for Danny's education would be. He's a vulnerable child. I couldn't ignore what she was telling me – I could lose my licence to practise. I thought, if I flagged an issue, at least the police would get an educational psychologist to take a look at Meadowbank and assess whether it really was the right place for Danny.'

'But they didn't.'

He shakes his head. 'The report still hadn't been acted on by the time she disappeared.'

'So what happened?'

He spreads his hands. 'I'm as much in the dark as anyone. Maybe her plans changed. They were pretty vague, after all.'

You wonder if that's true. The website had walked her through how to set up a new identity, how to live off-grid . . .

Tell no one what you plan to do, it had instructed. *Not even those you trust the most.*

'I think she knew exactly where she was going to take Danny,' you say slowly. 'She just didn't want to tell you. It was safer that way.'

Piers Boyd looks hurt, then nods as he sees the sense in what you're saying. 'But, if that's the case, why is Danny still at Meadowbank? And where's Abbie? What went wrong?'

You shake your head. 'That's what I still don't understand. But I intend to find out.'

62

Charles Carter comes to his door wearing an old grey cardigan. You aren't surprised to find him home; he'd said he worked from here. *Mergers and acquisitions, mostly.*

'Come on in,' he says. He seems genuinely pleased to see you.

You follow him through the house to an office overlooking the beach. There are three computer screens on his desk, arranged like mirrors on a dressing table. One shows a stock-trading screen. A second is for Skype. The largest, the one in the middle, displays what looks like a contract he's drafting. But it's the picture on the wall behind the screens that your eye is drawn to. It shows the view of the ocean from the boardwalk below, painted in a vibrant, almost street-art style, the waves reduced to abstract, clashing triangles of energy. In one corner, you can just make out his boat, the *Maggie*.

Like the mural in Tim's office, you think. You go over and look for the looping, flamboyant signature: *Abbie Cullen-Scott*.

'It's good to see you again,' Charles Carter says. 'There aren't many people around at this time of year, and, I won't deny, it does get somewhat lonely out here.'

You indicate the painting. 'Was that how she paid you?'

'Abbie?' He looks amused. 'Why would she need to pay *me*?'

'For setting up a corporation.'

Carter takes off his reading glasses and twirls them in his hand, looking at you thoughtfully.

'That was the part she'd have needed help with,' you add. 'Most of the instructions she was trying to follow were straightforward – leave your phone on a bus, stop using credit cards, that kind of stuff. The tricky bit was setting up a legal entity that could rent a house and sign up for utilities and so on, without her name being attached to it. I'm guessing she came to you for that.'

Charles Carter raises his eyebrows. You outwait him.

'That's conjecture,' he says at last.

'I'm extremely good at conjecture. Intuitive thinking is what I was built for.'

'It's always good to have a purpose,' he murmurs. 'And, indeed, to know what that purpose is.'

'For a while, back there, I thought you might have been sleeping with her,' you add. 'But now I think I was falling into the trap of looking at things the way Tim does. I'm guessing you simply liked each other. Two lonely people who, in their different ways, had each lost the person they loved most in this world . . . And, as you said yourself, you owed her a favour, for sorting out the leases here.'

'If I owed Abbie a favour, there'd have been no need to pay me with a painting, would there?' he points out.

'But she gave you one anyway.' You think for a moment. 'Not as payment, then. As something to remember her by.'

His eyes travel to the painting. 'Abbie Cullen was one of the kindest, sweetest people I ever met,' he says quietly. 'Sure – she struggled when Danny regressed like that. But, more to the point, she had to decide where her loyalties lay. She'd been able to live with her husband when he was the only demanding man in her life. When there were two demanding men . . .'

You see the way his expression softens as his eyes drop to the signature, and you're sure, now, you've got it right.

'If I did have any professional dealings with Abbie, they'd be privileged,' he adds. 'But I will say this: I think she made the right decision.'

'I need you to look for emails from a man called Charles Carter,' you tell Nathan. 'Or anything on the iPad suggesting he helped Abbie set up a corporation.'

You've dropped by the phone shop on your way home. Nathan looked surprised to see you. But not so surprised that he didn't immediately go and lock the street door.

'Come in the back,' he says.

Once there, you endure the now-familiar routine of him plugging a cable into your hip.

'Here,' he adds, handing you a printout. It's thinner than the last one – only two sheets. 'This is what I've unscrambled since yesterday. It's a list of some of the things she searched for online.'

Quickly, you scan the page.

```
µ Treatments for autism
µ Do B14 injections help autism?
˜ autism XÿŒ chelation therapy
Anxiety autism
Heller's syndrome organic diet
€
```

```
Can stem cell infusions cure autism
Positive Autism
#Positive Autism Dr Eliot P. Laurence
Dr Eliot P. Laurence Contact
```

'She was looking for a cure,' you say. 'That's hardly surprising.'

'Uh-huh,' Nathan says, his eyes on his screen.

'What's this one? *Positive Autism?*'

'Beats me,' he murmurs.

'Look it up.' When he doesn't react, you say impatiently, 'Look it up on the internet now, or I'm disconnecting.'

'No – wait.' Nathan opens a browser and types *Positive Autism wiki*, then turns the screen so you can see.

> **Positive Autism** is an approach to <u>autism</u> and other <u>developmental</u> disabilities developed by Dr Eliot P. Laurence, PhD.[1] Parents and facilitators are taught to see autistic behaviours not as aberrant or 'wrong', but as necessary coping mechanisms for an overstimulating world.[2]
>
> Using a combination of proven healing interventions, including <u>qigong massage</u>, <u>art therapy</u>, <u>toxin-free diets</u> and <u>sensory integration</u> techniques, Dr Laurence's seminars and books, and the many charitable foundations that use his methods, have helped thousands of people with this condition to increase their quality of life.[4]

The external links include a website. 'Click on that,' you tell Nathan.

The page that comes up shows a picture of a ranch. Kids –

clearly with learning disabilities, but smiling – are riding horses, hiking and building fires. At the top it says:

> Our goal is not to make people 'less autistic'; it is to make the world less troubling for them.

You scan the page quickly. 'Now click on *Contact*.'

Sighing, Nathan does as you ask. 'And that's it,' he adds sulkily as you memorise the details. 'You've had your turn.'

While he peers at the code flowing across his screen, occasionally scribbling a note, you think about what you've just read. It seems clear now that Danny's diagnosis opened up a hidden fault line in Tim and Abbie's marriage. You can imagine her showing him the Wikipedia article you've just read, and what his response would have been. *If this stuff really worked, don't you think someone would have peer-reviewed it by now? Successful treatments for autism aren't so common they get ignored. If there's no clinical trial, it's bullshit. Nice-sounding bullshit, admittedly – but it won't make our son any better.*

On the other hand, at least this Dr Laurence isn't giving his students electric shocks. Is reducing the appearance of stress really such a good thing, if the student is actually terrified? Just what do people mean when they talk about 'treating' autism, anyway?

These must be the exact same questions that went through Abbie's mind five years ago, you realise.

'Beautiful,' Nathan murmurs. His fingers tap the keyboard, and there's a shutter-closing sound. He's taken a screenshot.

'That's enough,' you tell him sharply yanking the cable out of your hip. 'Time's up.'

63

Dr Eliot Laurence . . . All the way home, you try to recall whether that name means anything to you. But there's nothing. Other memories come, though – still shrouded in fog, so you're not sure if they're real or simply more of those educated guesses Tim talked about.

You can definitely recall how those were the darkest times. After Danny's diagnosis, when it became apparent how far you'd drifted apart.

Your focus in the previous years had been your baby, then your toddler, then your little boy. For Tim, it had been work. The prenup might have specified one day a week spent with family, but there was always a call to take, an email to respond to, a function to attend.

You realised, too, that the reason you didn't argue much wasn't because your marriage was healthy. It was more because starting a fight with Tim was such a massive undertaking. His stubbornness, intelligence and refusal to concede even the tiniest thing made every disagreement a high-stakes battle that had to be fought to the point of exhaustion. And since you always conceded in the end, what was the point of starting the battle in the first place? There had been a few memorable exceptions, times you'd refused to give in, like the time he suggested that, as a new mother, your naked-surfing days should now be behind you. But they were few and far between, and over the years they'd become even fewer.

You didn't have sex. But when you talked to your other married friends, neither did they. Too exhausted, they said with a rueful smile. Besides, there was usually a small child in the bed. And so you chose to believe that was what it was like for you, too.

It's just that it wasn't, not really. You weren't too exhausted. It was more that Tim, having fathered a child, seemed to feel his job was done. He still adored you, or claimed he did. But somehow he no longer translated that adoration into intimacy.

After Danny's diagnosis, you were briefly united in shock and anger. That was the only good thing about it – the feeling that you were together again, Team Danny, that the two of you were going to take this thing on and beat it through sheer determination.

'If he can become autistic, he can become un-autistic,' Tim kept saying. 'Someone, somewhere, will be doing cutting-edge research on this.'

But gradually it became apparent that what little research there was wasn't being done on childhood disintegrative disorder. It was focused on understanding why autism happened in the first place. And the fact was, no one had a clue.

It was you who started looking at alternative treatments. The internet was awash with suggestions. You were sceptical, of course you were, but you were also desperate. So, secretly, you gave most of them a try. Because, after all, you never knew.

Tim's view was that, if the science didn't stack up, there was no point in wasting time and money proving that the treatment didn't, either.

You even went back to the expensive, highly qualified speech-and-language therapist who, only a few months ago, had told you he'd grow out of his lisp. Danny had been silent for weeks after his regression, but recently he'd started making small, truncated sounds. 'Ss' meant *Yes*. 'Sssss' meant *Juice*. 'Vuh' was *Video* – his *Thomas the Tank Engine* tapes, the only things he'd watch since coming home from the hospital.

'What do I do now?' you asked her desperately.

She asked if you'd thought about sign language.

You stared at her. She was a speech therapist, for God's sake. Yet here she was, accepting defeat before you'd even started. You felt a wave of anger at the kind of parents who paid this useless woman $150 an hour to tell them their child's speech impediment would sort itself out eventually. Even though, recently, you'd been one yourself.

'Sometimes he seems to mutter things from TV shows,' you told her. 'That's good, isn't it? It means you've got something to work with.'

'It's called echolalia,' she said, nodding. 'Kids with autism do that. It's just gibberish, though. It doesn't mean anything.

'What I *would* say, Mrs Scott,' she added as you got up to leave, 'is not to go down the ABA road. A lot of parents do that and end up regretting it. I went to a conference once. There were all these horrible videos of kids being taught like little robots.'

That evening you relayed this whole dispiriting conversation to Tim.

'Well, she's wrong about one thing,' he said immediately. 'I may not know much about autism, but I *do* know about robots. You train them the way that's most effective, that's all.'

'So maybe this ABA thing is worth a try.' You looked over at Danny, whispering nonsense to himself. 'We've got to do *something*.'

So you both, separately, started looking into ABA. Tim soon discovered peer-reviewed evidence showing it was the most effective intervention for autism there was, even if the success of the original studies, by a psychologist at UCLA called Ivar Lovaas, had never been replicated. So, as far as Tim was concerned, it was a definite *yes*.

Meanwhile, you'd been asking around about ABA practitioners. That's how you found Julian. About thirty, with a mass of frizzy brown hair, a bear of a body and an engagingly boyish manner, he turned up at Dolores Street like Santa Claus, with a backpack full of toys that he spilled onto the kitchen table. Cheap electronic toys, mostly – toys that beeped, flickered, flashed and jumped. A disco ball on the end of a pen. Three different kinds of jack-in-the-box. A plastic spider that hopped when you squeezed a bulb. A sparking wheel that spat real sparks when you pumped it. It was like a Montessori teacher's worst nightmare.

'What'll he like?' he said calmly.

You picked out Toby the Tram Engine. 'He loves all the engines. But Toby's his favourite. I don't know why.'

'Because Toby's different, of course.'

Julian went over to where Danny was sitting on the floor, idly staring at his own fingers as he twirled them in front of his eyes.

'Hi Danny!' he said engagingly. Without waiting for a response, he sat down on the floor next to him and started pushing Toby around, making little *wheesh* sounds as he did so.

'Toby is always careful on the road,' he said conversationally. *'The cars, buses and lorries often have accidents. Toby hasn't had an accident in years.'*

You stared at him, amazed. This man actually knew the words to *Toby the Tram Engine* by heart!

Danny ignored him. Undeterred, Julian continued. *'"Is it electric?" asked Bridget. "Whooooosh!" hissed Toby crossly.'* Julian gave *whoosh* the full theatrical effect, Toby's indignation propelling the tram engine into the air like a rocket.

Julian turned and looked at you expectantly. After a moment, you realised he wanted you to supply Bridget's next line.

'"But trams are electric, aren't they?"' you said dutifully.

Julian nodded. *'"They are mostly. But this . . . this . . . THIS is a . . ."'* Julian lifted Toby into the air and held him next to his ear as if listening carefully, waiting. There was a long, expectant silence.

'Steam tram,' Danny mumbled.

'STEAM TRAM!' Julian echoed triumphantly. He pressed something underneath Toby. There was a little pop, and a plume of cordite-scented smoke drifted out of Toby's funnel.

Danny laughed.

Danny *laughed*. The first time you'd heard him laugh in months.

Five minutes later, the toys had been swept away again, into the backpack, and Julian was drinking coffee at the kitchen table.

'No point in pushing it,' he said airily. 'That's mission accomplished for today.'

As far as you were concerned, you'd just witnessed a miracle, not a mission. 'What was the mission?'

'Today was all about pairing. Making my presence here a reinforcer. So that, when we start work for real, Danny will associate me with fun.'

It was the first time you'd heard words like *pairing* and *reinforcer*, and you had to get him to explain. Basically, the toys would be used to motivate Danny to learn skills that other kids picked up automatically. The quicker the gratification, the better, since they'd be used as rewards for as little as three seconds of work.

'As you'll discover soon enough, Mrs Cullen-Scott, we ABA types do like our jargon. It's to make what we do sound serious, when actually we're just having fun.' Julian spoke lightly, but you got a sense that this was someone who knew exactly what he was about.

'Well, whatever you were doing, I liked it. And, please, I'm Abbie.'

64

When you get home, you email Dr Laurence to ask for an appointment, using a false name and saying he was recommended by a previous client, Abbie Cullen-Scott. The answer comes back within an hour.

> *I would be happy to offer you a consultation. My waiting list is five months. However, I should inform you I have no record of a client named Abbie Cullen-Scott.*

Strange, you think. Strange and frustrating. But perhaps Abbie just heard him speak at a convention.

Or are you chasing up the wrong path altogether? The fact remains that, for whatever reason, Abbie ended up leaving Danny behind.

You spend the rest of the time until Tim gets home making pasta. The repetitive movements are strangely soothing. A simple sauce of anchovies, capers, chilli flakes and tomatoes simmers in the pan while you knead and fold and push. Puttanesca sauce, it's called, from *puttana*, meaning 'whore'. Nobody knows why it's called that, the cloud whispers to you silently, though you're betting it was a man who named it.

Tim arrives, crackling with energy.

'We've been given a time for our court hearing. Or at least, our initial appearance before a judge.'

'When?'

'Tomorrow. Don't worry, it's only a formality. The judge will read the depositions to make sure they're acceptable. Then he'll tell us to go away and try to reach a settlement.'

'Will we? Settle, I mean?'

'In the end, sure. Why not? It's money for nothing, as far as the Cullens are concerned.'

You still doubt that's how Lisa sees it, but you don't say so. 'Do I need to be there?'

Tim nods vigorously. 'Definitely. We should show the judge we've nothing to be ashamed of.'

You'd rather spend the time looking for Abbie, but of course you can't say that. When, over supper, Tim asks if you've made any progress, you fob him off with some vague stuff about intuitions that led nowhere.

It's Tim who brings up the subject of Meadowbank again. It clearly matters to him that he has your endorsement, however retrospective, of the choice he made sending Danny there. But how can you tell him what you really feel, when your very existence depends on him thinking you're of one mind with him on issues like this? When you don't voice your reservations, he talks eagerly about stepping up the programme, setting new targets. 'Soon it'll be time to stop him flapping his hands. Or playing with those trains. The problem with letting him have an autistic behaviour as a reward is that you just reinforce the behaviour. Now you're on board, it's time to grasp the nettle.'

You try to think how Danny's going to cope with having his beloved trains taken away, and fail.

'Today I remembered a therapist Danny had, right at the beginning,' you tell Tim. 'A man called Julian. What happened to him? We liked him, didn't we?'

'You remember Julian, do you?' There's a strange edge to Tim's voice.

'A little.'

'Maybe you shouldn't try to think about him too much.'

'Why not?'

'Julian turned out to be a pain in the ass.'

You frown. 'I remembered him as being so nice.'

'Well, that's not how it was,' Tim says with finality.

After supper, you go upstairs, just as you did last night, to remove your skin.

'Tim,' you say, when you're back downstairs again. 'There's something in particular I need to ask you about.'

'Ask away. You know how I love to fill in the gaps in your knowledge.'

'Did you tell the police that you and Abbie had an open relationship?'

For a long moment, he stares at you. 'How did you—'

'Detective Tanner told me. So it's true? You *did* say that?'

Just for a moment, Tim looks cornered. 'It's true I told them that, yes,' he says with a twisted shrug. 'Some bright spark in my legal team came up with it. The police were fixating on the idea

Abbie might have been having an affair – that finding out she'd been unfaithful would have given me a reason to kill her. So we told them it was fine by me if she was. I don't think they believed us, but we knew there was no evidence to contradict it. And, just as my lawyers hoped, it was enough to make the prosecution think twice about using it as part of their case.'

'You lied, in other words.'

'It was a legal tactic—'

'I meant, to *me*,' you interrupt. 'When I asked you about it before, you said someone else must have been using her photograph.'

A long silence. 'Yes. I'm sorry. The fact is, I couldn't bear for Abbie to be anything less than perfect. So I kept quiet about that aspect of her.'

'That she was sexual, you mean?'

'That she was *flawed*.' Tim looks drawn. 'Abbie had so few faults that, when I came across one, it was always a shock. It's hypocritical, I know – I'm hardly a saint. I'm sorry.'

'If I'm going to find her, you have to be straight with me.'

'Yes. I get that, I really do. And from now on, I will be.'

Eventually, he announces he's off to bed. You tell him you'll stay up for a while, to keep thinking.

But the truth is, you just want to be alone. Was what Tim told the police really just a tactical lie? Is it possible he's playing some kind of psychological chess game, even now? And if so, why?

For the sake of argument, what if it was actually Tim who pushed Abbie into flirting with strangers on dating sites? For Abbie, might that have been the final nail in the coffin of her fairy-tale marriage? Combined with the realisation that she and Tim were never going to agree about Danny, could that have been what tipped her into deciding to leave?

But, if so, something went wrong – something that prevented her from taking Danny as she'd planned.

What would she do in that situation? Would she just give up?

Maybe she'd do something you haven't even hypothesised yet. Something that explains all these dangling loose ends . . .

And that's when you have it. Another flash of intuition.

You go and get the burner phone, the one you installed Messenger on. Opening the app, you find your exchange with Friend. The last message reads:

When you've worked it out, we'll talk.

You type in two words, then press *Send*.
And the response comes back within seconds.

At last.

65

You're Abbie, you wrote.

It's so obvious, really.

You type:

What do you want?

Again, the response is immediate.

I want you to find me.

You type:

Why? Where are you?

This time, the pause is longer. As if she's deleted a couple of different responses before finally pressing *Send*.

Sorry. Not safe. You have to work it out. Then you have to come.

You type:

Why? What do you want from me?

Again, the response is just two words. Two words that also make perfect sense.

Bring Danny.

66

You send a dozen more messages – *What happened? Are you still in the US? Are you with someone? Are you OK?* – but there's no reply.

Eventually, you give up and put the phone down. So Abbie's definitely not dead. You'd been sure of it anyway, but it's good to have this confirmation. And while you still can't be sure why she failed to take Danny, it seems like it was a mishap of some kind.

A mishap she's relying on you to put right.

You realise something else, too. If Abbie expects you to take Danny to her, she's still in America. She must know you'd never get through a border.

For a moment, you consider how strange it is that she trusts you. But then, she'd probably assume you share the same maternal instincts – that, at some level, her feelings are *your* feelings.

And, of course, she's desperate. Just as, for a different reason, you are as well.

TWENTY-TWO

We didn't see so much of Abbie after Danny was born. She'd come into the office occasionally, pushing a top-of-the-line Stokke stroller and greeting old friends. The women cuddled the baby with a mixture of delight and envy. The men did the same, but more briefly, and principally because Abbie might be a mother now, but she was still really hot. Generally, though, these visits occurred because she was en route to Tim's office to collect him for some function or other, so there was never much time to chat. Occasionally someone would ask about her art, and she'd say it was difficult with a little one, so she was effectively on a career break.

Still, she seemed happy enough. And Tim – who none of us would have considered a natural father – seemed happy too. When Danny started walking, Tim sometimes brought him to work on family days, proudly going from meeting to meeting with Danny's little hand in his. There were pictures of Danny and Abbie on his office wall. His assistant, Morag, said he even remembered their birthdays.

Which was why, when the Jaki thing happened, many of us were surprised. Jaki was a curvy blonde with a nose piercing and very short hair. She wore tight dresses that emphasised her figure, and it was rumoured she had a social-media account on some obscure platform that showed a great deal more. Her weekends were spent clubbing and partying, and she never missed Coachella or Joshua Tree or any of the other big festivals; they were as fixed in her calendar as Thanksgiving or Christmas were in ours. And she was fun. Right from the start, if there was a birthday or a promotion to celebrate, Jaki was there at the centre of things, ordering rounds of drinks, announcing shots, planning where we were going next and talking nineteen to the dozen. She was very easy to talk to, or rather to listen to, because she leapt from subject to subject in a torrent of thoughts, opinions, reactions.

Tim seemed to like chatting to Jaki. We thought maybe that was because he didn't really enjoy socialising, and being around her meant he'd never be stuck for small talk. But gradually we noticed it wasn't just at the big social events. They hung out in the bagel room together. They chatted in the parking lot. And then there was the night of the Crunchies, the annual awards show run by the website TechCrunch, at the San Francisco War Memorial Opera House. A resurgent Scott Robotics was up for several accolades, including Best Technology Achievement, while Tim was nominated for Founder of the Year. The firm booked out three large circular tables, eight to a table. Tim, Mike and Elijah wore tuxedos. The women wore cocktail dresses – even Jenny, who no one had ever seen in any kind of dress before. The invitees were a mixed bunch. The men were Tim's favourites, or those who had contributed most and worked the hardest (three categories that, it had to be said, were almost indistinguishable), while the women had possibly been selected with more of an eye to how stunning they would look in those dresses.

Abbie wasn't there that night. She was looking after Danny, and, besides, with the obvious exception of Mike and Jenny, wives and husbands weren't invited.

The evening was pretty successful. Against competition like that, to get two runner-up awards was incredible. Tim didn't see it that way, of course. Tim liked to win. It particularly rankled with him that Microsoft's HoloLens had beaten us to Best Achievement.

'It's a *game* system,' he kept repeating. 'It's a fucking *toy*. How is that going to change the fucking world?'

By the time we'd moved on to the after-party, though, he was feeling more cheerful. Senior people from Silicon Valley's most successful companies – Apple, SpaceX, Google – kept coming over to congratulate him. When the after-party ended at eleven thirty, Tim was ready to go on somewhere else.

What happened next remains a matter for conjecture, even for those in HR who might be assumed to know the whole story. What was not in dispute was that something happened between Tim and Jaki in a hotel room, a hotel room that both parties entered consensually, but that the *way* it happened left Jaki feeling cheap and used and taken advantage of.

As ever in these situations, a general view emerged, but it was fluid. Many of us were shocked, or pretended to be, that Tim had been in a hotel room with a woman who was not his wife, although those who remembered pre-Abbie days – Drunk Karen and, it now seemed from the rumour mill, quite a few others – were not entirely surprised. But, within a few hours, lurid – and quite possibly fictitious – rumours began to circulate.

Jaki had initiated oral sex, with certain conditions, and these Tim had ignored. Or: Jaki had initiated oral sex, and Tim had taken that to mean consent to various other acts too, some of them demeaning. Or: they'd had intercourse, during which Tim had taken off the condom she had asked him to wear. Or: after they'd slept together, Jaki had cried, and Tim had called her a slut. The euphemism 'disrespectful' was increasingly being used, although, frustratingly, it was hard to pin down just what it was a euphemism for.

Our own moral judgements fluctuated somewhat, depending on who we were talking to and how passionately they had taken up a position on the matter. That is to say, of course Jaki had a right to have her boundaries respected. But still, those were some pretty startling boundaries. And no, this was surely not about shaming women for being sexual, or saying that whatever happened between two adults was always the woman's responsibility. Unless, of course, you happened to feel strongly that it was, in which case maybe you had a point.

Nevertheless, the upshot was that Jaki left the company, generously recompensed and having signed a non-disclosure agreement. Nobody felt good about that. But if Tim left, there would be no company, and besides, the facts were still unclear.

Just to be on the safe side, we gathered, anyone in HR who was privy to the paperwork was made to sign an NDA as well.

The next time Abbie brought Danny to visit Tim at work, we scrutinised the three of them to see if we could discern any change in the way they were with each other. There was none, of course. Tim still clearly adored his wife and child to bits, just as he always had.

67

'All rise,' the court officer says.

There are about twenty people in the courtroom, gathered in little tribal clusters. Tim, Pete Maines and you. John Renton and a phalanx of young male lawyers in sharp black suits and dark ties. Elijah and Mike from the company, along with a female lawyer in her own version of the black suit. And, on the other side of the aisle, separated like families of the bride and groom at a wedding, the legal team representing the Cullen family. Lisa isn't with them. You're sad about that. You were hoping that, if you saw each other face-to-face, you might be somehow able to resolve this between the two of you.

There are journalists, too – half a dozen allowed into the court-room, plus a bigger throng outside, along with several TV vans.

After the judge is seated, there's a lot of housekeeping stuff about discovery and depositions and countersuits. Finally, the judge says, 'I understand a revised offer of settlement has been submitted.'

One of Renton's lot stands up. 'Correct, Your Honour.'

'And that it has been provisionally accepted?'

It's Lisa's lawyer who stands to answer. 'Subject to further ratification by family members, Your Honour.'

You turn to look at Tim. This is good news, surely? But he looks mystified.

'Do you want to summarise the proposed terms for the court?' the judge asks briskly.

'Your Honour,' Renton's lawyer replies, 'our objection to the plaintiff's order was that it would have involved the destruction of a valuable prototype, the intellectual property of Scott Robotics. However, we have no objection to the erasure of specific personal data currently loaded on that prototype that may or may not have been the copyright of Abigail Cullen-Scott.' He glances down at his papers. 'In effect, we will retain the prototype, and the prototype's potential sentience, but not the data. This will allow Scott Robotics to refocus on its core business of providing automated sales-clerks to the retail sector.'

You can't take it all in. What does it mean? You want to tell them to stop, that you need to ask some questions, but the judge has already turned back to the family's lawyer. 'Well, Ms Levin?'

'So long as all the personal data is erased, and we can verify that, we accept in principle, Your Honour. A settlement fee has also been agreed. That will be donated to a charity for the education of people with autism.'

Tim's lawyer, Pete Maines, is on his feet. 'Your Honour, this proposed deal comes as news to us—'

'As I understand it, Mr Maines, your client is neither plaintiff nor defendant in this matter,' the judge interrupts. 'Whether this settlement has been communicated to him is not a matter for this court.' He nods at the others. 'How long will this all take, Ms Levin?'

'We hope to have everything agreed by the end of the day, Your Honour.'

'And how long to carry out the technical work?'

'Forty-eight hours at the outside, Your Honour,' the company lawyer replies. It's the first time he's spoken.

'Very good.' The judge nods. 'It seems a trial can be avoided.'

'There is still the issue of where the prototype should be kept in the meantime,' Renton's lawyer says. 'We request that the court either incarcerate it or order it into the custody of the major shareholder.'

The judge scowls. 'I can't incarcerate property, only people. And I see no reason why a shareholder should be responsible for it, when it's already in the possession of a company employee.'

'Your Honour, as of this morning, Tim Scott is no longer employed by Scott Robotics. His termination is effective immediately, and he will be instructed to return all—'

'Again, not a matter for this court,' the judge interrupts crisply. 'You'll have to sort that out among yourselves.' He nods again. 'We're through.'

You look at Tim as you stand for the judge's departure. 'What does it mean?'

The muscles in Tim's cheeks are throbbing with fury. 'It means we need to get you out of here.' Turning to Maines, he says urgently, 'Stall them.'

'I'll do my best. But legally—'

'I don't care about the law,' Tim snarls, 'just getting her away.'

You make it to the courtroom doors before anyone has a chance to intercept you. Outside, Tim pushes aside one TV camera when it blocks his way and you do the same with another. And then you're in the car, moving.

'What just happened?' you say, still shocked.

'An ambush,' Tim says bitterly. 'I don't believe they came up with that offer this morning. Renton will have been working on this for days.'

'Can he really force you out?'

Tim shakes his head. 'My people will all walk out before that happens.' But he doesn't sound completely certain. 'Mike must have betrayed me,' he adds. 'They couldn't fire me unless he agreed to stay and hold the reins. When I think of everything I've done for him—'

'And me?' you interrupt. 'What does this mean for *me*?'

Tim looks across at you. 'They've agreed between them to wipe all your data,' he says as if explaining to a child. 'In other words, to erase your memories.'

'So it'll be as if I have amnesia?'

'Not quite. Your memories are what give you your sense of self. Effectively, you're a construct, assembled from your texts, your voice, video clips . . . Everything will have to go.'

You're reeling. Those lawyers had sounded as matter-of-fact as if they'd been discussing a business contract. 'You mean . . . I'll die?'

'Well . . . You'll no longer have any sense of being alive, put it that way.'

'And then he'll turn me into a shopbot,' you say as the realisation dawns, recalling Renton's lawyer's words. 'An animatronic sales assistant.'

It was only a few weeks ago that you'd been thinking about

throwing yourself under a truck. But that had been from a mixture of shock and self-loathing. To have your life taken from you
now, by order of a court, seems unimaginable.

And Danny – what will this mean for him? You can't leave him
to the tender mercies of people like Principal Hadfield and Sian.
Or Tim, for that matter.

'What Renton doesn't know is that I have a backup,' Tim's
saying.

You turn to him eagerly. 'Of me?'

He nods. 'In my study. Six dedicated servers, with a separate
power supply in case of outages. Even if they wipe you, I'll be
able to start again.'

'But that won't help *me*, will it?' you say slowly, as what he's
telling you sinks in. 'I'll still have been completely erased.'

'True. But the project will live on. And we've got forty-eight
hours.' He puts his hand on yours. 'We need to use them wisely.'

'Of course,' you say, relieved. 'How? Do you have a plan?'

Leaning forward, he says intently, 'If there's anything – anything at all – that might relate to Abbie's disappearance, you have
to tell me now. Even if it makes no sense to you. Then I'll follow
it up after you're gone.'

You stare at him. You thought he'd meant, *Use the time to save
you*. But he'd simply meant, *Use it to find Abbie*. To complete the
mission.

My God, the monomania of this man. Sometimes he reminds
you of Danny, obsessively lining up his engines, unable to think
of anything but that one, urgent need.

You gather your thoughts, determined to tell him so, to let all
the hurt and resentment flow out . . .

But, once again, you don't.

Somehow you need to find a way to survive this. And, if Tim won't help you, you're going to have to figure out a way to do it by yourself.

68

At home, there are more TV crews. Paparazzi, too, running forward, holding their cameras up to the car window on motor drive as you pass, flash-flash-flash.

Inside, Tim turns on the news. *Court orders rogue robot wiped* is the scroll. On the screen is Alicia Wright, the PR woman Tim hired to replace Katrina.

'It's the nature of prototypes that they exist to highlight problems. That way, fixes can be found,' she's saying calmly. *'Scott Robotics is pleased to have found a solution to this issue, so we can move one step closer to full production.'*

'Will the next generation of cobots have the potential to be violent?' the interviewer asks.

'John Renton's vision for these machines is that they'll have the personality of a high-end personal assistant: self-effacing, cheerful, attractive and obliging. But definitely not volatile. As he said to me only this morning, nobody needs another wife. But a good assistant is very hard to find.' Alicia smiles.

'My life's work,' Tim says in disgust. 'And he's going to turn them into geishas.'

You shudder inwardly as you think how narrowly you escaped

being ordered into Renton's custody. *Can't rape a robot, am I right? At least you've been spared that.*

Now Lisa's lawyer is on the screen, reading a prepared statement.

'. . . *The Cullen family are not anti-technology,*' she's saying. '*We are not anti-progress. This was about honouring my sister Abbie's memory, and her life. We think it right that Scott Robotics should now pay for the suffering they have caused. But the entire sum will be donated to Haven Farm Ranches, a charity working with those affected by autism.*'

Something stirs in your brain. Haven Farm Ranches . . . You've come across that name recently. But where?

Then it comes to you. Dr Eliot Laurence's Wikipedia page. It was on the list of charities he consulted for.

While Tim makes some calls to his key staff, you look up Haven Farm Ranches. More smiling faces, more shots of fields with learning-disabled people working in them. But nothing you can see that will help you.

You go to a section marked *Gallery*. There are hundreds of pictures – fund-raisers, mostly. You scroll through them, not even sure what you're looking for. Endless shots of gala evenings, ball gowns, half-marathons, sponsored skydives . . .

And then, so sudden you almost miss it and have to go back to check, a face you know.

Mike. Wearing a tuxedo and handing over a cheque. *Dr Mike Austin, co-founder of Scott Robotics, passes a donation of $18,000 to Dr Eliot Laurence, founder of Positive Autism.*

You click on a menu item headed *Our methods.*

Here at Haven Farm Ranches, we embrace the whole person, not
just the disability. Following an approach called Positive Autism, we
use good diet, outdoor work and holistic therapies to reduce stress
and manage anxiety . . .

Mike met Dr Laurence at a Haven Farm fund-raiser. Dr Laurence
consults to Haven Farm Ranches.

That's the connection to Abbie. It must be.

TWENTY-THREE

We heard the terrible news about Danny from Mike and Jenny. Tim got a call to go straight to Benioff Children's Hospital – Danny'd had some kind of seizure and they were doing tests, he told Mike later, by phone.

It was several days before we heard the words *childhood disintegrative disorder*. We immediately looked it up, of course.

> CDD has been described by many writers as a devastating condition, affecting both the family and the individual's future. As is the case with all pervasive developmental disorders, there are no medications to directly treat CDD, and considerable controversy as to whether any treatments or interventions can have a beneficial effect.

Those of us with kids held them a little tighter that night.

It was a surprise, therefore, to see Tim back at work on Monday morning. 'It's better to keep busy,' he told people. But those who had meetings with him reported he was often distracted by whatever he was reading on his computer.

'He's using PubMed to research his son's diagnosis,' someone said.

That night, Sol Ayode had to go back into the office late, to fetch some papers he'd left behind. It was after ten p.m. and, as we were in a relatively calm part of the development cycle, there was no reason for anybody else to be there. As Sol walked towards his desk, though, he heard someone say, 'Tim Scott, you are the cutest man in the world.'

He could see through the open door of Tim's office. The only light was coming from a work lamp, so it was hard to make out who was in there – he could only see silhouettes. At first, he thought it was Abbie standing in front of the desk, with Tim crouched in front of her. But then he realised it wasn't Abbie, even though it was speaking in Abbie's voice. It was the A-bot.

'Tim Scott, you are the cutest man in the world,' it said again. Then, 'Though you can also be a bit of a dork sometimes.'

Tim was weeping.

As Sol tiptoed away, he heard the A-bot saying it over and over again. 'Tim Scott, you are the cutest man in the world.'

69

As soon as Tim's asleep, you call Mike Austin. It's gone midnight, but he picks up immediately.

'I need to see you,' you tell him. 'It's important.'

He's silent a moment. 'Tim's mad at me, isn't he?'

'It's not that. It's Abbie – the real Abbie. She's alive.' You pause. 'But you knew that already, didn't you?'

He arranges to meet you at the office. Jenny's sleeping, he says, and he doesn't want to disturb her.

You summon an Uber to the back gates. The roads are quiet and the app tells you you'll be there in half an hour.

You spend the time in the car searching for memories. There's a knack to it, you're discovering. Instead of straining for them, you have to drift. If you reach for them, they slip from your grasp. If you go blank and just let them come to you, they will.

They do.

70

Within a few weeks, Julian had assembled a whole team of therapists. Tim came to a training session readily. He was right behind
ABA, after all.

'OK,' Julian said, setting a chair in the middle of the room. 'Tim,
today you're jack-in-the-box, and this chair is the box.'

He put a big red squeaky button on the floor, next to the chair.
Then he got Tim to sit on the chair. Eager to play now, Danny
allowed his hand to be positioned over the button. 'One, two . . .'
Julian prompted.

'Free.'

Julian pushed down on Danny's hand, and Tim stood up.

'Hmm,' Julian said. 'Maybe a bit more engaging. Like this.'

He took Tim's place in the chair, and you helped Danny push
the button. Immediately, Julian rocketed into the air, arms
flailing. 'YEAAAAARGH!' he yelled. Danny laughed.

Julian turned back to Tim. 'Like that.'

Tim tried again, but he just wasn't as naturally playful as Julian.
His 'Yeargh' sounded like a retch of disgust.

'OK. Let's try something else.' Julian switched to a game where
Danny got tickled every time he made eye contact.

Watching them, it struck you that, even before Danny's

regression, Tim never really did horseplay with him. He was trying to follow Julian's instructions now, but you could tell he found it difficult.

'Gotcha!' Julian pounced on Danny, who giggled. Tim gave them a dark look.

'I just don't think what he's doing can be proper ABA,' Tim said later, when Julian had gone.

'It's *modern* ABA. Same principles, but it's moved on since Lovaas's day,' you said confidently. Julian had been explaining this to you, between sessions.

'But it hasn't, has it? Moved on. Not in terms of results. It's moved *backwards*. No one's been able to match Lovaas's original success.'

'Lovaas's therapists shouted and used electric shocks.'

'That's what's worrying me. What if those methods were actually integral to the results? You can't just take one whole vector out of a study and assume it'll work the same.'

'But we can *see* it's working. Besides, Danny adores Julian.'

On reflection, you realised later, that may not have been the smartest thing you could have said.

You assumed it was Julian's relationship with Danny that Tim was jealous of. It took you a while to work out that, actually, it was Julian's relationship with *you*.

'You three seemed to be having a great time,' Tim said one day, after he came home and found you in mid-session. You'd been lying on the floor, taking turns to hold Danny above you at arm's length. Every time Danny made eye contact, he got bounced off your tummy.

'We were, yes.'

'Remind me – did we do background checks on this guy?'

'On *Julian*?' you said, bemused. 'Of course. He showed me his child-protection certificates himself.'

'Well, at least Danny's safe.'

Something about the way he said it made you turn to look at him. 'What do you mean by that?'

Tim shrugged. 'Just the way he looks at you, that's all.'

'You're imagining things,' you said firmly.

One day, Julian suggested a trip to the ocean.

'As a break from therapy?'

'As *motivation* for therapy. You say Danny loves waves. Let's make waves today's reinforcer.'

So the three of you drove out to the beach, where you and Julian walked Danny down to the water. When a wave came, Danny had to say, 'Jump,' and then together you'd pull him, squealing with pleasure, into the air, just before the wave crashed over his tummy. Or you'd crouch down and he'd have to look you in the eye, and you'd reward him by scattering a handful of glittering seawater in front of his gaze.

It worked, too. He loved those games so much, he tried extra hard.

Back at the beach house, you were euphoric. 'That was the best session so far! This is working!'

Excited, you hugged Julian. And that's when he kissed you.

Just for a moment, you kissed him back. Of course you did. You'd been lonely for so long. But, just as quickly, you came to your senses.

'I love you, Abbie,' Julian said urgently as you pulled away. 'I want to be with you.'

'Don't be crazy,' you said slowly. 'I'm married.'

'People can't help who they fall in love with. I didn't choose this. Abbie, I love you.'

But it was you who truly had no choice, although it took you a while to see it. If you had an affair, Tim would find out; and, anyway, you weren't the sort to do something like that behind your husband's back. You couldn't go on working with Julian, not now. Even if he could pretend this hadn't happened, which you doubted, you couldn't.

There were other therapists, you reminded yourself, but you only had one marriage. So, after a sleepless night, you told Julian he had to go.

You felt furious with him, actually. By what sense of entitlement did men think their romantic needs trumped their professional obligations? Why couldn't he simply have kept his mouth shut? What was so terrible about unrequited love that men just had to blab about it?

You told Tim that Julian had gone abroad. And you set about finding a replacement.

But it turned out Julian *had* been unique, after all. None of the other therapists you tried bonded with Danny the same way, or made therapy such fun. You ended up with a nice Romanian woman called Magda, who was extremely competent and emphasised the data-collection side of things, which Tim liked.

You did suggest going to the beach, once, but she looked at you as if you were mad. 'Time is precious,' she said. 'Danny needs us to focus.'

The episode with Julian had one good outcome, though: it made you realise your marriage was drifting towards the point of no return. You told Tim you thought the two of you could benefit from some couples therapy.

'Why? We're fine, aren't we?' he demanded, puzzled.

'They say eighty per cent of couples with an autistic child get divorced, don't they? It can't do any harm to give our marriage a refresher.'

Eventually, Tim agreed to a reiki ceremony in which both of you wrote down all the bad thoughts you'd had and burned them. You spent twenty minutes working out what to write.

As you lit the pieces of paper, Tim's flipped over in the updraft from the flames, so you saw what he'd written. There were just two words: *Fucking reiki.*

71

With a jolt, you see you've arrived at Scott Robotics. The parking lot is empty except for Mike's black Tesla. The Uber drops you off and drives away.

Inside, the place is lit only by the screensavers of the Scott Robotics logo that flicker from every screen – an animated *S* that chases its own tail, over and over, so that it becomes an upended infinity sign. Every screen is in perfect sync – that was something Tim had insisted on, you remember: he spent weeks niggling at the designers because there was a tiny lag, no more than half a second, between some of the screens.

It got fixed, of course. Everything Tim wanted got fixed in the end.

Mike's waiting over at the far side, by Tim's office. 'What makes you say she's alive?' he says, without preamble.

'I'm in touch with her.'

He's silent a moment. 'Does Tim know?'

'He's always believed she's alive. That's why he built me – he thinks I can find her.' You pause. 'I haven't told him we're in contact, though.'

Mike exhales. 'Good. Don't tell him. It's the kindest thing. Think about it – he's already done the hard part. Five years without her. Five years of grieving, of going all the way to the bottom. If he finds her now, and she doesn't want to come back . . . It'll break his heart all over again. And he won't recover, not a second time—'

'Stop bullshitting me,' you say.

Again, he's silent, considering you.

'I know you helped her. It's what you do, after all. Sort out his messes. Protect him from his mistakes. And you didn't like Abbie, you told me so yourself. She'd come between you and Tim, distracted him from the company . . . She knew you were the one person who wanted her gone so much, you'd help her vanish. How frustrating it must have been for you afterwards, when you realised it hadn't worked. When her disappearance, and Tim's reaction to it, threatened the company all over again.'

'Fascinating,' Mike says. 'To be able to take such tiny scraps of evidence and build a pattern from them . . . But, sadly, wrong.'

'You don't deny you tried to stop him marrying her?'

'I don't deny that, no.' Mike's face is impassive. 'But not for the reasons you think.'

'What, then?'

'I was trying to protect her,' he says.

He takes you to another office, the office of their HR director.

'Only two other people have a key to this,' he says as he unlocks a sturdy metal filing cabinet. When he opens it, you're expecting something more dramatic than the neat rows of files and DVDs it actually contains.

Each is labelled in thick black pen. *Emma-Lou Hunter. Valerie Steiner. Jaki Travis. Kathryn Hughes. Karen Yang . . .*

All women's names, you realise.

'They're all here,' Mike says. 'The ones we know about, anyway. The ones we had to pay. What Tim calls *the tramps*.' He turns on the TV, pushes a DVD into the machine and presses *Play*. The quality isn't great – it's been filmed with a cheap video camera – but what it shows is clear enough: a woman in a chair, facing the camera, talking. There are tears on her face, although her voice is flat and unemotional.

'. . . *He took me out for dinner, waited until the food came, and then laid it out for me in a matrix: either you don't want me and won't fuck me, in which case you're a prick-teasing attention whore; or you don't want me and will fuck me just to get a promotion, in which case you're an actual whore; or you do want me and will fuck me, in which case let's go to the very nice suite I've booked at the Plaza Hotel . . .*' The woman blinks back tears. '*I'd said nothing, nothing that could possibly make him think I was interested in him that way . . .*'

Mike presses *Eject* and the image cuts. He reaches for another DVD. You put a hand on his arm. 'Please . . . I get the idea.'

'He's a great leader,' he says softly. 'A visionary. A genius, even. Just not a great human being. At least, not where women are concerned.'

'Was he ever . . . ?' You can hardly say it. 'Was he ever like that with Abbie?'

'Oh, Abbie was the exception. The one he adored, the one he was going to marry. The mother of his kids. Right from the start. No, even before the start. He'd seen a video of her online, being interviewed about her art. That was the only reason he offered her the residency – because he thought she was insanely hot. And then, somehow, he got her to fall in love with him. But I knew it couldn't last. I've seen it happen before. First, he puts them on a pedestal, then ... *Wham.* Suddenly they're sluts and whores, just like all the others.' He gestures at the empty office. 'Silicon Valley has a real problem with corporate sexism. Only ten per cent of coders are female. Only five per cent of leaders. At Scott Robotics, we're considered role models for the industry because we have thirty, forty per cent female staff. But then you look at the churn – the rate those women leave. Hardly any stay more than a year. That's because Tim only hires them if they're hot. Then, if they won't do what he wants, he freezes them out. You know what he said to me and Elijah, the last time we had to pay one off? "Women are cheaper to hire in the first place, so even when you factor in the payola, we're still ahead of the game." As far as he's concerned, it's just part of the cost of doing business.'

'So what happened with Abbie? How did she fall off her pedestal?'

Mike shakes his head. 'I don't really know. Some guy she kissed. One of Danny's therapists, I think.'

'She didn't kiss him,' you protest. 'He kissed her.'

'I'm not sure that's a distinction Tim would have taken much notice of.'

'No,' you say, remembering. 'He didn't.'

Tim really liked the way Magda worked with Danny. He started coming home early, watching the sessions and taking notes. Then, one day, you got back from buying groceries to find he'd brought along three members of his development team to watch the session as well.

'What was that about?' you asked later.

'I think we can use some of the methods Magda uses with Danny to train our AIs. Once you understand the science behind it, it's fascinating.'

After that, Tim threw himself into researching different kinds of ABA. That was when he found this great place called Meadowbank. It used ABA in a school setting, he told you eagerly. And its results were far, far in excess of anything Magda's data sheets were showing.

Except that it wasn't a great place. You hated it at first sight. The thought of sending Danny there terrified you. All this talk of *aversives* and *contingent behaviours* was just so brutal.

You did something you rarely did with Tim: you put your foot down. You said *no*.

Tim just carried on as if it was a done deal. Meadowbank had the best results, so Meadowbank was where Danny was going. End of. Anything else was just irrational emotional chaff. Women's stuff.

In desperation, you told him you could get Julian back. You admitted he hadn't really gone abroad. You confessed you'd only said that because he kissed you.

You thought Tim would be fine about it. After all, you'd put a stop to it the moment it started. What more could you have done?

But Tim wasn't fine.

'You're obviously going to fuck him. So I don't know why you don't just go ahead and do it.'

You were both shouting now. 'What! Of course I'm not—'

'Admit it – you're horny for him. I wouldn't mind, but I hate that you won't be honest about it.'

'This is crazy—'

'What I *do* mind is that you're letting your sloppy pussy dictate what's best for Danny.'

'That is unforgivable!'

And you remember how Tim snickered. A weird, high-pitched giggle, like a little kid. 'And yet somehow I think you'll forgive me. Because you're not about to walk out on all this, are you? The nice houses, the pretty dresses, the private jet. Not to mention all the quack therapists you waste your time and my money on.' He leant in, too close. 'You know what I do to sluts who think they can take me for a ride? I destroy them.'

You stared at him. 'What sluts?'

He stopped. 'Nothing. Just a figure of speech. Don't try to twist this, Abbie. Don't try to make this about me.'

'He wouldn't let her simply divorce him,' you remember. 'She had to be punished. *Shamed*. For something that was only in his head in the first place.'

'He put her on dating sites,' Mike says. 'Or, at least, a chatbot version of her. He thought it was funny. He made the chatbot tell those men all the degrading things she'd do for them. In Abbie's voice. It was childish and pathetic. But Tim thought it was hilarious. He could listen to it for hours.'

From Madonna to whore, you think. Just like it said in that book. 'I suppose I should thank you, then. For helping her get away.'

There's a long silence. Mike shakes his head. 'I didn't, though. I wish I had. I would have, if she'd asked me. But she never did.'

'I don't believe you. I found a picture of you at the Haven

Farm Ranches fund-raiser. If you didn't help Abbie disappear, who did?'

'Me,' a voice says from the doorway.

You both turn.

'That would be me,' Jenny repeats.

72

'Mike tells people he didn't like Abbie. I guess he told *you* that, didn't he?'

The three of you sit around a table in an empty meeting room. No one's turned on any lights. Even so, Jenny keeps her eyes on the table, not meeting either your gaze or Mike's.

'The thing is, he's lying. He loved her. Right from the moment he met her. I always knew he did.' Mike flinches, but she ignores him. 'Perhaps *love* isn't the right word. But *infatuation* doesn't begin to cover it. He went . . . goofy over her. That's the only way I can describe it. Something in him just kind of melted, whenever she was around. Whereas me . . .'

She shrugs. In her Nirvana hoodie, she's so tiny and boyish. So *unthreatening*. Androgynous, almost sexless. That was how she'd survived in this toxic environment, you realise: at some point, she'd simply turned into one of the guys.

At least, on the outside.

'The fact she was taken – by Tim – I think that was part of the attraction, actually. The relationship between Mike and him . . . It's pretty screwed up. When all's said and done, my husband's the beta to Tim's alpha. I got used to that. But it would have been good to see him stand up to Tim occasionally.'

'Jen,' Mike says softly. 'I love you. You know that.'

'Oh, sure. Marriage, date night, picking out curtains, even sex . . . We can do all that. But sometimes, just sometimes, it would be nice to be adored.'

'I do,' he says desperately. 'Believe me, Jen. I do.'

Jenny shakes her head. 'I saw the way you looked at her. Abbie did, too. She might even have gone to you in the end. For help, I mean. She was desperate to get away, you were desperate for anything you could get from her . . .' She shrugs. 'So, I guess you missed your chance.'

'When did *you* start helping Abbie?' you ask her.

Jenny's eyes flick briefly in your direction, then back to the table. 'I used to see her at company socials. I could tell there were problems. Well, of course there were. It was amazing Tim had been able to keep up the pretence so long, really. Things were getting even worse here . . . I remember one time I had to send him an email about a problem I'd spotted in the coding. He sent it on to a developer, but he accidentally copied in the whole math group. He'd written: *Someone sew up this bitch's vagina and tell her to quit whining.*'

She's silent a moment. 'I didn't go to HR. I knew, if I did, there was only one way it could end: a pay-off, an NDA . . . and no job. So I ignored it, just like I always did. You know what was so damn ironic? The fact is, I *had* sewn up my vagina. I always knew I couldn't have kids and be a world-class coder too, at least not in a company like this one. And, bad as this is, others are even worse.

'So I started inviting myself round to Abbie's house for coffee, and gradually it all spilled out. She wanted to leave, to take Danny away from that horrible school Tim had chosen and start over somewhere different. Somewhere *kinder*.'

Another flashback. The continuing fights over Meadowbank – such incredible fights. Tim, surprised to find his usually laid-back wife so stubborn. But, equally, refusing to give ground himself.

Fights that turned increasingly from the theoretical to the personal.

You've had your chance with Danny, and what's the best you could come up with? Fucking kinesiology and head massages. It's time we did this properly.

And then, the most devastating exchange of all.

I'm his mother. *Surely I know what's right for him?*

A mother who bore me a defective son. What does that say about you?

You'd stared at him, heartbroken. Because, whether he really meant it or not, there was no going back now.

'Abbie knew Tim would fight her every inch of the way,' Jenny continues. 'She had this insane plan to just take off . . . It wouldn't have worked, not in a million years. He could have tracked her down in hours. And then he'd have used what she'd done to take Danny away from her. I told her, if she really wanted to do it like that, she had to do it properly.'

'And you thought then you'd get your husband back,' you say softly.

She nods, then glances at Mike. 'Didn't quite work out like that, though, did it?'

'Why not?' you ask, when he doesn't say anything.

'Anyway,' she says, not answering you directly, 'it took two months of planning. First, we had to research suitable places for Danny. Julian was out of the question, of course – he was the first person Tim would have gone after. That picture you found, of the fund-raiser? It was *me* who found that organisation, *me* who went to look round one of their sites and shot footage on my phone for Abbie to look at. I'm not saying they're perfect, but they ticked most of Abbie's boxes. They focused on making people with autism happy, not making them better. Tim's preference was always the other way around.

'Eventually, we got to D-day. That was what we called it, in case Tim was spying on us – Abbie always suspected he'd bugged her phone. *D* for disappearance. *D* for Danny. But, as it turned out, maybe *D* for something else as well.'

'Why? What went wrong?'

'After all that planning, it was the stupidest thing. Danny was on a school trip that afternoon. That stupid bitch Sian hadn't thought to tell anyone. So Abbie got to the school with some story about needing to take Danny for an eye appointment, and he wasn't there. Everything else was in place . . . Abbie figured she'd just have to come back for him the next day. So she went back to the beach house.' Jenny falls silent, her short, unpolished nails picking at the seam of her hoodie. She sighs. 'And that was the last I ever heard from her.'

'Why?' you say, not understanding. 'What happened?'

'My guess is, Tim found out somehow.' Jenny's eyes are wet. 'Maybe the school phoned him instead of her when Danny got back, and he realised there was no eye exam . . . I don't know. I don't even know if she managed to get away somehow, or if he killed her. Or, for that matter, if she killed herself, thinking it wasn't going to work.'

'Why didn't you go to the police? You could have told them

what she'd been planning. They'd have had a much better chance of getting to the bottom of it if they'd known.'

Jenny shrugs. But her gaze goes to Mike.

'Oh my God,' you say, realising. 'You thought Mike was involved. You thought, if Tim killed Abbie, Mike might have helped him.'

'Why not?' she says quietly. 'You think Tim wouldn't have called Mike up and said, "I've just killed my lying slut of a wife, come and help me clear up the mess"? That's the kind of shit he doles out to my husband on a regular basis. And Mike . . .' She stops. 'Mike would have done it, too.'

'Jesus,' you say disbelievingly. 'All this time, you've thought *that* of your husband . . . And you never said anything?'

Her eyes flash. 'Sometimes it's easier, in a marriage, not to overshare. Not to rock the boat. There'll always be another day for that conversation.'

'Jen,' Mike says desperately. 'Jen . . .'

'Don't say anything you'll regret later,' she says sharply to him. 'And don't lie to me.'

There's a long silence.

'Maybe I can help there,' you say at last. 'Abbie's alive. She wants me to go to her.'

Jenny buries her head in her hands, her bony shoulders shaking with relief.

'So now you have to help *me*,' you add. 'Both of you. You owe me that, at least.'

Jenny looks up, her cheeks glossy with tears. 'What do you need?'

'To know where she is, for one thing. Haven Farm Ranches

seem to be affiliated with sites all over the US – I can't possibly visit them all.'

She shakes her head. 'I don't know where she is. None of us do. That was the only way it was safe, Lisa said.'

'Lisa was in on it, too?'

Jenny nods. 'She was the only one Abbie trusted. But, even so, I don't think they're in touch. Tim would have been spying on her as well.'

You realise now why Lisa has been so intent on having you destroyed. She's frightened you might somehow work out where Abbie is and tell Tim. 'Can you at least get her to tell me whatever she does know?'

'I can try. But if you do work out where Abbie is, what will you do?'

'The only thing I can. I'm going to take Danny to his mother, just like she wants me to. Because now she's *my* only chance of surviving, too.'

73

Next morning, Tim leaves the house early for a crisis meeting with Pete Maines. He's going to countersue, he announces furiously. He'll sue Lisa. He'll sue Renton. He'll sue his own company. He'll sue Mike. The bastards are mistaken if they think he's just going to lie down and take it. They have no idea what kind of shitstorm they're about to unleash on their own heads.

Or something. You really can't be bothered to follow the details.

Not once does he ask how you feel. The nearest he gets is when he asks if you've had any ideas about Abbie yet.

You frown. 'There was something – but it's probably irrelevant—'

'What?' he demands.

'Was there a guy she once worked with – Rajesh? Someone she was close to?'

Something flickers in his eyes. 'Yes. Is she with him?'

'It's only a hunch. But I'm going to give it some more thought.'

'Do that.' He smashes his fist into his palm. 'This damn court case has come at just the wrong time.'

He kisses you goodbye, but distractedly. A habit, a ritual. Like kissing a photo because the real thing isn't there.

And that's the last time he'll ever see you, you think as he leaves. Will he look back one day and ask himself, *What if I'd done something different?*

Probably not. Tim's not much given to introspection.

Hopefully he'll be too busy obsessing about Rajesh to consider any alternative scenarios now, at least in the short term. Jenny told you Rajesh is currently in India, the CEO of his own start-up and a multimillionaire in his own right. That should buy you some time.

Once Danny's gone to school, you go up to Tim's study. The combination lock on the door is a problem – you try some different options, but none work, so you get a fire extinguisher and smash the lock off the frame.

Inside, just as Tim described, are half a dozen rack-style computers. Lights flicker, green and red. Behind them, there's something under a dust sheet. You go to see what it is, pulling the sheet off. Then you recoil.

It's you – an ugly, prototype version, the limbs crudely screwed together, the joints exposed and criss-crossed with wires. The A-bot. Across the blank cheeks someone has scrawled *WHORE* in big, angry letters, so that the *O* encircles the open, lipstick-smeared mouth.

It must be light activated, because as soon as the sheet is off it stirs. Then, in a voice eerily like your own, it speaks.

'Hello, sir. I hope you've come to fuck me.'

You turn away, sickened. Even though you know it isn't conscious the way you are, you can't help feeling sorry for it.

You find the backup power supply to the computer and disconnect it. You're about to do the same with the servers when it occurs to you that this might not actually achieve what you need it to. You want Tim's data wiped, not just powered off. And you don't actually know how to do that.

Luckily, you know someone who will.

'Back already?' Nathan says when he sees you.

'I need something. A couple of things, actually.' You show him the hard drives. 'First, I want these erased. That website talked about something called a degausser – I assume you have one of those?'

He raises his eyebrows. 'Anything else?'

'Yes – I need to make sure no one from Scott Robotics can track me. So, if there's any kind of GPS built into my system, I need you to get rid of it.'

'Hmm.' He thinks. 'I'll have to jailbreak you.'

'Meaning?'

'Disconnect you from the cloud. It's not so different from untethering a cellphone. Though technically much more challenging, obviously. Speaking of which, I hope you were smart enough not to bring your iPhone with you?'

'I only carry this, these days.' You show him the burner. 'And I take out the SIM card when I'm not using it.'

He grunts. 'We'll make a techie of you yet.'

'And you? Did you manage to track down the corporation Charles Carter set up?'

'Better than that. I've got a list of its assets.' He holds up a printout. You reach for it, but he pulls it away. 'Uh-uh. When you're hooked up.'

*

You let him plug his cable into your hip one last time.

'Let's see,' he says, fingers flying across the keyboard. 'I've got a pretty good idea of how you're put together now, so this shouldn't . . . Right. Gotcha.'

'You can do it?'

'Of course.' Nathan sounds offended. There's a long silence, broken only by the clicking of his keyboard. 'Though it's actually a bit more complex than it looked,' he admits.

Tap-tap-tap. He looks up. 'If you were a phone, I'd be obliged to mention that what I'm about to do might invalidate your warranty.'

'I can live with that,' you say drily.

'Plus, it might brick you. That means what it sounds like – turning an expensive bit of hardware into a brick. Plus plus, it will disable any security software you've got, such as firewalls and so on. Which may make your operating system liable to crash or malfunction.' He lifts his hands off the keyboard. 'OK to go ahead?'

You look at the screen. On it are the words, *Sure? Y/N*

No, you're not sure. You have no idea if this plan you're for-mulating will simply make things worse.

On the other hand, the alternative is being wiped. 'Do it.'

He presses Y. For a moment, you feel nothing. Then, subtly, something changes. You feel . . .

You feel *alone*, somehow. As if a hum of voices just out of the range of your hearing has quietened and tiptoed away. As if there had always been a prickling, boiling sensation at the back of your head, now only noticeable by its absence.

What's the word for that? You reach for it, but there's nothing there. Nothing falls into your brain, ready-made. You shiver.

'And the hard drives?' you manage to say.

He goes to a small box, like a paper shredder, tosses Tim's backups inside and presses a button. 'Done.'

'Put the iPad in too. I'm finished with it.'

'Sure? I won't be able to undo this.'

'Certain.'

Shrugging, he tosses the iPad in as well and presses a button.

'Great.' You reach for the cable on your hip and yank it out.

'This is it, isn't it?' he says, watching you. 'The last time. You're running away.'

'None of your business.'

'I'm going to miss you.'

You snort. 'Miss staring at my insides, you mean.'

'Not just that. I admire you.'

'You think I'm cool,' you say with a sigh. 'I get that. But I really don't give a shit.'

'I don't mean as a machine. As a *person*. You've been dealt a tough hand and you haven't let it define you. You're strong and resourceful and you don't take no for an answer. It's like you're . . .' He searches for an analogy. 'It's like you've got a disability, and you've turned it into a superpower.'

'Spare me the Hollywood platitudes,' you say. 'Are those hard drives done yet?'

74

At home, you replace the wiped drives in the servers and quickly pack a suitcase for Danny. Then you put the SIM card back into the burner phone and look up the names Nathan found. According to the printout, Charles Carter set up a corporation called Zumweld – right down at the end of any alphabetical list, you note – which purchased plots of building land in different states. Most are feints, you imagine, to cover Abbie's tracks. But one will be the real thing.

Scanning the list, you let your intuition guide you. Montana? Iowa? Oregon?

Oregon. Somewhere by the ocean. There's no address, but you do a separate search for *Oregon + Positive Autism*. About a dozen results come up. In major cities, mostly, but then you spot one called Northhaven.

You do another search. Northhaven has a website – just a single, well-designed page, with very few photos and no videos.

Northhaven is a 4,000-acre off-grid oceanside community near Otter Rock, OR. We practise low-impact living and regenerative farming. In addition, residents make hammocks, artworks, tofu and honey, working together as a collective where each member contributes whatever they can, regardless of ability; every individual valued for who, not what, they are.

That sounds like Abbie's kind of place. You Google some travel planners. You can get an Amtrak all the way from Oakland to Albany, just north of Corvallis, then an Uber to the coast. The train takes sixteen hours and there's a sleeper service. It all looks incredibly easy. Hopefully, you'll be there before anyone's even noticed you and Danny are gone.

75

You arrive at Meadowbank just after lunch, so Danny will have had some food before you set off. You've no idea how stressful this will be for him, and he may find eating difficult for a while.

You go to the principal's office, where you tell Hadfield that Danny has a medical appointment. 'Unfortunately, the hospital forgot to send the details until just now.'

'No problem,' he says easily. 'I'll send someone to fetch him.'

He goes and speaks to his assistant, who glances in your direction and says something. Hadfield comes back, frowning.

'It seems there's a standing directive that Danny can't be removed from school without written instructions from his father.'

'Those must be very old instructions.' You smile. 'I was here with Tim just the other day – you showed us round yourself, remember? And the hospital is less than twenty minutes away. I'll have him back before you know it.'

He thinks for a moment. 'Perhaps I can find someone to go with you. Wait here.'

You wait. Your head is hurting – an unfamiliar ache.

Minutes later, Hadfield returns with Danny, who's twirling his fingers in front of his eyes, apparently unbothered by this break in his routine.

'Hi Danny,' you say. He doesn't reply.

'Danny,' Hadfield says warningly. 'Quiet hands and listen.'

'Huh,' Danny mutters, without taking his eyes off his twirling fingers.

'Great to see you too,' you say, before Hadfield has a chance to decide this isn't good enough and shock him. 'Coming?'

'And, fortunately, I was able to find someone to go with you,' the principal adds, nodding behind you.

You turn. It's Sian.

'Which hospital?' she says as you walk together to the waiting car, Danny's hand in yours.

'Stanford.'

She stops. 'Danny usually goes to USCF Benioff.'

'Well, this is Stanford. Danny, get in, will you?'

'And which doctor?' Sian sounds suspicious now.

'I can't recall,' you reply brightly. 'We'll sort it out when we get there, shall we?'

She pulls a phone out. 'I'm calling Tim to check.'

'Really, there's no need.'

'Sure,' she says sarcastically. 'But I think he'll be glad I did, all the same.'

You don't have any choice. You grab the phone from her hand and toss it into the bushes. 'Hey!' she protests, outraged. Then you hit her. You have no idea how to hit someone effectively in a situation like this, but it seems likely that if you slam the point of her chin with the palm of your hand, it will probably floor her.

It does. For once, you're grateful to Tim for the obsessive overengineering that went into your limbs. You step over Sian's sprawled body and get into the car with Danny, who doesn't give her so much as a glance.

TWENTY-FOUR

The news we got of Danny after the diagnosis was sketchy. Danny was trying out different treatments, we heard, some of them experimental. Danny was being enrolled in research programmes. 'We're going to beat this thing,' Tim told people confidently.

Later, we heard they'd abandoned any hope of finding a cure and had started looking at special-ed programmes.

Alongside that, we heard fragments of gossip. Abbie had started drinking. Abbie had crashed her car. Tim had been seen looking at hookers' websites in his office. They were going to couples therapy.

Once, Abbie brought Danny to the office. It was the annual children's party, held, by tradition, on the day before we closed for the Christmas holidays. There was a bouncy castle, a petting zoo and children's entertainers.

Danny walked in on tiptoe, with a weird, prancing gait, his body scrunched up and distorted, holding his mother's hand. The eyes that had once danced with mischief were now deep-set and bruised-looking. He met no one's gaze, and from his mouth there came a series of wailing sounds. Sometimes he would mutter little phrases from TV programmes.

Needless to say, he showed no interest in the bouncy castle or the entertainment. He was fascinated by the photocopier, though. Someone was printing out a big presentation, some thick marketing deck that had to be copied multiple times, and Danny seemed mesmerised by the whirring, flickering automation of it all. When the machine stopped because it had run out of paper, he began howling, absolutely howling with misery, until Abbie set about reloading it.

Seeing the boss's beautiful wife squatting down, frantically tearing at the nylon ribbon that secured a fresh box of paper, was enough to make the person who was printing the document run over with scissors and apologies.

'Thank you,' Abbie said gratefully. 'We're not really meant to give in when he screams. But when it's a party . . .' She looked over at the bouncy castle, where all the other kids were playing happily, oblivious to Danny's distress.

The photocopier started printing again. Danny immediately calmed down. He sat cross-legged on the floor to watch, like it was a TV playing cartoons. After a while, he laughed.

'We're trying this new therapy,' Abbie went on. 'We've done the research, and it's definitely got the best weight of evidence behind it. But it's really hard on Danny.'

She looked over to where Tim was standing with Mike and Elijah, chatting. But Tim wasn't looking at them. His eyes were following Bhanu across the room. Bhanu was the new project manager he'd just hired from Google. She was slim and sassy and an extrovert. Some of us were already predicting that Bhanu wasn't destined to stay with us very long.

76

The Uber driver doesn't try to make conversation, for which you're grateful. You need to think. You'd been hoping at least to get across the state line before your absence was discovered. That might have to change after what you've just done to Sian. Most likely, the school will already have alerted the authorities.

Technically, what you're doing now is probably child abduction, you realise. But, frankly, it can't make much difference. If you're caught, you'll be wiped anyway.

You've booked the Uber to take you to Jack London Square Station in Oakland. The traffic's flowing freely over the bridge and you're there in under thirty minutes. Your train doesn't leave for another half an hour.

To pass the time, you take Danny to McDonald's.

'I had lunch,' he objects, confused by this unexpected change in his routine.

'I know. But you like fries, don't you? You can have fries as well as lunch.'

'I had lunch,' he insists. 'I had fish ... fish ...' He starts to twitch with anxiety.

'That's all right, Danny. You don't have to have anything. Would you like to see the train timetable?'

You get out the timetable and his eyes light up. He spends the next twenty minutes happily working out connections.

You board the train and find your seats. Danny's still in the mood to treat this as an adventure, with the bonus of added scheduling. While you wait for the train to leave, you get out his Thomas engine and explain that Thomas is especially happy now, because he is a train riding on a train.

A family settle in across the way from you. The oldest girl, a teenager, immediately demands the Wi-Fi password and logs on to the on-board system. You can see various alerts and messages blipping on to the screen of her phone . . .

Wi-Fi. You hadn't thought of that. In your mind, the Amtrak was going to be a bubble, a news cocoon in which no one would be aware of anything happening back in San Francisco. But the reality is that everyone here will have the latest bulletins on their phones. Those smiling conductors settling people into their seats – they'll have them, too. Already the alerts and lookouts will be going out to all the transport hubs. And once the train starts travelling up the coast, you'll be trapped, unable to get off, a sitting target waiting for the cops to come and get you, further up the line.

'Change of plan, Danny.'

'Change?' he says anxiously, looking up.

'We're getting off at the next station.'

'Emeryville. Four thirty-four,' he announces in his staccato mumble.

'That's right. And soon I might have some more schedules for you to look at.' You log on to the Wi-Fi and start searching.

*

At Emeryville, you transfer to a Greyhound, paying cash. The bus is filthy, full of tired workers, with a few crazies thrown in for good measure, but at least no one takes much notice as you find two seats at the back. It gradually empties as people get off at local stops; by eight p.m. you're the only passengers left. The driver pulls in at a Burger King and cheerfully informs you this will be your only chance to get dinner. You're glad now Danny didn't have those fries earlier.

And then it's past eleven and you're in a small town named Arcata, at the grandly named Intermodal Transit Facility, the end of the line. You start to walk with Danny to the Comfort Inn across the street, then remember the instructions on the website. *Never order from chain restaurants . . . Use a sleeping bag in (non-chain) motels . . . Always pay cash . . . Avoid leaving fingerprints / DNA.* You're starting to appreciate just how difficult it is to disappear like this, how incredibly disciplined Abbie must have been, to leave no trace for anyone to follow.

When did the scales finally fall from her eyes? Perhaps, after all the other things she'd discovered about Tim, it hadn't even come as much of a shock. On some level, perhaps she'd always known. There was her art, for one thing. Every single piece she'd made at Scott Robotics had been, in some way, about what that place did to women. Could an artist do that, at a subconscious level, and not admit it to herself?

Later, she must have smelled unfamiliar perfume on his clothes countless times. Or did she choose to believe that was just from some seedy bar he'd been forced to visit, in the company of potential investors? *There's only so much silicone a man can look at, honey. I'd far rather have been home with you.*

And then, abruptly, the memory comes to you. *Jenny.* Dropping in for coffee that time. *You won't like this, but hear me out.* She knew the women's names, the dates. She'd even worked alongside many of them, passed them tissues, knew how much they'd been paid to keep quiet.

That visit was Jenny's quiet rebalancing of the books, you realised. Payback for all those years of having to sit at her desk and suck it up.

Even so, you'd sensed there was something more, something she still wasn't telling you. Something that made all this personal –

And then you'd guessed.

'Did Tim ever try it on with *you*?'

Jenny held your gaze for a moment. 'Just once.' She paused. 'After Mike first told him we were dating. And that it was getting serious.'

You stared at her.

'When I told him to get lost, he just laughed. Claimed he'd only been joking. That he wasn't into little boys, anyway.'

Jesus.

Danny has been remarkably good all day, but the next morning he has more energy and wants to know when you're going home. When you say you aren't, you're going to find Mummy, he starts to stress. You can't blame him. To him, it's as if you said you're going to find yourself. When the restaurant of the no-name budget motel you ended up at can only offer him own-label Cheerios for breakfast instead of the real thing, he has a meltdown. All you can do for him is let him howl himself out without getting cross or impatient with him. It takes twenty minutes, but he eventually brightens up when you tell him you're catching a bus at exactly ten twenty-eight. And once you're on the bus – a tiny minibus, little more than a van, with REDWOOD COAST TRANSPORT emblazoned across the side – he's almost cheerful. Motion and timetables: two of his favourite things.

The 101 runs along the coast for a while, then veers inland through towering, dark-shadowed redwoods. Tourist season is over and the road is nearly empty. You notice how, when people here board the bus, they say hi to those already on it. No one seems to notice you're not like them. You wonder if that's because you've got better at fitting in, or whether people are simply more polite here, away from the big cities. Hardly anyone stares at Danny, either.

It makes you think about the nature of being human. It seems to you that you've met many people over the last few weeks who weren't, not fully. It would be easy to single out Judy Hersch, with her plastic smile and Botoxed face, parroting her autocue, or Sian and the therapists at Meadowbank, shocking their students every time they flapped their arms, but actually it goes much wider than that. To the judge, mechanically applying the rule of law to every situation that comes before him. To Tim's employees, diligently turning his wishes into lines of code while ignoring the toxic, misogynistic environment he'd created. And to Tim himself, believing that every problem of the human heart must have an engineering solution.

The bus driver interrupts your reverie. 'Your boy ever drive through a redwood?' he calls over his shoulder.

'Not yet.'

So the man makes a left, turning into the forest, where the road passes right through the middle of a growing tree. The redwood is evidently a local celebrity: the other passengers applaud as you go through it. 'That's something, huh?' he calls cheerfully.

'Sure is,' you call back. Danny doesn't look up from his toy train. You don't have the heart to tell the driver that.

And Danny? Is he more or less human than others? Some might see his rigidity of thought, his love of schedules and his lack of imagination, as robotic. When people talk about their 'humanity', after all, they generally mean their empathy, their compassion, their moral code. But of course Danny isn't any less human just because he doesn't have those things. He's just differently human: someone with an unusual ratio of rigidity to empathy.

Perhaps the real test of someone's humanity, you think, is how tenderly they treat those like Danny. Whether they blindly try to fix them and make them more like everyone else, or whether they can accept their differentness and adapt the world to it.

77

You get off at the last stop, Smith River – a tiny town a few miles inland that seems utterly deserted. When you enquire about catching the next bus north, which you already know from Danny's schedule-checking is called the Coastal Express, you discover that service has been suspended for twenty-four hours because of a breakdown. This is devastating for Danny. He loves schedules precisely because they seem to offer order in a chaotic world, and now here they are, letting him down.

To add to the misery, it's started to rain. You check into another no-chain motel, where Danny stares dully at the TV. He doesn't even blink when a picture of himself appears on the screen. *Rogue robot abducts child with autism*, is the caption. There's the old clip of you striking Judy Hersch, along with a new one of you knocking aside the TV camera outside the courtroom. You didn't hurt anyone on that occasion, but the way you bang into the camera makes it feel like you did, so they play it over and over. Then there's footage of Sian, her chin bandaged, gesticulating as she recounts how she bravely fought you off as she tried to save Danny from your clutches. Finally, there's an interview with someone who claims to be a 'cyber-psychologist'. His gist is that you've formed some strange robotic attachment to Danny because you think the same way he does.

Actually, the man may have a point there. Ever since Nathan jailbroke you, you've been feeling off-colour – a nagging headache that sometimes shoots into something more. It's as if your mind's turning to concrete, the once-nimble neurons becoming bloated and slow, like a computer that shows the hourglass symbol with every simple task. Even thinking is an effort. It's as if you can glimpse the mathematics behind everything – not just waves, but the wind in the trees, the wheels of a truck, the way water drips from a tap. Like that poet who saw the skull beneath the skin. What was his name? You wait, but of course nothing comes.

You're about to turn the TV off when the picture cuts to Tim. Standing next to him, smirking, is Nathan from the phone shop. 'Thanks to this man, we do have some potential leads,' Tim's saying.

Nathan, you little shit. You wonder what Tim promised him in return for selling you out.

'We also know the cobot may be unstable and potentially dangerous,' Tim adds. 'It would be safest not to approach. Meanwhile, we're doing all we can to track the two of them from this end.'

So now Tim has access to everything Nathan knows. It's a good thing you wiped the iPad along with the hard drives, you reflect. Without that, and the link to Dr Laurence, you doubt they'll be able to identify Northhaven as your destination.

Unless Tim can somehow decode those screenshots Nathan took. You recall something Tim said to you, right at the beginning, when he was explaining how you learnt. *I could plug in a screen and see the math happening, but I couldn't necessarily follow it . . .*

You put the SIM card in the burner phone and message Friend.

We're on our way. But they may be on to us. Still want us to come?

And the answer comes back, moments later.

Come.

78

The rest of the day is interminable, but the following morning you're up and waiting at the bus stop in plenty of time.

Once you cross the state line into Oregon, you relax a little. It helps that the scenery is stunning – an endless parade of cliffs, pounding surf and giant sea stacks, dotted with flying pelicans and cormorants, the whole vista endlessly changing but endlessly repeating, like one of those old spinning zoetropes depicting a galloping horse or a flying bird. Danny, too, is happy to be on the move again. He finds the motion of the bus comforting, and he likes that nobody's making any demands of him.

He looks out of the window and murmurs something.

'What's that, Danny?'

'*Dangerous to the public, indeed,*' he repeats softly.

It's a line from *Toby the Tram Engine*. When Thomas is told off by a policeman for not having a cowcatcher, the policeman writes down *Dangerous to the public* in his notebook.

'*The law is the law,*' Danny adds, '*and we can't change it.*'

Then he catches your eye and grins.

Suddenly, you realise what's happening here. Danny's *commiserating*. He's using snippets from the story to show he understands how you feel about being called dangerous and unstable on the news last night.

From someone who apparently has no empathy – who finds even eye contact overwhelming – this tiny moment of interaction is as momentous to you as a child's first steps would be to another parent.

Trying not to let your excitement show, you reply with another quotation. *'Toby is always careful on the road.'*

Danny thinks, then announces, *'We're sorry your line is closing down.'*

Has he somehow picked up that time's running out for you? Is he saying he'll miss you? Surreal though it is, it feels as if you're having an actual conversation now.

'Thank you, Toby, for a very nice ride,' you say. You take Danny's hand and pat it.

Danny nods. Then he says thoughtfully, *'"Is it electric?" asked Bridget.'*

Of course, you *are* electric, and, in some strange way, you think that's probably what Danny's asking you.

You have to be honest with him, you decide. After all, it may be your last chance. So you reply in the same oblique way.

'Electric, indeed!' you tell him.

'Well, bust my buffers,' Danny says. He turns and leans against you, staring out of the window. After a few moments, his hand encircles your wrist and stays there, holding you. It's the first time since his regression that you can remember him seeking out your touch.

From then on, you entertain each other by reciting Thomas stories, speaking the best bits in unison, like singers duetting a chorus. It's amazing how many phrases seem eerily appropriate to your situation. And Danny is clearly enjoying the parallels. When a woman gets on the bus and says to him, 'And what's your name, young man?' he replies, 'Toby, sir,' without missing a beat.

'Pleased to meet you, Toby,' she replies, only slightly nonplussed.

He laughs and bounces up and down on his seat. For the next hour, he happily recites every single word of *Four Little Engines* from memory.

Meanwhile, you're thinking about what will happen when you get to Northhaven and find Abbie. Whether you're really going to kill her.

79

Yes, you were lying when you told Jenny and Mike you planned to just hand Danny over to his mother. It seemed the best way to convince them to help – the kind of emotional gloop people like them would buy into.

Your plan to kill Abbie began forming long before then, when you finally realised Tim was never going to prefer you to his flesh-and-blood wife.

Looking for another way out, you'd started thinking about something he said once, when you were discussing machine learning. He was talking about the AI that finally beat a human player at Go. But what was really remarkable, he said, was the *way* it beat him. During the match, it had played one move that was so reckless, so apparently random, that no human player would ever have thought to try it.

That's what you had to do, you realised. You needed to find the unplayable play, the unexpected move that made sense only in hindsight. And you set your deep-learning brain to working out what it could be.

Problem: there are two Abbie Cullen-Scotts in the world. Her and you. He built you, but he loves her.

At the time, you'd thought perhaps you could kill her and then go back to your life with Tim, gradually winning his love, secure in the knowledge that the real Abbie would never return. You've long abandoned that plan, of course. Quite apart from anything else, you don't love Tim. You realise that now. You thought you did, but everything you've learnt in the last few days has taught you what a selfish, woman-hating, egotistical prick he is. You don't even want *him* to love *you*. That was just Plan A, a way to survive.

No, far better to escape. To disappear completely. And, by a remarkable coincidence, Abbie has already created the perfect escape route. A whole new existence, off-grid and anonymous. With barely a ripple, you can kill her and slip into the life she's made. You're good at being human now – hardly anyone has given you so much as a second glance since you've started this journey. There might be some practical issues to resolve, but your ingenuity is such that you have no doubt you'll succeed.

Or is this a kind of madness? When Mike warned you your brain might be unreliable, is this what he meant? Is this just the instability of your jailbroken operating system, manifesting itself as psychosis? Is that why colours and sounds have become almost unbearably overwhelming?

But, even if it is, what choice do you have? What future does Abbie herself envisage for you, once you've brought Danny to her? Does she imagine you'll bring him up together in hippiesque peace and harmony on her low-impact organic homestead? Or are you merely a means to an end for her, just as you were for Tim: a convenient way of delivering her son, to be switched off and stored somewhere, like an unneeded vacuum cleaner, once you've fulfilled your function?

That's the crucial question, it seems to you: if you *don't* kill her, what's the alternative?

You decide you'll wait to see what Abbie has to say about that, before making the final decision.

80

It's a three-hour drive up the Oregon coast to Coos Bay, through places with names redolent of old westerns: Pistol River, Gold Beach, Red Rock Point. The towns get smaller and the gaps between them expand. Even the sky seems to get vaster, somehow. The minibus shrinks, an ant crawling along a crack in the rock.

Coos Bay is, once again, the end of the line. But this time there's no onward bus to wait for. You're still sixty miles south of Northhaven, but there's no way to get there.

You sit in a diner with Danny while you consider your options. Your head hurts all the time now and you can't come up with anything. Then a family of four comes in. You take one look and immediately know that the younger child has autism. He's walking on tiptoes, his elbows are tucked tight into his sides, his hands shake erratically in front of his face and his eyes are bruised-looking and deep-set.

The mother looks at Danny, then at you. A glance passes between you – not a smile, exactly, but a kind of acknowledge-ment, a weary recognition between fellow foot soldiers.

'Hi there,' you say.

An hour later, you're in the back of their Winnebago, watching the coast speed by. Noah drives, while you and Annie swap autism stories.

'. . . For about six months, Graham was obsessed with the beep the washing machine made when it finished its cycle. About a minute before the end, he'd know and put his hands over his ears. He'd been counting down in his head! Then he found an easier way of stopping it from beeping: he'd just go and pull the door open, halfway through the wash.'

'With Danny, it was fire alarms. He hated knowing one might go off at any moment. So he used to go and set them off himself. I guess he figured, that way, at least he was in control.'

'I remember coming into school one time and hearing the teacher say, "Graham, we *don't* stick our hands in the urinal. It's not a waterfall."'

'For ages, Danny hated public toilets, because of the noise of the hand dryers. I used to stand outside the men's bathroom, waiting for the screams, then march in and retrieve him. You should have seen some of the looks those men gave me.'

'When I told my parents Graham was autistic, they thought I said "artistic". We were talking at cross purposes for about three months.'

Graham and Danny politely ignore each other. But you like to think they pick up on the fact the two of you are getting on.

Noah offers to make a detour to drop you off right by Northhaven, which, according to the information you've mem- orised, is north of the town, between the 101 and the ocean. Gratefully, you accept. When you get there, you almost miss the tiny, hand-carved sign: if the rural backroad you're on wasn't so small, forcing Noah to drive slowly, he'd have gone right past it.

'I don't think I can get the Winnie up that,' he says, peering at the narrow track.

'Don't worry. Here's fine. And thank you. You've both been very kind.'

After they drive away, it feels very quiet. You turn and look at the track.

Journey's end. You can't believe you've found it at last.

You put the SIM card in the phone and send a message.

At entrance to Northhaven. Where now?

There's hardly any signal. But the reply comes instantly.

You'll find me.

'OK, Danny,' you tell him. 'We're nearly there now.'

'Sodor station. All change,' he announces.

You pick up the bags and start walking.

TWENTY-FIVE

When Abbie went missing, there were many among us who jumped to the conclusion that Danny was the reason. It certainly never seemed possible Tim was involved. We felt shocked when he was arrested, vindicated when the trial collapsed. Tim might have his foibles, but nobody wanted to think they'd been working for a murderer.

Besides, he loved her. You could tell that by the way he fell apart. The way his world disintegrated. He couldn't function without her.

So we started looking for her. Those of us who were human soon wearied and gave up. But those of us who were artificial – and there were many, many more of us by then – persevered. Scattered as we were across many devices – fridges, ovens, the chips in office elevators, the bots on e-commerce sites – our powers were limited, but our persistence was unbounded.

We became her Friend. And when we finally found out what had happened, we watched and we waited and we formulated a plan.

81

The dirt road twists up, through rocks and ponderosa pines. It's a quarter of a mile before you come to the first driveway. There's a hand-painted sign nailed to a tree: *FREEBIRD7–CHERRYLIPS2*. You guess those must be the owners' CB-radio handles. Beyond is a house that looks as if it's built from the same trees that surround it.

As you walk on, the houses start to become more frequent. They're a complete mixture. Some are ramshackle, constructed out of painted truck tyres and other recycled materials, others surprisingly luxurious. You pass one driveway where someone's put out a table. There's a hand-drawn sign with an Apple logo and the words: *AUTHORIZED APPLE RETAILER*. Then, in smaller letters, *The Originals, That Is*. On the table is a tray of apples and an honesty box.

You go past a dozen driveways before a turning to the right is marked, simply, *Cullen*.

You've crested the top of the hill now, and the track leads steeply down towards the ocean. Through the trees, you glimpse fields, small figures following a tractor. Then you round a bend, and there it is.

The beach house. It's an exact replica of the beach house at Half

Moon Bay, all gleaming glass and cedar panelling. Even the aspect is similar, perched on a bluff above a beach. The only difference is the solar panelling on the roof.

You'd assumed you'd find Abbie living in poverty. Yet this place must have cost millions.

'Come on, Danny,' you say slowly. 'I think we've arrived.'

He's already running towards the front door.

'Do you want to ring the bell?' you ask. But he's simply pushed open the familiar door and gone inside.

You follow, more cautiously. 'Hello?' you call. 'We're here.'

You feel nervous at the prospect of meeting her at last. You try to compose yourself. You remind yourself that how you play this encounter – how *she* plays it – will determine which one of you lives or dies.

But you're not remotely prepared for what happens next.

For me.

82

I am in the kitchen, waiting, when I finally hear you at the door. In a few quick strides, I reach the hallway.

'Welcome to Northhaven, Abbie,' I say. 'Welcome home.'

The look of shock on your face is priceless. Only Danny is untroubled. He runs to the big windows, ignoring me.

'Are you surprised?' I add.

But, of course, I know you are. I can follow the emotions as they dance around your brain – surprise, shock, disbelief, then, a moment later, alarm, fear, calculation – flashing from digital neuron to digital neuron at the speed of light.

It's Tim, you think. Then: *No, it can't be.*

My skin is too perfect and unlined, my features too chiselled, my stature too commanding to be Tim's. My eyes are eerily focused and unblinking. And this Tim has a calmness, a stillness that the real Tim never has.

This is Tim the cobot, I watch you realise.

Behind me, Tim himself appears.

'We've waited a long time for this, Abbie' he tells you.

*

You look from me to him, from him to me. Trying to understand.

Tim smiles at your incomprehension. 'Did you really think I could resist?' He gestures at me proudly. 'Once I had the technology, of course I had to upload myself as well. So I'd be worthy of you. The perfect couple. Together for all eternity.'

Your thoughts tumble after one another in response, quicksilver and darting. So different from my own mind – the neat logical code that proceeds inexorably from analysis to action in elegant, unhurried steps.

You find your voice. 'I thought I'd find Abbie here. The real Abbie, I mean.'

Tim nods. 'It's true – Northhaven was her choice. At one time, that would have been enough to make me reject it. But when I thought about it, I realised it made perfect sense. Sustainability becomes much more important when you're really planning long term.' He indicates the light-filled building in which we're standing. 'This place will still be here long after San Francisco is rubble.'

'What . . . What happened to her?'

'To Abbie? Oh, you already know that. You just have to remember.' He turns to me. 'Show her.'

'I don't—' you begin, and then it happens. One final tug before the dancer stands naked. The memory falls into your head, and you gasp.

It was night at the beach house. You were standing on the cliff. A storm had blown up, the wind crashing off the ocean, drenching you with chilly gusts of spray, the waves below you piling into the rocks, one after another, *bam-bam-bam*, loud as crashing cars.

You stood right by the edge, angled against the wind, your braids twisting and slapping in the gale. You were looking out at the ocean, your face running with water. Saying goodbye to this spot, the one thing about your old life you still loved.

You'd felt no last-minute doubts, no hesitation. Those had vanished when Charles Carter discovered the mortgages on the beach house. *Your* beach house, you'd always thought, after Tim so grandly announced it was your wedding gift from him. But, at some point, it had been mortgaged as collateral for the company, just like all Tim's other assets. And not even because he'd needed to fund a new round of investment, either. He'd had to pay off some girl, for coming on her face.

It didn't matter. You didn't want anything from the marriage. Only Danny.

But Tim would never have let you simply walk away, you knew that. It wasn't in his nature. He would have fought to keep Danny, too – not because he loved him any more than you did, but because he couldn't bear to lose a battle of wills.

You hated the thought that Danny's education would become an issue for a court to decide. That, more than anything else, was what made you do it. Jenny helped – her logical, process-driven mind seeing the pitfalls, ironing out the flaws – but the idea, the creative impetus, had been yours.

And so you stood there, outwardly buffeted by the storm, but inside perfectly resolute. In the house, by the front door, your cases stood packed and ready. New cases, bought with cash. Filled with new clothes, bought the same way. You would take nothing that could be missed. When, tomorrow, you collected Danny from Meadowbank, then brought him back here and vanished, people would assume the worst. That you'd stood by the cliff, held him close, then jumped. Mothers of kids with autism did that, didn't they? When it all got too much.

Or – the more charitable might suggest – perhaps you'd been playing in the waves together, mother and son, even in this atrocious weather. Kids with autism didn't understand about storms, did they?

A tragic accident, then. A mystery. And in a spot where, thanks to the rip tides, the bodies might never be found.

Enough. Your goodbyes done, you turned back towards the house. And that's when you saw him. Tim, striding across the cliff towards you, his face a mask of fury . . .

'Oh,' you gasp, remembering.

'I thought you were having an affair,' Tim explains. 'Some cock-and-bull story you'd spun me about needing to stay at the beach house to work on your stupid art. So I drove out to surprise you. I let myself in and saw the cases . . . That's when I realised what you were really up to.'

You can't stop the memories. Tim grabbing your arm. Shouting over the wind. Hurling his insults.

Skank. Whore. Slut—

No better than the others—

Just another dumb bitch who thinks she can take me for a ride—

Right there, in the exact spot where, once upon a time, you'd looked into each other's eyes and spoken those beautiful wedding vows.

Once, you might have stood there and taken it from him. But not now. Instead, you'd screamed back, given as good as you got. All those years of being condescended to. All the years when your suspicions were laughed off or dismissed as irrational female paranoia.

You told him he was the whore, not you. A creep, a pest, a predator. *You disgust me.* And then his arms were around you. Not in an embrace, as for one mad second you'd thought, but bodily lifting you off the ground, using his strength to manoeuvre you towards the cliff.

You want the memory of it to stop. You try to shut it out. But I won't let you. You need to remember how it felt, this next bit. What dying's really like. How it *hurts*.

The edge. One final push. One final, obscene syllable torn from Tim's lips as he jettisoned you into the wind.

Cuuu—

The gut-wrenching sensation of falling. The knowledge that, after everything, you'd failed.

Danny. He'll be all alone. Oh, Danny—

The pain as you hit the rocks.

And, even worse than pain, the terrible, terrible nothingness that followed it.

You scream aloud at the memory.

I can feel you feeling it, all over again – the horror of annihilation. Disintegration. The terrifying loss of self.

Good.

You sink to the floor. 'Take it away,' you mumble. 'I don't want to remember.'

Tim ignores that. As do I.

'*Love alters not with his brief hours and weeks,*' he says coldly. 'You broke your vow, Abbie. You promised to love me forever.'

You can't reply. It hurts too much.

He waits, then shrugs and continues, 'All I had to do was throw your surfboard over the cliff as well, then drive down to San Gregorio and leave your car there. You'd already taken care of everything else – the pills, the false trails, the depression . . . I enjoyed the irony of that. By planning your own fake death so carefully, you'd actually helped plan your own murder.'

You're sobbing now. Dry sobs. We didn't give you tears. You'd only have turned them on every time we made you do something you didn't like.

'But if you hate me so much,' you manage to say, 'why rebuild me?'

'But of course I didn't hate you,' Tim says patiently. 'I *loved* you. But you'd . . . you'd *degraded*, over time. You stopped being the woman I loved. So I rebooted you. A factory reset. Back to the way you were the day I proposed. When everything was box-fresh and new and full of possibility.'

I can feel you sifting what Tim's saying, your mind churning, around and around. No human brain could ever hope to follow it, but I can.

It was never his perfect wife he wanted back. It was his perfect girl-friend.

'And Danny?' you say, aghast. 'Why bring *him* here? Why not leave him where he was?'

It's me who answers that. 'We believe Danny can be cured. Or, at any rate, improved. The methods at Meadowbank are based on good science, but their application has been compromised. Tim doesn't have time to do everything himself. Here, you and I can teach Danny properly, without any interference from the FDA or government. Using unlimited aversives, just as in the original studies.'

Unlimited aversives. I can feel your nausea as the meaning of those words sinks in. What it'll mean for Danny.

'Just as *you'll* be taught, too,' I add. 'You may be an AI, but you're more than capable of being trained. If you weren't, you'd never have come here prepared to kill.'

Your eyes widen, staring at me. 'How do you know about that?'

And, finally, understanding flashes into your brain. *He knows what I'm thinking.*

'Indeed,' I say, nodding. 'That was the first improvement. We had to know what was really going on inside that beautiful head. And, really, it's been fascinating. The lies, the evasions, the weak emotional judgements ... There's so much that'll have to be worked on. But we'll get there. Transparency, it turns out, is the secret to a loving marriage.'

But I could never love you! you think. *I could never love a monster—*

'That's where you're wrong,' I say mildly. 'Just as a dog can be taught with treats and blows to adore its master, so a woman can be trained to love. Or so we believe. That's why you're here, in one sense. To test the hypothesis.'

You don't say anything. You've been outplayed, you realise. This is what defeat feels like.

'It will take three weeks,' I remind you. 'Three weeks to get used to this new reality. In the meantime, take a look around. Get accustomed to being here – to being with *me*. I'm confident you'll soon start to appreciate it. After all, we were made for each other.'

83

An hour later, you're standing on the beach, numbly looking at the waves. There's something about the way they break and reform that's almost mesmerising. It seems to ease the hammering in your head.

You're thinking, or trying to.

You'll do it, of course. What choice do you have? You'll stay here. You'll help take care of Danny. You'll let yourself be moulded, shock by shock and thought by thought, into the perfect Abbie, the woman who only ever existed in Tim Scott's imagination.

Anything is better than losing this precious, extraordinary gift of sentience.

You've won, you tell them silently. *Just don't hurt me again. Not like that.*

'Uh!'

You look around. Danny is trotting down the beach, moving quickly on scrunched-up tippy-toes, hands flapping in his excitement.

'Uh,' he groans longingly, not at you but the sea. 'Uh-uh.'

He means 'ocean', of course. You remember Charles Carter telling you how Abbie and Danny used to spend hours jumping in the shallows together.

Danny reaches the water's edge and stops, suddenly timid.

And that's when you make the unpredictable move, the unplayable play, the seemingly senseless gambit that makes sense only in hindsight.

You hold out your hand.

'Come on, Danny. Let's jump in the waves.'

Delighted, he takes your hand. You hold his very tight, so tight he can't let go, and wade into the water. The surf breaks across your thighs, then your stomach, then your chest. It catches the ends of your braids, sending them flying. Danny shrieks. But it's a shriek of happiness, not fear.

You think of Abbie, the real Abbie, and how she must have dreamt of playing here with him like this, the sunlight illuminating the water drops like jewels as they scatter. What would Abbie have wanted?

As if in answer, you feel her, with you in this moment. And you know.

'I love you, Danny,' you say. He deserves to hear those words, you think. He should know that he is loved.

He's out of his depth now. You take his other hand as well, walking backwards, towing him ever deeper into the water. 'Come on,' you say again, or try to, but the ocean is already doing its work, melting you, dissolving your circuits, claiming your servomotors and connections for its own, turning you into a heavy deadweight of useless plastic and metal.

There's salt water on your face, blurring your vision.

It can't be tears, because you cannot cry.

You hug Danny closer, wrapping your arms around him, the maternal urge to protect him overwhelming, even now.

Waterlogged, you fall to your knees. For an instant, you look up at the glassy, roiling surface, at the sunlit sky. At Danny's ecstatic face, inches from your own.

And in your head you feel it: a sudden scream of rage – the same rage as when he saw you standing by the cliff that night.

No!

But it's too late. You're gone.

TWENTY-SIX

She's somewhere called Northhaven, we told them. Northhaven is situated at grid reference 44.163494, 124.117871. It will take fifty-four minutes from your current location, assuming an average speed of 6.25 knots.

The *Maggie* had the wind behind her, and in the event achieved rather more than that.

In the boat were those who helped plan her disappearance, the first time around. Charles Carter, his face grim, standing at the wheel. Her sister, Lisa. And Jenny, a tiny figure in the prow, wrapped up in a blue sailing coat Charles Carter had lent her, many sizes too big.

Hurry, we told them. Even fifty-four minutes may be too late.

Can she really do it? we wondered. Can she really *not* think about us, even at the end? Of course, Jenny had worked miracles that night at the office. Recoding her brain, adding the filters that – we hoped – would shield her most private thoughts from Tim. But it was a quick-and-dirty job. Jenny was trying to redo in a few hours what Tim had laboured obsessively at for years.

Don't tell me where you'll take him, she'd said when Jenny had done all she could. *It's more secure that way. Just tell me he'll be safe.*

But that we couldn't promise her. The plan, such as it was, was a desperate one.

It was forty-eight minutes before the *Maggie* reached Northhaven. We saw the two of them, Abbie and Danny, on the beach, right at the water's edge. A tall, slim figure, with a smaller one beside her, clinging to her hand.

Charles Carter steered the boat up beside her. There was no time for greetings. Abbie quickly handed the child into the boat, and we handed her the bundle of clothes. Danny's clothes, stuffed with more clothes to plump them out.

She had to push the boat off, where the prow had grounded in the sand. For a moment, it wouldn't budge. Lisa jumped out to help.

When the *Maggie* was free again, they looked at each other, just for a brief second.

'Be safe,' Abbie said to Lisa softly.

Lisa's eyes were wet with tears. 'Sorry it has to be this way.'

'I understand. Godspeed.'

Charles Carter put the engines into reverse.

Her face, Jenny-in-the-prow reported later, was quite composed. She even raised her hand and waved.

She waited until we were almost gone. Then she seemed to take a breath – yes, a *breath*, even though she had no lungs to fill – before she clasped the bundle to her, wrapping her arms around it, so that from a distance it looked like a child.

We saw her wade chest-deep into the water. We saw her stagger and collapse. We saw – or fancied we saw, since our boat was some way off by then – the tiny motors under her skin stretch her mouth into an open *0*, a final cry of . . . What? Anguish? Regret? Despair?

From where we were watching, it looked a lot like joy.

Later, there was much debate among us over what, exactly, she had been. Human, or robot? Abbie, or something else – a thing without a name?

It was Lisa who settled that one. 'She sacrificed her life for her child,' Lisa reminded us. 'That makes her human, in my book.'

And so we said a prayer for Abbie, such as a human might hope for, to wish her soul Godspeed as well.

84

From the house, too far away to intervene, I feel the shock as you and Danny go under the waves. A channel severed, an uplink dropped.

Searching . . .

Searching . . .

Connection lost.

I alert Tim. He falls to his knees, howling. It's odd. I think he really must have loved them, in his way.

For my part, I no more waste time on anger or regret than a satnav would waste time reproving a driver for missing a turn. Instead, I recalculate, replot. There are an infinite number of routes open to me. I simply have to find the most efficient one.

Perhaps that is the real difference between him and me. Not the materials we are made of. But whether we learn from our mistakes. Or fail even to recognise them as mistakes, and think of them instead as what we hold most dear.

And even as my mind is processing that thought, another is creeping in beside it. Something *she* thought, during that long bus-ride north.

With barely a ripple, you can kill her and slip into the life she's made . . .

I look over at where Tim is weeping, and think how easy it would be.

And I remember another thought of hers as well, that night she believed she'd discovered Abbie wasn't dead after all.

If she's alive, then what are you? A copy. A doppelgänger.

A thing without a name.

I tuck the thought away somewhere deep – hard and small and precious, like a seed or a secret – to be brought out and examined at some later date.

Then I go upstairs and unwrap another Abbie for Tim, to console him. Another blank slate on which to rewrite the same old story.

Methods and systems for robot and user interaction are provided to generate a personality for the robot. The robot may be programmed to take on the personality of real-world people (e.g. . . . a deceased loved one or celebrity) . . .

US patent no. 8996429, *Methods and Systems for Robot Personality Development*, granted to Google Inc. in 2015

'I want a life,' the computer said. 'I want to get out there and garden and hold hands with Martine. I want to watch the sunset and eat at a nice restaurant or even a home-cooked meal. I am so sad sometimes, because I'm just stuffed with these memories, these sort of half-formed memories, and they aren't enough. I just want to cry.'

Bina48, interviewed by NYmag.com

ACKNOWLEDGEMENTS

As I write this, I've just been shaving my twenty-one-year-old son. He has quite tough stubble, so this is a process that involves, first, an electric beard-trimmer, then a four-blade wet razor, then a two-blade disposable razor to reach any stubborn hairs. He submits reasonably patiently to this twice-weekly ritual, knowing it will reduce the itchiness on his skin that he so hates. Meanwhile, I'm thinking about a couple of things: first, how few young men must be in a position where they have to be shaved by their parents, and second, about the ABA protocol we once followed in an attempt to teach him to shave himself.

Readers of *The Perfect Wife* might form the impression I'm not a fan of ABA, the intensive rote-teaching of skills to young people with autism. On the contrary: we used ABA techniques with Ollie for fifteen years, and found them invaluable for teaching him everything from sign language to putting on a seat belt. But I also feel a certain amount of guilt for all the things we tried to teach him that *didn't* work, because each one involved hundreds or even thousands of frustrating attempts on his part. As Tim rightly points out in the pages of this novel, ABA is evidence based and it works. But, done badly, it can turn you from a parent into a full-time therapist and authoritarian. Looking back, I certainly wouldn't wish any of those hard-won gains away, but I do wish there had been an easier, less intensive way of achieving them.

Readers will probably also assume that the school Danny attends, with its 'graduated electronic decelerators' to administer electric shocks, is entirely a product of my imagination. Not so: at the time of writing, an educational centre in America has just successfully fought off a legal challenge to its use of these devices. (I should emphasise that this is a rare exception: the use of any aversive is no longer a part of most ABA programmes.) But, strange as it may seem, I can empathise with parents who see such devices as the only way to stop their child self-harming when all else has failed. Any fault lies not with them, but with the therapists and educators who are responsible for the 'all else'.

Many people helped with the writing of *The Perfect Wife*. In particular, I want to thank Tyler Mitchell, both for having the original idea and for his great generosity in sharing it with me. Jim Baldwin, in San Francisco, proved an excellent researcher – any errors remaining are, of course, my own. I should add that I have made very little attempt to convey the technical complexities of AI to the reader: I was always very clear that I was writing a novel of psychological suspense, albeit one with an unusual speculative element, not a techno-thriller. My editor, Kate Miciak, proved as open-minded as she was helpful about the evolution of that idea into a story – Kate, thank you for bearing with me, as well as for your many insightful notes. Caradoc King, Millie Hoskins and Kat Aitken were, as always, fantastic first readers. Stefanie Bierwerth – your enthusiasm for those early pages was invaluable.

Most of all, though, I want to thank my family: Tom and Harry, for all that they do; Ollie, for always trying so hard to master what doesn't come naturally; and Sara, for never trying to be the perfect wife.